THE BLOOD
RED CITY

Also by Justin Richards

The Suicide Exhibition
(The Never War: Book One)

THE BLOOD RED CITY

THE NEVER WAR: BOOK TWO

JUSTIN RICHARDS

THOMAS DUNNE BOOKS

ST. MARTIN'S PRESS ≋ NEW YORK

THOMAS DUNNE BOOKS.
An imprint of St. Martin's Press.

THE BLOOD RED CITY. Copyright © 2014 by Justin Richards. All rights reserved. Printed in the United States of America. For information, address St. Martin's Press, 175 Fifth Avenue, New York, N.Y. 10010.

www.thomasdunnebooks.com
www.stmartins.com

Designed and set by Steve Tribe

Library of Congress Cataloging-in-Publication Data

Names: Richards, Justin, author.
Title: The blood red city / Justin Richards.
Description: First U.S. edition. | New York : Thomas Dunne Books/St. Martin's Press, 2016. | 2014 | Series: Never War, book 2
Identifiers: LCCN 2015043226 | ISBN 9781250059215 (hardcover) | ISBN 9781466863781 (e-book)
Subjects: LCSH: World War, 1939–1945—Fiction. | Human-alien encounters—Fiction. | BISAC: FICTION / Science Fiction / Military. | FICTION / Science Fiction / Adventure. | FICTION / Alternative History. | GSAFD: Alternative histories (Fiction) | Science fiction.
Classification: LCC PR6118.I365 B58 2016 | DDC 823/.92—dc23
LC record available at http://lccn.loc.gov/2015043226

Our books may be purchased in bulk for promotional, educational, or business use. Please contact your local bookseller or the Macmillan Corporate and Premium Sales Department at (800) 221-7945, extension 5442, or by e-mail at MacmillanSpecialMarkets@macmillan.com.

First published in Great Britain by Del Ray, an imprint of Ebury Publishing, a Penguin Random House Group company

First U.S. Edition: March 2016

10   9   8   7   6   5   4   3   2   1

For Julian & Chris

RE: Los Angeles Incident 24 February 1942

The President has asked me to inform you that while we still have no tangible evidence of an airborne incursion it seems likely that the incident the press have called "The Battle of Los Angeles" was triggered by an unidentified aircraft.

The airplane was probably Japanese and may be connected to the submarine that shelled the Ellwood fuel facility, north of Santa Barbara, on 23 Feb. Reports that the plane maneuvered and departed at extremely high speed and was of an unusual design cannot yet be discounted. Following that initial alert, RADAR later detected a trace 120 miles west of LA at 02:15 on night of 24/25 and tracked it in to the coast, where it was lost as it headed inland.

The positive news is that our emergency plan was operated as soon as the potential hostile was reported. A total blackout was enforced throughout the city and the 37th Coast Artillery Brigade responded with machine guns and anti-aircraft fire. In excess of 1400 shells were fired.

The all-clear was sounded at 07:21 on morning of 25 Feb.

We now know as well as minor material damage to buildings and vehicles, there were 5 fatalities as an indirect result of the incident. 2 were heart attacks, the other 3 due to traffic accidents.

Although local press sources are already announcing a cover-up, our official position, as articulated by the Secretary of the Navy yesterday, remains that the incident was a false alarm due to anxiety and war nerves. The differing opinion of Secretary Stimson and the Army is noted.

No further action.

CHAPTER 1

Officially, it was not a battle at all. But to Jed Haines, watching from the safety of his apartment, it certainly looked like one. He'd been up late, planning to finish notes for an article on the shelling of Ellwood. But now it looked like that would take second place as evidence of the USA's lack of readiness for war on its own mainland.

Another shell exploded high above the city, the smoke caught like clouds in the misty glare of the searchlights. The windows of the apartment rattled alarmingly. He had lost count of the number of percussions and flashes. He'd given up taking photographs – everyone in the city must be awake, and every other newspaperman in Los Angeles who possessed a camera must be taking photos. There would be nothing special about his own snapshots.

Unless, Jed thought, he managed to get a photo that no one else could. He had a good view from the apartment – at the top of one of the higher blocks in the area and on raised ground. Maybe from the roof he'd even see one of the attacking planes.

The night was cold and bitter. Smoke drifted across the roof of the apartment block, making the air taste acrid. Searchlights intersected above Jed as he negotiated a low brick wall and made his way along a lead-lined gulley to find the best vantage point.

He couldn't hear the planes, just the crump of exploding anti-aircraft shells and the distant chatter of heavy machine guns. Now he thought about it, although the sky was aglow with light and fire, he hadn't seen a single airplane. Was it just some sort of false alarm brought on by panic? Or a drill for the air defences?

Jed only had the camera for the occasional portrait shot to accompany one of his pieces for the paper. Anything important and they sent out a photographer along with Jed. He discarded the flash – it wouldn't help tonight.

He scoured the searchlight beams for a sign of anything other than smoke, taking a couple of shots that would probably be completely black. He should have grabbed a coat, but there was no point in staying here long. Give it five minutes and he'd head back inside and make coffee.

When the five minutes was up, or near enough, Jed took another photo. He might have been lucky enough to catch an explosion right overhead. Or he might not. He was too cold to care any more. He was turning to go when he saw it.

Just at the edge of a searchlight beam, off to the east. A dark shape moved smoothly through the night. It looked as if it was *part* of the night. Darkness given shape. Jed tried to focus on it, but the shadowy form seemed to slip from his vision just as it slipped from the beams of light. It wasn't an airplane – there were no wings, just a stunted, oval fuselage. Its shape was defined only by what it obscured.

Instinctively he raised the camera. From here, high up and off to the side, he actually had a perfect shot. He clicked the shutter, wound the film on, clicked again. And again.

Through the tiny viewfinder he saw the dark shape moving away, gathering speed. He lowered the camera, and watched as it accelerated suddenly into the distance – inland towards the desert.

The air continue to crackle and explode around him, but Jed barely noticed. He clutched the camera like it was his most valuable possession – which it quite possibly was.

*

The battle, if it was a battle, continued for several more hours. Jed changed the film in the camera and snapped a few more pictures from the relative warmth of his apartment. Light and confusion, sound and fury.

When he arrived at the office next morning, calm restored, the talk was of nothing else. But Felix, Jed's editor, was less than enthusiastic. He had already got the official story that the night's fireworks had been nothing more than panic and nerves.

'I called a friend who worked in London last year,' he told Jed wearily. 'He said, if you have to ask if it's an air raid, then it ain't an air raid.'

'It wasn't just panic,' Jed countered. 'They were shooting *at* something.'

'Shadows and ghosts. That's what the military say, that's what the government say. I know because some guy from Washington called to tell me first thing so this morning. No bombs fell, right?'

'If you say so.'

'I say so. No bombs, no raid. No planes even. End of story.'

'There was a plane,' Jed said. 'A weird one. I got pictures.' He brandished the camera as if that proved it.

Felix frowned. 'You sure?'

'Won't know for certain till the film's developed. But I think so.'

Felix gestured for him to hand over the camera. 'The army want any pictures we have. They don't want people thinking the Japs can bomb mainland USA when it was all just a false alarm.'

Reluctantly, Jed handed Felix the camera. 'If it was a false alarm, why do they want the pictures?'

'Hey, don't get smart with me. Because they're the military. You may not like it, and I certainly don't like it. But there's a war on, so what they say goes if we want to keep publishing.'

'You think they could close us down?'

'They could stop giving us war news.'

'So much for a free press,' Jed muttered.

'You've got a lot to learn,' Felix told him. 'Now get out of here and do something useful. Mike's running the story about the false alarm. Help him with that, and if there's anything good on this –' he waved Jed's camera – 'I'll let you know.'

If there was, Jed reckoned the military would keep it to themselves. But he knew there was nothing of interest on the film in the camera. The plane or whatever it was that he'd photographed was on the film he still had in his pocket. He sure as hell wasn't giving that up.

'Mike says you saw something,' Cynthia called out to Jed as he passed.

'We all saw something.' He forced a smile.

She took off her glasses, letting them dangle on their chain across her impressive bosom, and leaned forwards across her desk. 'I mean *really* saw something. That what you told him? What did Felix say?'

'He doesn't want to know.' Jed perched on the other side of her desk. 'But yeah, I saw a plane or something all right. Don't believe me?' he added, seeing her smile.

She looked round before she answered, her voice low and conspiratorial. 'Had a few people phone in and say they saw something moving northeast over the city. Must have passed right over your place.'

'Nerves and panic,' Jed said warily. 'Mass hysteria.'

'That'd be it.' She leaned back, rolling a pencil between her forefinger and thumb.

'So what else are people saying?' Jed asked.

'It'll cost you dinner.' She tapped the end of the pencil against her lips.

'OK. Dinner.'

'Got one guy says he reckons this mass hysteria came down somewhere out past Pasadena.'

'You told Felix about this?'

She put down the pencil and retrieved her glasses. 'Like you said, he's not interested. But I thought you might be.'

'Yeah,' Jed murmured. He had his hand in his jacket pocket, holding the roll of film from last night. 'Yeah, I'm interested.'

*

The cellar was lit only by candles. The flickering light did little to dispel the shadows. Darkness clung to the edges of the chamber like a shroud, spilling out of arched alcoves across the flagstoned floor. The stone table in the centre of the vaulted space was like an altar. The figures' faces were concealed by shadow within the hoods of their cloaks as they processed round the table, their chanting voices echoing off the brickwork.

The young woman lying on the table stared up at the ceiling, watching the smoke drift and shimmer in the flickering light. The stone was cold through the red velvet sheet draped over it and the thin white cotton dress that was all she wore. It reached down to her knees, her bare legs and feet stretching out towards the corners of the table.

As the chanting reached its peak, she blinked, and slowly sat up. Her dark hair was cut short, reaching to the nape of her neck at the back and fringed like a schoolboy's over her green eyes as she stared into the distance. Her pale face was expressionless.

The chanting died away. The cloaked figures bowed and stepped back, moving to the edges of the room.

The leading figure pushed back his hood to reveal the bald scalp and craggy features beneath. 'It is done,' he said with grim anticipation. 'Now we can only watch and learn.'

A wide trail was scorched through the scrubby woodland. Although it was right next to the road, Davy almost missed it. He drove past, Buster beside him with his head stuck out of the window as usual. Davy saw the damage in the rear-view mirror.

'Hold on there, buddy,' he said to the dog as he slewed to a halt. 'Let's take a look at that.'

He jumped down, Buster following, tongue hanging out as he trotted after his master. Davy stood by the edge of the road, putting his hand out for the black Labrador to lick at as they both stared into the woodland.

It looked like someone had driven a truck through. But a

truck thirty feet wide and so hot it had charred the ends of the broken branches and the dry grass and undergrowth. Lucky it hadn't started a fire, Davy thought. Whatever it was.

Walking slowly along the pathway that had been created, he examined the ends of the branches. Brittle and burned. The woodland would soon recover. A good fire could clear out and revitalise a forest. But this was something different.

The trees got taller and denser further in. Soon there was a canopy over them – the lower branches ripped and burned away, leaving the upper layers still intact. The weak winter sunlight filtered through dappling the charred ground. Unsettled, Buster kept close to Davy, making small whimpering noises.

There was something there, at the end of the trail. The scattered sunlight glinted on metal. Maybe it *was* a truck. Except it looked smooth, rounded, like a structure rather than a vehicle. Had it always been here, whatever it was?

Davy stopped, peering at it from a distance. He wasn't one to get nervous or scared. He'd been farming this land, or as much of it as *could* be farmed, for over thirty years. He reckoned there was nothing left that could surprise him. He was wrong.

But nervous or not, there was something unsettling about what he could see. As his eyes adjusted to the gloom, Davy could make out a dark patch on the curved side of the structure. An opening. Something moved in the darkness. He was aware of Buster tensing beside him, teeth bared and a deep growl emanating from the dog's throat.

The shape detached itself lazily from the darkness, slowly approaching. Picking its way carefully through the damaged undergrowth. Eyes gleamed as they caught the filtered light, and Davy almost laughed.

It was a cat. Probably one of the farm cats wandering in search of food. This time of year, there weren't so many mice in the barns or out in the fields. Black as a shadow, the cat didn't seem at all intimidated by Davy and Buster. It continued towards them, eyes flicking from side to side before stopping abruptly. Suddenly alert.

Buster was still growling. The dog took a shuffled step backwards and gave a bark. Buster never barked.

'What's wrong, lad? It's just a cat.'

She swung her legs off the side of the stone table and leaned forward. She half jumped, half fell forwards to the floor, landing on feet and hands together. The cloaked figures retreated to the edges of the chamber, giving her room. But she seemed oblivious to their presence.

For a moment the woman was still, looking round, exploring a landscape only she could see through the smoky haze. Candlelight played across her features as they contorted, lips drawn back from her teeth. Shadows elongated and sharpened her features, made her curled fingers more like claws as she scratched at the floor in front of her.

Slowly she moved forwards, on all fours. The muscles of her shoulders tensed through the thin cotton of the dress. Her body seemed to elongate as she arched her back. Her mouth opened in a hiss of satisfaction.

She moved slowly through the dim light, eyes flicking from side to side before stopping abruptly. Suddenly alert. She stretched out her arms in front of her, leaning backwards, mouth opening. Her eyes glittered as they caught the light.

The cat was right in front of them now. It stretched out its front legs, leaning backwards and yawning. It shook its head suddenly, as if to rid itself of fleas. Something glittered as it moved, something behind the head. A collar, perhaps?

Davy stepped towards the cat. None of the farm cats had collars. Maybe this was a pet. An expensive collar might mean a reward. He could see it now, as the cat stared back at him through unblinking emerald eyes. The collar looked heavy, dark metal inlaid with a tracery of intricate silver lines which caught and reflected the light.

Crouching down, Davy reached out his hand, encouraging the cat towards him. It stared back, eyes narrowing slightly. At the edge of his vision, Davy was aware of sudden movement.

Noise – the sudden barking as Buster shot past him. Straight at the cat.

'No – Buster, leave!'

But Davy's voice was drowned out by the dog's barks and the screech of the cat. The two animals were a rolling mass of fur and claws. The poor cat wouldn't stand a chance against the large gundog. All Davy could do was shout at Buster to stop.

A blur of motion in the guttering light as she rolled backwards. Her hands curled into claws, slashing at the air.

The bald man licked his pale lips as he watched, eyes gleaming.

Her face was a mask of anger and determination as she lashed out again at the invisible attacker. A red streak appeared in the front of the white dress, blood seeping through from inside, as if a knife had been drawn from her shoulder down to her navel. Another stain close to the hem. Patches of blood diffused through the white cotton.

The thin dress was soaked red, clinging wetly to her body, emphasising every curve in scarlet. Her hands were slick with blood, grasping it out of the empty air...

Something splashed against his cheek and Davy instinctively glanced up to see if it was raining. He wiped his hand across his face. It came away red. Blood.

The dog's barks were howls. The cat's screeches unabated. Somehow the cat was on top of the dog, raking its elongated claws down as Buster rolled and thrashed, desperate to throw the cat off. But it clung on with its hind legs, claws deep in the dog's fur, biting into its flesh with unnatural strength and determination.

Fur slick with blood, the dog was weakening – losing blood from a ripped artery. It collapsed panting on its back. The cat forced its way from underneath, then suddenly it was on top of the dog again, forepaws whipping out and claws slashing across the dog's exposed throat, where the fur was thinnest.

Barks became liquid howls. The cat jumped down, arching its back as it watched the lifeblood pumping from its opponent's neck.

Davy stared in horror, rooted to the spot, sick from what he'd just seen. The cat tilted its head slightly, staring up at him. Its fur was matted and stained and damp. Davy took a step towards it, rage building within him. He'd stamp on the bastard thing. He'd rip its scrawny head off.

The anger mixed with sorrow as he watched Buster's frantic panting slow to a halt. Became fear as he realised he couldn't move his leg. He looked down – and saw the dark, bulbous shape like a huge spider that held him tightly wrapped between its front legs.

Then he was falling, legs pulled from under him. His face was level with the cat's, staring into the image of his own terrified face reflected in its unblinking green eyes. Behind the cat, another of the dark spider-like creatures scuttled through the burned undergrowth towards him.

Norma Wiles was dozing by the fire when she heard the familiar sound of the truck pulling up outside. She went through to the kitchen to put some coffee on for Davy.

He watched her from the doorway, silhouetted by the low afternoon sun behind him.

'You've been gone a while,' Norma said. 'Reckon you'll be feeling the cold.'

His reply was dry and devoid of inflection. A simple 'No'.

Norma frowned. It didn't sound like Davy at all.

A black cat pushed between her husband's feet and padded into the kitchen, looking up at Norma. Its fur was matted, a thick metal collar gleaming beneath.

'Where's Buster?' she asked. The dog was usually into the kitchen before its master, looking for food and water.

'We don't need the dog.'

Davy stepped into the light and Norma gasped. 'What's happened to you. Look at your clothes – and you've got blood across your face. Are you all right?'

'Never better.'

'That's not how it looks, let me tell you.'

He shook his head. 'You can't tell me anything. I already know everything you do. Everything I need to know.'

He reached out for her, and she let him put his hands on her shoulders, drawing her towards him. She felt his familiar callused hand on her cheek, stroking. Down to her throat.

The cat jumped up onto the kitchen table in a single elegant movement, as if to get a better view of them. It tilted its head slightly, watching.

As Davy Wiles held his wife's neck carefully between his hands. Then twisted.

She padded across the floor, hands and feet stained red. At the stone table, she paused, then jumped easily up in a single elegant movement, as if she weighed almost nothing, landing on all fours.

Norma's body slumped to the floor. The cat closed its eyes and lay down on the table. It understood that it needed to rest. Soon it would start on a long journey.

Blood was streaked across her face, running down her chin and neck, trickling between her breasts where the sodden fabric clung to her body. The dress was as scarlet as the velvet sheet over the stone table.

Head tilted slightly to one side, she seemed to be watching something. Her bloodied mouth twisted into a cruel smile. Then her eyes blinked rapidly and she toppled sideways in a dead faint. She lay across the table, one arm thrown out over the edge, legs twisted under her. Her chest rose and fell slowly, rhythmically, in peaceful sleep. Bloodstained scarlet across crimson velvet in the dying light of the candles.

CHAPTER 2

February was cold in London, with a hint of snow in the air. Major Guy Pentecross and Colonel Oliver Brinkman walked the short distance from the car through the darkness of the blackout, taking the chance to discuss their imminent meeting. In the months since he had been recruited to Station Z, Guy Pentecross had seen things he never would have imagined. But the prospect of meeting Aleister Crowley again still made his skin crawl.

'It's not just the fact that he's a practising expert in the occult,' Guy told his commanding officer. 'I just find him so...' He struggled to think of a word to describe it.

'Reptilian?' Brinkman suggested.

Guy nodded. 'You can see how he got the reputation of being the most evil man in the world.'

'That was before Hitler and his cronies came on the scene,' Brinkman pointed out. 'And the competition is confined to humans.'

A year ago, even a few months ago, before joining Station Z, Guy would have thought that Brinkman was joking. But now he knew all too well that there were creatures that were far from human which could be described as 'evil'. Station Z's mission was to discover all they could about the Vril, as the creatures were called, and formulate a strategy to deal with them.

Fighting a war at the same time made it more complicated. Much more complicated, since they knew Himmler and the SS also had a group dedicated to learning about the Vril. But the Nazis planned to exploit the creatures, using whatever they learned and perhaps even the creatures themselves to their advantage, harnessing Vril knowledge and technology against the Allies.

Though the threat of the Vril was real and serious, Station Z's resources were limited and their mission kept secret. Seconded from his job at the Foreign Office after being wounded serving in the British Expeditionary Force at Dunkirk, Guy was now second in command at Station Z.

Not that there were many people under his command. The entire staff consisted of Brinkman's secretary Miss Manners, though she was far more than a mere filing clerk; Segeant Green, who was responsible for liaising with the regular military forces when necessary; Leo Davenport from the Special Operations Executive; and Sarah Diamond, a pilot from the Air Transport Auxiliary, who had joined at the same time as Guy.

There were others too whose expertise Brinkman and his team could call on – like David Alban at MI5, Elizabeth Archer at the British Museum, and Dr Wiles at the top secret code-breaking centre at Bletchley Park.

And Aleister Crowley.

Guy tried to keep his disgust hidden as he sat in Crowley's office with Colonel Brinkman a few minutes later.

Crowley faced them across his desk, chubby fingers laced together on the blotter. He wore a dark robe, hood pushed back from his craggy, bald head. Behind him the unpleasant figure of Ralph Rutherford leaned against a bookcase, arms folded, watching Guy and Brinkman without disguising his own contempt.

'The results were rather ambiguous, I'm afraid,' Crowley said. He unlaced his fingers and opened his hands briefly in an apology that didn't reach his face. 'But I shall tell you what I can.'

'Why?' Rutherford said. 'Why tell them anything?'

'Ralph, Ralph, Ralph,' Crowley soothed without turning. He pronounced it 'Rafe'.

'Any help you can give us will be greatly appreciated, sir,' Brinkman said. 'For the war effort.'

Brinkman and Guy had agreed they would focus only on the advantages Crowley's information might give them against the Germans. There would be no mention of the Vril, since Crowley seemed to regard them with something approaching reverence. He saw them as higher beings, if they existed, that promised power and enlightenment.

But Guy knew from his own experience that what they brought was blood and death. What Station Z lacked most was information about the Vril, knowledge they could turn to their advantage. They tracked the strange wingless aircraft that the Vril used. They had survived attacks by the superhuman Ubermensch creatures into which the Vril could somehow convert ordinary people. But they still didn't really know where the Vril came from or what they intended. They were hostile, and they had bases of operations hidden below ground around the world.

Some of the Vril's technology apparently relied on a form of science that humanity did not yet understand – closer to the occult or psychic and paranormal than conventional science. Their communications could be picked up not only by the listening Y Stations around the British Empire where enemy radio signals were intercepted, but also by more arcane means. Which was why they were here, talking to Crowley. Or rather, listening to him.

'We held a ceremony – a form of séance – as I promised,' Crowley was saying. 'A connection was formed, though whether directly with the Vril I cannot say.'

'Were you able to discern their intentions?' Guy asked. He didn't add 'sir'.

Crowley fixed him with his dark, deep-set eyes. 'The Vril are the benefactors of humanity. The Coming Race, the bringers of power and enlightenment. If our enemies crave their secrets, then the Vril and we are of one mind, one purpose.'

Guy was aware of Brinkman's warning glance. 'But did you discover anything that might help that purpose?' he said, careful not to contradict anything Crowley had said.

In answer, Crowley turned slightly to address Rutherford. It was an awkward movement, as Crowley's neck was almost as thick as his head. 'See if Miss Roylston has recovered enough to see us, would you, Ralph?'

Rutherford pushed himself away from the bookcase. 'She should have tidied herself up a bit by now,' he said as he strode from the room.

'I'm afraid Ralph is not convinced we should be helping you,' Crowley said as they waited.

'We're very grateful that you are,' Brinkman said.

Crowley's lips curled into a thin bloodless smile. 'We all do what little we can. I imagine life under the Reich would be a rather tedious proposition.'

'I thought Hitler was a devotee of the occult and all that sort of thing,' Guy countered.

'He surrounds himself with people who have some knowledge and vision, but no – the Fuhrer himself believes only in the tangible aspects of power. Only in himself. I gather he is one of those unimaginative people who has to see to believe. What about you, Major Pentecross?' Crowley asked, smile still fixed in place. 'Can you believe in things you cannot prove? Are you a churchgoer?' He made it sound like an insult.

Guy was saved from answering by the return of Rutherford, accompanied by a slim young woman with short, black hair. She wore a simple grey dress that seemed plain and ordinary in contrast to Crowley's robes. Guy recognised Jane Roylston from a previous meeting.

'Miss Roylston is our most sensitive colleague,' Crowley said, gesturing for her to sit.

Jane perched nervously on the edge of an upright chair. Rutherford returned to his position at the bookcase, watching her with ill-disguised loathing as she spoke.

'I established a connection,' she said, voice trembling slightly. 'But what I saw...'

She paused, glancing at Crowley. He nodded for her to go on, but Guy sensed there was more to it than simple encouragement.

'Just snatches, images, I'm afraid. I don't think it was anything useful.'

'Tell us anyway,' Brinkman said gently. 'Let us decide.'

'I had no sense of place,' she said. 'A wooded area, but it could have been anywhere. Trees, undergrowth...' She waved her hand. 'I'm sorry, does anyone have a cigarette?'

Crowley snapped his fingers impatiently at Rutherford, who scowled and produced a packet of Pall Mall. Jane took one, and Rutherford held his lighter awkwardly for her, so she had to twist uncomfortably to light the cigarette.

She seemed calmer after inhaling the smoke. 'Sorry. As I said, just images really. A fight – with a dog, I think, But it seemed very big. Then a man, in a car. Or maybe a lorry.'

'Were you with him, or did he drive past you?' Guy asked.

'I was with him. We drove to a house. Hardly more than a wooden shack. We went inside, and there was a woman.' She blew out a long stream of smoke and looked away. 'That's all.' She glanced again at Crowley. 'That's all.'

Crowley nodded. 'Thank you, Jane. That is most helpful.'

Guy and Brinkman did not linger. Rutherford showed them out, all but slamming the door of the house in Jermyn Street behind them.

The evening was drawing in, a chill in the late February air. Further down the street, a car flashed its lights, their beams mitigated by dark hoods that allowed only a thin slit of light through.

Sarah Diamond got out of the car to open the door for Brinkman. Even in the gathering darkness, Guy saw that she looked immaculate in her dark suit. She closed the door behind Brinkman and smiled at Guy.

'You can open your own door.' Her voice was accented, American. Guy knew her father was English, though he lived in the States, where Sarah had grown up. She and Guy had both started at Station Z at the same time – having worked together to try to find out what Brinkman's team was up to. They would never have guessed the truth. Guy still found it hard to believe.

He had been working at the Foreign Office, after being wounded at the Dunkirk evacuation and invalided out of the army. But Sarah was a ferry pilot with the Air Transport Auxiliary – technically a civilian, responsible for helping to deliver aircraft where they were needed all round Britain. She drove the staff car on sufferance, and almost as fast as she flew planes.

As soon as they were all in the car, Sarah twisted round in the driver's seat. 'You get anything out of the old goat?'

'Nothing useful,' Guy confessed.

'He doesn't trust us,' Brinkman said. 'He thinks the Vril are coming to save the human race, though I'm not sure what from.'

'Hitler, maybe?' Sarah suggested.

Brinkman shrugged. 'Whatever he thinks, Crowley will help us against the Germans, but he won't do anything to disadvantage the Vril.'

'The woman – Jane Roylston,' Guy said. 'I think she knows more than she was saying.'

'I think you're right,' Brinkman agreed. 'But perhaps Miss Manners will get more out of her.'

The room was small, but there was just enough space for a narrow upright chair between the tiny dressing table and the door. This was where Jane Roylston found Miss Manners sitting when she returned to the room. As well as being Brinkman's secretary at Station Z, Miss Manners was well versed in the occult practices of Crowley and his colleagues. For a time, she had been one of his acolytes – which was where she had met Jane. But that life was behind her now, and she never regretted escaping from it.

'Penny,' Jane exclaimed in surprise. 'What are you doing here?' She glanced nervously over her shoulder before shutting the door quickly behind her. 'You shouldn't have come,' she hissed.

'You shouldn't stay,' Miss Manners countered, peering at her friend over the top of her severe spectacles. 'We can look after you. Keep you safe.'

'No one can keep me safe. You know that. Not even Colonel Brinkman or your friend Pentecross. Of course,' she realised, 'you came with them.'

'And they're waiting for me outside now. You could come too. You can get away from him, you know. *I* did.'

Jane sat on the narrow bed, hands clasped in front of her. 'Perhaps you're braver than me. But no, I have to stay. Anyway, while I'm here I can help you. Crowley won't help, you know. Oh, he says he will. I'm sure he seems very cooperative. But he won't help unless he thinks he's getting something in return.'

'He told us about the ceremony.'

'Keeping you sweet.'

'He let you talk to Brinkman.'

'He told me not to say anything. Or as little as possible. I probably told them more than Crowley wanted. That bastard Ralph would rather I said nothing at all. I'll pay for it later, I'm sure.' She looked away, eyes glistening.

'All the more reason to come with me now.'

Jane shook her head. 'I was seeing through the eyes of a cat, but Crowley told me not to tell Brinkman that. And there was an image. I didn't tell Crowley about that, though. It was in my mind when I was... connected. That was the overriding impression – a shape.'

'What shape?'

'A bit like a figure of eight on its side, but flattened rather than rounded. Two inward facing triangles, with their tips overlapping. Symmetrical.'

Jane looked round for inspiration. 'Here, I'll show you.'

The room was so small that the bed itself served as a stool for the dressing table. Leaning forward, she could reach the mirror. She breathed heavily on it, misting the glass, then drew the shape she had described with her finger.

Miss Manners turned in the chair to see. 'What is it?'

Jane shrugged, wiping her hand across the mirror and smearing away the image. 'A shape. I don't know. It's tangible, though, not symbolic. Not a letter or a drawing. An actual *thing*. And whatever it is, it's important to *them*. Very important. They want it.' She frowned, struggling to remember. 'No, more than that – they *need* it.'

'Do you know why?'

Jane shook her head. 'I could see details, symbols engraved on it, whatever it is. I'll make a drawing and send it to you.' She glanced nervously at the door. 'You should go. It's not safe here.'

Miss Manners stood up. 'I know.' Her voice was tinged with sadness. She reached out and took Jane's hands between her own. 'Last chance.'

Jane smiled weakly. 'I've had so many last chances. But I have to stay. And one day I'll get even with Rutherford, even if I never get away from Crowley.'

Miss Manners sighed. 'You know where to find me.'

He watched her leave from the shadows of a doorway across the landing. Rutherford knew Penelope Manners, of course. The one that got away – that thought fuelled his anger.

He gave her time to get down the stairs. So quiet, so certain she had not been seen. Rutherford doubted that Jane had told her anything. He doubted she had anything useful to tell. But she'd pay for it even so. Without really thinking about it, he had unbuckled his belt. He slid it out of the loops and wrapped it several times round his fist, gripping the buckle and letting the length of leather hang free.

Nearly five and half thousand miles away, a black cat melted into the shadows beside the highway. It paused for a moment, an image fixed firmly in its mind – the thing it was hunting for. It could feel it, getting closer, stronger with every step.

But the cat still had a long way to go. The heavy metal collar round its neck glinted in the sunlight as it emerged from the shadows. It had a long way to go, but it would get there. Soon the hunt would be over.

It stopped for a moment to stretch in the weak winter sunlight, reached out its front paws and scraped at the hard ground beside the road.

The sleepers all had numbers. The nurse doing her rounds spared each of them little more than a glance. Her heels echoed on the stone floor of Wewelsburg Castle, headquarters of the Nazi SS, as she walked between the rows of beds. She stopped at one to adjust the drip feeding into the old man's wrist.

In the next bed was a young woman, perhaps 20 years old. A single sheet draped over her body, her blonde hair splayed over the pillow. Number Seventeen. The nurse glanced, moved on. Unless they were reacting, unless a sleeper was somehow connected to an Ubermensch and could *see* what the creature saw, the nurse wasn't interested. She let them sleep on, oblivious.

If she had passed on the other side of the bed, the nurse might have seen Number Seventeen's hand moving. Lying on top of the sheet, the woman's hand was curled into a fist, shaking. As the nurse moved on, the woman's breathing became ragged, sweat breaking out on her forehead.

Slowly she uncurled her fist, the fingers stretching out and scraping at the cotton. Clawing urgently at the sheet beneath the high vaulted ceiling of the castle room.

CHAPTER 3

It was unusual for all of Station Z's main staff to be able to get to a meeting at the same time. But Brinkman was pleased to see that he and Miss Manners were joined not just by Major Guy Pentecross and Sarah Diamond but also by Sergeant Green, recently returned from interviewing a pilot about an Unknown Detected Trace. UDT was the designation given to any aircraft sighted or detected but unidentified.

Many were misreportings or Allied aircraft that were later identified. But some were undoubtedly Vril craft. Sarah Diamond had seen one in her previous job in the ATA ferrying aircraft to where they were needed – that was how she came to the attention of Station Z in the first place. While many UDTs turned out to be conventional planes, barrage balloons, or other easily explained phenomena, some pilots had described similar strange, wingless aircraft. Guy Pentecross and Leo Davenport had seen one hidden in a Vril base beneath the desert of North Africa.

Davenport, a well-known stage and screen actor, had been recruited from the Special Operations Executive – the organisation set up by Winston Churchill to 'set Europe ablaze' with acts of sabotage and espionage against the Nazi occupying forces.

Given Davenport's continuing acting commitments, always in service of the Allied war effort, he was keen to point out, it was surprising he could spare the time. Brinkman thought that Davenport's frequent absences from briefings were as much down to his low boredom threshold as to his civilian schedule.

'Just popping in, if that's all right,' Davenport announced as he took his place at the table in the main meeting room. He made a point of checking his watch. 'I'm on the radio at eight-thirty.' He looked round at everyone, his expression decidedly smug, even for him.

'It's Thursday today, isn't it?' Green said.

'Absolutely it is,' Davenport agreed.

Miss Manners peered over her glasses, unimpressed. 'Would you like to make a start, sir?' she said to Brinkman.

He suppressed a smile. Trust her to keep them focused. 'Don't mind if I do,' he said in his most officious tone.

There was a moment's pause, then Davenport guffawed, pointing at Brinkman. 'Didn't have you down as an *ITMA* listener.'

'Everyone listens to *ITMA*,' Brinkman told him. 'Even Miss Manners, I suspect.'

'Occasionally,' she admitted.

'Since you are clearly going to be insufferable until we hear all about it, Leo, tell me,' Brinkman went on, 'are you by any chance appearing in *It's That Man Again* on the wireless this evening?'

'Oh, I've been on it before,' Davenport said, doing his best to sound offhand.

'I think you may have mentioned that,' Guy said. 'Several times.'

'I have appeared on it several times. In fact, they're talking about giving me my own catchphrase.' He smiled at Brinkman, 'So in future you can quote me rather than Colonel Chinstrap's "Don't mind if I do".'

Brinkman allowed Davenport a few moments of showing off before he brought them back on track. 'Since you have to shoot off, Leo, we'd better get started.'

'Mrs Archer sends her apologies,' Miss Manners said. 'She's

busy with something down in her cavern under the British Museum. I didn't really understand what.'

Brinkman nodded. 'And I assume Dr Wiles won't be joining us.'

'I doubt he even remembers we're having a meeting,' Sarah said.

She was right. Henry Wiles was a brilliant cryptographer who headed up a small team at Station X – Britain's secret code-breaking centre at Bletchley Park. His job was to try to make sense of emissions intercepted from the UDT craft and other Vril sources. The same emissions that Crowley's séances seemed to pick up.

The main topic of discussion was Crowley's information from their meeting a couple of days previously. Brinkman summarised the little he and Guy had learned. Then Miss Manners gave a brief account of her subsequent meeting with Jane Roylston.

'This arrived in this morning's post,' she said, unfolding a foolscap sheet of drawing paper and pushing it into the middle of the table.

Everyone leaned forward to see. On the paper was a pencil drawing, just as Jane had described to Miss Manners. But now the shape was shaded, symbols drawn across it as if engraved in whatever material it was fashioned from.

'What is it?' Sarah asked.

'That's the question,' Miss Manners replied.

'Could be Sumerian,' Davenport mused, rubbing his chin. Of all of them, he was the most versed in history and archaeology. 'Have you shown Elizabeth?' he asked. They all knew that his knowledge was minuscule compared with Elizabeth Archer's expertise.

'Not yet,' Miss Manners said. 'But I shall.'

Curator of the British Museum's Department of Unclassified Artefacts, Elizabeth Archer was knowledgeable in areas that very few people knew existed. She was also responsible for a collection of artefacts that even fewer people knew existed – a secret archive of whatever could not be explained, or ought not to exist according to conventional science and theory. Her experience, advice and insight were invaluable to Station Z.

'Wiles may have some idea about these symbols, whatever they are,' Brinkman said.

'Runes?' Green suggested. 'They remind me of some of the stuff in that burial site in Suffolk.'

'If it's something related to the Vril, then that would make sense,' Guy agreed. 'We saw some very similar symbols in their base in North Africa.'

Davenport nodded. 'Several of them were the same, I'm sure.'

Brinkman sat back in his chair. 'It seems to me that before Leo heads off to entertain the nation, we have a few things to follow up on. We need to know what this drawing represents. So wrack your brains, check any sources you can. Miss Manners will show it to Mrs Archer, and a copy to Dr Wiles too please.'

'There's the cat as well,' Miss Manners said.

'I'm sorry?' Sarah said.

'Jane – she said she was somehow connected to a cat. She saw through its eyes.'

'So if we knew where this cat is, it might give us a clue as to what it's doing,' Guy said.

'And why it's important,' Sergeant Green added. 'There's a reason the Vril want this thing, whatever it is. If we knew that, we'd know if we want it, or want to stop them getting it, or really don't care either way.'

'Oh, that reminds me,' Miss Manners said as she retrieved the drawing, 'I shall need your pencil sharpeners.'

'May I ask why?' Leo Davenport enquired.

'There's a memo going round. Pencil sharpeners are now banned within the civil service, to conserve pencils. There's a shortage.'

'That's ridiculous,' Guy said.

'I don't make the rules,' Miss Manners told him. 'But don't let me catch you sharpening anything you shouldn't.'

'You're not getting mine,' Davenport said. 'For three very

good reasons.' He counted them off on his fingers. 'First, I'm not a civil servant. Second I don't have one, though I do possess a pocket knife. And third, I prefer a fountain pen anyway.'

'Leaving our pencils to one side for a moment,' Brinkman said, 'as usual we have more questions than answers. So let's see if we can't find those answers.'

'Assuming the Germans don't arrive this evening,' Sarah said. 'I'll blame you, Leo, if they do.'

There was a smattering of laughter. It was a national joke that if Britain was invaded on a Thursday evening at 8.30pm, the landings would be unopposed as the whole of Britain – including its armed forces – would be listening to *It's That Man Again* on the wireless.

'A cat?'

It was one of the rare occasions when Sarah had seen Dr Wiles show surprise.

'You want me to find a *cat*?' he repeated. He buttoned his threadbare tweed jacket, then changed his mind and unbuttoned it again before peering at Sarah and Guy over his wire-rimmed spectacles. Then he sniffed, all trace of surprise abruptly gone. 'Well, I suppose anything's possible in this game. You'd better tell me all about it. Find yourselves somewhere to sit.'

It wasn't as easy as he made it sound. Sarah and Guy finally managed to unearth two chairs from beneath piles of papers and message transcripts. Wiles fussed round, making sure the papers were properly transferred to the floor, which was the only other available surface.

'Debbie,' he called across to a young woman in army uniform.

'It's Eleanor,' Sarah corrected him, but the woman didn't seem to mind.

Wiles ignored the comment in any case. 'I think we're going to need tea. Lots of tea.' He frowned as she turned to go, and pointed to the far wall. 'And whose bicycle is that?'

Eleanor glanced at it. 'Yours,' she said.

'Ah. Good. Well, just leave it there, then, will you, in case I need it? Thank you.' Wiles slumped down behind his desk. He was almost invisible behind the piles of documents. 'Now then. Tell me about this cat.'

'It's transmitting,' Guy said.

'Is it indeed?' Wiles raised an interested eyebrow. 'Like a UDT, you mean? We monitor transmissions from them all the time, though we still don't really understand what their purpose might be.'

'More like an Ubermensch,' Sarah said.

'The men somehow controlled by the mysterious Vril.' Wiles nodded. 'Then it's likely to be a two-way communication. Instructions coming in, and experiential data going out. What the cat sees, hears, smells… How do you know about it?'

'From some sort of occult ceremony,' Sarah admitted.

Wiles's eyebrow rose higher. 'Glad I asked.'

'It seems significant,' Guy explained. 'The Vril are looking for something, so far as we can tell. Using the cat.'

'Ah! So that's why you want to know where this cat is, so you can find out where they are looking.'

'Exactly.'

Wiles leaned back, staring up at the wooden ceiling of the hut. 'We haven't picked anything up. But we can double-check what the Y Stations have been sending in. Can't we, Eleanor?' he added as she handed him a mug of tea.

'He knows who I am really,' she murmured to Sarah as she passed across another mug. 'I'd offer you sugar, but even if we had any, I wouldn't know where to find it.'

'If the Y Stations didn't pick it up, but Crowley's ceremony did, what might that mean?' Guy asked, accepting his own tea.

'Could just be bad luck. The coverage is pretty comprehensive, there are Y Stations listening and intercepting enemy traffic all over the Empire. But there are some places we don't cover very well. Maybe the source – the cat – is in one of those areas.'

'And where are they?' Sarah asked.

'Mostly uninhabited and in the middle of nowhere.'

'We know the cat was with people.'

'South America, then. Or North America, come to that. The US have their own stations and we share data now that we're all friends together.'

'They know about this place and what happens here?' Sarah asked.

'I believe the number of Americans who know about us can be counted on the fingers of very few hands,' Wiles told her.

'Are you counting me in that?' Sarah asked.

'I'll use my little finger to count you,' Wiles said. 'But the point is, your half-countrymen probably share as much and as willingly with us as we do with them.'

'So they might pick up signals from this cat, this Uber-whatever the German for cat is, and not tell us,' Sarah said.

'Uber-Katz,' Guy told her. He was fluent in German as well as many other languages. That was one of the main reasons he had been at the Foreign Office both before and after his time in the army, though he was glad to be back in his major's uniform now.

Wiles drained his tea and looked for somewhere to set down the empty mug. He finally perched it precariously on a pile of papers. 'I'll look for your cat. If it's in the data we have, we'll find it. I'll get Douglas to go through the transmissions intercepted from the UDTs again. And any other transmissions that we've intercepted and which can't be identified. If you can give me a timescale to narrow the search, that would be helpful.'

'Thank you,' Sarah said.

'And we'll pass on anything else that we find out that could help,' Guy promised.

They chatted on the way back to London, easy in each other's company. Guy watched Sarah as she drove the staff car, her eye occasionally leaving the road to look back at him. They talked about how the war was going – the fall of Singapore a few weeks previously, and how long it would be before

America was fully committed to the conflict in Europe. They discussed Wiles and agreed that if anyone could find a single cat that could be almost anywhere in the world, it was him.

Back at the Station Z office just off St James's Square, they found the place apparently deserted and stole a quick embrace. They leaped apart as Miss Manners appeared from Colonel Brinkman's office at the end of the main room. She returned to her desk, glancing at the two of them over her severe spectacles.

'Afternoon,' Guy ventured.

'You know,' Miss Manners told them, settling herself in front of her typewriter, 'there are many secrets in these offices. But how you two feel about each other is not one of them.'

Sarah suppressed a smile. She was amused to see that Guy – the hardened soldier – had gone rather pink.

There was an image in SS Sturmbannfuhrer Hoffman's head, and he couldn't get it out. Since the Vril creature had scratched him in the secret Vault below Wewelsburg Castle, all manner of strange images had been appearing in his thoughts, vying for attention. He hadn't realised at first that he was infected by the creature. Hadn't told anyone – who could he tell? Perversely, the only people he trusted were the British agents Pentecross and Davenport who had been with him in the Vault. Even his own people seemed to have abandoned him. His increasingly infrequent reports disappeared into the ether, unacknowledged and perhaps unheard.

But this latest image was more 'insistent' than the previous shapes and thoughts that had insinuated themselves into his mind. A shape, little more than a shadow unless he concentrated on it. Then details became apparent. But he didn't want that. He wanted it out of his head.

He did his best to ignore it, concentrating instead on his memories of Alina, the girl he had left behind in Russia when he 'became' a German. When he took the identity of Hoffman, and embarked on the life he now lived. With every day, the memories seemed to fade, and all that was really left was the cracked, brittle photograph he kept hidden in his room. It showed her sitting on the step outside her house.

But the image displaced the Vril in his mind. For years now, Hoffman had held two people inside his mind and learned to switch between them. The Russian soldier he used to be was kept in check, hidden so deep even he barely remembered who he had been. Mikhael had died the moment Stalin sent him to infiltrate the SS.

Now he struggled to suppress another part of his mind in the same way. Just as he was both German and Russian, so he was now human and Ubermensch. It had been hard at first – almost impossible to resist the urge to put on one of the bracelets in the Vault. But he knew that if he did he would be entirely suborned to the Vril cause, their thoughts and instructions amplified by the bracelet. Every day, every hour that he resisted it got a little easier.

But still the images rose unbidden in his mind. A Vril bracelet allowed one of the Watchers to see through the eyes of an Ubermensch, forming a connection between the two. Similarly, the bracelet allowed the Vril to control the Ubermensch. But even without a bracelet Hoffman saw what they wanted him to do, just as some of the Watchers could see through the eyes of an Ubermensch without the need for a bracelet. How long before he was fully Ubermensch himself, he wondered? How long before one of the sleepers awoke and saw through *his* eyes?

There were advantages, if you could call them that. Hoffman knew from his own experiences that an Ubermensch could survive all but the most destructive of wounds. If he cut himself, he did not bleed, but the thin orange filaments that now grew inside him curled out and repaired the damage. At first, the sight of them had made him feel sick. But he had managed to come to terms with the fact that they were a part of what he had become.

Another change was that he barely needed to sleep. But even so, he was tired. He was tired of the deception, tired of the unforgiving stone walls of Wewelsburg Castle. Tired of not knowing whether his reports made a difference, or were even received. Of not knowing how Alina was – even if she was still alive. Tired of everything.

He wanted to go home.

If Jed had sent the film to be developed at the paper he would have had prints back the next day. But he didn't want Felix to know he had another set of photos. Not until Jed himself had seen them. Not after the way Felix had practically confiscated the camera from him and dismissed the whole 'battle'.

There was a little place Jed knew off Seventh Street. The main shop was a dispensing chemist, but they developed photos too, sending them away to Kodak. Jed could have done that himself, but he was naturally wary. He didn't really believe that Felix was keeping tabs on him, but Jed was taking no chances. He wasn't sure what he had on the film but he was sure he wanted to keep it to himself for the moment.

The chemist was short and balding, with a sheen of perspiration across his forehead as he checked a ledger for Jed's name.

'Haines, Haines, Haines,' he murmured as he ran a sweaty finger down the page. 'Ah yes… Yes.'

'There a problem?' Jed asked. There was something in the man's tone that made him suddenly uneasy. 'The film is back, isn't it? It's been over a week.'

'Oh, it's back. Yes…'

'But?' Jed prompted.

Behind him the bell hanging over the door jangled as another customer came into the shop. The chemist frowned, and Jed glanced back. A man in a dark suit and blue tie was examining a display of shaving brushes.

The man spoke without looking at them. 'No hurry. I'm just looking.'

The chemist turned back to Jed. 'I'll be right back.' He disappeared into the back room. He returned a few moments later with an envelope stamped with the Kodak logo. He handed it to Jed. 'There's no charge.'

'What?'

'A fault, they said. With the film.'

Jed pulled open the flap of the envelope and tipped out the glossy photographic prints inside. They were all completely black, except for the narrow white border.

'It happens, apparently.' The chemist smiled apologetically.

'So I see,' Jed muttered. He stuffed the prints back into the envelope. On the way out, he brushed against the man now approaching the counter and muttered an apology.

The man in the suit smiled thinly, looking at Jed through watery, pale blue eyes. 'No problem.'

No problem, Jed thought as he stood outside, breathing in the cold March air. There certainly was a problem. But was it really with the film, or was something more sinister going on? You're just getting paranoid, he told himself. Pictures taken in the middle of the night without a flash. Of course they were dark. Maybe he'd make out some detail if he examined them closely.

He slid the envelope into his coat pocket and set off back towards the office.

Inside the shop, the chemist handed another envelope to the man in the suit. It was identical to the envelope he had given Jed. Except that the photos and negatives inside were not blank. The man in the suit glanced through them, checking everything was in order.

'You looked at these?'

The chemist shook his head quickly. 'No, no, of course not.'

'Good.'

The man in the suit handed over several dollar bills. Enough to make the chemist raise his eyebrows.

'Keep the change,' the man in the suit told him. Whoever had already seen the pictures when they were developed would be persuaded to forget about them in a similar way. It was a shame, the man thought, that they hadn't known about them sooner – they could have intercepted the film on the way to the lab.

He pushed the prints back into the envelope. As he closed it, he glanced at the name written in block capitals on the flap: 'JED HAINES'.

CHAPTER 4

It was the speed at which things happened, or rather didn't, that frustrated Sarah the most. The war itself went in fits and starts – nothing for what seemed like an age, then a flurry of action and activity and news. It was the same in the battle against the Vril.

After the information from Crowley and Jane, there was a few days of excitement as they tried to interpret what they had discovered. But soon the interest dwindled and the theorising and investigation became a chore. Not that Sarah could do much investigating. She didn't have an aptitude for code-breaking or seeing patterns like Wiles. She didn't have the patience for research of Elizabeth Archer or the interest in the occult of Miss Manners. Guy seemed used to the lulls between the action, and Leo Davenport never seemed at a loss for things to do.

Sarah felt she was rapidly being reduced to Brinkman's driver. That wasn't what she'd signed up for, and she wasted no opportunity to tell him so as she ferried him from meeting to conference and back to the Station Z offices.

So when he called her into his office, she suspected it was to give her yet another pep talk and explain the importance of what they were doing.

'I know you're frustrated that you can't get more involved,' Brinkman said.

'And that everything takes so long.'

Brinkman held up his hand. 'I know. In many ways it's the nature of the job. Which is why I'm sending you to Cheshire.'

Sarah stood up, suddenly angry. 'You're having me transferred? Just to keep me out of trouble? How dare you!'

Brinkman suppressed a smile. 'Sit down. Cheshire is just where you start. I'm not having you transferred. I'm having you *trained*.'

Sarah sat down, still wary. 'Trained? What do you mean, trained?'

'As a Special Operations Executive agent. They have a, well, a sort of school for agents. I'm putting you through it. If you're going to get involved properly then I want to make damned sure you've got the skills you need to stay alive.'

'What sort of skills? I can fly planes and shoot, but you can't train someone for the work we do.'

'That's largely true. But there's a lot you can learn that will be useful. Now, while there's something of a lull in things as you've been at pains to point out to me whenever you can, seems like as good a time as any. You start with parachuting and then I believe it's sabotage techniques. Just don't practise them in the office. You report to SOE on Monday.'

The first thing that was made clear to Sarah when she reported on the Monday was that no one used their real names. Even the SOE instructors, Sarah suspected, were not who they said they were. She was 'Sparrow Hawk', which she thought was actually quite appropriate. There didn't seem to be any system to the names: a shy mousy brunette girl was 'Boxer' and a middle-aged man with thinning hair who seemed to be constantly sweating was 'Sardine'.

What surprised Sarah most was the variety of training. She had started at RAF Ringway in Cheshire, parachute training. They moved her on quickly from that when she told them she knew what she was doing, and had parachuted into Germany.

'Well, not really,' she confessed to the instructor. 'Back in 1934 I was working in a flying circus and we did shows all across Europe. My plane crashed, engine failure. I had to bail out. That was in Hamburg.'

The instructor, whose name like so many of the instructors was apparently 'Smith', nodded. 'That's good. You'll have to be convincing where you're going.'

Whether he thought she was going into occupied territory or simply meant the rest of the training, she wasn't sure. It took her several minutes to persuade him she wasn't making it up.

Sabotage training at Brickenbury in Hertfordshire was exhausting and Sarah wasn't sure how useful it might be. She was good at the practical side of things, but the theory she found tough going. It was one thing to set explosives and rig them to go off, quite another to read through pages of notes about which devices to use when, and what different types of explosives, fuses, and detonators were called. But there was a perverse satisfaction in twisting the handle of a detonator, or waiting for a fuse to do the job, and watching a small building or the shell of a vehicle explode into flames and smoke.

She was more convinced by the Commando combat course – which involved a train journey to Scotland that was almost as much of a test of endurance as the outdoor survival training that was included when she got there. A group of grizzled, experienced men who were obviously itching to get back to some real action taught Sarah and her anonymous colleagues all they needed to know about finding food, locating water, creating a shelter, and how to make a smokeless fire. She also learned the basics of a form of unarmed silent killing which the instructors called 'Defendu'.

Gradually, over the days and weeks, Hoffman was able to suppress the images – to keep them at the back of his mind rather than overprinted on his every thought. He felt some affinity with the Watchers, though he could never tell anyone that, of course. Kruger, the scientist in charge of them, probably put it down to macabre curiosity that Hoffman spent so much time here with them, watching them sleep.

The girl, Number Seventeen, in particular intrigued him. She had connected to an Ubermensch without the need for a bracelet. The link had been weak and indistinct, but a link nonetheless.

Looking down at her, apparently sleeping peacefully, Hoffman wondered who she was. Most of them were volunteers, so she had probably been plucked from the League of German Girls – the female equivalent of the Hitler Youth. Had she volunteered for the tests that revealed her innate psychic ability, he wondered?

He heard the noise as he turned to go. A scratching, scraping sound, so quiet he almost missed it. Hoffman walked slowly round the bed, trying to trace where it came from.

Her hand was scratching at the sheet, describing a shape on the cotton.

Hoffman wanted to go home. But for the moment he must continue to be the person he had become, whatever the consequences. Drop his guard for a second, and he would be dead, no matter how resilient his body had become. So he strode over to where a tired nurse sat making notes at a small desk in the corner of the room.

'Get a pencil and paper quickly,' he ordered. 'I think Number Seventeen is drawing.'

The cat didn't need much sleep and it rarely had to rest. Even so, it was a long way to the city. It could have got there quicker by jumping into the back of a truck that stopped for fuel at a gas station on the highway. But the cat didn't want to be noticed. It kept to the shadows, off to the side of the road.

When it was hungry, which was not often, it ate, creeping up on small rodents – even unwary birds – and pouncing. With its senses and speed and viciousness all sharpened by the Vril that controlled it, the cat rarely lost its prey.

It didn't get impatient, it was just following instructions. But even so, there was a hint of satisfaction somewhere in what remained of its feline brain as it padded to the top of an incline and saw the city in the distance ahead. The tops of the taller buildings appeared first, and then gradually the whole vast expanse of Los Angeles was laid out before it.

They propped her up in the bed and she stared straight ahead, eyes unfocused. The pencil in her hand swept over the paper, sketching out a horizon. Then the detail – the buildings, streets, a car approaching along the road leading down the incline.

One last detail – the same on every sheet – and the drawing was done.

The cat watched the car approaching. Not wanting to be noticed, it moved silently and swiftly to the side of the road.

Kruger pulled away the drawing as soon as it was finished and handed it to the nurse. She numbered it and added it to a pile at the foot of the next bed.

Hoffman watched as Number Seventeen started on a fresh picture. Grass and trees, seen from a low angle.

'They are moving off the road,' Kruger said. 'Whoever they are.'

'Whatever they are,' Hoffman said. 'See how low the point of view is.'

'An animal?' Kruger wondered. 'A dog perhaps? And this image over the picture, always the same shape...'

The cat watched the car as it drew level. It caught a glimpse of the driver – a young man with curly dark hair.

The cat turned to watch the car speed away, hissing with irritation that its journey had been interrupted, even though only for a few moments. Mouth wide, teeth bared, saliva spotting the nearest grass.

The girl turned, staring directly at Hoffman. Her mouth opened wide in a sudden hiss of anger – teeth bared, saliva spotting his face.

He stepped back, surprised, wiping the back of his hand across his cheek.

'I think it's a cat,' he said.

The cat made its way back to the side of the road. Once it finally reached the city, then the search would begin in earnest. It knew roughly where to start, but it would still take days, perhaps weeks or even months, to find what it was looking for.

There was an image constant and clear in its mind. The artefact it needed to locate. It could feel it, the slight trembling in the air that drew the cat onwards, growing almost imperceptibly stronger as the cat headed in the right direction, as it drew closer to its goal.

Jed glanced down at the map unfolded on the passenger seat of his car. It looked like it would take him about another hour. Keeping his left hand on the wheel, he traced his finger along the paper road towards his destination.

It had seemed simple enough back in the city. Just set off towards where he had seen the strange aircraft heading and see if anyone had seen anything. But now he was on his way, driving through miles of deserted countryside and wasteland, he realised what a mammoth task it really was. The empty space on the map translated into hundreds – maybe thousands – of miles on the ground.

Even if someone had seen it, the chances of Jed finding them were probably minuscule. Even if they remembered – it was weeks ago now, but this was the first chance he'd had to get out of the city. Looking up from the map, Jed ran his hand through his curly, dark hair and continued down the road.

He hated touching them. Hoffman was quite sure it wouldn't work, but it was still the obvious thing to do – and if he had not suggested it, Kruger probably would have done.

The Vault was deep beneath the castle, secured behind a huge metal door, like the airtight hatch of a submarine. The guard snapped out a 'Heil Hitler' as Hoffman approached, then spun the locking wheel in the centre of the heavy door and swung it open.

Hoffman entered what looked at first like an operations room. Maps hung on the walls, plans and documents were spread out over wooden tables under a high, vaulted ceiling. Alcoves stretched into the distance, shadowed in darkness though Hoffman knew exactly what each contained.

He walked briskly down the long chamber, past the tables and into an area that was more like a laboratory. At the end of it was another identical hatchway door. Few people knew what lay beyond that, and Hoffman shuddered at the memory of what he had seen there.

But his interest was in a workbench to one side, against the wall. Laid out on it was a variety of artefacts – pottery, glass, metal, ceramic, all neatly labelled. All ancient. At one end of the workbench lay several bracelets, rings of chunky metal inlaid with a gleaming silver tracery.

He reached out a tentative finger towards the nearest bracelet. Nothing. Carefully, warily, he picked it up, holding it only by the edges. Immediately the silver tracery glowed a brilliant white and the inside of the bracelet erupted. Thin orange filaments sprang out, probing, searching for flesh. If he put the bracelet on, Hoffman knew, the filaments would find his wrist. Metal spikes would spring out to hold him immobile as the filaments burrowed through his skin.

Hoffman had a wooden box in his other hand, already open. He dropped the bracelet into it, and at once the filaments drew back inside the metal.

Number Seventeen was still drawing – a hazy view of a street with hollow doorways and scattered dustbins. Nothing to distinguish where the city or town might be. And over the top, the same symbol sketched again as on all the other drawings.

'The Reichsfuhrer should be told,' Kruger said to Hoffman as he handed him the wooden box.

'I shall inform him when he returns,' Hoffman said. Himmler

was at meetings with Hitler all week. Often, Hoffman went with him. He didn't enjoy the experience.

Kruger opened the box. If he thought it odd Hoffman had put the bracelet inside, he didn't comment. He removed the bracelet. It was hinged and he pulled it open. He closed it round the girl's right wrist. It hung heavy and inert as she drew.

'Nothing,' Kruger said, disappointed.

'Hardly surprising,' Hoffman told him.

'I suppose not. But we can always hope. I wonder if it is worth trying the other bracelets we have? One of them may be a match.'

'It needs to establish a link at both ends,' Hoffman pointed out. 'It must match not just the girl but whoever, whatever she is seeing through. We can establish a link at one end with the ritual but even that doesn't always work, and we never know which of these it might link to.' He waved his hand to take in all the sleepers across the whole room.

'Then this is probably as good as it gets,' Kruger said.

'We are lucky she is picking up anything at all,' Hoffman said. He gently pushed back a strand of the girl's hair that had fallen forward across her face. Not that she noticed.

Sarah hardly noticed the passage of the days – the weeks. Spring was turning to summer without her really noticing. Most of the time she had no idea where she was. The people she was with changed constantly, as everyone seemed to do the training stages in a different order. Maybe, she thought, it was a deliberate policy to dissuade any of them from becoming friends. Not just a security consideration, she realised, but because for many of them this training would lead to almost certain incarceration or death.

Knowing that meant she saw her colleagues in a different way. She realised that the bluster and arrogance of some of the men, the spiky abruptness of some of the women, was down to nerves more than character.

The final stages of the training seemed more sedate. Sarah

spoke some French, and learned more. She was shown how to forge documents – which required a lot more patience that she'd ever believed she had. She spent a day learning to fire and handle enemy guns and explosives – almost as long as they'd spent teaching her about Allied weapons.

Arriving at the Beaulieu estate in Hampshire to complete the final stages of her training was almost a rest.

'Here you will learn surveillance techniques as well as deception,' the chief instructor, Major Woolridge, informed Sarah and the others. He was a tall, slim man with a plummy voice and a thin moustache. About a dozen trainees were assembled outside the impressive country house, standing on the gravel driveway. 'But don't believe for a moment that the heat is off, because it isn't. So I'll see you back here at oh-six-hundred tomorrow for a visit to the assault course.'

Every day started early with the assault course, or a run through the extensive grounds, or both. Sarah reckoned she was fitter than she had ever been. As exhausted as she had ever been. It was a surprise as well as a relief to be given some free time one sunny, warm afternoon. One of the instructors gave Sarah and several other trainees a lift into Southampton. He 'suggested' that they should not be seen together, so they each went their separate ways.

It was a refreshing change of pace just to wander round the town. But it wasn't long before Sarah realised she was being followed. She first saw the man as she was walking along a quiet street. He paused to light a cigarette as she glanced back, turning out of the wind, but also so that his face was hidden. She recognised the same man from his raincoat and hat later as she turned a corner. Then she saw him reflected in the plate-glass window of a large shop on the main street. He stood on the opposite side of the road, obviously watching. As she turned, he also turned away, and pretended to walk on.

Was this part of her training, Sarah wondered? Or was it more sinister – someone actually watching her because of her connection to Station Z? Either way, her best option was to lose him, and as soon as possible.

She wandered apparently aimlessly round the main streets as she decided what to do. When she finally decided, she walked into the largest clothing store she had found, and made for the ladies' underwear department. There were a few other people browsing, all women. As she had hoped, the man kept his distance rather than make himself obvious.

Taking a selection of items to the changing rooms, Sarah smiled at the attendant. 'I'm so sorry,' she said. 'I don't really want to try any of these on.'

The middle-aged woman outside the line of changing rooms raised an eyebrow. 'Oh?'

'It's just that...' Sarah hesitated, feigning nervousness. 'There's a man following me. He's been following me round all the shops. I know him slightly, but I would really rather not see him.'

The woman smiled back. 'Oh, I quite understand.' She glanced past Sarah to where the man was making a pretence of examining a rack of women's coats. 'He does look rather an unpleasant type,' she agreed.

'I just wondered if there is a back way out of the shop, or something?'

The woman pointed past the changing rooms. 'Turn left at the end, you'll find a door that leads out into Melvyn Street. I'll distract him for a moment for you.'

Without another word, the woman marched off towards the man. He glanced up as she approached, while Sarah made sure he saw her step into the nearest changing room. She put down the clothes and peered out again, watching as the woman took the man by the arm, turning him expertly as she showed him one of the coats.

As soon as the man's back was turned, Sarah hurried from the changing room and round the corner. Soon, she was sitting in a tea room several streets away, positioned so she could see the street outside without being seen herself. There was no sign of the man who had been following her.

'Is this seat taken?'

She thought at first it was the same man. But he was

younger, wearing a jacket rather than a coat.

'No, please.' Sarah gestured for him to sit down opposite her.

'Have you been here before?' the man asked as he waited for the girl to come over. 'The tea cakes are very good. If they have any.'

'My first time,' Sarah said, returning his smile.

She was happy to sit and chat for a while, all the time keeping a discreet watch on the street outside for the man who had been following her.

He introduced himself as Charlie. 'I work down at the docks,' he told her. 'Boring, really. An office job, but they say it's too important for me to be allowed to join up, so...' He shrugged. 'What about you? What do you do?'

'I work in an office too,' Sarah said, choosing her words carefully.

Charlie sipped his tea. 'Doing what?'

'Oh, this and that. I'm a sort of secretary.'

'Sort of?'

She watched him carefully, noting how intent he suddenly seemed. The bead of sweat above his left eyebrow. She hadn't noticed before, but there were several empty tables further into the tea room, so why had he sat here with her?

'Very boring,' she said, forcing a smile. 'Typing mainly. I'm sorry, but I have to go.' She drained the rest of her tea in a swallow and stood up.

Charlie – if that really was his name – seemed amused. 'Will I see you again?'

'I doubt it.' She left without looking back, pausing only to pay at the till on the way out.

'Charlie' got up almost immediately. He handed a few coins to the girl at the till, not waiting for his change, and followed Sarah out into the street.

As soon as he stepped through the door, a man appeared in front of him. Charlie made to step round him, but the man moved with him.

'Leave her,' the man said.

'I beg your pardon?' Charlie frowned, tried to push the man out of the way.

But the man resisted, catching hold of his arm. 'I said leave her. You had your chance, you did you best, and she didn't fall for it.'

'I don't know what you're talking about.'

'Yes you do. So don't be a poor loser. She passed the test, she didn't tell you anything about herself, did she? Probably not even her name.'

Charlie's silence gave the man his answer.

'So make your report and leave it at that.'

'Afraid she might crack if I keep at it?' Charlie demanded. 'Isn't that the point?'

The man smiled. 'Usually, perhaps. But Sparrow Hawk is a very special case. I don't want her upset or intimidated.'

Charlie made to go, but the man's hand clamped down on his shoulder, squeezing it painfully tight. The man's eyes were flint-hard and there was an unpleasant edge to his voice. 'Understand?'

'Yes,' Charlie muttered. 'Yes, you've made your point.' He stared at the man for a moment as he tried to twist free, seeing him closely for the first time. 'Hey – aren't you…?'

The man let go of his shoulder. 'I get that a lot,' he said.

Sarah's suspicions were confirmed the next day. Summoned to Major Woolridge's office, she was surprised to find that there were already two other men in the room.

'Come in, Sparrow Hawk,' Woolridge said. 'I believe you already know Captain Philcox, and Corporal Innes.'

Sarah nodded. 'Hello, Charlie,' she said to Philcox. She turned to the corporal. 'And I assume you're the man who wanted to buy me a new coat. Or was it a pair of knickers?'

Innes coloured and stammered a greeting.

'You did well,' Woolridge told her. 'Not many people spot they're being tailed on the first outing. Even fewer manage to lose their minder.'

'And what about Charlie?' Sarah asked.

'You'd be surprised how many of the ladies fall for a handsome young man with a plausible manner. Though I have to say a higher proportion of the men are taken in by a pretty young woman. It gives the secretaries here an amusing side line.'

'And if I had been taken in, as you put it?' Sarah asked. She glanced at 'Charlie'. It would have been easy to succumb, easy to tell him a bit of what she did to try to impress him.

'Well, you're something of a special case, I gather,' Woolridge said. 'But for anyone else, it's the end of any career they might have thought they had with SOE.'

'So, a lucky escape,' Captain Philcox said with a smile.

'Or,' she told him, 'it's just possible I know what I'm doing and wasn't taken in for a second.' She smiled back at him, as his own expression froze. 'And anyway,' she added, 'you're not my type.'

For weeks she drew similar pictures. Hoffman checked through them whenever he could, but the initial novelty had worn off, and both he and Kruger left the nurses to take shifts providing paper and pencil.

Streets, people, cars and buildings. But the drawings were indistinct, with not enough detail, despite the quantity of images, to identify where the place was. Obviously somewhere industrialised and modern – but it could be Britain, the USA, even Germany...

Over each image Number Seventeen drew the same symbol. Two triangles pointing in at each other, overlapped at the tips. Just an outline, but Hoffman could see the details. It was the same image he saw in his own mind, but his image was stronger, focused, detailed. He could see the runes carved into the stone the artefact was fashioned from.

But what was it? On the one hand he didn't want to show too much interest in it, afraid that might somehow give him away. On the other, Hoffman was desperate to know.

'This shape,' he said to Kruger finally, 'why does she draw this on every page?'

Kruger shrugged, inspecting the latest sheet. 'Some sort of interference, perhaps? Or maybe it represents some defect in the creature's vision. Perhaps this is how cats see the world.' He smiled to show he was not being serious. The smile faded as he caught Hoffman's answering expression. 'I don't know,' he admitted.

'Does it represent something?' Hoffman asked. 'Have you seen it before?'

Kruger looked back at the drawing he held. 'There is something about it,' he admitted. 'It did seem familiar when I first saw it. Something held in the Vault, perhaps.'

Hoffman shook his head. 'There's nothing like that down there.' He had checked. As soon as the image had appeared in his own mind, he had checked.

'Even so...' Kruger leafed back through the past few drawings, although the shape was identical on them all. 'I'll tell you where it might be,' he said at last.

'Yes?'

'Have you seen the archive footage?'

'Not all of it,' Hoffman admitted. 'And a long time ago.'

'Just a thought,' Kruger said. 'But perhaps the answer lies in what happened back in 1936.'

One of the most surprising courses that Sarah took was 'Deception Training'. What surprised her was not being taught how to lie convincingly, how to tell when someone else was probably lying, or the importance of apparent self-confidence and techniques to suppress any outward signs of fear or unease.

What surprised her was that the instructor was Leo Davenport. He smiled at her as their eyes met, but made no comment. So she too did her best to give no sign that they knew each other. Everyone else knew who Davenport was of course, which made it easier to keep up the pretence.

She made sure she was the last to leave at the end of the day, waiting until there were just the two of them.

'Making a little extra on the side?' she asked. 'I thought

you were off on a film somewhere.'

'Cover story,' Leo told her. 'Brinkman knows I moonlight here from time to time. Part of the conditions of SOE letting me leave them to join Station Z in the first place. Between you and me, no actor can stay as busy as I claim to be. More often than not, the film or radio work you think I'm doing is down here bringing light and enlightenment to potential agents. Well,' he added, packing away his notes into a leather briefcase, 'if what I teach ends up saving the life of just one of them, then it's time well spent.'

Sarah had to agree. 'You down here for long?'

'Heading back this evening. Just as soon as I've delivered my reports on each of today's students.'

'Oh?' She raised her eyebrows.

'Don't worry, you'll pass with flying colours.' He grinned suddenly. 'And I am glad to see you're taking this new "Bare legs for Patriotism" campaign seriously.'

Ralph Rutherford didn't wait for an answer. He knocked on the study door, and went straight in. He knew immediately that he shouldn't have done.

The bookcase behind Crowley's desk had been pulled back from the wall on one side – hinged like a door. Before Rutherford could retreat, Crowley himself stepped out from behind the bookcase. He saw Rutherford immediately, and Crowley's deep-set eyes seemed to recede even further into his head as they narrowed.

Without comment, Crowley swung the bookcase closed again, concealing whatever lay behind it.

'I'm sorry,' Rutherford said. 'I shouldn't have come in.'

'No,' Crowley agreed in a monotone. 'But what's done is done.' He raised his hand so that Rutherford could see he was holding a heavy bracelet made of dull metal. 'Is everyone ready?'

Rutherford nodded. 'I was coming to tell you.' He smiled apologetically, trying to make light of his mistake. 'So what else do you keep in there?'

Crowley didn't answer for a moment, and Rutherford felt suddenly cold and empty inside. Another mistake. Then the older man's long face cracked into a grim smile.

'Pray that you never find out,' he said.

'I promise you, it won't hurt,' Crowley had told her. Either he was wrong or he was lying.

The chanting reached its peak, echoing round the candlelit cellar. One of the robed women held a silver tray out in front of her. Her head was bowed so that her long, fair hair spilled over the tray, obscuring what was on it. She raised her head as the chanting stopped, revealing the bracelet.

Crowley lifted the bracelet from the tray, murmuring the words of power. He opened the bracelet and turned to Jane Roylston standing beside him. She raised her right arm and Crowley slid back the sleeve of her loose gown with one hand. With the other, he placed the bracelet over her forearm and snapped it shut.

The pain was immediate and intense, like fire burning, stabbing, and burrowing right through her. It started in the arm, shooting up to her neck then out through the whole of her body. Her vision swam as she struggled to contain the fire. When it slowly subsided, and her eyes refocused, she was somewhere else.

Crowley's words were faint and muffled, as if he was speaking to her from another room.

'What do you see?'

She was close to the ground, padding along a deserted street. Rubbish blew across the pavement in front of her. Jane knew she was the cat again. But now she didn't just see through its eyes like she had back in February. She could feel what it felt, she knew what it knew. She closed her eyes, taking a deep breath. Smelling the rancid decaying food and the traffic fumes.

When she opened them again, she was back in the cellar. The scent in her nostrils was the smoke from the candles. The bracelet burned on her arm, but she could cope. She was used to pain – she had Rutherford to thank for that. She could detach herself from it, use it to give her the strength to be herself.

'Los Angeles.' She was surprised how strong and assured her voice sounded. 'I was in Los Angeles. Whatever the Vril are searching for is there.'

'Very good, Jane,' Crowley breathed. 'Thank you. Do you know what it is?'

She shook her head. 'Only what it looks like.'

At a gesture from their master, the robed figures bowed their heads and backed away. All except one.

'Will you tell Brinkman?' Rutherford asked, throwing back his hood.

'Perhaps. I haven't decided.'

'I don't think we should.'

Crowley pushed back the hood of his own robe and stared back at Rutherford impassively. 'I repeat, *I* have not decided.'

The discussion over, Crowley turned back to Jane, reaching for the bracelet on her arm. It was warm to the touch, the inlaid silver tracery glowing faintly in the dimly-lit cellar. And when he tried to unclasp it, the bracelet didn't give. It was like it was a single ring of solid metal welded to her arm above the wrist.

CHAPTER 5

The death of Reinhard Heydrich on 4 June cast a shadow over Wewelsburg. He had been injured in an assassination attempt in Prague on 27 May, taking a week to die from his infected wounds.

Himmler was in a foul mood. He had visited Heydrich in hospital two days before his death, and found the man in philosophical mood, resigned to his fate.

Hoffman didn't really care either way. He had never much liked Heydrich – the man was too full of himself, like so many of the higher-ranking Nazis. The blood on his hands was thicker than on most. This was the man who more than anyone else devised the Final Solution to the Jewish problem. But Hoffman knew that he would soon be replaced, and the reprisals against probably innocent Czechs would be brutal and extensive.

The only good thing to come out of it was that Himmler was preoccupied. Heydrich had been on his way to Berlin when he was attacked.

'The Fuhrer had decided to reassign him to France,' Himmler had told Hoffman. Another irony, Hoffman thought – if the Czechs had only waited, they would have been rid of their 'Protector'.

'The situation in France has worsened,' Himmler went on. 'The resistance there is gaining traction. We need a man of

Reinhard Heydrich's drive and commitment to subdue the subversive elements entirely.'

Determined to have a say in how to fill the power vacuum left by Heydrich's death, Himmler departed for Berlin, leaving Hoffman in Wewelsburg. It was the first chance he'd had to follow up on Kruger's suggestion that the answers to his questions might lie in what had happened back in 1936...

Station Z's continuing pursuit of the artefact Jane Roylston had seen in her visions took place largely below ground. In a vast chamber built beneath the Great Court of the British Museum, in the centre of London, Elizabeth Archer worked through days, nights and the increasingly infrequent air raids without distinguishing one from the others. When he was available, Leo Davenport helped, but for the most part it was a lonely and painstaking task. Exactly as Elizabeth liked it.

The department of the British Museum for which Mrs Archer was responsible was different from all the other departments in two important ways. First, its greatest treasures and most valued acquisitions had not been removed from the Museum to be stored safely down disused tube tunnels or Welsh coalmines. They were safer left where they were, in this deep, cavernous vault beneath the Museum's Great Court well away from prying eyes and – it was hoped – German bombs.

The second difference was that the Department of Unclassified Artefacts, ironically given its name, did not officially exist. It was a secret kept from all but a few. The artefacts for which Mrs Archer was curator did not fall into any other department's remit for the simple reason that they should not, according to accepted science or history, exist. Or if they did then they, or what they implied, were certainly too dangerous to be made public.

Over the years the collection had grown, stored in a vast chamber that even most of the Museum's staff had no idea existed. Shelves, crates, and boxes were home to ancient Egyptian canopic jars, manuscripts written in human blood, sophisticated electrical componentry found beneath an Iron

Age burial mound, and much more. Almost all of it was meticulously catalogued, almost none of it fully understood.

Now old and increasingly frail, Elizabeth had worked here almost all her adult life, starting unofficially in the 1880s until finally she succeeded her husband George Archer as curator when he died. Her knowledge of the department's collection and of the more arcane corners of history and science was almost unparalleled.

If anyone could track down a mysterious artefact from a rough sketch drawn by a woman who saw it while in an occult trance, then it was Elizabeth Archer. Leo Davenport had no illusions about that – here, for once, he was relegated from lead role to spear-carrier. His task was to help, to encourage, and to keep Elizabeth company. But as a keen amateur historian and archaeologist, and as one who enjoyed academic discussion, it was a role he was very happy to accept.

Thursday 18 June 1942 was the day that Winston Churchill arrived in Washington for meetings with Roosevelt and the US military. And it was the day that the months of research paid off and Elizabeth Archer finally found what she was looking for.

'I think this might be it,' she said with typical calm understatement, and so quietly that Davenport almost didn't hear her.

He hurried over to where she was working her way through a pile of ancient manuscripts and volumes. 'Let me see.'

Elizabeth held Jane Roylston's drawing in one thin, bony hand. The skin was stretched tight and her veins stood proud of the skin. She held the drawing next to another, this one on yellowed parchment showing a similar artefact, but fixed at the end of a pole or rod.

Davenport nodded. There was certainly a distinct similarity. 'You'll have to enlighten me, my ancient Greek isn't as good as yours.'

'The Axe of Theseus,' she told him. 'Or rather, just the axe-*head* in Miss Roylston's drawing. Probably all that survives, since the handle was wooden. If this is it.'

'Oh this is it, all right,' Davenport told her. 'An axe-head, yes…' He headed back to the table where he had been working.

'What is it?' Elizabeth watched as he sorted through more modern papers and documents.

'I should have paid more attention. These are catalogues and lists of artefacts in various museums and collections in Los Angeles.'

'Where Crowley claims the Vril are hunting for our artefact.'

Davenport nodded. 'I had Jack Warner tear himself away from his work in the studios for long enough to send over anything he could get his hands on. He thinks I'm mad. He's probably right. But he owes me a favour for stepping into the breach at the last minute when one of his so-called stars threw a tantrum and walked off set. Then there was that potentially embarrassing business with the showgirl and the slide trombone… Ah – here we are!' He pulled out a printed booklet and leafed through it. 'I saw it listed as native American and didn't look to see if there was a photo as we were hunting for something more classical in origin. Yes.'

He brought the booklet back to Elizabeth and waved it triumphantly in front of her. Sure enough, the photograph showed a very similar artefact, made of stone and carved with the strange curling symbols visible in both the drawings.

'That's not native American,' Elizabeth said.

'It is according to the description. It's supposed to be the axe that cut the wood that was used to create a doll-child who came to life and reawakened the winds when they were lost.'

'Nonsense.'

'Don't say that to J.D. Sumner.'

'Sumner? The collector?'

'The reclusive collector of all things valuable and ancient,' Davenport agreed, 'who is opening a new wing of his private museum to show off more of his acquisitions. Including this so-called Doll-Child's Axe.' He handed Elizabeth the booklet. 'This is an advance copy of the catalogue for the new wing.'

Elizabeth sniffed. 'Well, a story about an animated doll has some resonance with the Ubermensch, I suppose.'

'Got to be worth following up anyway,' Davenport decided. 'It's in the right place, and the resemblance is close enough that it has to be what we're looking for. I'll see what else I can find out about it. And if anyone knows how we can get to see the reclusive Mr Sumner.'

'Good luck with that,' Elizabeth told him. 'From what I hear he's a very private person. He sees practically no one these days. Even your charms may be wasted.'

'One can but try. Unless you'd like to see if he'll talk to an eminent curator of the British Museum.'

Elizabeth was already absorbed in the documents on her desk. 'Not really,' she said without looking up. 'There's some interesting provenance on this axe-head I'd like to follow up.'

Davenport nodded thoughtfully. 'So could this artefact of Sumner's be your Axe of Theseus, do you think? The same artefact? And if so, how did it end up in America with a different history?'

'If it did,' Elizabeth said. 'Perhaps there are two of these things. Which begs an obvious question.'

'Are the Vril after just one, or both of them? And why?'

The cat didn't feel the heat. In the height of summer, the streets of Los Angeles were oven-hot. But the cat padded along them methodically, slowly but surely getting closer to what it was seeing.

By late June, it had covered most of the enormous city, and was working its way out towards the suburbs. It was close – it could feel it. Rarely resting, occasionally eating, the cat had kept to the shadows. The closer it got, the less it wished to attract attention.

Even without Himmler, Hoffman was kept busy. The Japanese offensive in the Pacific seemed to be stalling, and there were rumours that the Russians were preparing to counterattack on the Eastern Front. Hoffman hoped that was true. He kept his real emotions and thoughts masked as he effectively ran several SS operations from Wewelsburg in Himmler's absence.

But eventually he got the chance to escape from the rigours and demands of the war.

The whole of the forest was burning. It was only six years ago, but the flickering black and white made the images seem older. There was no sound on the film, just the chattering of the projector. They had warned him not to stop the film, or the celluloid would melt from the heat of the projector's bulb. But he could play it backwards and forwards over sections he wanted to see in more detail.

The images were distorted and given texture by the stone wall they were projected onto. Hoffman had not bothered with a screen. He stood beside the projector, occasionally walking closer to make out the detail. Occasionally slumping down in a chair. His eyes never left the screen.

He had seen it before, seen most of the films before. But now he was looking for something more specific than information and enlightenment. An image that resonated in his mind's eye. The more he thought about it, the more he was sure he had seen it somewhere else, before the Vril clawed their way inside his consciousness.

This first film was almost like a shadow play. The dark silhouettes of SS soldiers against the pale flames licking up from the crash site. The trail of devastation composed a nightmare landscape of skeletal branches from shattered trees punctuated by small fires – a scar through the heart of the Black Forest.

The cameraman didn't get close enough for detail. Maybe it was too hot, or he was scared, or the SS team wouldn't let him. Instead he recorded their retreat, carrying what they could salvage. Blurred, indistinct, some of it still burning.

The second film was less frenetic. A calm, almost measured tour through the debris and devastation, lit by the pale morning light. The trail through the trees where the craft had come down was more evident. What it was that had crashed was not. The ground was churned up, blackened and charred. Roped off, waiting for the investigation team.

Then suddenly, on the third reel, there was Streicher – the SS archaeologist brought in with his team at Himmler's express orders to excavate and catalogue the site. In rapid edits that belied the time and care actually taken, they marked off the site into metre-squares and painstakingly excavated each one. Flashbulbs flared on the stone walls as everything was photographed and removed.

But still Hoffman had not found what he was looking for.

He knew, because of what he now was, that the Vril that survived the crash would have burrowed into the ground. They liked the darkness and the shadows, the weight of the earth above them, surrounding and protecting them. But the surprise on the celluloid faces of the soldiers and archaeologists as the creatures burst from the ground was total.

The camera was on a tripod, left to get footage of the archaeology. It captured a confused mêlée – the ground erupting; dark shapes emerging; flashes of gunfire; people running... Then the image skewed suddenly sideways. Something dark spattered across the lens. The picture cut to blackness.

The final reel from the crash site showed the aftermath. The dead bodies being taken away. Humans dumped into a heap, and then burned, the Vril by contrast carefully photographed in situ then delicately removed.

He returned the reels of film to the Vault, passing Kruger on the way.

'Did you find any sign of whatever she is drawing?' the scientist asked.

Hoffman shook his head. 'Not so far.'

'You could review the Ubermensch footage,' Kruger said. 'But I doubt there is anything much in it that's relevant.'

Hoffman had also seen that footage before, and he was inclined to agree. There were photographs of the Ubermensch after it was brought back from Tibet, and more taken after it woke. But what they showed was not the same as the moving pictures captured on the films. The images in the still photographs were... different. What they showed bore no resemblance to a human being. Hoffman did not know why that was. No one knew.

This film had sound with it – documenting the creature's progress as it learned to talk. Or rather, as it learned to talk their modern language. Its own was ancient and forgotten, it had slept – had been *dead* – for so long. It assimilated knowledge at a rapid pace. Occasionally, there were flashes, moments where the Ubermensch's form blurred and became like the still photographs. Then it shuddered back to the emaciated form that Hoffman himself had seen when he met the Ubermensch.

In the recordings of the interviews, the Ubermensch, educated and invigorated, looked more as Hoffman recalled – more like an emaciated human than a desiccated corpse. This was when the Ubermensch made its proposal. Hoffman had been there for that of course. He had been as surprised as anyone that Himmler accepted the Ubermensch's suggestion that it should lead a raiding party to England.

Of course, it promised them knowledge, power, more Ubermenschen in return. 'And what would you gain from this?' Hoffman had asked.

He never got used to its rasping, tortured voice. 'I hear, although that is not the word for it, I *sense* information coming from England. If I go there, it may become clear. If I go there, I can recover another like me. I shall have comradeship. You will have two of us to study and to learn from.'

Except that the Ubermensch did not survive the mission to Shingle Bay. The British – Davenport, Pentecross and their comrades – had destroyed the second Ubermensch too, though no one here knew that except Hoffman. Was the 'information' the creature sensed actually from a group of Vril in Britain, or was it some sort of interference – either deliberate or unintentional?

'You're right,' he told Kruger. 'I don't think the Ubermensch footage will help. And there is nothing in the Vault.'

'Not everything is still in the Vault,' Kruger pointed out. 'But everything they found was photographed, before it was stored or sent on to von Braun and the others. Kammler was in charge. Now he oversees some sort of construction project.'

Hoffman knew exactly what sort of construction project Kammler was working on. But Kruger's suggestion was a good one. He thanked him, and continued on down to the Vault.

Even now that her SOE training was complete, a summons to Colonel Brinkman's office usually meant that he wanted Sarah to arrange transport for him. If she was busy, she arranged for an army driver. Sometimes Sergeant Green was happy to oblige. Often she drove him herself, grateful for an excuse to get out of the office. If she was lucky, she might need to fly Brinkman or some of the team somewhere.

But today it was not about transport. At least, not in the way Sarah imagined. Leo Davenport was already in the office, leaning nonchalantly against a filing cabinet and smoking a cigarette. Brinkman waved Sarah to a chair.

'We've found the artefact,' Brinkman said. 'Or at least, Mrs Archer and Leo have.'

'That's great,' Sarah said, wondering what it had to do with her. 'So where is it? *What* is it?'

'It's an ancient axe-head, it seems.' Davenport pushed himself away from the cabinet and leaned past Sarah to stub out his cigarette in the ashtray on Brinkman's desk.

'Do you know J.D. Sumner?' Brinkman asked.

'I've heard of him, of course,' Sarah said. 'Everyone has. Eccentric millionaire who collects, well, just about everything. He endows arts funds, sets up museums, buys art and antiques. But I don't think anyone actually *knows* him, do they? He's some sort of recluse. Does he own this axe-head then?'

'Apparently,' Brinkman told her.

'Well, sorry to disappoint you, but just because one of my parents is American doesn't mean I know everyone else who's American. I doubt if I can help.'

'You might be surprised,' Davenport said.

'Oh? I'd have thought you'd have more chance of knowing Sumner. You must have contacts in LA.'

'I do,' Davenport agreed. 'And it's my contacts in LA who

tell me that Mr Sumner entrusts artefacts in his extensive collection to just one shipping company. He wants anything moved, then there's one man he calls.'

Sarah could guess where this was leading. 'My father, I suppose.'

'You suppose correctly.'

'And you want to know if I can persuade my dad to get you an appointment with J.D. Sumner?'

Brinkman shook his head. 'No. I want your father to get *you* an appointment with him. I'm sending you and Sergeant Green to Los Angeles.'

'Sergeant Green?' That surprised her more than anything else. 'Surely to deal with Sumner we need a trained diplomat, not an army sergeant and an ATA girl. Why not send Guy?'

'It's a good point,' Brinkman conceded. 'But I think you'll find Green is more than up to the job. As are you, now that you've completed the SOE course. And in any case, although he doesn't know it yet, I need Guy to go with Leo, to France.'

CHAPTER 6

It didn't seem to Jed Haines that the paper's readers would be at all interested in the sixty-eighth meeting of the American Astronomical Society. Especially as it had taken place a couple of weeks previously, and at Yale University. But Felix was keen to publish what he called 'lighter' material to distract from the news of the war.

The challenge for Jed was coming up with some sort of local angle to give the story some interest. He hadn't been out of the city for months. For one thing he was too busy, with the paper and with seeing Cynthia. For another, the few times he had driven out in the hope of finding someone who had seen the mysterious aircraft back in February had soon convinced him he was looking for a needle in a field full of haystacks. Now, looking back, he couldn't be sure he hadn't imagined the whole thing.

But on his last trip, he'd driven past a sign to the Mount Wilson Observatory. Maybe that was his local angle? The astronomers on our doorstep... He found the number and gave them a call. The next afternoon, he was driving out of Los Angeles again – but this time with a defined destination and a specific purpose.

The Mount Wilson Observatory was a collection of small buildings hidden away amongst the trees. The pale structures could be glimpsed through and above the woods as you approached. A narrow lane afforded the only way in.

The interviews went better than he had expected. It turned out that one of the senior staff at the observatory had actually been at the Astronomical Society meeting. They were happy to show him the telescope and explain what they did – some of which Jed understood. He took copious notes and snapped a few photos.

He waited until he was leaving before asking, as casually as he could, if any of them had seen anything on that night back in February when it seemed like Los Angeles was under attack. There were some exchanged glances, but it seemed that no one had seen anything unusual.

'Hell of a light show though,' the senior guy – Meredith – said. But no, he assured Jed, no one had seen anything. There were no unexplained sightings in the sky on the night of 24 February. And thank you for coming, it had been a pleasure.

It was a disappointment, but hardly unexpected, Jed thought as he returned to his car. The photos had come out blank and even under a magnifying glass they'd remained defiantly devoid of detail. No one had seen anything that would help him find out where the strange craft he had seen was from, or where it went. If he *had* seen it – he could barely recall now what he had witnessed. A shadow, a trick of the light… Time to let it drop. Again.

The tap on the window made him flinch with surprise. It was one of the men from the observatory, probably come to check he knew the way back to the main road. Jed wound down the window.

'It's OK, I remember the way. And I've got a map.'

'A lot of what we do here is government funded,' the man said. Trevor, Jed remembered his name was, though that could be his first or last name. 'Or at least, dependent on the government's good will.'

'I guess it is,' Jed replied wondering where this was leading.

'So you can believe us when we tell you we saw nothing. Back in February, I mean. We saw nothing at all.'

'I don't doubt it.'

Trevor nodded. 'Good. That's good. Because,' he went on, 'if we had seen something it probably would have been to the south east of here. There's a few farms out that way – let me show you.'

He gestured for Jed to pass him the map he had open on the passenger seat. 'This is the area I'm talking about.' He pointed to the empty space on the map south east of where the observatory was marked, broken only by a few thin roads on their way to somewhere else. 'Just to save you the journey, you understand. But there are a few farms and a couple of homesteads in that area. If you ask people down there, they probably won't have seen anything either.'

There were photographs of everything in the Vault. Even of himself, soon after he arrived, helping to catalogue and label some of the artefacts and one of the dead creatures.

Hoffman paused, his fingers glossing against the surface of the photograph. He looked so young. So naïve. So human.

He set aside his emotion, like flicking a switch he turned on his concentration and returned to the task, leafing through each picture. A steady, systematic movement. As soon as he finished one box, he returned it to its place on the shelf and started on the next. No pause for sleep or food. Like a machine.

Until he found it.

There were two photographs. One of the artefact lying on the ground in the forest where it had been found. The other was on a plain background, a measuring stick laid alongside to give the scale. He was surprised how small it was. It would fit into the palm of his hand. It was made of a single piece of stone, the symbols carved into it, just as the girl had sketched. An angular hourglass with a reference number displayed on a card at the edge of each photograph: V-962-X7.

The number yielded a single card in the index drawer. Neat block handwriting told him:

Stone implement. Likely buried at the site in antiquity and disturbed by the crash.

Given the location it was found, suggestion that it could even be the mythical 'Axe of Thor'. The runic markings support this theory. Thor is said to have used the axe to hammer on the Gates of Asgard to awaken Odin and the other gods when they slept through the Long Dark Night of Damnation.

Hoffman turned over the card. On the back, someone else had written:

Artefact removed from Archive on 27 October 1938. Authorisation – Standartenfuhrer Hans Streicher.

Streicher was dead, so Hoffman couldn't ask him. But where was the artefact now?

Papers and manuscripts were spread across the table of the conference room at Station Z. Guy and Leo sat one side of the table, Elizabeth Archer and Miss Manners on the other. Brinkman, already briefed by Mrs Archer, left them to get on with it. All Guy knew was that he and Leo were going to France. He had yet to discover why.

'Sumner is holding a reception to open the new wing of his personal museum or gallery or whatever he calls it next week,' Leo was saying. 'He's already sent out a catalogue to various local collectors and luminaries, which is how we found the axe-head.'

'Assuming it's the same artefact as Miss Roylston saw,' Guy said.

'It's the same,' Miss Manners confirmed. 'I showed her the catalogue at lunchtime when she managed to slip away from Crowley's house for a while. There's no doubt.'

'What I do doubt,' Elizabeth said, 'is the supposed provenance.'

'How do you mean?' Guy asked.

'Its apparent origin. According to the notes in Sumner's catalogue, he believes the axe-head to be an ancient artefact that originated in North America.'

'That's possible, surely,' Guy said.

'It is,' she agreed. 'But it is also possible that the artefact in Sumner's possession is this.'

She pushed an ancient parchment towards Guy. He leaned forward to inspect it. The writing was Greek, he could tell that much. But it wasn't modern Greek, which he could read fairly easily. He didn't spend time trying to interpret what he did understand. His attention was focused on the picture.

It was a drawing of an axe, complete with its wooden handle. But the head of the axe looked identical to the photograph in Sumner's catalogue.

'It's the same,' he murmured, pulling the catalogue closer so as to compare the two.

'Perhaps,' Miss Manners said.

'Or,' Leo added, 'we think it's possible that there are two of these axes.'

'If not more,' Elizabeth said. 'But we have to be sure. We know the Vril are after the one in Sumner's possession. Or we have to assume that they are.'

'Though we don't know why,' Guy said. 'And of course, they may be after this Greek one as well, if there are indeed two. We have no way of knowing. It *is* Greek, I take it?'

'From the text,' Elizabeth explained, 'this is the axe that Theseus took from Procrustes.' She pulled the parchment back and started to gather up the other papers and documents, obviously assuming this explained everything.

Guy looked at Miss Manners, who seemed to be trying not to smile. Leo cleared his throat.

'I'm sorry,' Guy said at last, 'all I know about Theseus is that he killed the Minotaur in the Labyrinth.'

Elizabeth looked up, and caught Guy's puzzled expression. She sighed. 'Procrustes had a bed.'

'So do I,' Guy offered. 'Did he also have an axe?'

'Procrustes, also known as "the Stretcher", was a son of Poseidon. He was a smith, and he waylaid travellers on the road between Athens and Eleusis. He forced them to try out his bed for size.'

'Doesn't sound too bad,' Guy ventured.

'If they didn't fit the bed,' Miss Manners said, 'then he stretched them out and hammered at them until they did.'

'Hence "the Stretcher",' Leo said. 'The process killed the poor travellers, of course.'

'Unless they were too long for the bed,' Elizabeth went on. 'In which case, he cut their legs off. With an axe.'

'Ah, I see. *That* axe.'

'Exactly.'

'So you had to be a perfect fit to survive,' Guy deduced.

'Well, no,' Leo told him, 'because Procrustes cheated. He actually had two beds of different sizes. So he'd produce the one he knew you wouldn't fit.'

'And how does Theseus come into it?'

'He got the better of Procrustes,' Leo said, 'which must have been a huge relief to everyone else. He made him lie on his own bed, and sure enough Procrustes didn't fit either. So, according to one version of the story, Theseus took his axe, and cut his head off with it.'

'Theseus was trying to find a way to the underworld, and Procrustes guarded the Sixth Entrance to Hades. There is also a version of the legend that says Theseus used the same axe to slay the Minotaur,' Miss Manners said.

'Ah, the Minotaur.' At least Guy knew that story.

'But let's not get carried away,' Elizabeth told them. 'These are just myths, after all. But it's interesting that the axe was known as the Labrys, from which the Labyrinth took its name. And from that, it's come to mean a maze, of course.'

'The double-headed axe has always been important in Minoan legend and ritual,' Miss Manners said. 'Which would tie in with the Minotaur and the Labyrinth.'

'I'll tell you something else that's interesting,' Guy said, 'if only to prove that I do know something about Greek history as well as their language.'

'And what's that?' Elizabeth asked.

'Well, it's probably just a coincidence, but until very

recently the double-headed axe was also the symbol of the Greek Fascist Party.'

'You never know,' Leo said, 'like the Nazi adoption of the Swastika, ancient symbols seem to have a resonance with the fascists. Harking back to an earlier, purer age or something, no doubt.'

'Perhaps the French manuscript will enlighten us,' Elizabeth said.

'Finally we get to France.' Guy smiled. 'I was wondering what the connection might be.'

'The connection is a manuscript, as Elizabeth says,' Miss Manners told him. 'It is said to be a copy of writings by Plutarch, though he himself took the ideas from his grandfather, Lamprias, whom he almost certainly paraphrased.'

'So what's it about?' Guy wondered.

'It is unique,' Leo told him, 'in that it apparently brings together and reinterprets myths and legends from the ancient worlds of Greece, Rome, Scandinavia and Northern Europe.'

Elizabeth nodded. 'It seems to suggest a common thread, possibly a common origin, for all these myths. Which is obviously unusual. But Lamprias, the original author of much of it, seems to be the original source for the story of the Axe of Theseus, including the embellishments about the Minotaur. So this manuscript may well give us more background information about the axe itself and its history and relevance. By drawing together the different legends, it may give us a common origin for both these axes, or make it clear there is only the one.'

'So if this manuscript is so important and unusual, how come there is only one copy?'

'Suppressed by the Catholic Church.' Miss Manners' tone made it clear what she thought about that. 'They're so closed-minded. But at least they preserved the manuscript rather than burning it.'

'And they preserved it in France?'

'It's held in the library of a monastery just outside Paris,' Leo said. 'And Elizabeth thinks it would be a good idea for you and me to go over and fetch it.'

Guy laughed. 'Easy as that?'

'Not quite, old boy, no. Apart from the fact that we'd be stealing a priceless manuscript from a collection of monks who won't care to part with it, we have to get into occupied France, and then survive long enough to identify the right manuscript.'

'The library at St Jean-Baptiste de Seine has a large collection of ancient writings,' Elizabeth said. 'It's quite famous for it.'

'But if you can recover the manuscript,' Miss Manners said, 'then it might tell us more about the Axe of Theseus, how it relates – if it does – to the axe that Sumner has, and why the Vril are after it.'

Elizabeth smiled. 'Exactly.'

'All right, let's go and get it, then.'

'There is just one other complication,' Leo said as Miss Manners helped Elizabeth gather up her papers. 'The Monastery of Jean-Baptiste de Seine has been requisitioned by the occupying power.'

'So it's no longer a monastery?' Guy said.

'Oh, the monks are still there, apparently,' Leo assured him. 'And the library, and hopefully the manuscript. But the buildings are now also home to the local headquarters of the Gestapo.'

CHAPTER 7

They flew from Prestwick on the south-west coast of Scotland. From here, BOAC, recently formed from consolidating the nationalised British Airways and Imperial airlines, operated the Return Ferry Service to Montreal. Sarah and Sergeant Green shared the converted RAF *Liberator* with several other pilots. They'd all flown American-built bombers across from Canada and were now on their way back to collect more.

Sarah and Sergeant Green sat alone in the back of the plane. It was draughty and cold and uncomfortable. It took about an hour for the other passengers to stop glancing back at Sarah. No doubt they were wondering who she was and why she was on the flight. It unnerved her slightly, until Green said quietly:

'I don't know why they keep looking at me like that.'

She laughed, drawing more stares. 'You realise I hardly know anything about you,' she told him. 'I don't even know if you're married.'

He smiled. 'You asking?'

'I'm spoken for,' she said.

He nodded. 'I know. And yes, I am married. But thanks for the thought.' He offered her a cigarette. She declined. 'To save you asking the next question,' he said, 'the answer's no.'

'No?'

'No, we don't have any children.' Green blew out a thoughtful stream of smoke. 'Doesn't seem like the best time to bring a kid into the world right now.'

'No,' Sarah had to agree. 'Wouldn't be easy for your wife either, with you away. I mean, looking after the child,' she added quickly.

Green grinned. He didn't smile often, but it changed his face from looking like a boxer's to something far more avuncular. Yes, Sarah thought, he'd make a good father – one day. If he got the chance. She hoped he would.

'You're right, she wouldn't have time,' Green said. 'Mable works in a munitions factory in Manchester. Lives with her mum, who works there too. It's boring but dangerous.' He took another drag on the cigarette. 'So, a bit like flying across the Atlantic, I suppose.'

'I suppose.'

One trip, Jed promised himself. Just one. Chances were he'd find nothing, because there was nothing to find. If he was lucky he might meet some old farmer with failing eyesight who might have seen something back in February. Or maybe he didn't, and perhaps it wasn't February he was thinking of anyway. But after the tip-off from the guy at the observatory, it had to be worth a look.

So just one trip. And even so, he was wasting time and gas, he thought as he turned down yet another narrow dirt track.

Or maybe not.

Jed slammed his foot down on the brake pedal, bringing the car to a skidding halt in a cloud of dust. It might be nothing, but the undergrowth on one side of the track had been ripped away, branches of trees broken off, the ground charred, a scar scraped through the landscape. The woodland had started to grow back over it, of course, but it looked as though something had ploughed through here – something large and fast and hot. And the damage was evidently several months old...

Could this be what he was looking for?

Jed left the car angled across the narrow road, running back to explore the area he'd seen. The trail led deep into the wooded area, the ground and branches and scrub charred and discoloured, thrust aside as something forced – burned – its way through.

In the distance, nestling under larger trees, he caught sight of something reflecting back the afternoon sun. The glint of metal. Whatever it was that had torn its way through the wood – it was still here.

Did he have the camera with him? Jed couldn't even remember if he'd bothered to chuck it on the back seat of the car. But he wasn't going back to check, not until he'd seen what was at the end of the trail of devastation.

He hurried forward, hardly daring to draw breath. Was it a plane? A Japanese bomber? The shape was obscured by the trees and the vegetation growing back over it. Then a figure stepped out in front of Jed.

He skidded to a halt. The man was dressed in rough work clothes, dishevelled and spattered with mud and dirt. There was a rip down one leg of the pants. His weather-beaten face was set hard as granite and he held a shotgun levelled at Jed.

'Wait – wait!' Jed cried out, afraid the man was about to shoot first and not bother with questions at all. 'I just want to see what's down there, in the trees.'

'Why?' the man's voice was strangely devoid of accent, flat and emotionless.

'Do you know what it is?'

'This is my land.'

Jed held out his hands. 'Look, sorry if I'm trespassing. I'm a reporter, from LA.'

The shotgun jabbed forward slightly. 'Reporting what?'

'For a newspaper. I know something came down here, one night back in February when there was all the noise and shooting over the city. Remember?' Maybe the guy was a bit simple. But Jed didn't doubt he would shoot if he didn't like what he heard.

'You're a newspaper man.'

'That's right.'

'You got connections.'

'I suppose. But whatever you have here, on your land, it could be valuable. Why not let me take a look?'

The man tilted his head slightly to one side. Maybe he was considering this. 'Then what?' he asked.

'Then I could come back with a camera. Take some photos. Get you and whatever it is in the paper. Make you famous. Maybe,' Jed added, 'make you rich.'

'You'd pay me to let you see what's down there?'

'Depends what it is.' He didn't want to commit to anything until he knew what the guy had here. 'Let me see what you got, and I'm sure we can come to an arrangement.'

The man nodded. But he didn't lower the gun.

'I'll make it worth your while,' Jed said. 'I've got some cash on me now, if it helps. Not much...' He reached into his pocket for his billfold. 'I'm Jed – Jed Haines. What's your name?'

'Davy Wiles. I don't need money.'

'Then you're a remarkable man.'

'Yes.' He said it like it was a simple statement of fact.

'So what *do* you need?'

There was a pause. The man looked up, as if he was listening. 'I need to see Sumner.'

'You what?'

'J.D. Sumner. I need to see him. You know Sumner?'

Jed shrugged. 'Sure I do,' he lied. 'But why would a farmer like you want to see Mr Sumner? They say he hasn't been outside his mansion in years.' A thought struck him. 'You want to sell him whatever you've got back there? He's a collector, might make you a good offer.'

'Nothing like that,' Wiles said. There was still barely any inflection in his voice. 'We share an interest, me and Sumner.'

'Oh?'

'An interest in...' He paused, glancing upwards again as if listening to something in the distance before continuing: '... in native American artefacts.'

'Stuff the Red Indians left behind, you mean? Yeah, I've heard he goes for that stuff.' Jed remembered subbing an

80

article about it recently. He struggled to recall the details.

'Found some pieces on my land. Might interest Sumner. So, can you arrange for me to meet him?'

'Sure.' Jed smiled. He remembered the article now. 'Sumner's opening a new gallery of his museum this week, going to show off some more of his collection. Including some of these Native American Artefacts. He's having a reception for the opening, on Friday evening.' Sumner probably wouldn't even show up, but Jed wasn't about to mention that. 'I can get a press pass for you if you want. I'll talk to Felix, my editor. Won't be a problem. We'll sort something out.'

Now Wiles did lower the shotgun, just slightly. 'Good. You do that, Jed Haines. Then you can see what's here.'

'No, I want to see it now.'

The gun swung back up. 'After I see Sumner.'

Despite the lack of emotion or accent, there was something in the voice that told Jed he meant it. 'OK, OK. I'll sort out that press pass, like I said. We can arrange somewhere to meet. I'll be going too. Then next day, I come back here and see what you've got. I'll bring a camera, all right?'

Wiles nodded. 'Come back before and I'll know. Then I'll kill you.'

Jed's mouth went dry at the matter-of-fact way he said it. He forced himself not to show how afraid he suddenly was. 'Hey, we got a deal, right?' He tried to smile, tried to sound in control. 'This reception will be a big deal, you know. Loads of important people there. Rich people too. You'll need a suit.'

There was a plane waiting for them at Montreal. If Sergeant Green was impressed with Sarah's father's hospitality, he didn't show it, but settled back in the rather more comfortable seat of the DC-3, and was almost immediately asleep.

Sarah spent the journey down to Los Angeles staring out of the window, enjoying the tangible motion of the flight as it bumped gently through the clouds, and wishing she was at the controls.

It didn't surprise her that Dad was there to meet them

when they landed. She hadn't seen him since before the war. His face was a little more lined, his hair no longer streaked with grey but a uniform gunmetal. He was a tall man, lean and confident, and enfolded Sarah immediately in his arms.

'How's my favourite daughter?' There was a trace of accent he'd picked up from his years living in the States.

'I'm your only daughter,' Sarah pointed out as she untangled herself from the embrace.

'You can still be my favourite.'

Sarah introduced Green, and her father led them through the airport, assuring them their luggage would be at their hotel before they were. A limousine was waiting for them at the kerb, the uniformed driver already holding open the back door for Sarah to climb inside.

'You'll want to freshen up, I'm sure,' Anthony Diamond told them as he settled himself in the front beside the driver. He twisted round to look back at them. 'But then I'll stand you both dinner.'

'That's very kind, Mr Diamond,' Green said. 'But—'

Diamond waved away the protest. 'But nothing. Least I can do.'

'We're here to work, Dad,' Sarah pointed out.

'Not today, you're not. You want to see Jonny Sumner, you'll have to wait until he wants to see you.'

'And when is that?' Green asked.

'I ship goods around the world for him, but he's not at my beck and call. More's the pity.'

'So you can't help us?' Sarah couldn't keep the disappointment out of her voice.

'It would help if I knew why you're so desperate to see him.'

Green shook his head. 'Can't tell you that, I'm afraid, sir.'

'I know, I know – there's a war on. Not that you'd notice it much over here yet. But for what it's worth, I do have an invitation to the reception on Friday when Sumner's opening the new gallery you seemed so interested in. If that's any good.'

'That's great,' Sarah told him, leaning forward to put her

hand affectionately and gratefully on his shoulder. 'There's something in the gallery we need to see as well as Sumner, if we can.' She was aware of Green looking at her, and knew she'd said more than he thought she should have. 'Thanks, Dad.'

'Yes, thank you, sir,' Green added. 'That's really good going.'

'Not as good as you might like, Green,' Diamond said, turning back to face the windshield. 'My invitation is for me and one guest. I'm not missing it for the world, and my guest is my daughter. So you'll have to sit this one out.'

There was the hint of a smile on Green's face. 'Oh I've never been one for sitting things out, Mr Diamond. Invitation or not, I'll be there, I promise you.'

While it was late afternoon on the west coast of the USA, it was the middle of the night over occupied France. A plane smaller and quieter than the DC-3 that had taken Sarah Diamond and Sergeant Green from Montreal to Los Angeles made its clandestine journey from RAF Tempsford in Bedfordshire. The Westland Lysander banked away from Paris, evading German observation posts with practised ease and descending towards a field to the east of the city.

The plane was on the ground for less than a minute. As it took off again, its two passengers set off across the countryside and disappeared into the night. Not for the first time, Guy Pentecross and Leo Davenport were risking their lives in occupied France.

CHAPTER 8

It wasn't the sort of place Jed had expected at all. The bar was upmarket and expensive in a good area of the city. But the note from Davy Wiles, delivered to Jed at the office that afternoon, said to meet him here.

Jed almost didn't recognise the man. Wiles was sitting at a table in a booth towards the back of the dimly lit room. A glass of beer sat untouched on the table in front of him. But perhaps it wasn't the man's first.

Jed waved to the barman for a beer of his own, and slid into the booth to sit opposite Wiles.

'You all set?' he asked.

Wiles fixed him with an unsettlingly focused stare. 'All set.'

'You look smart,' Jed said as he waited for his drink.

The man had shaved and generally cleaned himself up. He was well dressed too. Very well dressed in a dark blue double-breasted suit.

'You said I'd need a suit.'

'So I did.' Jed's own suit was in need of cleaning and pressing. But it would have to do.

'You have the invitation?' Wiles demanded.

Jed patted his breast pocket reassuringly. 'I do indeed.'

It had taken all his charm and more to persuade Cynthia to go to the considerable trouble of getting it. She'd been livid when she found out Jed didn't intend to take her with him.

He'd promised to make it up to her. If this evening – and more importantly tomorrow morning – went as well as he hoped, he'd be able to afford to.

'I've got the car outside,' Jed told Wiles as he drained his beer. Wiles, he noted, still hadn't touched his drink. 'You staying in town tonight? If you are, I can give you a ride back to your place tomorrow. I've got the camera with me,' he added, hoping to provoke some clue from the man about what he might see in the morning.

But Wiles remained impassive. 'I have a ride arranged for tonight,' he said.

'You're full of surprises, ain't you,' Jed said, buoyed up by the beer. He signalled the barman for another. 'Nice suit, by the way. Did you get it specially?'

There might have been the hint of a smile on Wiles's lips as he watched Jed start on his next drink. 'Yes,' he said, 'I got it specially.'

The barman took Jed's empty bottle and tossed it into a crate full of other empty bottles. The crate was almost full, so while the bar was fairly quiet he decided to dump it out the back.

The back door of the bar opened into an alleyway. It was already dark, and the nearest streetlight was out. Scrumpled paper caught what light there was as it blew down the narrow street. The barman heaved the crate up and emptied it into a large dumpster. The bottles rattled against the metal sides. Usually they smashed on the bottles and other trash already inside, but this time they didn't. The barman barely noticed. He was already thinking about how long he still had to work and what he'd do when he got off tonight.

Inside the dumpster, deadening the fall of the bottles, lay the twisted form of a man's body. He had been killed by a single, powerful blow to the head. Until recently, he had been a the manager of a small bank three blocks away. Until recently he had cared about his appearance, but now he was lying amongst a stale mass of discarded restaurant food and broken glass, flat beer dripping onto his lifeless body.

Until recently, he had been wearing a dark blue, double-breasted suit.

The beaten-up, muddy car looked as out of place beside the smart, gleaming limos parked on the forecourt as Jed felt among the smartly dressed people arriving at Sumner's house.

'House' was an understatement – it was a mansion on an estate outside the city. The house was lit with floodlights. The grounds were sculpted out of the landscape, designed to show off the grandeur of the place. A long driveway curved its way to the house so as to afford the best possible views. Even in the dark of the evening, it was an impressive sight.

As they joined a group of other guests heading up the wide steps to the main entrance, Jed tucked the bulky camera under his coat. He pulled the crumpled invitation card from the pocket of his crumpled jacket.

'I'll get you in, as agreed,' he said quietly to Wiles. 'But once inside it's up to you to find Sumner and talk to him, all right?'

'All right,' Wiles repeated, without looking at Jed. 'I will find what I need.'

'Then I get to see whatever came down on your land. That's the deal, right?'

'You will see it,' Wiles promised, still not looking at Jed. 'You will see it very soon.'

It was a long time since Sarah had dressed up for an evening out. Drinks or even a meal with Guy after a day at work were special, but not in a dressing-up sort of way. She had spent a pleasant afternoon shopping in the city, forgetting for a while all about the war and rationing and how difficult it was to find anything to wear in London apart from the drab utility clothing everyone bought.

Now, walking up the steps to what looked like an English stately home dumped down outside Los Angeles, she felt like a million dollars. She had a coat that had some shape to it and actually kept out the chill of the evening. A dress that fitted – fitted very well, she was happy to admit, and in all the right places. For once she was wearing stockings. Real stockings rather than wiped-on gravy browning with a line of pencil to represent the seam. Lipstick was a luxury – she had never been able to stand using beetroot juice to redden her lips like some of the girls in the ATA. Or, come to that, soot from the fireplace to darken her eyes.

She didn't think of herself as vain. These were all things her father could have sent over from America for her if she'd really been that bothered. But that hardly seemed fair on the other women struggling to manage in a country under siege. Just for this evening, though, Sarah was happy to feel good about how she looked. The appreciative smile from the man who checked their invitation enhanced the feeling – even though he probably thought her father was a rich playboy showing off his latest gold-digging trophy.

'Is Mr Sumner here this evening?' Sarah's father asked the attendant. 'My daughter would very much like to meet him.' He stressed the 'daughter' – obviously reading the man's smile the same way Sarah had.

The smile faded. 'I believe he is, sir, yes.'

'Thank you.'

A maid was on hand to take their coats. Her own smile had been painted on with a lot of practice. They followed the general flow into a huge reception room with an impressive chandelier hanging from the high ceiling and wood-panelled walls. White-jacketed waiters moved through the crowd with bottles to top up glasses, and trays of food.

'Let's mingle for a bit,' Diamond said. 'If I spot Sumner, we'll try to grab a few words with him.'

'It's a nice home he has here,' Sarah said.

Diamond laughed. 'Oh, he doesn't live here. This is his collection of art and artefacts. It's open to the public, notionally.'

'What's that mean?'

'It means by appointment. Sumner actually lives in a

penthouse at the top of one of the hotels in Los Angeles. Runs his company from there too.'

'And rarely leaves.'

'He's rarely seen in public. There's a difference.'

They were interrupted by a sudden flash of light close by. Sarah turned, startled – to see a photographer moving through the room, a young man with dark curly hair in a suit that had seen better days. He paused to take another picture of a middle-aged couple, nodding his thanks and moving on to take more.

'I doubt Sumner will take kindly to having photos taken,' Diamond said.

He was right. Two of the waiters, distinctive in their immaculate white jackets, were already hurrying after the photographer. They reached him as he framed up yet another picture. The flash went off again, just as one of the waiters put his hand on the man's shoulder. The other relieved him of his camera. The photographer's protests were shrugged away.

A short, rather nondescript man in a plain suit and slightly off-centre bow tie had appeared beside Sarah and her father. His dark hair was oiled and slicked back from his high forehead. He sipped at his wine and nodded to where the photographer was now defiantly scribbling in a small notebook. 'The press are always with us, it seems.'

'I'm afraid so,' Diamond agreed. 'I'm sorry, I don't think you've met my daughter, Sarah.'

'I don't think I have.' The man took Sarah's hand. She thought for a moment he was going to kiss it, but instead he gave a gentle shake and let go. 'You're every bit as beautiful as your mother.'

She hadn't expected that. 'Thank you, sir.'

'Oh call me J.D. – everyone does.'

'Sumner?!' Sarah mouthed at her father as the man turned away for a moment to speak to a waiter. Her father nodded.

'Tell him he can have his camera back tomorrow,' Sumner was saying to the waiter. 'But he's not to use any of the pictures without my express permission. And the permission of whoever is in them, of course. No real harm done.'

The waiter nodded and moved off. Sumner turned back to Sarah and her father, smiling. 'I hate these events,' he said. 'But thank you for coming. It's good to see some friendly faces in amongst the people you have to invite for...' He frowned. 'Well, I'm not quite sure why I have to invite them, but there must be a reason.'

'I confess we're not really here for the fun of it either, I'm afraid,' Diamond told him.

'Oh? You intrigue me, Anthony.'

'My daughter wanted to ask you some questions.'

Sumner's smile hardened slightly. 'You're not a reporter, are you?'

'No,' Sarah assured him. 'I work for the British military. We believe you might have something in your collection that is important to the war effort.'

The smile was back. 'Reduced to bows and arrows now, are you? I knew things were getting tight over there.'

'Not quite. But an ancient axe-head, actually. It's in the collection you're showing off tonight.'

Sumner nodded. 'There are several axe-heads. But I would guess you're interested in the Doll-Child's Axe.'

'That's the one.'

'Normally, I wouldn't—' Diamond started to say.

But Sumner waved away his apology. 'Fascinating. The Doll-Child's Axe has some significance, some relevance today?'

'It would seem so. Though we don't know what – just that...' She hesitated, not sure how to phrase it. 'The enemy are interested in it, and we want to know why.'

Sumner nodded. 'A puzzle. And one probably best discussed more privately.'

'I'd appreciate that,' Sarah agreed.

'Let's go look at it, then.'

'The axe?'

'Why not? Every man and his mistress, and there are quite a few of those here tonight, will be traipsing through to look at it when we open the gallery in an hour. If you want to take a look without the fanfare and the inane comments then now's the time.'

'You're sure?' Diamond asked.

'An excuse to get away from this lot?' Sumner said quietly. 'You're joking. Course I'm sure. Get yourselves another drink, I need to say hello to the Mayor, but then I'll be with you.'

Muffled sounds of the reception carried to the wing where the new exhibition hall had been set up. It was like a long corridor, with display cases along each side. Not all the lights were on yet, so the corridor was lengthened by shadows, stretching into the distance. At the far end was a large window giving out into the grounds. Since it was dark outside, the window acted as a mirror, making the gallery seem even longer.

The white jacket of a uniformed waiter almost glowed in the dim light as he stood a short way along the gallery. He nodded to Sumner and his guests, his face dipping deferentially into shadow as they passed.

Sumner led Sarah and her father to a display case about halfway along the gallery. Inside were various artefacts, all of them cracked and chipped and worn: a small wooden statue in a rough approximation of the female form but with hugely enlarged hips and breasts; several arrowheads; a hollowed-out stone bowl; a small cup that looked as if it had been fashioned from bone...

Resting on a small plinth behind these was the stone axe-head. Sarah recognised it at once, even without the small typed card that listed it as 'The Doll–Child's Axe' along with a reference number. It was in surprisingly good condition compared with the other relics in the case.

'It's smaller than I expected,' she said. The whole artefact was only about four inches across at its widest point.

'It's ceremonial rather than practical,' Sumner said. 'It belonged to a small town museum in Idaho,' he went on. 'They were losing money, looked like they'd have to close. So I made them an offer, and now they can stay open. For a while, anyway.'

'It's made of stone?' Sarah's father asked.

'Yeah, seems to be, though it's worn well as you can see. No way of dating it for certain, but it's thought to be from about the tenth century. So pretty ancient.'

'And it originated in Idaho?' Sarah asked.

'Who knows? If you asked me, I'd say it probably didn't originate in North America at all. But the museum curator swore blind the local Indians venerated it for centuries as the axe used to cut the tree in the legend of the doll-child.' He shrugged. 'I'm an enthusiastic collector, but I'm not an expert. So who am I to argue?'

'So why's it important, Sarah?' Diamond asked.

She shrugged. 'Blessed if I know. But people are looking for it.'

'Nazis?' Sumner asked.

'Probably. And others. You might do best to keep it in a vault.'

Sumner gave a nervous laugh. 'You really think someone's gonna try and steal it from here?'

They'd told Jed he could get his camera back tomorrow – provided he agreed not to use any of the pictures he had taken without permission. So what good was that?

He was annoyed – as much with himself as anything. He'd need the camera back before he returned to Wiles's farm. He should have waited, got photos of something worth photographing rather than the Mayor and some minor local celebrities. And Davy Wiles of course, he was in the background of a couple of the shots – just standing there looking totally out of place.

Jed looked round for Wiles to see if he'd managed to collar Sumner yet. He saw Sumner before he saw Wiles – leaving through a back door with a pretty young blonde woman in a striking backless dress. There was an older guy with them too – old enough to be the woman's father. No prizes for guessing what might be going on there, out of sight of the other guests.

As he watched, he caught sight of Wiles – distinctive in

his dark blue suit. Where the hell had he got that? Where the hell had he got the money to get that? Wiles was pushing past several other guests without a word of apology and following Sumner and the man and woman from the room. Well, that could be embarrassing. Jed smiled at the thought of how Sumner's heavies would treat Wiles if he got in the way.

On the other hand, he realised, he needed Wiles sweet and amenable for the moment. Best to warn him off – help him choose a better time. Jed hurried after them. He glanced round to make sure none of the waiters was watching before he slipped through the door after Wiles.

Something brushed against Sarah's ankle. She stifled a gasp of surprise and looked down. A cat glanced back up at her, before slinking off down the gallery. A black cat – was that good or bad luck? She could never remember.

Sumner was telling them he'd rather not remove the axe from the display case right now. 'After everyone's been through, wait behind then and you can examine the hell out of it. For all the good it will do you – it's just stone.'

The cat had stopped and was looking back at them. Its eyes glinted green with reflected light. And Sarah felt a sudden chill down her spine that had nothing to do with the cut of her dress.

'Do you have a cat?' she asked.

'What?' Sumner frowned. Her father was staring at her, equally surprised by the question.

'It's important – do you have a cat? Here at the gallery?'

'No, of course not.' Sumner peered into the darkness, at the cat staring back at them. 'I'll have someone put it outside.'

He turned to gesture to a figure approaching along the gallery. At first Sarah thought it was the waiter, but she could still see the white of his jacket further down the room. This man was dressed in a dark suit. Behind him, another man was running towards them. As he passed under one of the infrequent lights, Sarah saw that it was the photographer.

'Wait!' he called. 'Mr Wiles – Davy – not now!'

Sumner had seen him too. He was holding up his hand and shaking his head as he stepped forward. 'No, no, no. No interviews, no background pieces, no personal information. Tonight is all about the gallery, not about me.'

The man in the suit didn't break step. He grabbed Sumner by the lapels of his jacket, lifted the small man bodily into the air, then hurled him aside. Sumner crashed to the floor with a cry of surprise and pain.

The photographer was running towards them. The waiter too, stocky and well-built, barrelled down the gallery. Sarah grabbed her father, pulling him out of the way as the man in the dark suit smashed his fist into the front of the display case, shattering the glass.

'He's come for the axe-head!' she gasped.

'The hell he has!'

For a moment they were caught frozen in place. Sarah holding her father back. Sumner struggling to his feet. The photographer and the waiter running. The man reaching into the shattered display cabinet. The cat watching from further down the room.

Caught in a blinding flash of light as something huge and bright descended on to the lawn outside. There was a roar of sound and the whole window exploded inwards, showering glass along the gallery.

CHAPTER 9

They spent the best part of the morning watching the monastery. It was on the edge of the small market town of St Jean-Baptiste de Seine, one side bordered by extensive woods. The original stone-built medieval structure had been extended in the last century. From the vehicles parked outside the newer section, and from observing the various comings and goings, it was apparent that the newer block was where the Gestapo had set up their headquarters.

Guy and Leo Davenport were concealed in the woodland, lying in the dense undergrowth. From here they had a good view of the back and side of the buildings. Through an arched opening in the wall, they could see several monks tending a small kitchen garden. The dark, shapeless habits were a contrast to the smart uniforms the Gestapo officers wore, very similar to the uniform of the SS.

The ground was damp and cold. Guy was getting cramped, and with every minute he seemed to become more aware of the stones and sticks digging into him. He shifted to try to get more comfortable.

'So what do you suggest?' he asked.

'Well,' Leo replied, 'the simplest approach is often the best.'

'You think we can just wander in and ask to see their collection of rare historic books?'

'I think we probably can, actually.' Leo smiled at Guy's

surprise. 'We'd need a reason. A couple of academics visiting from Paris, perhaps?'

Guy looked at Leo's rather bedraggled appearance. It had rained quite heavily in the night and he suspected he looked just as dishevelled and unkempt. 'Do we look like Parisian academics?'

'Who knows? But we might. I'm open to any other suggestions. I guess we could wait until tonight and break in. But then we have to find the library, and the manuscript we want, and who knows what hours they keep in a monastery. Never mind our friends next door.'

He nodded at a Kubelwagon drawing up outside the Gestapo building. Two men in grey uniform dragged a young woman out of the back of the vehicle and pushed her roughly ahead of them towards the door. She stumbled, regained her balance enough to spit at them, and was shoved forwards again.

Guy felt his anger rising. His fists clenched at his side. Leo put his hand on Guy's shoulder, shaking his head. They both knew there was nothing they could do.

'We'll wait until late afternoon,' Leo said. 'Our clothes will have dried, so long as it doesn't start raining again. The monks should be tiring by then; they've been up since five. And if it's starting to get dark, they're less likely just to turn us away.'

'You hope.'

'Life is built on hope. Certainties just get in the way.'

Guy couldn't help but smile. 'Does that actually mean anything, or does it just sound as if it should?'

'I have no idea,' Leo confessed. 'It's probably a quote from something, I rather lose track.' He rolled onto his side and pulled something from his coat pocket. It was a pack of cards. 'Now then, how about a few hands of whist while we wait?'

It stayed dry for most of the afternoon, but it was starting to rain again as Guy and Leo approached the main door to the monastery. Guy hoped that might work in their favour. Surely it was part of the monks' remit to be sympathetic to the needs and comfort of others?

Leo worked an iron bell-pull beside the door. It had no discernible effect, but within a few moments they heard footsteps approaching, and the door opened.

The monk allowed them inside the hallway, which was as bare and spartan as Guy had anticipated. A plain wooden chest stood in an alcove, but that was the only furniture or adornment. Guy explained to the monk that they had travelled from Paris with the hope of being allowed access to the monastery's famous library. Leo's French was more than adequate, but he let Guy do the talking.

'We were delayed on the way. So many checkpoints, and the weather…' Guy shrugged. 'I am sorry we are here so late in the afternoon. I suppose,' he said, hoping his tone conveyed how much of an inconvenience this would be, 'that we could make arrangements to stay in the town for tonight and return in the morning.'

The monk was sympathetic. He would have to speak to the Abbot. Usually the library was open only to those who made appointments well in advance. Had they made an appointment perhaps? They had not. And the Abbot was currently occupied. He was at prayers and not to be disturbed.

'If you are happy to wait until he is free?' the monk suggested.

Guy assured him that they were.

'You can wait with Brother Pierre. We have no librarian as such, but Pierre knows the books better than any of us. Even if the Abbot is unwilling to allow you to see the library, Pierre may be able to help you.'

'You think the Abbot might not grant us access?' Davenport asked. 'We have come a very long way.'

The monk opened his hands sympathetically. 'Alas, it is not entirely up to the Abbot. We live in strange times, as you know. The library itself is in the building currently occupied by the German authorities. They would also have to agree.'

'The Gestapo,' Guy murmured.

'I'm afraid so,' the monk replied. 'Whether they will agree, I cannot predict. In this as in so much they are rather capricious. So let us hope Brother Pierre can help you.'

Brother Pierre was reading. He sat at a small, plain, wooden table in a small, plain, stone-walled room. He was a tall man, thin with wispy grey hair and deep-set eyes. His face was weathered and lined, and seemed to relax into an easy smile. He gestured for Guy and Leo to sit on the low bench on the other side of the table while they explained who they were and what they wanted.

'Ah yes, Plutarch.' He nodded. His voice was gentle and quiet. 'The Lamprias Manuscript, yes?'

'You know it?' Guy asked.

'I have read it, certainly. I recall certain sections of it, but of course there is no substitute for seeing the real thing. Tell me, why are you interested in such an obscure volume?'

Guy glanced at Leo before answering. It was difficult to know how much to divulge, but Brother Pierre's memory might be as close as they ever got to the actual manuscript. 'We are researching the myth of the Axe of Theseus.'

Pierre nodded slowly. 'How unusual. But it seems that scholarship becomes more narrow and focused all the time.'

'The manuscript mentions the axe, I believe,' Leo prompted.

Pierre leaned back, tapping the ends of his fingers together and closing his eyes. 'Let me see if I can remember. It mentions several axes. Three in total, I believe. You understand,' he went on, opening his eyes again and leaning forwards, 'that the manuscript recounts a variety of myths and legends gathered from across Europe during antiquity. Plutarch adds his own interpretations, but much of the time he merely recounts earlier work, in particular the writings of Lamprias.'

'So we believe,' Leo said. 'It is the details that interest us.'

'Then you may be disappointed. It is quite vague. There is a summary of the various distinct myths, but then the author – Plutarch or Lamprias or whoever actually wrote it, there is some doubt as to which sections derive from which sources – then the author attempts to amalgamate them and ascribe a common root to the stories.'

'Isn't that working backwards?' Guy said.

Leo shook his head. 'Oh no, it's just a question of whether you think there are several axes, each with its own story, or just one axe about which several stories have sprung up.'

'And there are similarities between the three axe stories that are cited, from what I recall. That is the point the author tries to make.'

'There are?' Perhaps this was useful.

Pierre counted them off on his fingers. 'Thor's axe awakens elemental powers from their long sleep – Odin and the other old gods. The Axe of Theseus is also related to sleep – perhaps tenuously, but he uses it to destroy the bed of Procrustes, which itself was a death bed. Sleep again, you see.'

'You mentioned three axes,' Guy prompted.

'The manuscript is vague about the third, but it's related to Roman mythology. So it would be a section that was added by Plutarch himself. This third axe was apparently used by the god of war, Mars, to break down the gates of a fortress where several of the other gods, including Jupiter, had been tricked into drinking a sleeping potion. But the author says the axe has vanished. Which is interesting as it suggests that for all his arguments for conflating the stories, the other axes could still at the time be accounted for.'

'Perhaps it found its way to America,' Leo said quietly to Guy.

'Where it brought the doll-child to life and awakened the winds, or something.'

The monk who had admitted them to the monastery returned with news that the Abbot was now available and waiting to see them.

Leo asked if Brother Pierre would come with them. 'You could perhaps help us to convince him that we are genuinely interested in the manuscript.'

In the event, it was not their interest that the Abbot doubted, but their academic credentials.

'You have no letter of introduction, nothing to identify

you as being from where you say you are.' The Abbot was an elderly man, completely bald, but with clear and alert blue eyes. 'Your papers tell me nothing. Oh, I don't doubt your academic interest, but you will appreciate we cannot simply open the doors of our library to anyone who turns up unannounced and asks to be let in. It would be highly irresponsible.'

'But we've come a long way. All the way from Paris,' Guy protested.

'So you say.' The Abbot sighed, and leaned back in his chair. 'I am not being obstructive simply for the sake of it, believe me. And if you are happy to stay with us until tomorrow morning I think there is a simple solution that will satisfy both my need for assurances, and yours for entry to our library.'

'And what is that?' Guy asked.

'Just give me the name of the head of your department, and when the university is open tomorrow I shall ask the Gestapo if I may use their telephone to call and check your references.'

Guy and Leo exchanged glances. This was not lost on the Abbot.

'Or is there a reason why I should not telephone?'

'I think we should tell him,' Leo said. It took Guy a moment to realise he had said it in English. So the decision was already made.

The Abbot and Brother Pierre listened without comment to Guy's rapid explanation that the manuscript might contain information that was vital to the Allied war effort. He was deliberately vague, acutely aware that the Abbot might simply call for help and then hand them over to the Germans.

He was certainly angry. As soon as Guy had finished, the man slammed his fist down on the table in front of him. 'Occupation by a foreign power is one thing. An inconvenience, an imposition. We don't like it. But this is more than that. You dare to bring your war in here? To a place of peace and prayer?'

'You do share it with the Gestapo,' Leo pointed out.

'And we came and asked. We didn't just break in and take what we need,' Guy added quickly.

'But if the Gestapo were not here, I think you might have done.'

He couldn't argue with that – it was certainly possible, if not likely. 'Look,' Guy said, 'we're not asking you to do anything other than let us see a manuscript in your library. It won't have any repercussions for you. The Germans will never find out, and if they did you can just say that you believed our story about being from the university in Paris.'

'You are assuming that I want to help you,' the Abbot said.

'But we must,' Pierre told him. It was the first time he had spoken. 'Anything we can do to liberate our country. I can't be the only one who hears what is happening next door. Even through the thick stone walls.'

'Next door is a police station. It is where they question criminals.'

'It is where they torture our countrymen,' Pierre countered. 'These men are right – the Germans will never know we have helped them. But to stand by, to send them on their way without helping, that surely would be a sin of omission.'

'But if they did find out, Pierre.' Despite his firm, calm voice, the Abbot's hands were shaking. 'What do you think they would do to us then?'

'Do you really think,' Pierre said quietly, 'that the Christian martyrs weighed up the probability of their own death before proclaiming their faith? Or if they did, it certainly did not deter them from their path. The possible consequences should not determine our ability to do what is right.'

The Abbot nodded, forcing a thin smile. 'I can see they have a powerful ally in you, Pierre.'

'Many – I would say most – of my brothers will think as I do.'

'You may be right…' The Abbot lapsed into silence, leaning back and staring up at the ceiling.

'Will you help us, sir?' Guy asked after a long pause.

'I must do what I believe is best for the monastery, for the brethren in my care,' the Abbot said. He sighed and looked at Pierre. 'Give them robes, so that if anyone sees them they look like brother monks. Then take them to the library and show them what they want to see.'

'I thought you needed to ask permission of the Gestapo?' Davenport said.

The Abbot shook his head. 'Only if you were outsiders. We may consult our own books whenever we choose.'

'Thank you,' Guy said.

The Abbot didn't meet his gaze. 'Do it quickly, and then leave us.'

The Abbot is a good man,' Pierre said as he unlocked a heavy wooden door. 'He only wishes to do what is best for those in his care.'

'We understand,' Guy told him. 'It's good of you to help us.'

'It is good of you to risk your lives coming here,' Pierre said. He pushed open the door, and led them down a narrow passageway. At the end was another, similar door, which he also unlocked.

The passage evidently connected to the newer building, and led directly to the library. The room had been purpose-built, wooden bookshelves fitted into alcoves and a gallery giving an upper level, also lined with bookcases. The only access to the gallery was an ironwork spiral staircase. Pierre led the way, and obviously knew exactly where he was going.

The oldest books were in a locked cabinet at the end of the gallery. Pierre produced another key and swung open the wooden door. Inside, Guy saw that the volumes were each attached by chains to the wall behind. He glanced at Leo – there was no way they would be able to remove the book and take it with them without considerable effort, causing substantial damage.

Pierre pulled one of the large leather-bound books from the shelf, and placed it on the reading table in front, arranging the metal chain so it did not impede his turning the pages. He spent a few moments finding the section they wanted, then stood back and gestured for Guy and Leo to take a look.

'I assume you can read medieval Latin.'

'A little,' Leo said.

Guy didn't comment. If they said they couldn't, it would be obvious they'd intended to take the book away and pass it on to someone who could.

Pierre smiled, and leaned across between them. 'Mine is a little rusty too, so please indulge me if I translate out loud. I'm sure you will tell me if I go wrong.'

'Of course,' Guy said. 'Thank you.'

'Here are the three legends, you see.' Pierre read them a few sections, but it added nothing to what they already knew.

The next page had drawings of the axes themselves. They all looked very similar, but the drawings were heavily stylised, and Guy reckoned the sketch Jane Roylston had made was probably more accurate to the real artefacts.

'Ah, now here we have the combined legend...' Pierre murmured to himself as he read. 'I must confess I was mistaken. He does not conflate the legends, not quite. But the author suggests that the three axe-heads were designed to be used together. Each is capable of awakening or opening a specific door, I suppose it means. It's not very clear. But all three together...' He paused to turn the page.

'Yes?' Guy prompted.

'The gods scattered the three axe-heads across the world, because all three together could open the Gates of Hell.'

'The Gates of Hell?' Leo echoed.

Pierre looked up. 'Well, it's obviously symbolic. And only a legend... But yes, and there the account stops. The next section is about the building of the Labyrinth and Theseus's battle with the Minotaur.'

Leo opened his mouth to reply. But before he could say a word, the main library doors crashed open. Grey-uniformed figures hurried into the room, hand guns drawn and aimed up at the gallery.

The last man into the room wore an officer's cap. He was lean and thin-faced, pulling on black gloves as he fixed cold grey eyes on the three robed figures in the gallery.

'I see the Abbot was right,' he said in German. 'We do indeed have guests. And all the way from England.'

CHAPTER 10

Sarah shielded her eyes as they gradually adjusted to the brilliant glow from outside. The roar of noise had died away and she could make out the silhouette of the man reaching into the display cabinet, pulling out the stone axe-head.

Sumner struggled to his feet. 'What the hell are you doing?' he demanded. 'Who are you?'

The man didn't answer. He turned from the cabinet, cradling the axe-head in his hands.

The photographer skidded to a halt a few feet away. 'Wiles – Davy!'

The man didn't answer. Just stared.

'Put it back. Look,' the photographer went on, turning to Sumner, 'I'm sorry – this is my fault. I brought him here, but I didn't know—'

The photographer's words were cut off abruptly as the waiter shoved him aside. Sarah stared in surprise as he pulled a revolver from inside his white jacket, levelling it at the man holding the stone axe-head. It was only when he spoke that she realised who it was.

'Put that down, or I fire.'

'Sergeant Green?' Sarah gasped.

For a moment it looked like the thief might obey. But then he stepped forward, swinging the axe-head in one hand like the weapon it had once been. Green leaped back, and the axe-head smashed through the air just in front of him. Sarah's father pulled her away as Green fired.

The shot slammed into the man's chest, hurling him back into the shattered front of the display case. But no blood oozed from the hole ripped in his suit. Instead, tiny orange tendrils licked out, exploring the wound.

'Ubermensch!' Sarah realised.

Green fired again. This time at the man's head. But he pushed himself upright again, the tiniest trickle of blood running from the hole in his forehead down his face. The axe-head fell to the floor as his hands went instinctively to his face.

'Get behind me,' Green ordered. 'Maybe we can hold it back. At least it's wounded.'

He was right, Sarah thought. Before, bullets had barely wounded an Ubermensch. Perhaps this one was newly infected – still largely human. How long did the conversion process take? Was it human enough to feel pain? Human enough to be stopped?

Without thinking, she pulled away from her father and ran to where the Ubermensch was straightening up, hands lowering. Before it could recover fully, she grabbed the stone axe-head – amazed at how heavy it was for its size. She staggered back, regaining her balance in time to dodge a clumsy blow from the creature as it started after her.

Green stepped in front of her, firing again. The Ubermensch lurched backwards. But it seemed to recover quicker this time.

'Davy?' the photographer was saying. 'Davy? What the hell?'

'What is that thing?' Sumner gasped. 'Cause it sure ain't human.'

'Explanations later,' Green insisted.

'And you're not with the caterers,' Sumner added.

'You noticed,' Green said, pushing Sarah behind him. Her father was close beside her again. He said nothing, but his expression was full of questions.

They were all backing slowly along the gallery, towards

the broken window and the lights outside. The Ubermensch stalked slowly towards them.

'If that's a UDT outside and there are Vril,' Green said quietly, 'then we're caught between a rock and a hard place.'

Holding the heavy, cold stone close to her, Sarah turned to see if there was movement outside.

'Someone will have heard the shots,' Sarah's father said. 'Help must be on its way.'

'How do we stop that thing?' the photographer asked, voice trembling.

Sarah's scream cut off any reply.

Intent on the lights outside, she hadn't seen the movement closer to them until it was too late. The cat launched itself at her, paws extended, claws out, A bundle of snarling, spitting, scratching fur hit Sarah full in the face. She dropped the axe-head and flailed at the animal, trying to get a grip on its fur and pull it away.

More hands tore at the cat as Sumner and Diamond struggled to help. But the animal clung on – scratching and biting, raking its claws down Sarah's face, hissing and spitting. Finally, they dragged it off her, and hurled it to the floor. Green fired – the shot tearing through animal's fur. But with no effect.

Orange fingers quivered in the wound, knitting together, binding it shut. The cat leaped again, but the photographer somehow managed to knock it away. As it fell, he kicked it hard – sending the cat flying into a display case against the wall.

Anthony Diamond immediately grabbed the top of the case, dragging it away from the wall. The whole thing crashed down in an explosion of glass and splintering wood. The snarling screech of the cat was cut off as the heavy case slammed down on top of it.

At the same moment, the Ubermensch attacked again. Green fired twice more, barely slowing it. Then the gun clicked on an empty chamber. The Ubermensch shouldered him aside, sending the bulky sergeant staggering away. With one hand, it scooped up the stone axe-head. The other grabbed the photographer by his jacket collar, pulling him along towards the windows at the end of the gallery.

'Leave him,' Sumner yelled. 'It's the axe you want – just take it. But leave that man alone!'

The photographer stared back at them, his face pale as ice and his eyes wide with fear. 'Davy,' he stammered. 'Davy – just let me go. Please let me go.'

Sarah made to follow, but her father held her back. 'You really think you can stop that thing?'

'We've stopped them before,' she said, shaking off his grip.

But now Green was between her and the Ubermensch. 'Not like this,' he said. 'We need fire or something. There's nothing we can do. Just hope he lets that fellow go when he's away and safe.'

The Ubermensch had reached the window. He let go of the photographer, and the man's relief was clear in his face. As clear as the renewed terror as the Ubermensch lifted him with his free hand, and hurled him through the remains of the broken glass into the grounds outside.

The force of the impact jolted all the air from Jed's lungs. He landed on paving slabs – a path round the building – and rolled across the hard ground. He could taste blood. He could feel it on his face weeping out of tiny cuts where he'd hit the shattered remains of the glass hanging in the broken window frame.

He struggled to his feet, rasping for breath. Trying to make sense of what the hell was going on. A robbery? Or something more than that?

The light had dimmed from its initial brilliance to a pulsing luminance. A figure loomed out of the glow, reaching out to Jed. To help him? Thank God. But it was Davy Wiles, or whatever Davy Wiles had become. He grabbed Jed by the back of the neck, turning him away from the building and towards the glow.

The shape was masked by the light coming from it. But Jed could see that whatever had come down on the lawn was huge. A great disc, surrounded by a halo of light. He could make out the gleaming metal between the lights, a dark opening. A hum of suppressed power and a metallic, bitter taste at the back of his throat.

There were shapes in the light. Dark shadows emerging from the even darker opening. Angular, skeletal silhouettes coagulated out of the darkness and scuttled towards him.

'What is it?' Jed gasped. The pain in his neck was increasing as Wiles tightened his grip.

'You wanted to see what was hidden on my land,' Wiles said. His tone was exactly as it had always been – level, uninflected. Bored. 'I said I'd show you. That was the deal. Well, here it is. Seen enough?'

Jed tried to nod. Tried to twist away from the man's superhuman grip. 'Yes,' he managed to splutter. 'Yes, I've seen enough. Now – let me go!'

'Of course.'

The Ubermensch tightened its grip on the man's neck, a sudden searingly painful clench of his hand. Then he let go, allowing the body to crumple to the ground. Jed's eyes stared sightlessly at the craft he'd been so desperate to see.

Dark shapes scuttled out to surround the man who had been Davy Wiles, escorting him and the precious stone axe-head into the craft. Then the dark opening in its hull sealed over. The engines roared back into life, the lights blazed out again, and it lifted majestically into the night sky.

Sarah shielded her eyes from the glare. For several moments the UDT hovered above the grounds, lights pulsing and engines throbbing. Then it was a smudge of light blurred across the heavens. The noise faded, and the sky was empty.

Sarah's father hurried over to the body lying on the grass. Sumner continued to stare in disbelief at the sky.

'What the hell was that?'

'To be honest, sir,' Green told him, 'we don't really know.'

People were running from the front of the house to see what the noise and lights signified. Sarah had no idea what they could tell them. 'Nothing happened here tonight' would hardly cover it, especially as a man was dead. A robbery was a far more plausible explanation. Maybe it was best to let them all make up their own minds and hope the resulting rumours and stories would somehow counter each other out.

Another man who had a passing interest in how events might be interpreted watched from the shattered remains of the gallery window. Well, it was someone else's problem now. He had more important things to do.

He turned and walked slowly back down the gallery, his dark suit seeming to soak up the light as he passed. He paused in front of a fallen display cabinet, set down the large metal briefcase he was carrying, and straightened his light blue tie. Then he bent down and heaved the cabinet aside.

Beneath it lay the body of a black cat. Incredibly, the cat moved, stretching, turning its head to look up at the man weakly.

The man drew a gun from a holster inside his jacket. He stared back at the cat for a moment, through watery pale blue eyes.

Then he gripped the gun by the barrel and hammered the heavy handle down on the cat's head. There was no anger or emotion in the action, just a ruthless efficiency. Soon the head was nothing more than a bloodied pulp, orange tendrils sprouting from the mess like the first shoots of spring grass.

He lay the metal briefcase on its side, sliding the catches and opening it to reveal an empty plain metal interior. The man carefully picked up the cat by its tail, dropping its twitching body into the briefcase. The orange filaments swayed and danced, as if trying to feel what was happening. But the man snapped shut the briefcase.

He pulled a plain, spotlessly white handkerchief from his top pocket and wiped first his fingers, and then the bloodied handle of his gun. Then he replaced handkerchief and gun, picked up the briefcase, and walked away.

*

They had moved Number Seventeen to a desk in the cloister room down near the Vault. Her last picture was an image of a woman's face – her mouth open as if screaming. In extreme close-up.

The nurse supervising lifted the sheet of paper away, numbered it and placed it on the pile. Number Seventeen was already drawing again. Shading black across almost the whole sheet.

She stopped abruptly. The pencil fell from her fingers and clattered down on the stone table before rolling off and falling to the floor. The girl's eyes widened, as if she was seeing the nurse for the first time. Her hands bunched into claws. She gave a hiss of anger, saliva spattering across the paper. Then her eyes rolled upwards until only the whites showed, and she pitched backwards, falling after the pencil.

CHAPTER 11

The bed was drenched in sweat, the bottom sheet crumpled and torn. Jane Roylston was awake suddenly – no slow surfacing from the dream, but an abrupt plunge into the real world. Her hand clawed at the ripped sheet, nails shredding the cotton. Her whole body was slick with perspiration.

At some point in the nightmare she had thrown off the covers – sheet, blankets, eiderdown lay in a heap on the floor. She tumbled out of the bed, scrabbling for something to put on. She needed to see Crowley. Had to tell him what she had seen played out in her dreams.

Crowley heard her urgent footsteps as she clattered through the house. He emerged from his bedroom, tying the cord of a paisley-patterned silk dressing gown. Through the open door behind him, Jane could see Edith, one of the newer acolytes. She was sitting up in the bed watching, her mass of red hair tumbling untidily forwards and cascading over her breasts. Crowley pulled the door closed behind him.

'What is it, Jane?'

'The cat's dead,' she told him. 'At least I think it is.'

'My study,' he ordered, leading the way briskly across the landing.

As they entered the room, Ralph Rutherford appeared, bleary-eyed and hastily dressed. Jane hoped Crowley would send him away, but he followed them into the study and

113

slumped down in one of the chairs.

'More visions?' he asked.

Crowley ignored him. 'Tell me what you saw. As much detail as you can recall.'

She sat down, closed her eyes, and let the dream play out again in her memory. She described it as it happened, what she could remember of it. The long gallery. The display cases. The people. The fight. The light outside. Attacking the blonde woman – claws raking her face. Biting, scratching, spitting... And the sudden terrible darkness as the cabinet pitched forwards, falling towards her.

Jane opened her eyes. She was breathing heavily. Sweat prickled down the middle of her back. 'Will you tell Brinkman?'

'No,' Rutherford said. 'There's no need, surely,' he added quickly as Crowley turned to stare at him.

'And what if he finds out anyway? We don't know who was there, who witnessed these events. Who they will tell.'

'About a dead cat?'

'There was a fight,' Jane pointed out. 'A robbery.'

'We don't know they got away with it.'

'An attempted robbery, at least,' she snapped.

Rutherford turned to Crowley. 'We can't just tell these people everything we know. All the time.'

Crowley sniffed. 'Why not?'

'I thought we were after power for ourselves, not to give it away to others.'

'You think knowledge is the only power?'

'It's a damned good start.' He got up and went over to the desk, reaching for the whisky decanter.

But Crowley put his hand over it. 'Do you really have such little understanding of the sort of power that we have? That *I* have?'

Rutherford met his stare, but only for a moment. Then he turned away. 'Oh, I meant to tell you – I'm leaving,' he said.

For a brief instant Jane was elated.

But Rutherford added: 'Just for a couple of days. I have some business I need to sort out.'

'Yes,' Crowley agreed. 'Take a break, by all means. But come back with a better attitude. A better understanding of yourself and of us.'

Rutherford looked like he was going to say something in reply. But then he changed his mind, and walked quickly from the room.

Crowley stood up and came over to where Jane was sitting. He held out his hand, and she lifted her own to take it. The metal bracelet was heavy and loose on her thin wrist. As she moved her arm, it shifted, a thin trail of blood oozing out from beneath.

'Interesting,' Crowley murmured. 'Hold still a moment, my dear.'

He unclipped the bracelet, and it swung open, coming off easily. There was a band of congealed blood round her wrist where it had been attached, droplets of blood still oozing out from the tiny holes drilled into her flesh.

There was time only for hastily exchanged whispers on the gallery before the Gestapo men arrived and took the two spies away. Guy didn't like what was decided, but he could appreciate it was the most pragmatic approach. It might yet save all their lives. Or it might condemn an innocent man to death.

But Kriminaldirektor Fleisch, the senior Gestapo officer at the facility, knew nothing of his prisoners' hasty and desperate plan. He was a lean man, with angular features and dead, grey eyes that he fixed on the three men.

'Take them to the cells,' he ordered.

'But I've done nothing wrong,' the monk protested.

'You collaborated with enemy spies,' Fleisch told him.

'Because the Abbot asked me to. He said to bring them here and make sure they stayed until you arrived to arrest them. I was helping. Please,' the monk continued, 'I have to report back to the Abbot. And I am due at prayers in a few minutes.'

'Prayers?' Fleisch gave a snort of derision. 'In that case, thank your God that I am a reasonable man.' He nodded to the guards to let the monk go, and turned his attention to the real spies. 'If either of you believe in a God, then perhaps you should make peace with him now.'

Amused and pleased with this quip, Fleisch stepped back to allow the two spies to be taken away.

He started with the shorter, stockier man. But it was soon apparent that he spoke almost no French at all, and Fleisch wondered how long he had hoped to survive here. One of his men, Helmut Blau, spoke some English, but it was slow work punctuated by punches and kicks to encourage the man to open up.

What they did learn was unedifying. His name was Carlton Smith and he was a History professor from Harvard University. An American, surprisingly. His story that he was interested only in examining the medieval volumes held by the monks in their library for research was plausible. But Fleisch didn't believe it.

Keeping the men in different cells meant he could double-check the story. Fortunately, the second man spoke excellent French – better than Fleisch did in fact. Except he refused to speak at all, even to give his name and tell them he would say nothing more. After a fairly comprehensive beating, the man still remained silent, staring back defiantly through eyes almost hidden in his swollen face.

'This is just the beginning,' Fleisch assured him. 'In the morning we shall start in earnest. Heat, cold, electricity, water, knives and shears. I confess, I am rather looking forward to it.'

The man was too weak for his saliva to reach Fleisch. It splashed to the floor, and the Gestapo chief was pleased to see it was red with blood. Soon he'd be spitting out his own teeth.

Fleisch looked in on the woman on his way back to his office. They had brought her in yesterday, suspected of helping the resistance. Maybe she had, maybe she hadn't. On balance, having heard her scream her innocence, Fleisch thought she probably hadn't. But he didn't really care either way. She was manacled to the back wall of the cell, wrists and ankles held outstretched tight in metal clasps. Her clothes were shredded and stained, and her face was streaked with blood. Fleisch nodded with satisfaction as she lifted her head weakly to stare at him, her eyes wide and frightened.

Back at his office, Fleisch was surprised to see the Abbot waiting for him, together with the monk who had been with the spies.

'They are no longer any concern of yours,' he told them. 'You did your duty, and the Reich is grateful.' He pushed past them to get to his desk, knocking the two men aside. It was only when he sat down that he realised the mistake he had made.

As soon as Fleisch had dismissed him, the monk had hurried back through the monastery to the Abbot's room. He did not bother to knock, but threw the door open and walked straight in.

The Abbot was kneeling beside his plain wooden bed. He looked round in surprise when the door opened.

'Praying for forgiveness, Abbot?' Guy Pentecross asked angrily. 'Because for what you've done, you're going to need it.' He crossed the room and hauled the man to his feet. 'Prayers can wait. My friend, and your Brother Pierre, need our help.'

'Please,' the Abbot stammered, 'I was doing what I thought was best for the monastery.'

'Well you were wrong, and you're going to help me put it right.'

It had taken Guy almost an hour of constant arguing and cajoling to persuade the Abbot to help. Even then, he refused to allow any of the other monks to be involved and of course there were no weapons in the monastery.

So Guy was pleased he had been able to remove Kriminaldirektor Fleisch's gun from its holster so easily when the man pushed past them to get to his desk. He levelled the Luger at the Gestapo chief.

'It was a surprise to the Abbot too,' Guy told him. 'Now, are you going to arrange the release of my friends, or do I need to shoot you as well as our holy friend?'

With luck, Fleisch would believe the Abbot was innocent of any deception and had genuinely tried to help the Gestapo. Well, he'd be half right. Provided the Abbot kept Brother Pierre out of sight for a while, it was unlikely anyone would connect a hooded monk with one of the British spies who had been captured and then escaped...

Like so many cruel and sadistic men, Fleisch was frightened when his own safety was at risk. With his own gun jammed into his ribs, he opened the door of his office and shouted for the two prisoners to be brought in.

'I've agreed with the Abbot that they can make a final confession,' Fleisch told the men who led in Leo Davenport and then dragged in the barely conscious Pierre. 'Who knows what they may say as their final words to God?'

If the men were surprised to be dismissed from the room, they were disciplined enough not to show it.

The Abbot's feelings at seeing his brother monk bruised and bleeding were more obvious. Guy gave him a warning look – he couldn't show sympathy. Not yet. He undid the cord round his own robes and handed it to the Abbot.

'Tell him to take off his uniform, then tie him up.' Guy nodded at Fleisch. 'In his chair. Then,' he added, making sure Fleisch could hear, 'you are coming with us as a hostage. Who knows, we might even let you live.'

While the Abbot tied Fleisch to his chair, Davenport did his best to clean up Pierre's wounds. There was a carafe of water on the desk, and he wet his handkerchief to dab at the blood. Pierre winced with each movement.

'You see the sort of people you're dealing with?' Guy asked quietly when the Abbot had finished.

The Abbot was staring at Pierre's battered face. 'I... I had no idea.'

'You didn't want to have any idea.'

Fleisch's uniform just about fitted Guy. So long as no one

looked too closely, he reckoned he would get away with it.

'They will know you are a fraud as soon as you open your mouth,' Fleisch told him defiantly.

'I doubt it,' Guy told him in perfect German. 'I am here at the direct instructions of Gruppenfuhrer Muller, Generalleutnant der Polizei. Would you dare to doubt me? Would any of your men?'

Fleisch looked away. Guy took hold of his chin and turned his face back, stuffing his mouth with the bloodstained handkerchief Davenport had used to clean up Pierre.

The monks' robes served to disguise that Leo and Pierre were former prisoners, and cover their wounds. With the hoods raised, they became anonymous. If Pierre was leaning heavily on his fellow monk for support, it was not too obvious. Leo himself seemed remarkably resilient. He admitted that he'd taken a bit of a beating – though nothing like the punishment meted out to Pierre. His apparent willingness to cooperate while actually revealing nothing had paid off. Not for the first time, Guy guessed.

Guy himself did his best to walk tall and proud, not showing how nervous he actually felt. Perhaps he should have changed clothes with Leo – the actor was more than capable of pulling off the role of a major working for the head of the Gestapo. But unfortunately, his German wasn't up to the task.

In the event, they were not questioned as they made their way past the cells and back towards the library. Being the small hours of the morning, there were few people about. Those who were had evidently become conditioned not to speak out of turn. It seemed that Fleisch's cruel grasp on his own people as well as others had done them a favour.

Several of the cells were occupied, pale, haunted faces staring blankly back at them as they passed. Pierre shook his head sadly. The Abbot crossed himself and murmured a blessing. If the prisoners appreciated it, they made no sign.

The last cell contained the woman that Guy and Davenport had seen brought in while they were keeping watch. But she was barely recognisable, manacled to the wall and spattered with her own blood.

The Abbot drew a deep shuddering breath. 'Madeleine,' he breathed. 'I remember her baptism.' He turned to Guy, eyes pleading. 'We have to help her. We can't let those… those animals—' He broke off, unable to continue. In the cell, the girl raised her head slightly at the sound of voices.

'We can't just release her,' Leo said.

'Why not?' the Abbot demanded.

'She's in no fit state to escape, and they'd just drag her back again. We have to hope that when they're done with her they'll let her go.'

'You think that's likely?' Pierre asked. He coughed violently with the effort of speaking. He suppressed it quickly as a figure entered the cell corridor through a door further along – one of the guards.

'The Abbot is right,' Guy murmured to Leo. 'Let's worry about sorting it out later.' He didn't wait for a response, but walked briskly up to the approaching guard.

'The woman is to be released at once,' he said. 'She obviously has nothing to tell us. She can go.'

'Go?' the guard laughed. He tried to turn it into a cough as he saw Guy's expression. 'I doubt she can even stand, sir.'

'The Abbot and brothers are here to take care of her.'

The guard nodded. 'Of course, sir.'

The Abbot and Guy had to almost carry her through to the library. Leaving the Abbot looking after the girl as she sat on one of the benches, leaning heavily against him, Guy and Leo helped Pierre up to the gallery. The volume they had been inspecting was still out on the reading table.

'I can't let you take it,' Pierre said weakly.

'We can't risk the Germans discovering what we were looking for,' Guy said. 'We know what it says now. If you copy it down for us, that will suffice. But can we risk the book staying here?'

'They can't know that it is this book you were interested in,' Pierre pointed out. 'But I can hide it. Replace it with another volume, in case they come looking.'

'There is another problem,' Leo said. He glanced down at the Abbot below, the woman still leaning weakly against him. 'Fleisch will know there was no order for her release. And the guard knows she is in the monastery.'

'We just have to hope he'll have other things to worry about,' Guy said. It wasn't a perfect solution, and they all knew it. 'Maybe when news of this gets out Fleisch will be replaced before he can do anything. Or if it doesn't, he'll need to keep things hushed up and won't dare to act.'

'You hope,' Pierre said.

'I hope,' Guy agreed.

But when they returned to the lower floor, the Abbot had a different idea.

'Find a room for her. Let her rest,' he said, helping the girl to her feet. 'Brother Francois can tend to her injuries. And yours, my friend,' he added, gripping Pierre's shoulder.

'What about you?' Pierre asked.

'I'm going back to Fleisch.'

'What?' Guy said.

The Abbot nodded. 'I shall give you a few minutes to get away, then I shall go and tell him I escaped from you. I shall also tell him that in return for my silence about his incompetence, I want safety for the girl. I will tell him she is innocent, and that we will look after her until she has recovered.'

'You really think that will work?' Guy asked.

In answer the Abbot pulled him into a sudden embrace. 'I pray that it will.'

Leo nodded. 'I think your plan is probably the only one with a chance of success,' he said. 'You are a brave man, sir.'

'I'm merely putting right what I helped to make wrong.'

'I hope you find peace,' Leo told him. Guy thought it was an odd thing to say.

They helped Pierre get the girl to a room and settle her on the plain, hard bed. It would be luxury compared with her earlier predicament. Leo had Guy's own clothes bundled under his robes.

'Best wait until we're clear of this place before you change back into civvies,' he suggested. 'Just in case we need to bluff our way out again.'

They left Pierre and Brother Francois with the girl and let themselves out through the door they'd arrived by just a few hours before. Guy had folded in his pocket the sheets on which Pierre had transcribed the relevant section of the manuscript.

Only when they were well clear of the monastery and leaving the village of St Jean-Baptiste de Seine behind them did Guy realise that he no longer had the Luger he had taken from Fleisch.

'I must have put it down in the library,' he said. 'Unless I dropped it in the cell when we were helping that poor woman.'

'No,' Leo said, a tinge of sadness in his voice. 'When the Abbot embraced you, he took it from the holster.'

'But – why?'

'Because, like I said, his plan is the only one that will guarantee no one ever discovers that Fleisch didn't order the release of the girl.'

The Abbot closed the door behind him. The relief in Fleisch's eyes was apparent from across the room. The Abbot walked slowly over. He turned the chair away from the desk, and leaned down so he was staring into Fleisch's eyes.

'I have sinned,' he said quietly. 'I have stood by and allowed terrible things to happen. And today, I was confronted with those things. Today I saw for myself what I have ignored. I saw *your* sins. I am horribly afraid,' he said, 'that despite a lifetime of devotion, so many prayers that I cannot count them, so much love for my brothers... I am horribly afraid that today I am going to Hell.'

He reached for the bloodied handkerchief stuffed into Fleisch's mouth, and gently pulled at it.

'But at least I have the satisfaction of knowing,' he went on, 'that you are coming with me.'

Fleisch's eyes were wide with horror. The handkerchief fell from his mouth, but before he could cry out, the cold barrel of his own Luger replaced it.

The Abbot was surprised how loud the sound of the shot was in the confined space, echoing off the stone walls. He did not hear the second shot.

CHAPTER 12

Fritz Weingarten saw more time-wasters than anyone else at the embassy. There were usually several every week who wandered in off the streets with something to sell. Or, mostly, nothing at all to sell. He was sympathetic, a good listener. But his patience wore thin when local down-and-outs who spoke not a word of English and barely any German turned up and suggested they could somehow become the best spy Germany had ever sent to Britain.

Occasionally – just occasionally – he found gold. That was why he was here, and it was what kept him going. With his ample frame squeezed into the chair behind his large desk, blowing cigar smoke across the room, he reflected that today he just might have hit gold again.

The man sitting opposite him in Weingarten's office at the German embassy in Lisbon was also smoking. He held a cigarette between his fingers, unconsciously making a V sign. Ironic really, as he was British. It was rare for a real Brit to turn up and offer information.

That said, what he was offering seemed rather arcane. Weingarten's interest was in what the man could discover on his return to England rather than what he was offering right now.

'A stone axe,' Weingarten said, wanting to be sure he had it right. 'I'm sorry, Mr Rutherford, but I cannot see the significance of an archaeological artefact to the British war effort.'

'Neither can I,' Rutherford admitted. 'I just know that it's important. I thought you should be told.'

'Thank you. I will pass on the information, along with your written description. And, of course, we will be grateful for any further information you can provide. Either on this same subject, or about other things.'

Rutherford frowned. 'What other things?'

Weingarten made a show of shrugging, his enormous shoulders lurching with the effort. 'Oh, I don't know. There may be things you see or hear that we might find useful. Troop movements, ships at the docks in London. Supplies being moved or loaded. We may send you specific questions from time to time. And money, of course. We can't expect you to work for nothing, and I'm sure there will be expenses.'

'How will I pass this information on, assuming I can get it?' Rutherford asked. 'I can't keep coming to Lisbon.'

'That might raise suspicions,' Weingarten agreed. 'Although between you and me, the British seem rather incompetent in the area of counter-espionage. We have a significant network of agents already working across Britain. You will be joining a team.'

'Really?' It was gratifying that Rutherford seemed surprised at this. The British really had no clue, Weingarten thought with satisfaction.

'I shall give you the name and address of an agent you can contact. We refer to her as Magda, but in London she uses a different name of course.'

'Of course.' Rutherford leaned forward to stub out his cigarette.

'I will write down the details. You will memorise them, then destroy them. Understood?'

'Understood.'

There it was, in his voice. Weingarten could hear the thrill, the excitement, the hint of nerves. Rutherford was trapped now – involved, intrigued, ensnared. Yes, he could prove a most valuable agent. Weingarten wrote out the details of how and where to contact Magda, and her assumed name. He stood up and handed them to Rutherford before seeing the man out.

Easing himself back into his chair, Weingarten thought about what the man had told him. He doubted that any of it was of any interest to anyone in Berlin. But he had nothing else to do this afternoon, so he might as well include it in his report. Along with details of his latest agent. He smiled at the codename he had selected for Ralph Rutherford – 'Thor'. Well, the man seemed to be interested in axes.

'Progress meeting' was a misnomer, Miss Manners thought as she listened to the others talking round and round the same subjects. She glanced down at her shorthand minutes of the discussions so far.

The axe-head that J.D. Sumner had in his possession was gone – taken by the Vril before Sarah or Sergeant Green could even examine it properly. They had photographs and notes from Sumner, but so far Elizabeth Archer at the British Museum had made little of them. The cat that Jane had been able to connect to, which gave them an insight into what the Vril were doing, was also gone, probably dead.

Leo Davenport and Guy Pentecross had not brought back the manuscript from France. But they had at least escaped with their lives, and they had a transcript. It suggested there might (or might not) be two other axe-heads, but so far no one knew where.

Colonel Brinkman was getting frustrated, but hiding it fairly well. With the Y Stations reporting an increase in UDTs over mainland Europe, he was under increasing pressure from the Prime Minister to offer some advice and insight. But all he could suggest was that this increase might merely mean more enemy aircraft were being deployed but not being identified.

The most positive suggestion of the meeting came from David Alban. Although he worked for MI5, Alban had been caught up in the affairs of Station Z, tracking down an

Ubermensch and saving Sarah from it. Initially cynical about the team's usefulness, he was now a convert – and a useful ally within the intelligence services.

'This transcript,' he said, 'is it in English? Or is it the original medieval Latin or whatever it is?'

'We have both,' Davenport told him.

'Do you understand Latin?' Sarah asked. The marks on her face where the cat had attacked her were almost gone, but one stubborn scratch persisted down the side of her face.

'Precious little,' Alban said. 'But I was just wondering if we shouldn't treat it like any other data we've recovered.'

'Mrs Archer is examining both the translation and the Latin,' Guy told him. 'Is that what you mean?'

'Not exactly. If we see it as data rather than prose, as some sort of cipher…' He shrugged. They had got the point. 'I deal with coded text and hidden messages all the time. Sometimes one set of symbols is jumbled up, other times they stand in for a completely different set of symbols or language. Numbers instead of letters, that sort of thing. Just a thought, but what it says and what it means may be very different things.'

Brinkman nodded. 'A good thought. Yes. Leo – you and Elizabeth know as much about these legends as anyone, take the transcripts up to Wiles at Bletchley and see if he can make anything of them.'

Guy waited for Sarah as the meeting broke up. 'Feeling left out again?' he asked.

'Not yet,' she told him. 'To be honest I'm glad of the rest. And there's not a lot for you and me to do right now. Best to leave it to the experts.'

Guy agreed. 'I don't think there's a training course for how to understand Wiles and his team.'

'I did have one idea,' Sarah told him as they followed the others out of the room. 'Someone it might be useful to talk to. If I can set it up, will you come with me?'

'Of course. Who are you thinking of? Just so long as it's not Adolf Hitler.'

*

One whole wall of the wooden hut was covered with a map of Britain. It was a composite picture, made from a tessellation of several maps, overlapping and fixed to the wall with drawing pins. Coloured threads criss-crossed the map, some red and some blue, held in place by round-headed map pins.

Elizabeth Archer had not been to Bletchley before, and examined the map with interest. To Leo Davenport, it was old news. He watched the two of them absorbed in their studies – Elizabeth intent on the map; Professor Wiles poring over the transcript of the ancient text they had brought with them.

'These lines in red…' Elizabeth said thoughtfully after a while.

Wiles glanced up, peering over the top of his spectacles. 'What of them?'

'They're Ley lines, aren't they?'

Wiles took off his glasses and dropped them on his desk. 'You know about Ley lines? I mean, yes, yes, they are. And you can see there's a good correlation between the UDT tracks, the blue lines, and the Ley lines.'

Elizabeth nodded. 'Someone did mention your theory, but it's only when you see it laid out like this that it's so obvious. I assume these numbers –' she pointed to a label at the end of one of the blue lines – 'tell us how many UDTs have been tracked along this route.'

'That's absolutely correct.'

'They do seem to stick to particular flight paths,' Davenport said. 'And those paths correlate, as the professor says, to Ley lines.'

'Miss Diamond suggested that the ancient sites that are thought to define the Ley lines might be navigational markers of some sort,' Wiles explained. 'Not whatever is at the site now, but the place itself.'

'It would explain why some sites gain a mystical status,' Elizabeth agreed. 'An emanation of some sort. We sense it but can't define it. The Vril make use of it.'

'Perhaps they even put it there,' Davenport said. 'Whatever it is. But what about our manuscript?' he went on. 'Any joy with that?'

Wiles retrieved his spectacles. 'Well, if it's a cipher we won't know from this. But I think it's unlikely, as the original stories have been told and retold. They will have changed over the years and as a result of translation and transcription. So any message explicitly encoded in the actual words and phrases won't be recoverable.'

'You think there was one?' Elizabeth asked. She sounded dubious.

'Oh, I doubt it. What would be the point? Who would it be intended for? And anyway, these myths and legends originated with human beings, not with the Vril. Probably. And they'd be recounted orally, not in written form to begin with.'

'I agree.'

'So there's nothing you can tell us?' Davenport said, disappointed.

'Oh, I wouldn't say that. We have three stories here, more or less. Three being the minimum for a series or a progression. In mythology, there are almost always three choices, or three giants to defeat, or three tasks to perform. It shows development – of narrative and character. Sorry,' he went on without breath, 'where were we?'

'The manuscript,' Davenport prompted. 'You were telling us what you learned from the three stories.'

'Ah yes, yes yes. Well, it's interesting because they are *not* a progression. In fact, in many ways it's the same story over and again.' He waved a piece of paper that was covered with jottings and a spider's web of lines. 'I've noted down the salient points and linked them together as you can see.'

'Perhaps a quick summary?' Elizabeth prompted.

'Well, in all the stories, the same elements occur. Most obviously, and therefore we must assume most importantly, in each, our hero journeys, or attempts to journey, to the underworld or some equivalent. He must pass through a metaphorical Valley of Death. And in each we have an awakening – from death, or from sleep. A powerful being or group of beings returns.'

'And the axe features in them all, of course,' Davenport

added.

'Of course, yes. In fact, the axe is the instrument of awakening, see.' Dr Wiles pointed to a nexus of lines on his notes. 'The axes are therefore key. Or rather, I think they are keys, plural.' He smiled at them, evidently pleased with his deductions. 'It's an allegory.'

'An allegory for what?' Davenport asked. 'You say the axes are keys, which certainly ties in with what Pierre told us in France.'

'To awaken the powerful beings,' Wiles said.

'And these beings,' Elizabeth said slowly. 'You think that's the Vril?'

'It seems likely. Which is why they want the axes. We know from Bulwer Lytton's writings that they have bases underground.'

'And from our own experience,' Davenport reminded him.

'So, here's my conjecture. At some point in antiquity, someone stole the keys to the underground chambers where the Vril are sleeping. Those people were venerated as heroes, and the keys, which happen to look like stone axe-heads, became almost mystic symbols. Perhaps axes were modelled on the shape of the keys, or perhaps it's a coincidence that they're similar. Who knows. Some of the legends have got confused or conflated, so it sometimes seems that the keys will awaken great heroes. But other times, as your friendly monk suggested, they are said to open the gates of Hell. But it always comes back to releasing something hidden deep underground.'

'And now the Vril are collecting the keys that will unlock these hidden underground chambers?' Davenport said.

'That's about the size of it. If I'm right. I wonder where those three axe-heads are now.'

'The Vril already have the axe from Los Angeles,' Elizabeth said.

'Thor's axe could be anywhere,' Davenport said.

'But it's likely to be in Central Europe, judging by this,' Wiles told them, brandishing the transcript they'd brought.

'Probably in Germany, knowing our luck. The Black Forest region seems likely.'

'Theseus used his axe to slay the Minotaur,' Davenport recalled.

'Underground again, you see,' Wiles said. 'But according to this text, he left the axe behind when he followed the thread back out of the Labyrinth. Which is all a legend, so goodness knows.'

'Not if Arthur Evans is right,' Elizabeth said. 'He believed his excavations on the island of Crete about forty years ago had uncovered the Labyrinth at a place called Knossos.'

'I wonder if he found a stone axe-head,' Wiles said. 'Perhaps we should ask him.'

'He died last year,' Davenport said.

'Shame,' Wiles said. 'That is, of course, if I'm right about any of this. It's all deduction and supposition really. There's no empirical proof.'

'But if you are right,' Elizabeth said, 'I wonder how many of these things there are in hibernation or whatever they're doing. Waiting to be woken up.'

'And why wake them, I wonder?' Wiles said.

'Well we know they're not exactly friendly,' Davenport said. 'Perhaps they are the army the Vril intends to use to conquer the world.'

Wiles frowned. 'That's a rather sobering thought,' he said. 'You could be right, though. Yes...' He stared off into the distance. 'Yes, you could well be right.'

CHAPTER 13

Luckily for Hans Meyer, he had not been at headquarters that night. As deputy to Kriminaldirektor Fleisch, Meyer faced the problem of explaining events at the monastery. It was a mess, but Fleisch's death made things easier. There was already a scapegoat, and Meyer for one would not shed any tears for the man. Especially if he could organise things so that he got Fleisch's job.

Clearly Fleisch had somehow allowed the prisoners to escape – dying in the process. The Abbot was another casualty, presumably killed by the British for turning them over to the Gestapo in the first place. How Fleisch's own gun came to be in the Abbot's dead hand was a detail that failed to make it into Meyer's final report.

He expected an investigation, but it was a shock when an SS Hauptsturmfuhrer arrived at Meyer's (formerly Fleisch's) office two weeks after the incident. The man introduced himself as Dieter Grebben and sat without asking.

Meyer forced a smile. 'And how can I help?'

Grebben teased off his black leather gloves. 'These spies – you are sure they were British?'

'I was not here myself at the time,' Meyer pointed out. 'But the men on duty felt that at least one of them was British. Another seemed to be American. He spoke no French apparently.'

Grebben considered this, although he must already have read it in the report. 'So why send a man who speaks no French into occupied France, do you suppose?'

Meyer shrugged.

'And why send them to a rather insignificant Gestapo office?' He smiled. 'No offence.'

'They were arrested in the library of the monastery,' Meyer said. 'It is in the report.'

'Yes. The library. We are very interested in this library. Or rather, in whatever the British were looking for.'

'You think that was why they came here?'

'I don't think it was to confess their sins, or for the scintillating conversation. No offence. The American was perhaps an expert of some kind. A man who had to be here in person to identify or study whatever they were after. He was clearly unsuitable in operational terms for the mission, therefore his presence was unavoidable. What were they doing when arrested?'

'Doing, Hauptsturmfuhrer?'

'Your report says simply that they were found and arrested in the library. It doesn't state whether they were looking for something, or copying down information, or drinking tea. I repeat – what were they doing?'

Meyer bit back his instinctive confession that he had no idea. 'I wasn't here at the time, you understand.'

'Oh yes, you have made that very clear. Several times.'

'So it is probably best if you hear it from one of the officers who was. A first-hand account is always better, I find.'

Meyer excused himself and, after hurried enquiries of his men, established that Witzleben had been there and helped make the arrest.

'They were on the gallery of the library,' he told Grebben, standing stiffly to attention and not meeting the SS captain's stare.

'Standing?' Grebben asked. 'Sitting? Talking? Silent?' Before Witzleben could answer, Grebben stood up. 'Show me. I wish to see exactly where they were.'

A few minutes later the three of them were standing on the gallery.

'They were here, three of them. Standing. Talking, I think. They stopped when we entered the room, of course.'

'Why here, do you think?'

'Well, because they were reading a book.'

Grebben turned to glare at Meyer. 'What book?'

Witzleben opened the door protecting the ancient volumes. He pulled one out, its chain jangling across the wooden reading table. 'This one.'

'You are sure? You saw the title?'

'No, sir. But I remember where it was on the shelf.'

Grebben nodded. 'Very well. I shall take it with me. Also the volume either side, just in case your memory is at fault. But keep them separate. Cut the chains and bring them to my car.' He turned and started down the spiral staircase without a backward glance.

It was almost a month since Colonel Brinkman had last seen his family. He telephoned to let his wife know that he was coming. As he approached the house, he could smell the bread she'd been baking.

Dorothy hurried out to greet him, wiping the flour from her hands on to her apron before embracing him. Brinkman tried not to hug her too tight.

'Oliver,' she chided, 'you've lost weight.'

He laughed. 'You haven't.'

'No,' she agreed.

'Where's James?'

'Back garden,' she told him. 'I didn't mention you might be coming, in case you couldn't get away.'

The boy was digging in a corner of the vegetable patch with a small trowel. When he saw his father, he leaped up, dropping the trowel and ran to Brinkman, wrapping muddy hands round his father's legs.

Brinkman laughed. 'Hello, son. You looking after Mother for me?

135

'I'm growing carrots for tea.'

'Good.'

'Are you staying at home now? Is the war over?'

'Not yet, I'm afraid.' Brinkman extricated himself from the boy's embrace, and crouched down so he was at eye level with the three-year-old. 'But I hope it won't be long, and then I'll be home for good. But until then you have to be brave and you have to be the man of the house, all right?'

James nodded. 'All right,' he conceded, disappointed.

Brinkman stood up and ruffled the boy's hair. 'Good man. Now you get back to your digging while I have a chat with Mummy.'

'Yes, sir.' James attempted a salute, then ran back to retrieve his trowel.

Brinkman was aware of Dorothy standing behind him in the doorway, watching them both. He put his arm round her shoulders. She had taken the apron off, and the bulge of her stomach was more noticeable now.

'It must be hard,' Brinkman said. 'It'll be even harder with two of them to look after.'

She nodded. 'I know. So you'd better win this war pretty damn quick and come home to help.'

'I'm doing my best,' he assured her with a smile. But beneath the smile he wondered which of the wars he was fighting would be the harder to win – the one against the Nazis, or the one against the Vril?

'I'm not at all sure how I can help,' the old man said. His thinning hair was still dark, though his moustache was grey. 'Some propaganda thing, is it? You want me to write a piece for a newspaper, perhaps?'

'Nothing quite like that, sir,' Sarah said. It had been her idea to come, but she hadn't realised how old he would be. Perhaps Guy was right and they were wasting their time.

'You could reprint passages from *The Rights of Man*, of course. Funny how your opinions change and develop, isn't it?' he mused.

'In what way?' Guy prompted.

'Hmm? Oh, thirty years ago – twenty even – I'd have said that eugenics was a good thing, broadly speaking. Impractical, of course, but generally a way to advance the human race through selective breeding. Now of course, I'm arguing that it restricts the rights of the individual – as we can see from what's happening on the continent, and in the United States before that.'

'Yes, actually,' Sarah said, 'we were hoping to talk to you about one of your novels. About where you got the ideas for it, whether any specific research helped.'

'You know, last year, I said in my preface to the new edition of *The War in the Air* that my epitaph should be "I told you so, you damned fools". So if you've come to tell me I was right, it's not exactly news.'

'It was actually *The War of the Worlds* we wanted to ask about,' Guy said.

Mr Wells blinked. 'Really? Never really rated that one myself. Wasn't all that successful until that other Mr Welles did his radio show of it a few years ago in America. And people believed it was actually happening.' He shook his head. 'I should write something about human credulity.'

'So where did the idea come from?' Sarah asked.

'Where do any ideas come from? Blessed if I can remember now.'

'But it's a very imaginative idea, isn't it,' Guy pressed. 'What made you think about beings from another world invading us?'

'Well they had to be from a more advanced civilisation, that was the point. There was no more advanced civilisation than ours on this world, so I had to look further afield.' He shifted in his chair. 'It's not actually a book about creatures from another world, you know. No, no, no – it's about imperialism. It's about the hardship wrought on nations and peoples that are unwillingly absorbed into a larger, foreign empire.' He sighed. 'Perhaps it's *too* imaginative – no one seems to understand what the book is saying. Still, that's the thing with books, isn't it?'

'What is?' Sarah said.

'You can always write another one.' He leaned forward suddenly, fixing Sarah with a steely look. 'Why are you interested?'

'Um, well, it's an interesting idea for a book.'

'I mentioned *The War in the Air* just now. People suddenly became interested in that because the fiction became fact. Because it was suddenly and unpleasantly relevant. So let me ask you a slightly different question – have the ideas behind *The War of the Worlds*, the notion of invasion from another planet, have those ideas suddenly become unpleasantly relevant?'

Guy glanced at Sarah before he answered. 'I'm afraid we can't discuss our interest in detail. But you said yourself, the novel is about one culture being conquered by another more advanced civilisation and the consequences of that. I believe there is relevance to what is happening now, perhaps not here in Britain, but across Europe. The German war machine is even now crushing the relatively backward peoples of the Soviet Union.'

'So any insight you can offer us that might help in the fight against them,' Sarah said, 'would be appreciated.'

Wells nodded. 'I'll give it some thought,' he promised.

'Disappointed?' Guy asked as they made their way back from Regent's Park to the Station Z offices.

Sarah nodded. 'All our clues at the moment are coming from myths and stories. I just thought here was another one that seems to fit, and the author is actually still alive and we can ask him. I guess it's just coincidence.'

'Probably. Or he may remember something – something he read or that he was told, which might help.'

'We keep chipping away at things, but I don't know if we're getting any closer.'

'I know what you mean,' Guy agreed. 'Frustrating, isn't it? But something will happen soon enough. Too soon, probably.'

'How can you be sure?'

'I'm not. Not really. But it just seems like things are coming to a head. Reaching boiling point. The manuscript from France, the axe and the Ubermensch in Los Angeles. I just feel that something's about to happen, and we have to be ready. Don't you feel it?'

'I do, yes. But how can we be ready?' Sarah demanded, her exasperation coming out in her angry tone. 'We don't know what's going to happen.'

'No, but we are making progress. Maybe...' He stopped. 'Yes, that's possible.'

'What is?'

'I was just thinking – perhaps Rudolf Hess knows what's going to happen. He seemed pretty informed before he clammed up and refused to say anything more.'

'I thought Alban said MI5 got everything out of him that they could,' Sarah said.

Guy nodded. 'Brinkman spent some time with him too. He wanted me in on it, except he couldn't get me clearance. And you're right, Alban has had a team going to town on Hess, for all the good it did. But how much of what he says can we believe anyway? From what Leo and Miss Manners say, he's a narrow-minded, credulous occultist. Even Crowley agrees. Anyway, like you said, he won't talk to us. But,' Guy went on, 'maybe he will talk to someone he thinks actually understands and appreciates what he has to say.'

'You mean Crowley? I don't trust Crowley, and I doubt Brinkman would let him near Hess.'

'I wasn't thinking of Crowley,' Guy told her. 'I was thinking that Rudolf Hess might talk about an imminent invasion from another world to the man who wrote a future history of just such an event. I was thinking he might talk to H.G. Wells.'

CHAPTER 14

A cork board had been fixed to the stone wall. It was covered with paper: handwritten notes, typed reports, drawings and maps. There was an order to it all, Hoffman saw. The papers were arranged in clusters, grouped together. Lines drawn across the board, from one cluster to another, or sometimes to several others.

Hoffman's eyes were immediately drawn to a pencil sketch – a drawing of the artefact he saw in his dreams and whenever he closed his eyes. He made an effort not to react.

'You have been busy in the last few days,' Heinrich Himmler said. He waved his hand at the cluttered board. 'All this comes from Streicher's notes and files?'

The third man in the room was tall and lean, with thinning grey hair. He was older than Himmler, probably in his fifties, Hoffman thought. His voice, like his manner, was confident and assured.

'Much of it, Reichsfuhrer,' SS Standartenfuhrer Ritter Nachten said. 'But a lot I have also gleaned from other sources.' He stepped forward, standing in front of the board, like the university lecturer he had been before the war. 'I see connections. That is how I operate.'

Himmler nodded. 'And what connections have you seen that you believe warrant my attention?'

'Isolated incidents. Reports and information that on their

own mean nothing, but when connected and taken together...'
Nachten turned to examine the board.

Hoffman sensed that the man might circumnavigate the
subject for a while if left to his own devices. For all their sakes,
and spurred by his own impatient curiosity, he walked up to
the board and tapped the drawing that interested him most.

'This would appear to be the centre of your web of
connections,' he said. 'Perhaps you could explain to the
Reichsfuhrer and to myself its significance?'

'Of course.' Nachten cleared his throat.

Hoffman glanced at Himmler, and was rewarded with a
thin smile and raised eyebrows. 'Proceed, Standartenfuhrer,'
Himmler murmured.

'The drawing was part of a report forwarded to Berlin
by our embassy in Lisbon. The drawing is apparently of an
ancient axe-head, and was provided by an Englishman who
gave his name as...' Nachten crossed quickly to his desk on
the opposite side of the office and leafed through papers until
he found the report he sought. 'Here we are – Rutherford. He
now has the codename "Thor".'

'And it is significant for what reason?' Hoffman prompted.

'Rutherford did not know. Or he did not say. The Abwehr's
people in Lisbon clearly felt it was irrelevant. The covering
letter that accompanied the report of Rutherford's visit to the
embassy was apologetic. But it is clear from what Rutherford
did say that the British are extremely interested in this artefact.'

'Why?' Himmler asked sharply. The light glinted on his
glasses as he stepped forward to examine the drawing.

'We don't know,' Nachten admitted. 'But they clearly see
it as important. According to Rutherford, they dispatched
personnel to the United States, to Los Angeles, to recover this
axe-head.'

'Los Angeles?' Hoffman said.

Nachten traced his finger along one of the lines from the
drawing to a news clipping pinned further along.

'Los Angeles, where a rare and ancient native artefact was
stolen from a private collection on the day it was opened to the

public. It made the newspaper as one of their own reporters was apparently killed in the incident.'

'Stolen by whom?' Hoffman asked.

'The report is vague. But from my own researches, it seems this axe-head is a close match to two others described in antiquity.'

'And where are they?' Himmler asked.

'One was thought to be connected to the Black Forest region. I am not sure about the other.' Nachten traced another line, to a set of papers fanned out at one side of the board. 'I thought this might provide the answer...'

'And what is that?' Hoffman asked.

'Reports from the Gestapo, of an enemy incursion into a monastery outside Paris. It seems the spies who went there were interested in the monastery library, which is noted for its collection of ancient texts.'

'You think the texts mention these axe-heads?'

'That was my first supposition. I sent one of my best men to obtain further information. He came back with this.'

Nachten gestured to a side table standing in an alcove. Three leather-bound books lay on it. They were all clearly old, with thick parchment pages. The leather was as scuffed and faded as the pages were curled and yellowed. Nachten opened the top book. It creaked as he turned the pages.

'This was the book that the spies examined. The others were next to it in the library, but are unrelated.'

'And this book describes the provenance or history of one or more of these axe-heads?' Hoffman asked.

'So I thought. But no. There is nothing.'

'You are saying there is no connection after all?' Himmler said.

'Yet without a connection, the British interest in the monastery library makes no sense. The library itself is in the building which the local Gestapo use as their headquarters. Clearly to risk an operation there it must have been vitally important.'

'And the spies told the Gestapo nothing of their intentions?'

Himmler demanded. 'Where are they now?'

'It seems they escaped, killing the Gestapo chief and perhaps the Abbot of the monastery in the process.' Nachten shrugged an apology. 'There is some confusion about what actually happened.'

'Some anxiety to avoid blame, most likely,' Hoffman said.

'Most likely,' Himmler echoed. 'How do we know that is the book they were after?'

'One of the arresting officers identified it as the volume they were consulting when they were taken.'

'Identified it how?' Hoffman asked. 'Did he recognise a particular page or the title?'

'No, but he remembered where it was on the shelf. Hauptsturmfuhrer Grebben took the books either side as well, in case the man was mistaken. I have examined them too.' He sighed. 'Nothing.'

'What is the connection between the three books?' Hoffman wondered.

'The other two are Latin translations of older texts. This one is an account of a journey through the Holy Land made in the eighth century by a French monk. There is no connection.'

Hoffman looked at Himmler. 'There are three possibilities that I see here.'

Himmler nodded for him to go on.

'First, there is some relevance to one or all of these volumes that has so far escaped us. I assume that is unlikely?'

Nachten nodded. 'I would have found it.'

'Then the second possibility is that the information the British spies were seeking has nothing to do with these axes at all.'

'Possible,' Nachten conceded.

'And the third possibility?' Himmler prompted.

'The most likely in my opinion,' Hoffman said. 'Simply that the British did not find what they were hoping to, any more than the Standartenfuhrer did. They were searching in the wrong book, or more likely it was not there to find. Their information, whatever it was, was wrong.'

Himmler nodded slowly. 'The monastery is a dead end,' he decided. 'Leave it. Concentrate on other leads. Find out about these ancient axes and why they interest the British.'

Nachten clicked his heels. 'Of course, Herr Reichsfuhrer.'

'With your permission,' Hoffman said to Himmler, 'I shall do some research into the axe supposed to be associated with the Black Forest.'

'An excellent idea, provided it does not interfere with your other duties. Nachten,' Himmler ordered, 'you will provide Sturmbannfuhrer Hoffman with all the information you have. Then on your return we shall see what collectively we have discovered.'

'One other thing,' Hoffman said. 'The Englishman, Rutherford...?'

'He is keen to help the Reich all he can,' Nachten said. He hurried back to his desk to retrieve the full report.

'Of course.'

'Lisbon put him in touch with an agent in London. I have arranged with Admiral Canaris's office for any information he provides to be forwarded immediately to me...' He leafed through the typewritten pages. 'Here we are. He is to make contact with one of the Abwehr's best agents, apparently. Her codename is Magda.'

It was a disappointment but not a surprise that Sarah was not permitted to sit in on the meeting. Brinkman apologised, and promised to brief her immediately afterwards.

'It's a good idea,' he told her. 'But to be honest, I doubt if anything will come of it. I was there when they interrogated Hess last year, and he clammed up like a corpse.'

'Was that at the Tower of London?' Sarah wondered.

'No, this was before they took him to the Tower. It was in a place on the Brompton Road, used by the Royal Artillery as a base for all their anti-aircraft operations. It's above a disused tube station, so I assume it's easy to evacuate. But Alban's spent time with Hess since he was moved, and got precious little out of him. For all his schoolboy humour and looks that man could get blood out of the proverbial stone, believe me.'

Brinkman's reservations turned out to be justified. He called Sarah in to his office when he returned from the meeting and gestured for her to sit down.

'I'll brief everyone properly later, though there's not much to tell.'

'But something?' Sarah asked hopefully.

'Hess was his usual helpful self. He's worried, but how much of that is because of his knowledge of the Vril, and how much is just down to being a prisoner of war and the way the tide is turning against Germany...' Brinkman shrugged. 'There were just the three of us, I insisted on that. I translated, as Mr Wells doesn't speak German.'

'And did Hess appreciate speaking to him?'

'Hard to tell. He'd read some of Wells's books, which was a help. They discussed colonialism as much as anything. Hess believes, if what he says is true, that the Vril are essentially imperialists.'

'That all makes sense,' Sarah said. 'In fact it's pretty much what we'd concluded already. But did he give any reason why they have been here for so long?'

Brinkman shook his head. 'I had Wells suggest to him Elizabeth Archer's theory that they have been waiting for civilisation to reach a stage where it's useful to them. But Hess didn't seem to have any thoughts on that. He sees the Vril as creatures of darkness, lurking underground, and interested in causing death and destruction for its own sake. Conquest as a means in itself.'

'Maybe it's not the Vril he's describing there,' Sarah said.

Brinkman nodded. 'That's what I thought. Guilt and regret can take many forms.'

'So we've learned nothing new, really, have we?' She shook her head, disappointed.

'It was a good idea,' Brinkman told her. 'And to be honest, the relevance and value of what we have discovered may not become apparent for a while. Maybe we've gleaned some nugget of information that will be important later. We'll just have to see. And Mr Wells himself may yet come up with some useful insights.'

The instructions were precise, and imprinted indelibly on Ralph Rutherford's memory. He found the house easily enough, in a leafy suburb that seemed largely unaffected by the bombing. Exactly seven o'clock, the instructions had said. He waited in the street, smoking to calm his nerves.

He was excited as well as nervous. Finally, he was doing something. He was making decisions that were not dictated by others – by Crowley. He wouldn't tell the Germans much, he decided. Just enough to get well paid for his services. To get enough money to be able to do what he liked. Maybe he'd buy a house like this one. Maybe he'd take over from Crowley – the man was old, he couldn't go on for ever.

There had been a time when Rutherford believed Crowley saw him as his successor. But increasingly he felt side-lined and insulted. And now that Crowley was pandering to MI5 or whoever they were...

He checked his watch, and made his way up the drive. The revolver was a reassuring weight in his jacket pocket. There were four doorbell buttons beside the door. Each had a name against it, apart from the top button. That was the one he pressed. Two short presses and one long one. He listened, but could hear no response from inside the house.

After what seemed an age, the door was opened by a young woman wearing a dressing gown. Her auburn hair was a mess and there were dark rings under her eyes. She looked at Rutherford warily.

'I don't know you,' she said.

'I don't know you either,' he told her.

She started to close the door.

'No, wait! I'm here to see...' For a moment, the name escaped him.

The door paused. 'Here to see who?'

'Lucy.' Yes, that was it. 'Lucy White.'

The door swung open again. 'Then you'd better come in.

Top floor, second door on the left. Knock the same way as you rang the bell.'

The woman disappeared down the hallway, leaving Rutherford to make his own way up the stairs. There were four floors, the top being almost an attic. The carpet was threadbare, and the walls a plain white that was fading to a dull ivory colour. Rutherford knocked on the second door on the left as she had said – two knocks, a pause, then another.

'It's open,' a woman's voice called.

It was like entering another world. Soft carpet under Rutherford's feet, and deep red wallpaper patterned with black swirls. Matching velvet curtains were drawn although it wasn't yet dark outside. The light came from a central chandelier and several lamps on tables round the walls. The room was dominated by a large bed. Rutherford saw that there was another door on the other side of it.

The woman was lying on the bed. She glanced at Rutherford, then put down the book she had been reading. 'You looking for me?' Her voice was soft as the carpet.

'I am looking for Magda,' he replied, just as the instructions had said.

'Then you've found her.'

Magda, or Lucy, or whatever her name really was, sat up and swung her feet off the bed. She went over to a side table and helped herself to a cigarette from a wooden box. She didn't offer Rutherford one, but lit it and stood regarding him with dispassionate interest.

His own interest was anything but dispassionate. Magda had flame-red hair curling over her shoulders, and dark, smouldering eyes. She was wearing a red satin corset, black silk stockings, and very little else.

'Well, at least you're punctual,' she said. 'Our mutual friends said you'd be dropping by. So, what can you do for me?'

CHAPTER 15

Despite her attire, or lack of it, Magda evidently took her business seriously. All aspects of it, Rutherford suspected. He realised she had stopped speaking. She had been explaining how to write a hidden letter in invisible ink between the lines of a real letter. How she would pass the letter on, and give him instructions written in the same way.

But now she was silent – watching Rutherford watching her. He had been staring. It was hard not to. She was sitting at the small desk, facing him as he stood watching.

'Eye contact,' she said, 'is usually made above the neck.'

'Sorry.' Rutherford was used to seeing women literally in the flesh. But something about her unnerved him. Her easy confidence and business-like manner, perhaps.

'Business before pleasure.' She leaned back in the chair, running her hands down the front of the corset. 'If you're a good studier, perhaps I'll teach you some other tricks. But afterwards.'

Then she was straight back to explaining how Rutherford should contact her in an emergency. She spent several minutes cross-questioning him on what she had covered. He made an effort to concentrate. After that she wanted to know why he was working for the Germans. It seemed easiest to say it was for money.

'There's just one other thing you need to know,' she said at last, standing up. She stood in front of him, looking him up and down in much the same way he had examined her. 'Yes, I think you'll do nicely. If it's money you're after, then we can help you there.'

'You and the Nazis?' He meant it as a joke. But his mouth was dry and it came out more as a flat statement.

Magda gave a short laugh. 'I don't work for the Nazis,' she said.

She must mean she worked for money too, Rutherford thought as he watched her cross to the door beside the bed. The view of her from behind was as impressive as from the front. A deep warmth stirred inside him.

And froze to an icy chill as she opened the door and a man stepped into the room.

A man he recognised, though he didn't remember his name – if he had ever known it. A round, freckled face that looked younger than the thinning red hair above it.

'You!' Rutherford gasped. 'But – you were with Brinkman.'

The man stared back at him. 'I'm as surprised as you are,' he admitted. 'Magda told me she had a new client. I never expected "Thor" to be you, Mr Rutherford.'

'You're a German spy?' Rutherford said. It seemed incredible. But his surge in confidence in the reach of the Reich was dashed by the answer.

'Oh, please,' the man said. 'I'm here to persuade you to work for us. To feed back what we ask to your German masters, and to answer their questions exactly as we want you to.'

'They pay well,' Magda said. She was leaning back against the wall, smoking again.

Rutherford's mind was in a whirl. 'But – they'll know. If I lie to them, the real German spies…'

The red-haired man was shaking his head sadly.

Magda pushed herself away from the wall and blew out a stream of smoke. 'I'm the only German spy you'll meet,' she told him.

'Give it some thought,' the man said. 'It's either a generous salary or it's execution. I can't imagine it's that difficult a choice.'

Rutherford's head was throbbing. It felt like it was about to explode. He needed to think. What if he didn't agree? But if he did, then what if the Germans found out? What if *Crowley* found out? He thrust his hand into his jacket pocket, feeling the cold metal of the gun he'd brought.

'So what do you think?' the man was saying through the fog that filled his mind. 'Obviously you'll have to come with me while you decide.'

But Rutherford wasn't going anywhere with this man. If he did, he might never see the light of day again. He pulled the revolver out of his pocket. It snagged on the way out, and he had to disentangle it. But despite the fumble, the man looked surprised as Rutherford aimed at him.

'There's no way out for you,' the man said. 'Except to work for us.'

Magda moved away from the man, putting distance between them so that it was hard for Rutherford to cover them both with the gun. There was a hardness in her eyes now as she watched him. No one else knew he was here, Rutherford thought. He could shoot them both and just walk out.

Except – there was the woman downstairs who had let him in. Probably others too. They would hear the shot. And he didn't know if the man was alone. He backed away to the door, moving the gun from Magda to the man and back again.

'Don't try to follow me,' Rutherford ordered as he reached the door. Then he spun round and pulled open the door.

He slammed it shut behind him. There was no way to lock it, so he ran – clattering down the stairs, stuffing the gun back into his pocket. Hoping no one would see him or try to stop him.

Outside, he gulped in huge lungfuls of fresh air before hurrying off down the drive. A quick glance down the street assured Rutherford it was deserted before he set off back the way he had come.

Behind him, a dark shape detached itself from the shadow

of a driveway. A man in a raincoat, with his hat pulled down low over the eyes, followed Ralph Rutherford.

David Alban closed the curtains again.

'Thompson's following him.'

Magda stubbed out her cigarette in an ashtray on the desk. 'What if Thompson loses him?'

Alban smiled. 'He's good. And I doubt Rutherford is capable of losing an elephant in a maze. Anyway, I'm pretty sure I know where he's heading.'

Magda walked over to Alban, standing so close her body brushed against his. 'Then I assume you're in no hurry to get after him.'

She turned round so that he could undo the laces down the back of the corset.

'I suppose not,' he said.

The 'Twenty Committee' took its name from the Roman number – XX. Double cross. Closely affiliated with MI5, it was the group responsible for running all the German agents in Britain – identifying them, interrogating them, then imprisoning or executing or 'turning' them. To say it was an efficient operation was an understatement. During the course of the war, the only German spy to elude them did so by committing suicide. Despite what the Abwehr and other German intelligence organisations believed, there was not a single spy in Britain who wasn't actually working for the British and sending back a stream of disinformation. Many of the spies the Germans thought they had in play didn't exist at all.

As soon as he knew for sure where Rutherford was headed, Alban phoned the head of the Twenty Committee to report events. John Masterman listened carefully, as he always did, before asking Alban for his own recommendations.

'The only information Rutherford can provide to us concerns Crowley's activities,' Alban said. 'And Crowley, so far as we can tell, is cooperating anyway. I don't trust him, but I doubt Rutherford knows any more about what he's up to than we do.'

'Any value in turning him?' Masterman asked.

'Not a lot to be honest, sir. From what he told Magda, the Germans didn't seem terribly interested in what he had to offer, and as I say he has rather a limited field of operation. It just wouldn't be credible if he suddenly stumbled across the sort of information we'd really like to pass on. And we're not exactly short of other German agents.'

Masterman's chuckle echoed in the receiver against Alban's ear. 'Normally, I suppose we'd send him to Camp 020 for interrogation, find out all about him. But as he's British, we probably know all we need to already. And from what you say he's a pretty volatile character. We certainly can't have him wandering about knowing that you and Magda are involved in counter espionage.' There was a hint of rebuke in his voice as he added: 'It's a shame he got away from you.'

'I know where he is, sir. I can have him dealt with by a third party with no comebacks to us.'

'You're sure?'

'Positive.'

Masterman sighed. 'Well, there's no need to involve the whole committee for something as relatively insignificant as this. I'll mention it at next week's meeting. Since this Rutherford fellow's not left us a lot of leeway, I'll leave it with you.'

As soon as he had hung up, Alban redialled. The phone at the other end rang for a while before it was answered.

'Mr Crowley? You may remember me – my name is Alban, and I work with Colonel Brinkman. I have a small problem which I think, when I explain what's on my mind, you'll be happy to help with.'

There was no sound from inside the study. Rutherford listened at the door for as long as he dared. There was no sign of light from under the door, but that didn't mean the room was empty. He had to be fast – MI5 would be after him, and

Crowley might return at any moment. His only way out of the situation was to find something he could use to bargain with.

He was angry – with himself for getting into this mess, but mostly with Crowley and even more with Jane Roylston. It was her fault, the bitch – talking to the Manners woman, poisoning Crowley against him. If there was time, he'd find her before he left. But time was something he was short of.

So Rutherford took the chance, and eased open the study door. The room was in darkness. He closed the door behind him, calling softly, just in case: 'Mr Crowley? Aleister – are you there? I need to speak to you…'

No answer.

He felt his way across the room to the desk and fumbled for the lamp. It cast a pale glow across the blotter and he waited for a moment until his eyes were used to the gloom. Then he examined the bookcase behind the desk. It took a few moments, but eventually he found the catch, and eased the heavy bookcase away from the wall.

Crowley had been annoyed that he had seen the hidden doorway open. Whatever was concealed inside must be valuable. Valuable enough for him either to sell and get enough money to disappear for ever, or valuable enough for him to trade with the MI5 man for his freedom.

Behind the bookcase was a rectangle of darkness. He moved the light on the desk, pulling it across and angling it into the doorway. It revealed a small room, lined with shelves. Papers and ancient books were arranged along one shelf, a metal strong box on another. Something at the back of the small room glinted like metal…

He peered closer, moving into the room, but careful not to block the light. Yes, it *was* metal – strips of metal, or narrow bars. A cage, he realised. A metal cage on a low shelf at the back of the room. Inside the cage, the darkness itself seemed to move, to stir, to wake.

As he approached he made out the shape of the thing inside, dark and malevolent. A single eye snapped open, staring back at him.

Rutherford's hand went to his mouth as he stifled a cry of horror, tasted the bile at the back of his throat, and flung himself backwards out of the room.

'Why Ralph,' a voice said from the darkness behind him. 'Whatever is the matter?' And the main lights came on.

CHAPTER 16

'I gather you've been a bit of a naughty boy,' Crowley said. He handed Rutherford a glass of brandy.

Rutherford looked like he needed it – pale and shivering. He gulped the brandy down, and Crowley refilled the glass.

'Not me,' Rutherford managed to gasp. 'It's Jane you need to watch. She's telling the Manners woman everything, I'm sure of it.'

Crowley leaned back in his chair, amused. 'And that's worse than you running off to Herr Hitler's friends, is it?'

Rutherford didn't meet his gaze. He sipped at the brandy. 'I just…' he muttered.

'Just nothing!' Crowley roared. 'You were nobody when you came here. You had nothing. You knew no one. If it weren't for me, you'd probably be dead in a gutter by now, and don't you forget it. This is how you repay me?'

Rutherford didn't answer.

'Our friends at MI5 want me to kill you, you know.' Crowley's tone was offhand, conversational – as if he was remarking on the weather outside.

But it snapped Rutherford back to reality. He stared at Crowley. 'Kill me?' he echoed, his voice strung out with nerves.

'"Execute" was the word they used. And I ought to after this…' He nodded at the bookcase still standing away from the wall to reveal the hidden room behind.

'But – you can't!'

Crowley's voice was hard. 'Oh yes I can. I always could, but now I have official permission to kill you in cold blood any time I see fit. Don't forget that, not ever. But for the moment, well…' He smiled. 'We'll see, shall we? I might be able to persuade MI5 to keep you alive. Perhaps.'

'What do you want me to do?' Rutherford asked.

'As you are told, for a change. For a start, you say nothing of what you've seen here.'

Now he knew he was safe for the moment, there was a hint of the old defiance in Rutherford's voice. 'I don't know what I have seen.'

'Then perhaps I should enlighten you.'

'And Jane Roylston? I was telling you the truth – she's passing on everything to Brinkman and his lot.'

'Yes…' Crowley considered. 'I suppose that's hardly surprising.' He stood up. 'I think perhaps it is time for poor Jane to meet her destiny.'

'Kill her?' Rutherford breathed.

'I'm still deciding whether or not to kill *you*.'

'Then what do you mean?'

Crowley took Rutherford's empty glass from him, placing it on the desk. 'Bring her to the cellar. Just Jane and you, no one else. I'll meet you there.'

'What if she won't come with me?'

'I'm sure you can persuade her, Ralph. You're good at that, I know. And I'm sure you'd enjoy it.' Crowley turned to the dark opening behind the bookcase. 'I have someone else to bring.'

To Rutherford's disappointment, mention of Crowley's name was enough for Jane Roylston to follow him down to the cellars. She glanced warily back at him as they descended into the flickering light of the stone-lined chamber. But Crowley was already there, the candles already lit. A copper bowl of incense burned smokily on a stand close to the altar stone.

'You want me to try making contact again?' Jane asked. 'I

told you, the link has been broken. There's nothing there to make contact with, not any more.'

'You have a very special ability, Jane,' Crowley said. His craggy face was an escarpment of trembling shadow in the candlelight. 'I think it's time to take your talents to the next level. Into new territory – for all of us.' He gestured to the stone altar table in the centre of the chamber. 'Please.'

As she had done so many times before, Jane stepped up on to the dais surrounding the table. She glanced back at Crowley, and glared at Rutherford who stood smirking next to him.

'Naked, if you would be so kind,' Crowley said. His pale tongue licked quickly over his bloodless lips.

'I'll help you if you want,' Rutherford said. The anticipation was obvious in his voice.

'I can manage,' Jane told them. She was close to the burning incense, the smoke making her lightheaded and woozy. She kicked off her shoes and unbuttoned her blouse, all the while conscious of the two men staring at her. She was used to it, but she still found it unsettling. Especially Rutherford.

The table was cold under her back as she lay down. She stared up at the vaulted roof above, its details lost in shadow as the light danced over the stone surface. The perfumed smoke from the copper bowl beside the table drifted across, blurring the image and dulling her senses. 'I'm ready.'

'Not quite,' Crowley said. 'Don't resist, my dear. It will all be over soon.'

The smell of the incense was stronger now, the smoke thicker. Through it, she saw Crowley looking down at her, holding the copper bowl close to her face, letting the smoke drift across her. She breathed it in, feeling herself begin to slip away.

Someone took her hand, pulling it gently away from her body until it was stretched out to the edge of the stone table. She felt the metal clasp round her wrist, securing it in place. Then the other arm. Jane felt a moment's panic as her legs too were pulled apart. She tried to sit up, to see what they were doing, but her head felt so heavy…

Then cold metal closed round her ankles, holding her spread-eagled across the stone.

Crowley replaced the copper bowl on its stand and looked down at the woman stretched out on the stone.

'What are you going to do to her?' Rutherford asked. He too was staring at Jane. He'd never seen her look so beautiful. So helpless.

'I shall do nothing,' Crowley said.

For a moment, Rutherford thought Crowley would just leave, and let Rutherford do whatever needed to be done. But instead he stepped down from the dais and went to one of the alcoves at the side of the chamber, reaching down into the shadowy darkness.

When he straightened up and turned around, Crowley was holding the metal cage Rutherford had seen in the hidden room. It was covered with a black velvet cloth, and Crowley carried it carefully, almost reverently to the altar table. He set it down on the stone surface, between Jane's ankles.

'What's going to happen?' Rutherford asked, breathless.

'To be honest, I don't know.' Crowley gently pulled the cover from the cage, murmuring quietly as he did so. Rutherford could not hear the words, wasn't sure it was English – Latin perhaps? Or an even older tongue?

Darkness quivered inside the cage. A living shadow. Slowly, carefully, warily, Crowley undid the clasp at the front of the cage, and lifted up a section. He stepped back as the inchoate darkness reached out through the opening.

An angular limb, gnarled and grotesque like the leg of a giant spider, licked out of the cage. Then another. The creature inside pulled itself out, and squatted malevolently between the cage and Jane. Sensing something was happening, she tried to raise her head, looking down along the length of her body. Rutherford didn't know if she could see the nightmare creature that was moving slowly towards her. He hoped so. Her eyes were wide with fear, her whole body trembling.

One of the creature's skeletal limbs brushed against her

160

thigh, and Jane cried out in surprised terror. The cry was choked off as the creature moved on, upwards, reaching out across her flesh, hauling itself up onto her body. The single eye swivelled back and forth as it surveyed its prey. It paused, the pulsing, bulbous body resting on the woman's naked belly, gnarled legs stretching out across her thighs, her breasts, towards her face.

Jane's head lifted again and she saw the dark nightmare stretched out across her. Her whole body convulsed with the effort of screaming, back arched and limbs straining at the manacles. The creature's limbs curled round her in a macabre embrace, clutching her tight, then abruptly releasing her.

Her body slackened, fell back to the stone.

Crowley stepped forward, muttering urgently to the creature. A limb whipped out like a tentacle, narrowly missing Crowley's face. He stepped back with a snarl, gave an angry, guttural order. Slowly, reluctantly, the creature withdrew. Its crooked limbs gathered into a knotted mass beneath its dark, bulbous body. A single defiant eye glared for a moment back at Crowley.

Then it withdrew into the cage, and Crowley snapped the bars back into place and closed the clasp.

'How do you control it?' Rutherford's voice was a dry rasp.

Crowley glanced at him. 'Ancient words of power, handed down through the generations of natives in the Himalayan foothills of Nepal. I am never quite sure whether the words control it, or whether it merely does as I ask.'

Rutherford's heart was thumping and he was breathing heavily – part excited and stimulated by what he'd seen. Part horrified. He stepped up onto the dais beside Crowley, keeping well clear of the cage. Not daring to look at what it held. Instead he stared down at the body of Jane Roylston.

'Is she dead?'

'No, she's not dead,' Crowley said.

A thin trail of blood wept from a narrow slash across her left breast and down her chest. Several smaller lacerations criss-crossed her stomach and the top of her legs. A bead of blood welled up from a point close to her navel, running slowly across the undulations of her body and dripping to the stone table.

'What now?' Rutherford said, his voice a nervous whisper.

Crowley picked up the black velvet cloth and draped it back over the cage. 'Now we wait.'

CHAPTER 17

Before leaving for the Bertesgarten, Himmler insisted on a status report from both Hoffman and Nachten.

'Perhaps you will have some good news for me to pass on to our Fuhrer,' he suggested, looking from one to the other.

Hoffman was too familiar with Himmler to be intimidated, but Nachten – he was pleased to see – shuffled uncomfortably. They were sitting at a large, round stone table in one of the anterooms. Nachten had brought a plentiful supply of notes and papers, books and folders which were stacked in front of him. Hoffman had his notebook.

When he judged that Nachten has squirmed enough, Hoffman replied. 'As you know I have been researching the axe supposedly connected to the Black Forest. But, I am sorry to report, with little progress so far,' Hoffman admitted. 'I shall inform you both when I get a lead.'

He made a point of looking down at the notebook on the table in front of him. He saw to his surprise that while they had been talking he had drawn in the margin. Several small axe-heads. A few of the runic symbols. And a complex circular pattern, lines spiralling inwards to form paths – some blocked and some opening into other sections. It was a shape he had seen before, in his mind's eye and in his dreams. He closed the notebook and looked up. 'There are several possibilities I should like to follow up.'

Himmler nodded, and turned back to Nachten. 'What of the third axe?'

'I need to do more research myself. But I have discovered enough already to believe that my researches are pointed in the right direction.'

'And what direction is that, if I may ask?'

'Greek myths and legends. I believe the third axe-head is still in Greece.'

'Explain, if you would.' Himmler leaned forward, hands clasped together on the cold stone surface of the table. 'Briefly,' he added.

'You two are looking very pleased with yourselves,' Sarah said.

Leo was perched on the edge of Miss Manners' desk, the two of them talking quietly. There was no one else in the office, and Sarah had heard Leo's laughter from the stairs on her way up.

'We think we may have tracked down our elusive axe,' Leo explained.

'Dr Wiles and Mrs Archer suggested Crete as a possible location,' Miss Manners said. 'But it was just a theory, based on a myth and Evans' archaeological finds. Nothing very concrete to back it up.'

'And now?' Sarah asked.

'Now it looks as if there may be a connection to the Labyrinth in Crete after all,' Leo said.

'The legend of Theseus and the Minotaur?'

'That's right,' Leo told her. 'The Palace of Knossos on Crete where the Labyrinth was supposedly built was also known as "The House of the Double Axe".'

'So there's a connection.'

Leo sighed. 'Well, sort of. It may not be as clear cut as it seems, because actually any Cretan palace was known as a house of the double-axe. That said, it keeps us in Crete. We, by which I mean archaeologists and classical academics, tend to associate the island with the bull.'

'They had paintings and statues of bulls everywhere,' Miss Manners added. 'They sacrificed bulls, and of course there's the Minotaur.'

'Half man, half bull. However that happened,' Sarah said, mainly to show she knew what they were talking about.

Leo had stood up from the desk and was pacing back and forth as he explained. 'Well, keeping it brief, King Minos of Crete asked the god Poseidon to send him a snow-white bull from the sea as a symbol of support for his reign. Minos was supposed to sacrifice it, but the bull was so impressive he kept it and sacrificed a different one instead. As a punishment, the king's wife was made to fall in love with the bull and, well, the result of this relationship was the Minotaur.'

'That's...' Sarah struggled to find a word. 'Disgusting,' she decided.

'Yes, well, there's a lot of that sort of thing in Greek myth, I'm afraid. But anyway, apart from the prevalence of bulls in Minoan – Cretan – history, axes are also important.'

'The Cretans sacrificed bulls,' Miss Manners said, 'using double-headed axes like the one we're interested in, though rather larger of course. And remember the Thor legend?'

Sarah nodded. 'Wasn't the third axe supposed to belong to Thor?'

'That's right. Well, the Greek god Zeus used an axe to create storms, so there's another similarity.'

'And he's often depicted holding an axe,' Leo explained. 'In fact,' he went on, 'the Greek for "lightning" literally translates as "star axe".'

Miss Manners cleared her throat. 'But getting back specifically to Crete, Minoan priestesses carried these double-headed axes on ceremonial occasions.'

'So,' Sarah said, 'lots of connections.'

'Too many for it to be a coincidence, now we've looked at it,' Leo agreed. 'Or so we believe.'

'So, what next?'

'Since we talked to Dr Wiles at Bletchley,' Miss Manners told her, 'he has managed to trace several UDT sightings and transmissions in the Mediterranean back to Crete. Of course there are a lot of other places on those same trajectories. But there are also suggested Ley lines that meet in Crete. All that taken together…'

'Adds up to something worth investigating,' Sarah agreed. 'What about your friend Jane Roylston? Can she confirm or help with any of this, do you think?'

'I wondered that,' Miss Manners said. She was frowning behind her severe spectacles. 'But I've not been able to contact her. She's been out of touch for a while now. So long, in fact, that Guy and Colonel Brinkman are going to see Crowley. If nothing else, he may know something about occult connections to Crete which might help.'

The resentment was growing in him by the day. Ralph Rutherford felt he was being kept on a leash, like a dog. Crowley insisted he couldn't even leave the house, and he felt like every moment he was being watched. He had never really liked Crowley. He certainly didn't trust the man. And now, at any moment, he might decide to follow the advice of MI5 and stick a knife into Rutherford's back.

A knife… Like the one now in Rutherford's hand…

It was all Jane Roylston's fault. Since the bizarre ritual down in the cellar with the grotesque creature, Rutherford hadn't seen her. Jane was confined to her room – recovering, according to Crowley, though the way he said it made Rutherford sure the man was keeping something from him. He couldn't get back at Crowley, not easily, not yet. But Jane…

There was no answer when he knocked on the door. So he opened it and went in. She was sitting on the side of her bed, staring out of the small window. She didn't turn when he spoke.

'Jane.'

He walked round to stand in front of her, holding the knife where she could see it. 'Stand up,' he ordered.

She looked up at him, but made no effort to stand. Her expression was blank. Her eyes showed none of the fear and loathing he was used to seeing in them. She turned back towards the window.

'I said stand up!' he yelled, suddenly angry.

She stood. Slowly, almost dreamily. Her eyebrows raised slightly, but otherwise she did not react to the outburst.

'I can make life very difficult for you,' he said. Still no reaction. 'Difficult and painful.' Nothing. Feeling the tension and resentment building inside him, he reached out with the knife, tracing the point of it down her cheek. She turned slightly to look at him.

'Yes, that got your attention, didn't it,' he whispered. 'You're nothing, you understand. Crowley can do anything he likes to you. You know that. Well, so can I.'

He pressed harder with the knife, until it bit into the skin below her eye, producing a tiny bead of blood.

'I'm going to teach you to show me respect.'

A thin line of colour followed the blade as he drew it slowly down her face. She didn't flinch. That angered him even more, and he pressed harder. The skin parted beneath the blade. Rutherford smiled, looking for the pain and fear in her face.

But there was nothing.

And hardly any blood.

Instead, pale orange tendrils licked out from the cut – probing, feeling, gently pulling the skin back together. Rutherford felt his own skin begin to crawl at the sight. He took a step back, raising the knife again. But Jane's hand whipped out, grabbing his wrist in an impossibly firm grasp. He felt the bones compress and shatter. The knife fell to the floor.

Her other hand was round his neck, squeezing tight as Rutherford gasped for the air he needed to cry out. His vision blurred. But before it faded completely he saw that now at last her face was showing some reaction, some emotion.

She was smiling.

Then everything was darkness and silence as he crashed lifeless to the floor.

CHAPTER 18

'I did telephone Mr Alban a few days ago,' Crowley said. 'He said he couldn't speak as he had to go and look after a Mr Brown.'

They were sat in Crowley's study. Brinkman glanced at Guy Pentecross. He happened to know from a recent high-level briefing that Alban was at Chequers, the Prime Minister's country house, and 'Mr Brown' was in fact the Russian foreign minister Vyacheslav Molotov, who was meeting Churchill there.

'What did you want to talk to Alban about?'

Crowley shrugged. 'Nothing important. He asked me to do something for him a little while ago. I merely wished to confirm that I had done it. But,' he went on quickly, 'what can I do for you? It seems that our arrangement is all rather one-way at the moment, doesn't it?'

'How do you mean?' Guy asked.

'I scratch your back. And that's it. Although my own back does occasionally itch too, you know.'

'I'm sure there are many people who would happily scratch it,' Brinkman told him. 'But if there is anything specific?'

'Oh please.' Crowley's smile was almost predatory. 'You first.'

'Nothing too taxing,' Brinkman said. 'We just wanted a quick word with Jane Roylston.'

Crowley's smile hardened into a frown. 'May I ask what about?'

Brinkman considered for a moment before answering. 'We wondered if she knew of any connection between the Vril and Greece. Crete in particular.'

Crowley sat back in his chair. 'Well, you've answered one of my questions already, then.'

'Oh?'

'I'm afraid Jane isn't here. She disappeared, just upped and left about, oh, a couple of weeks ago, I should think. I did wonder if she had come to join your people. Obviously not, if you're asking me about her.'

'You've no idea where she went?' Brinkman asked. It seemed unlikely, but it was possible.

Guy voiced his next thought:

'That man Rutherford – could he have anything to do with her disappearance?'

'No.'

'You seem very sure,' Brinkman said.

'I am. Ralph is no longer with us either, you see.'

'Then perhaps—' Guy started.

But Crowley cut him off. 'There is no connection between the two, I can assure you. If you need confirmation, then ask your friend Alban. He knows what happened to poor Ralph, and if I tell you that Ralph, er, absented himself from us, shall we say, before Jane left then you will understand that the two are not connected.'

'I see,' Brinkman said, though in truth he didn't. He would leave a message for Alban and hope the MI5 man could clarify things. 'Then it seems we've had a wasted journey.'

'I'm sorry,' Crowley said. 'But I'm sure Miss Roylston will return to us soon. She probably just needs a little time to herself. But I must apologise that she isn't here to help you now.'

'Unless you can help us,' Guy said. 'Do you know of any connection between the Vril and Crete?'

'Not off hand,' Crowley admitted. 'There are various

sources I can consult. If I do find anything, I shall be sure to let you know.'

'And is your back no longer itching?' Brinkman asked.

'It has eased. But there is still one matter you can perhaps help me with.'

'Which is?'

'A term I have come across. Perhaps I heard it from one of you, I forget. Tell me, what exactly is an Ubermensch?'

Brinkman glanced at Guy, and found the major was looking back at him for guidance. Brinkman nodded.

'We don't really know,' Guy said. 'They are people who are somehow infected by the Vril. They become subservient to the creatures. But they also gain in strength and resilience as the infection or whatever it is spreads through their body.'

'I see.' Crowley nodded. 'Hence the name. Could this infection be spread through physical contact?'

'That is our best theory,' Brinkman agreed. 'It doesn't seem to be passed on by an Ubermensch to other humans, but direct contact with the Vril themselves could instigate the change.'

'And how can you spot these Ubermensch? Are there many of them?'

'To be honest, we don't know how many there are,' Brinkman said. 'We do know that at least one was working with the Germans, but how the alliance was arrived at or whether there was an element of coercion on either side...' He shrugged.

'And the only way to spot them,' Guy said, 'the only way we've found, is that when you kill them, they don't die.'

When he had found her standing over the body of Ralph Rutherford, Crowley had confined Jane to the cellars. He had no idea how dangerous she really was, but Brinkman and Pentecross had said nothing to allay his fears.

For the moment, Jane seemed docile. She lay on the altar table, wrists manacled to the sides as before. Her legs were free, and she was wearing a plain white robe of thin cotton as she did for séances and ceremonies.

Crowley wouldn't say that the young woman was back to herself exactly. But she was far more communicative, far more like the Jane she used to be than she had been when she killed Rutherford. He could only assume this was connected to the degree of infection. Was the restoration of self-will and individuality a stage in whatever process of transformation she was undergoing? Or was it a side effect of her not being directly controlled by the Vril?

Standing on the dais, looking down at her supine body, it occurred to Crowley for the first time that the answer might be obvious.

'Can I ask you something?' he said. Would she simply tell him what he wanted to know? Could it be that straightforward?

Jane turned her head to look up at him. 'Unchain me,' she said, her voice devoid of intonation.

'Perhaps if you answer my questions. But I can make no promises.'

'You always used to make promises,' she said. 'Promises you then broke.'

'I wasn't afraid of you then,' he admitted.

'If I tell you I could leave here whenever I wish, does that make you more afraid?'

He caught his breath. But she was lying, bluffing. Wasn't she?

'I see,' she said, turning away. She had her answer.

'If you can leave, why don't you?' he asked.

'I have no instructions,' she said simply.

'Jane? Are you still Jane?'

'Who else would I be?'

'You tell me.'

She turned back, staring at him angrily. 'You did this to me,' she said, her voice suddenly laced with emotion. 'And now you ask me what is happening? I am Jane – of course I'm Jane. But I'm not alone in here. I can feel them inside my mind. Always there, waiting to tell me what to do. It took a while to get used to it. To deaden their voices. But I've always heard them – in séances and ceremonies. When I wore the bracelet... Now I tell myself they're just talking louder and I can ignore them.' She stared up at the ceiling. 'I can ignore them,' she insisted through gritted teeth. 'I can.'

'Always?'

'Mostly.'

'When they speak to you...' Crowley licked his thin lips with a bloodless tongue. 'Do they ever mention Greece? The island of Crete?'

'That's not how they speak. I see in my mind what they are thinking. It's like voices, but it's also pictures. Thoughts...' She closed her eyes, the muscles in her face relaxing.

For a while there was silence. Crowley was about to leave when she suddenly opened her eyes again, staring unfocused at the vaulted stone above.

'I see darkness in the shape of the axe, carved into the living rock. Tunnels where the shadows dance on the rough-hewn walls. Passageways and steps, closing in around me, stale suffocating air that no one has breathed in centuries. In millennia.'

'In Crete?' Crowley breathed.

'A pathway that leads through hidden depths, down into the earth itself. The lair of the Guardians. The place where they sleep, patiently awaiting the time of awakening. The time when they will spew forth across the world and take what they believe is theirs.'

'Where?' Crowley demanded. 'Where is this place?'

She drew a sudden rasping breath, her chest convulsing with the effort. Her head rose from the stone, straining at the chains as she stared across at him.

Her voice was angry snarl of contempt: 'It is the gateway to Hell.'

CHAPTER 19

The pilot was more used to flying over Germany and occupied France. It had taken over a week for Colonel Brinkman's request to be actioned. The converted Spitfire was flown first to Malta. The island, close to German shipping lanes, was effectively under siege, the bravery and stamina of its small population recognised in April 1942 when they were collectively awarded the George Cross. It was still just as dangerous a place several months later when the Spitfire used Malta's airfield as the base from which to fly its mission over Crete.

Flying at a height of thirty thousand feet, the tiny plane was far above most other aircraft. Stripped of its weaponry, it relied for its survival on going unnoticed, and on the fact that its cruising speed was greater than anything else it was likely to meet in the sky. It was helped by the fact that the whole plane was painted a uniform pale blue, making it all but invisible as it flew high over the island. The five cameras under the wings and in the fuselage took stereoscopic photographs that would be delivered within days to a country house thirty miles to the west of London.

On the journey, they went over the notes from Brinkman's meeting with Crowley.

'What sources did he say he'd consulted?' Leo Davenport

wondered. 'We've come across nothing like this at the British Museum.'

'He didn't say,' Miss Manners replied. The two of them were sitting in the back of a staff car driven by Sarah Diamond. 'In fact he was quite vague about the whole thing.'

'You think he was making it up?' Sarah asked over her shoulder.

'No, I don't think so. He was too hesitant. Like he wasn't really sure if he wanted to tell us about it at all.'

'It's not a lot to go on, to be honest,' Leo pointed out. 'He confirms a connection with Crete – which we told him we suspected anyway. But he can't say what that connection really is or how he knows it exists. Instead he just waffles on about underground tunnels and the gateway to Hell, whatever that means.'

'But the Vril do seem to be subterranean by nature,' Miss Manners said.

'As Crowley probably knows. If nothing else, *The Coming Race* tells us that.'

'It's just a novel,' Sarah said.

'But a prescient one,' Miss Manners told her.

'Whatever the case,' Leo said, 'given that we suspect a connection between the axe and Crete, it's sensible to take a look. And the RAF can do that quicker and easier and more safely than we can.'

The grounds of Danesfield House were now dotted with temporary wooden buildings. Even so, the drive up to the main house was still impressive.

Sarah drove them towards the wide white frontage with its large central tower and prominent chimneys before following signs to park over to one side of the main building.

They were greeted at the main entrance by a thin man in a crumpled suit. His mass of hair was almost entirely white, and his eyes were pale and grey and watery. He introduced himself as Alan Blithe.

'Welcome to Danesfield House. Or RAF Medmenham

as we now have to refer to it,' he said in a reedy voice as they shook hands. 'They asked me to look after you as I'm an archaeologist by profession. If archaeology is indeed a profession,' he added, leading them inside. 'I sometimes wonder.'

'Isn't this a strange place for an archaeologist to end up?' Miss Manners asked as Blithe led them through the house.

'Oh we've all sorts here. Academics, of course. Geologists. Archaeologists like me. Even some bods from Hollywood, would you believe,' he said, turning to smile at Leo. 'But you'll know more about them than I do, I suspect.'

'I wouldn't count on it,' Leo told him. 'But I guess they're experts on photography and film.'

'Absolutely. We'll take anyone who can examine an aerial photograph and have some understanding of what the hell they're looking at, really. Horses for courses, as they say. The geologists look at the landscape, and maybe spot a feature that's out of place and might be artificial or camouflaged. I'm used to looking at how the face of the earth has changed over time, and making deductions based on partial evidence. But generally we all muck in together.'

'Analysing photographs,' Sarah said.

'That's what we do. "Image Intelligence" it's called. Or IMINT for short. Ah, here we are.'

Blithe ushered them into a large room with a high ceiling. Several large tables were set up down the length of the room. Round each, men and women sat poring over photographs. Some were staring at them fixedly. Others looked through jeweller's glass magnifiers. As Blithe led them towards a table at the back of the room, Leo saw that the magnifiers had two lenses so that the analysts looked through them with both eyes.

A man and a woman were already at Blithe's table. The woman was spreading out photographs while the man examined one through a double magnifier. Both wore RAF uniform.

'June, Philip, meet our friends from...' Blithe broke off.

'Well, I'm not sure quite where they're from, actually. So probably best not to ask. But this is Miss Manners, Miss Diamond, and Mr Davenport. I think that's right.'

Leo nodded. 'So what have we here?'

'These are all the photographs of Crete,' the woman, June, explained. 'We have pretty good coverage. Obviously we're most interested in the ports and the troop deployments usually. But I gather you're looking for geological features, is that right?'

'Or archaeological ones,' Miss Manners said.

'No shortage of those,' Philip said. His voice was clipped and sharp, but not unfriendly. 'Whole damned island is one big ruin. Well, up to a point.'

'Something of an exaggeration,' Blithe confessed. 'We discarded any images that really were just countryside. Oh, we checked them all meticulously first, of course. You can take a look if you like. But it's mainly grass and sheep and hills.'

Miss Manners picked up one of the photographs. There were two pictures on the same sheet, both looked identical. 'You can identify sheep on these?'

'Oh yes.' Philip took the photo from her and pulled a different one across the table. 'Here, take a look at this one. Through here.' He placed one of the dual magnifiers over the sheet. It covered both photographs, a lens over each.

Miss Manners lowered her head and peered through. After a moment, she straightened up, removed her spectacles, and tried again. 'That is very impressive,' she said. 'There's a man on a bicycle. You can make out his shadow and everything.'

Leo gestured for Sarah to go next. From the positioning of the lenses over the two photographs he had already guessed what she'd see.

'How's it done?' Sarah asked in surprise.

'Stereographic, I assume?' Leo asked, taking Sarah's place.

'That's right, sir,' Philip told him. 'The pictures are taken from slightly different angles. Look at them both, one eye seeing each, and...'

'Three dimensions,' Leo said. It was impressive – both the detail and the three-dimensional perspective.

'Size and depth are still the tricky things to work out,' Blithe said. 'The bicycle on that one means we can work out the scale. Shadows help too.'

'It's a shame the Germans don't play cricket,' Miss Manners said.

Blithe laughed. 'Indeed.'

'Why's that?' Sarah asked Leo quietly.

' A cricket pitch is a standard size,' he told her. 'One chain – that's 22 yards – between the wickets.'

'Now then,' Blithe was saying, 'there are three of you and three of us. So I suggest we pair up to examine the photographs together. June and Philip and I can help interpret what you're seeing. And I'm assuming you people will know what you're looking for.'

'Not necessarily,' Leo admitted. 'But hopefully we shall know it when we see it.'

Leo and Philip took one stack of photos. Leo would have welcomed the chance to chat to Blithe about archaeology and find out where the man's interests lay. But it made sense to spread the expertise. Sarah and June formed the second pair, with Miss Manners starting her partnership with Blithe by giving him a stern stare across the top of her glasses.

It was slow and methodical work. But they knew it would be, and had arranged to stay overnight if necessary. By mid afternoon when they took a break for tea, Leo was wondering if they might be here for several nights.

Blithe and his colleagues had other work to catch up on, so Leo, Sarah and Miss Manners took tea on their own. The mess hall had been a ballroom.

'The house isn't as old as it looks,' Miss Manners told them. 'Blithe was telling me it was only built at the turn of the century.'

'They made a good job of the neo-Tudor aspects,' Leo said appreciatively. The tea was acceptable too. 'You're very quiet,' he remarked to Sarah.

'I didn't realise just looking at photos would be so tiring,' she said. 'And I'm sure I'll end up boss-eyed from looking through that stereo-whatever it is thing.' She sipped at her tea. 'And I was thinking…'

'Yes?' Miss Manners prompted.

'About that poor fellow in Los Angeles. The reporter who died. He was taking photographs at Sumner's gallery.'

'Really?' Miss Manners set down her own cup and leaned forward. 'What happened to them?'

Sarah shrugged. 'Damned if I know. They confiscated his camera, long before the UDT arrived.'

'Even so, there might be something on the photos. The Ubermensch was there.'

'True,' Sarah said. 'You think it's worth tracking the camera down?'

'Chances are it's been returned to the newspaper,' Leo said. 'Though no one there will know what they're looking for on the photos, if they ever developed them.'

'I'll find out,' Sarah promised. 'I'll put a call through to Sumner and ask him what happened to the camera.'

'We'd better get back to work,' Miss Manners decided.

'Good of you to keep us in order,' Leo said, smiling.

'Someone has to,' she told him sternly. 'This could take a while.'

'Even if we knew what we were looking for,' Sarah said.

'Let's hope we really do know it when we see it,' Leo remarked, standing up. 'And the sooner the better.'

They did.

'The angle's not very good,' Miss Manners said, 'But I think I may have found something.'

She moved aside to let Blithe take a look. 'It's a narrow opening into the rock face,' he said. 'We can estimate the size from the German fuel depot on the coast nearby. There are people there, and vehicles… Yes,' he decided, 'it's probably a cave. Or possibly the way into some ancient ruin. It looks like there might be steps carved into the rock, though I can't be certain. Probably not as obvious at ground level, though.'

'May I?' Leo asked.

Blithe moved aside to let him look through the magnifier. Even though, as Miss Manners said, the angle wasn't the best, the shape of the opening in the sheer rock face was unmistakeable. There were two shallow depressions impressed into the rocky landscape on the inclined side of a slope leading down to cliffs and the sea. The narrow opening that Blithe had identified was between the two, just where the curved shapes met.

'What do you think?' Leo asked, making way for Sarah to take a look.

'It's bigger, obviously. But it looks like the axe-head,' she said. She straightened up. 'What is it?'

'Remains of an ancient building, probably,' Blithe said. 'That depression will be where the floor was. The opening might lead down into the cellars.'

'Or,' Miss Manners said quietly, 'like Crowley said, it might lead down into Hell itself.'

CHAPTER 20

Himmler was spending more time away from Wewelsburg. The Russian campaign continued and the American influence was beginning to tell. As a result, Hoffman was able to pursue his own researches.

Himmler's absence suited Hoffman. He had no intention of telling either Nachten or Himmler what he discovered. He worked long into the night. An advantage of his 'condition', as he thought of it, was that he needed far less sleep. The main disadvantage was the distraction of the constant pulling at his mind. But a man used to living a double life – a Russian playing at being a German – was able to compartmentalise that. He could shut away the voices and images that the Vril somehow injected into his thoughts.

Even so, the notepaper in front of him was scattered with unconscious sketches of the axe-head, or runic symbols, or the intricate spiralling circular pattern that invaded his thoughts. There was another pattern too – short dashes radiating out from a central point. Was it a variation of the spiral pattern, he wondered? The problem was that while he could sense what the Vril were transmitting to him, he had no idea what it meant. The only way to put it into context would be to surrender himself to them completely – put on a bracelet and lose his mind. That was not an option.

Even so, as he struggled to keep himself free of their

influence, he was only too aware that his body was changing. He was conscious that he needed to keep these changes hidden. He retired to his room when he was expected to sleep, though he needed almost none. He made a show of appearing at meal times, even though he ate and drank hardly anything and had no appetite at all.

Having a focus, something to concentrate on, certainly helped. A note on one of the inventory sheets was signed 'GK'. Could that stand for Georg Kruger, Hoffman wondered. Was the man here back when the artefacts from the 1936 crash were catalogued? There was an easy way to find out.

'I came here in '38,' Kruger told him. 'We were still sorting through the debris to see what we could salvage. I wasn't involved with the stuff that went to the Vault.'

'But you worked with the Ubermensch?'

They were in the Hall of Supreme Generals on the ground floor of the North Tower of the castle. With Himmler away, they could be sure they had the place to themselves. Hoffman was leaning against one of the twelve pillars round the outer edge of the room. Light streamed in through the recessed window behind him, illuminating the black 'sun wheel' symbol inlaid into the floor. With its central hub and twelve jointed 'arms' projecting to the outer circle it looked to Hoffman like a stylised image of one of the Vril. Like the grotesque spider-like creature had been crossed with a swastika.

Kruger seemed happy enough to talk about the past. For the most part he merely confirmed things that Hoffman already knew.

'We sorted the debris into what might have technical value and what was more esoteric.'

'And then what happened to it?' Hoffman asked.

'Much of it remains in the Vault, as you know. Catalogued and archived. Including the... organic material.' Kruger couldn't disguise the disgust he felt as he thought of the Vril.

'But not all. I know Streicher removed some items, back in 1938.'

'That would be about right. Some items were deemed of historical value. I wasn't involved with them; as you say, Streicher was responsible. There was a feeling that they were not connected to the crash. Though I always thought...' He shrugged. 'What I thought didn't matter back then. I was very junior. I'd only just arrived. You'd have to ask Streicher or Meklen. They were in charge back then.'

'And both of them are now dead,' Hoffman pointed out.

'This is war. It happens.'

He couldn't argue with that. 'What did you think? At the time, when no one listened? Because they'll listen to you now.'

Kruger nodded. 'It doesn't really matter now. Probably didn't matter back then. But I thought it was a hell of a coincidence that the craft came down on top of a previously undiscovered archaeological site.'

'Though that would explain the ancient artefacts that were found.'

'True.' Kruger took out a cigarette. He didn't light it, but jabbed it towards Hoffman as he made his point. 'But isn't it more plausible that the artefacts were on board the craft? That they were cargo?'

'You think the Vril were collecting them?' Hoffman waited while Kruger lit the cigarette.

'It seems likely.'

Hoffman had to agree. 'There is another possibility,' he realised. 'Did you consider that they might not have been collecting those artefacts, but delivering them?'

Kruger blew out a thoughtful stream of smoke. 'No,' he admitted. 'That had not occurred to me. It should have done. We know the Vril have been here before, long ago. Perhaps they never left.'

'So what did Streicher do with them? Where did the archaeological materials go?' Hoffman asked. He had the man interested – intrigued, even. Hopefully enough to help Hoffman trace the axe-head.

'There were several consignments sent out, as far as I remember. Not all archaeological. One consisted of anything we could salvage from the propulsion systems. That was sent to the Army Research Centre.'

'Where's that?'

Kruger shrugged. 'Some island on the Baltic. They set it up after the crash, once they realised von Braun's work actually had some potential. Peenemunde, I think it's called. Run by the Army Weapons Office, though the Luftwaffe are also trying to get in on the act, as you can imagine.'

'It's where they are developing the A4,' Hoffman said. He had heard of the place. The A4 was a ballistic rocket, also known as 'Vengeance Weapon 2', or just V2 for short.

'Then some stuff went to Messerschmitt. There was an idea it could help with new aircraft engine designs.'

'And the artefacts?' Hoffman prompted.

Kruger shook his head. 'Don't recall. Several places, I think. Museums and so on, depending on what it was. We did show the items to the Ubermensch,' he added. 'In case there was anything important we'd missed. Once it had agreed to help us, of course. Just before we crated everything up and shipped it off, that I do remember. It would have been in late 1938, I suppose.'

That fitted with the note Hoffman had seen saying Streicher had removed the axe-head in October 1938. 'Did it pick anything out?'

'Again, I couldn't say.' Kruger was apologetic. 'But you could check the film.'

'I've looked at all the films in the archive.'

'Ah, but not all the films are in the archive,' Kruger said with a smile. 'The films we made of the Ubermensch being interrogated and trained, those are in my office. Including the film of it examining the artefacts.'

There was no sound on the film. The first time through, Hoffman saw nothing remarkable. It was taken in the Vault. One of the long tables filled the foreground, covered with artefacts laid out neatly and labelled. The angle was such that it was difficult to distinguish the artefacts, but one of them looked as though it could be the stone axe-head that Hoffman was looking for.

The Ubermensch, dressed now in the uniform of an SS officer, walked slowly across the frame. The image flickered occasionally as it had before, flashing up glimpses of how the Ubermensch appeared in the still photographs. It examined the artefacts, even picked one up. Hoffman leaned closed, but he could see that the Ubermensch had picked up something far smaller than what he was after – a flint arrowhead perhaps? Several had been found and catalogued.

He ran the film again. And again.

The fourth time through, he saw it. He rewound it, played it through once more. The Ubermensch reached out, and picked up the arrowhead or whatever it was. But there was a hesitation. A change of direction. Again the angle didn't help, but the Ubermensch reached out for an object, hesitated, moved its hand to the side and selected instead the object next to the one it had initially reached for.

It had been about to pick up the axe-head. Then it changed its mind – not wanting to draw attention to the one item on the table that it was interested in. Hoffman was certain of it. He froze the film, with the Ubermensch's hand hovering above the artefact he was now sure must be the stone axe. He stared at the frame for several seconds before letting the film continue. Freeze it for too long and the film would melt under the hot light of the projector.

Relaxed now, having found what he was looking for, Hoffman nearly missed the more important clue in the film.

He was standing up, turning to shut off the projector when he saw it. Behind the Ubermensch, on a table at the back of the Vault: a wooden crate. The lid was propped against it. A bundle of straw on the table beside it. And on the front of the crate, a label with writing stencilled across it.

Another run of the film, and Hoffman stood as close to the screen as he could get without masking the crate. It was close enough to make out the writing on the label: 'Sonderauftrag Linz'.

So the artefacts had been crated up and sent to the Special Commission set up in 1939 to establish a Fuhrermuseum in the name of Adolf Hitler in the Austrian city of Linz. These must have been the first artefacts delivered to the commission, selected when its formation was still being debated. Hoffman knew that Speer was still working on plans for the museum. Eventually the museum would house artwork and artefacts looted from across Europe. But for now, the collection was curated by the Dresden Picture Gallery.

Back in his room, Hoffman put his notebook on his desk. He had actually made no notes during the film. Instead, he realised, he had sketched a detailed drawing of the circular, spiralling pattern. It took up a whole page of the book. He took hold of the page, about to tear it out and throw it away, when his eyes settled on a particular tile behind the washstand further along the wall.

He couldn't have replaced it properly, he realised. Gently, Hoffman prised the tile from the wall, and pulled out the roll of cloth behind it. He stared at the photograph curled inside the material. Brushed the tips of his fingers across the young woman's face. Yes, he must go to Dresden, he thought.

And after that, eastwards, to Russia. He wanted to go home.

CHAPTER 21

The submarine was incredibly small and cramped. Guy could not imagine spending more than a few days on board, let alone the months that the submariners spent on duty. He and Brinkman shared a cabin, which gave them considerably more privacy than most of the others on board.

'I'm surprised they let you come,' Guy said to Brinkman as they lay on their tiny bunks the first night.

'I didn't give them an option,' Brinkman replied. 'It's time I got out of the office and did something useful for once. That said, as you speak Greek and I happen to have a contact in Crete, we're obviously the best choices for the job.'

'I suppose so.'

'Though I have to admit that General Ismay wasn't entirely convinced.'

Guy could hear the smile in the man's voice. He could imagine how much he wanted to see some action. Guy too found it frustrating to be spending so much time in offices or libraries or museums rather than actively engaging the enemy in battle – whether that enemy be the Vril, or the Germans and their allies.

It took the best part of a week to reach the waters off Crete. The weather was turning as the submarine broke the surface on schedule and in position. The vessel they were rendezvousing with was less punctual. By the time the fishing boat appeared over the horizon, dark clouds were massing ominously overhead.

'So tell me about this contact of yours,' Guy said as they waited at the top of the conning tower. They could see how rough it was getting by the way the approaching boat was being tossed and tumbled by the waves.

'An old friend. British, but he's spent a lot of time in this part of the world. For our purposes, and as far as the Germans are concerned, he's a shepherd called Mihali.'

'I'm guessing he doesn't have that many sheep,' Guy said.

'I really couldn't say. Though knowing Patrick, he's probably set up his own farm and is turning a tidy profit.'

'And the fisherman?'

'One of the local resistance. Man called Dimitry. He can take us to Mihali.'

'And Mihali can show us the area we're interested in.'

'If the weather holds,' Brinkman agreed. As he spoke, the first spattering of rain fell across them.

Dimitry's face was suntanned and weather-beaten. He was short but stocky and communicated his greeting mainly in grunts. Guy put this down largely to the weather, which was deteriorating by the minute. As soon as Guy and Brinkman were on board, Dimitry thrust a bundle of ragged, scruffy clothes at them and pointed to a narrow set of steps leading down below the small deck.

'You're shepherds,' he said. 'So look like shepherds.' He didn't wait to see if they replied, but stomped off to the tiny wheelhouse.

The pitch and yaw of the boat seemed even worse below deck. Guy changed quickly in the confined space. Despite looking old and worn, the thick jumper and cotton trousers turned out to be warm and dry. Two rather scruffy-looking sheepskin coats and two pairs of scuffed boots were dumped in a corner and Guy guessed these were also for them.

'I think I'd rather be on deck,' Brinkman said, pulling on one pair of boots. He and Guy had put down the bags of equipment they'd brought in the corner where the boots had been. They contained rations, weapons, and a radio. There were false papers in waterproof oilskin bags, but it seemed sensible to leave those in the dry.

It was almost dark on deck. Their arrival had been timed so that the evening was drawing in when they reached the shore – fishermen returning at the end of the day. But the storm clouds had hastened the arrival of twilight. The other fishermen had probably returned hours ago when the weather first started to worsen. The island was a dark wall in front of the boat, much closer than Guy had expected.

'Looks like we're nearly there.' Guy had to shout above the sound of the rain and the sea. As he spoke, a spike of lightning streaked across the sky. Thunder exploded round them and the rain became torrential in an instant.

At the same moment, the front of the boat dipped down alarmingly. Guy grabbed for a handrail, catching hold of Brinkman's arm. Water washed over the deck and almost swept their feet from under them.

Dimitry leaned out of the side of the wheelhouse, shouting at them. But his words were swallowed up by another roll of thunder. Guy pulled himself along, using the handrail at the edge of the deck. Brinkman was close behind him.

'It's getting worse,' Dimitry was shouting. Guy translated the Greek's words for Brinkman.

'Like we hadn't noticed,' Brinkman yelled back.

'We're not going to make the cove,' Dimitry shouted. 'We'll have to try to ride it out. But we're very close to the rocks.'

Guy risked a look over the side of the boat. His stomach was pitching almost as much as the frail wooden vessel. Where the steep cliffs descended into the sea, rocks spilled out into the water. They were indeed very close. The waves broke over them in a white spay. The boat was turning, slowly, so that its back was towards the cliff. It looked like Dimitry was trying to put some distance between them and the rocks.

For a while, he seemed to succeed. The boat struggled forwards, engine whining in protest as it was pushed to the limit. Spray shot up in front of them as the nose of the boat plunged down into an oncoming wave.

Guy and Brinkman had managed to get to the wheelhouse, but it afforded little shelter. What Guy had assumed was a window was an empty space, the glass – if there had ever been any – was long gone.

'She won't take much more of this,' Dimitry told them. He pointed into the distance, to the slightest break in the cloud. 'Better weather is coming, though. If we can hold on for just a few more minutes.'

Guy kept his attention fixed on the brighter patch of sky. He tried to ignore the way the ground beneath his feet bucked and reeled. Slowly, the brighter area was widening, spreading towards them.

Just as he began to hope they were through the worst of it, there was another almighty crack of thunder as the sky was simultaneously splashed with lightning. The front of the boat dropped away like they'd sailed off the end of the world. Water poured across the deck. A wave rose up in front of them like a vicious animal about to pounce. Then it crashed down.

The sound of splintering wood was audible even above the noise of the sea. The whine of the engine became a stuttering cough, then stopped. The whole boat lurched suddenly backwards. Guy was hurled out of the wheelhouse, sliding across the slippery wooden deck, scrabbling desperately to catch hold of something fixed. His legs were over the edge by the time he caught hold of a metal stanchion.

He could see Brinkman clinging to the outside of the wheelhouse. Another wave burst through the glass-less window and swept him aside. When the water and spray cleared, Guy was amazed and relieved to see the colonel still holding tight, arms wrapped round the wooden roof support.

More water swept past Guy. Something heavy crashed into him, caught and clawed at him, then was gone. Shocked, he realised it was Dimitry. Guy twisted, staring out into the churning white water below, but there was no sign of the man.

Then they lurched again. Wood shattered and rock tore

through the bottom of the hull. The fishing boat twisted on to its side, breaking to pieces on the jagged rocks at the base of the cliff.

Somehow, Guy managed to scramble from the stricken boat to the rocks below. They were slick beneath his feet, water up to his thighs. He fought against the pull of the waves, desperately trying to make headway towards the base of the cliffs.

But first he had to find Brinkman. Was the colonel still on the boat? The vessel had almost completely broken up under the onslaught of the sea. Waves tore at it, ripping off planking. The main mast had fractured and was lying across the side of the boat, rolled back and forth as if it was a pencil on a desk.

'Guy!'

He thought at first it was the sound of the wind. But when he heard his name called again, he managed to locate the source. Brinkman was hanging from the side of the boat, his feet almost in the water. As Guy watched, Brinkman dropped into the boiling sea and disappeared from sight.

A moment later, he surfaced again, and struggled towards Guy – who was now frantically wading towards him. The water was deeper here – up to Guy's chest. He managed to grab Brinkman's outstretched arm and together the two of them half staggered, half swam to the cliff.

There was no beach, no dry land. They had to clamber up the steep side. The rock was firm, but made slippery by the sea spray. They managed to get to a point where there was a ledge wide enough to perch precariously and look down. Saltwater stung their eyes as they watched the boat finally break up. For a few seconds the mast was left dipping in and out of the water. Then it too was swallowed up in the spray and the waves and the deepening twilight.

'There goes the radio,' Brinkman said. 'Not to mention our papers and guns.'

'And Dimitry,' Guy told him.

Brinkman sighed. 'Really? I'd hoped he was further along these cliffs.'

'Went overboard. Didn't resurface. He may have survived, but it'd be a miracle.'

'Then we're on our own.'

'What about your friend the shepherd?'

Brinkman shook his head. 'Dimitry knew how to make contact with Mihali. And without the radio we can't ask London for any help finding him.' He glanced up at the cliff rising steeply above them. 'But we'll worry about that later. For now, we'd better concentrate on getting our breath back – there's some climbing to do.'

The cliff was steep, but there were plenty of hand and foot holds. The rain was easing as the better weather and clearer sky arrived at last. As they got higher, there were tufts of grass and spiky shrubs. They had to be careful, though, as some of them were rooted so shallowly that they just pulled out from the rock face. But others were secure enough to take their weight as Guy and Brinkman hauled themselves ever higher.

Finally, as the last of the light was fading, they reached the top. The cliff became a shallow grassy slope leading upwards. They crested the top, and flopped down on the grass. Guy's rasping breaths became laughs of relief.

But the relief was short-lived.

'There's someone there,' Brinkman said quietly.

Guy sat up. It was an effort even to keep his eyes open, he was so exhausted. Several dark figures were approaching through the gloom. One of them called out:

'Who's there? What are you doing?'

Guy understood what the man said perfectly, but there was something odd about his voice. Only when the figures were close enough for him to make out their uniforms and their guns did he realise what was strange.

They were speaking not Greek, but German.

CHAPTER 22

The large desk seemed tiny in such a vast space. It took Nachten a long time to cross the room. Long enough for his nerves to pique, which was no doubt the intention.

Himmler had demanded a report as soon as he returned to Wewelsburg. He did not look up as Nachten approached his desk, though he must have heard the man's boots ringing on the stone floor. Another technique for putting people at their unease.

Eventually, the Reichsfuhrer-SS glanced up. He switched on a thin smile that did not reach much further than his thin lips. 'You have made progress?'

Nachten clicked his heels and gave a formal nod. 'The research progresses, sir.'

Himmler leaned back, pressing the tips of his fingers together. 'I am pleased to hear it.'

'It seems the axe in the United States was indeed stolen. We did wonder if it was a ploy by the Allies to mask the fact that they have it. But the story seems genuine.'

'And have you traced the others?'

'Not yet. Sturmbannfuhrer Hoffman is following a lead on the second axe, the one linked to the Black Forest.'

'What lead?'

Nachten shuffled uncomfortably. 'I'm afraid I do not know. He mentioned to Kruger that he had found a clue to its current whereabouts, and he left here a few days ago. He did not say where he was going.'

Himmler considered. 'Hoffman is clever and Hoffman is efficient. But he is also a cautious man. He will report as soon as he has something tangible to tell us. And what of your own researches? You suggested that the third axe might be connected to ancient Greek myths.' Himmler leaned forward, his eyes glinting behind his spectacles. 'But, of course, Greece is a large country.'

'I am narrowing down the possibilities. I do have a theory...' His voice tailed away. Perhaps Hoffman was wise not giving away how much he had actually discovered.

But Nachten was not to be given the chance to keep his idea to himself. Himmler's smile was still fixed in place. 'And would you care to elaborate on that theory?'

'It is, you understand, only a theory. But the axe is important in particular to Minoan society. The Minoans lived in ancient—'

'Crete. I know.' The smile seemed more genuine now. 'The birthplace of civilisation, older even than the Greeks. According to Sir Arthur Evans, anyway. Yes... Yes,' Himmler decided. 'Crete is most certainly a possibility. Perhaps you should go there.'

'Perhaps, Herr Reichsfuhrer.' As soon as he said it, he realised his mistake. 'Of course,' he went on quickly. 'An excellent suggestion. I shall make arrangements immediately.'

As soon as he was out of the huge office, Nachten wiped his forehead with his handkerchief and took a deep breath. So he was going to Crete. Well, he consoled himself, Himmler was probably right, he could continue his researches more easily there than stuck here in the castle. It would be useful to talk to Hoffman before he left, but he had no idea when the man would be back.

There might be some clue in Hoffman's room as to where he had gone, Nachten thought. Of course it was hardly ethical to enter the man's quarters uninvited. But he should leave Hoffman a note, telling him of these latest developments and asking him to get in touch as soon as possible so they could compare their progress.

Hoffman's room was as impersonal and tidy as Nachten had expected. There were several books piled up on the side of a small desk. A notebook and pen. Little else, apart from the soap and towel by the washstand, to suggest the room was even inhabited.

Nachten picked up the pen and opened the notebook, riffling through to find a blank page. There were notes and sketches of the axe-head and its runic symbols. What Nachten could decipher was hardly useful. Mainly questions, but if Hoffman had discovered the answers he had not committed them to paper.

The last used page was a diagram or drawing. A complicated matrix of spiralling lines inside a circular boundary. Nachten turned past it, and wrote a brief note to Hoffman. When he was finished, he tore out the page and placed it prominently in the centre of the desk. Before replacing the notebook, he turned back a page to the circular diagram.

There was something about it that seemed vaguely familiar. He traced his finger along the lines as he thought. 'Of course,' he murmured as he realised what he was looking at. 'I was right. It has to be Crete.'

He tore the page from the notebook, folded it carefully, and put it in his jacket pocket.

There was a truck parked on a narrow track at the bottom of the hill. Guy and Brinkman were pushed roughly in front of it, so that the headlights dazzled them.

'Your papers,' one of the soldiers demanded in German.

Guy and Brinkman both feigned ignorance, shrugging.

'Papers,' the soldier said again, this time in passable, but accented Greek.

It seemed best for the moment to pretend they just didn't understand what was happening. It looked to Guy as if they'd been spotted on the skyline by a passing patrol – rotten luck that meant their mission was probably over before they'd even begun. If they were lucky they were off to rot in some POW camp for the duration. If not, they were off to rot in a shallow grave.

Confident that their prisoners didn't understand them, the soldiers debated what to do.

'Just shoot the idiots and be done with it,' one of them suggested.

Guy and Brinkman exchanged glances. Guy tensed, ready to run if he had to. There wasn't much chance either of them would get far, but that was better than just standing and waiting for the bullet.

'No,' the corporal in charge decided. 'We'll take them back to headquarters, and let someone else decide what to do. Then at least it's not our fault.'

Resigned to a long, arduous and most likely painful interrogation, Guy and Brinkman followed the mimed instructions to climb into the back of the truck. But before they reached the tailgate, there was a shout from further down the track. The Germans turned, weapons raised, as another figure appeared out of the gloom of the evening.

It was a tall man with wild, dark hair and several days of stubble. He was dressed like Guy and Brinkman in a crudely-stitched sheepskin jacket and shapeless trousers.

'Thank God you found them,' he exclaimed in Greek. Without further explanation he enfolded first Brinkman and then Guy in an enormous bear-hug.

'Stand back,' the German who spoke some Greek ordered. 'These men have no papers. We are taking them to headquarters.'

'No papers?' the Greek was outraged. 'Look at them – they're wet through. Half drowned. Who worries about their papers at times like this? But they don't need papers. They're Dimitry's cousins.' His eyes widened in sudden anxiety. 'But – where is Dimitry? What's happened?'

'I'm sorry,' Guy said, doing his best to match the man's rural accent. 'The storm – Dimitry was swept overboard when the boat hit the rocks. We were both lucky to escape with our lives, though of course we lost our papers. We managed to climb the cliff, and then the soldiers found us.'

'And thank heavens they did.' The Greek grabbed the nearest German's hand and shook it. He hugged another, tears in his eyes. 'You have saved them. Poor, poor Dimitry. But at least his cousins are safe.'

'Dimitry the fisherman?' the Greek-speaking soldier asked.

'Of course.'

'I didn't know he had cousins.'

'Everyone has cousins.'

'We help with the fishing sometimes,' Guy explained.

'You know Dimitry?' the Greek demanded. 'Because if you do, perhaps you can tell his wife what has happened? While I get these two into the dry and warm before the rain starts again.'

'Not me,' the German said quickly. 'I only knew him by sight. Better that it comes from a friend.' He glanced at Guy. 'Or a relative.'

The Greek sighed and nodded. 'I'm sure you are right. Thank you again. I'll make sure they apply for replacement papers as soon as they have recovered from their ordeal.'

The German nodded. 'See that you do. Or they really will be in trouble.' He turned to Guy and Brinkman. 'This is your last warning.'

'Yes,' Guy muttered. 'Thank you, sir.'

Brinkman made a vaguely appreciative sound.

As the lights of the truck disappeared into the distance, the Greek man started to laugh.

'You haven't changed a bit,' Brinkman told him. 'Though your dress sense has improved.'

The man gave a gap-toothed grin. 'Nor have you, old man,' he replied in English. His voice was surprisingly cultured – a contrast to the rural Greek accent he had adopted earlier.

'Thank you for that,' Guy said. 'How did you know we'd be here?'

'I was watching for Dimitry's boat from the cliffs further along, by the cove. So I saw what happened, and came as fast as I could.' The man reached out to shake Guy's hand. 'Call me Mihali,' he said.

They slept in a barn. It was cool but dry, if rather draughty. 'Mihali' had a stack of blankets ready for them as well as a couple of buckets of clean water for them to wash in. A pot of stew was bubbling on a small fire just outside the barn.

'Mutton,' he told them. 'Well, I am a shepherd. You'll feel better when you've eaten something hot. There's no tea, I'm afraid.'

He told them he had seen what had happened to Dimitry, shaking his head sadly.

'Will you tell his wife?' Brinkman asked. 'Do you want us to come with you?'

Mihali waved his hand. 'Dimitry wasn't married. No relatives. Not even cousins,' he added with a sad smile. 'But his friends will miss him.'

Guy slept well despite the conditions. He was completely worn out by the day's exertions. His sleep was deep and mostly dreamless. When he did dream, it was a confused version of his usual nightmare of struggling through the water at Dunkirk. But now Brinkman was with him, and Dimitry's lifeless body floated past – the man's cold, dead eyes staring up at the smoky sky.

Breakfast was water and hunks of coarse bread and hard cheese. Mihali laid a map out on top of a bale of straw. He showed them where the barn was in relation to the area they wanted to explore.

'It's not too far. Dimitry deliberately chose the cove because it's the closest we could safely get you.' He gave a humourless laugh. 'Safely…'

'How long will it take to get there?' Brinkman wondered.

'Three hours if we take it fairly swiftly, I'd say. It's not that far, but the terrain is quite rough. And we'll need to take a bit of a roundabout route to avoid any patrols. Especially as you have no papers.'

'Will that be a problem?' Guy asked.

'Probably not. I think they only asked you for them last night because they were bored and thought you might be British spies sneaking ashore.'

Guy smiled. 'As if.'

'Well, quite.' Mihali folded up the map and stuffed it into a backpack. 'If we start now, we can be there in time for a picnic lunch.'

'That sounds good,' Brinkman said.

'Don't get too excited,' Mihali told him. 'It's the rest of the bread and cheese.'

The weather was a complete contrast to the day before. The only clouds were pale wisps against the deep blue of the sky. It was already getting mercilessly hot as they set off. Mihali suggested they take their coats, stuffed into backpacks, as it would get cold in the evening and as they again approached the sea.

The landscape was rugged. It seemed to be composed entirely of hills covered with coarse grass and punctuated by outcrops of jagged rock. To Mihali the journey appeared to be a casual stroll. When Guy and Brinkman rested, Mihali stood impatiently, ready to get moving again almost immediately.

'I don't really know this area,' he confessed as they approached their destination.

Approaching the top of yet another hill, Guy could feel the sea breeze, and fancied he could hear the waves, though that might just be the wind. There was something else too, he realised as they got closer – metallic, industrial sounds, and voices. Brinkman had heard it too, and gestured for them to slow.

'Wait here,' Mihali said. 'I'll check ahead.'

He ducked down as he reached the top of the hill, crawling the last few yards. After a moment he beckoned for them to follow. Guy and Brinkman crawled up to join him.

Mihali had produced a pair of binoculars from his backpack and handed them to Brinkman. But Guy didn't need them to see they were in trouble.

On the other side of the hill, the ground sloped sharply down before levelling out. The sea was perhaps half a mile away, across the rocky plain below. Guy could see the vague outline of the axe-shaped indentation in the ground. But from this angle, he would never have noticed it if he had not seen the aerial photographs.

That wasn't the problem. The photographs had also shown what looked like a fuel depot close by. It had not been clear from the photographs just how close the depot was. The huge tanks of petrol and diesel were a good distance away, but a set of narrow pipelines ran across the plain to a jetty. They were laid right along the edge of the indented ground, curving round it. There was a huge ship at the jetty, either taking on fuel or delivering it.

Surrounding the whole installation – pipeline, fuel tanks, and jetty – was a wire fence. It looked to be about ten feet high, maybe more. Guy didn't need the binoculars to see that there were several guards patrolling the fence. And it was between them and where they needed to go.

'Looks like we'll be doing our archaeological investigations right under the nose of the Germans,' Brinkman said.

'I can arrange a distraction for a while,' Mihali offered. 'But you still need to get through that fence.'

'Do you have spare weapons?' Guy asked. 'I don't fancy going in there unarmed.'

'For this sort of operation we'll want quite a bit of equipment,' Brinkman said.

'I'll ask SOE to send us what we need,' Mihali said. 'I'm due to report in tonight. We don't keep in close contact, because the Germans monitor the radio and if they pick us up they try to triangulate where we are. Not very healthy if they find out. But let's make a Christmas list and I'll ask Santa if he can deliver it all.'

To her surprise, Sarah had discovered from her father that J.D. Sumner still had the photographer's camera from the night the man was killed. Sumner was happy to send it over, and it arrived on one of the ferry flights from Canada.

Miss Manners made arrangements to deliver the camera directly to Blithe at RAF Medmenham. Sarah drove them down, and they waited in the corner of the room where Blithe and his colleagues worked while he supervised developing the film.

June brought them black coffee, apologising that she had to get back to work. 'We're just getting pictures of the U-boat yards at Danzig. They used that new heavy bomber, the Lancaster, last night. We're all rather keen to see what sort of damage they inflicted.'

Blithe was back within an hour, clutching a handful of prints still wet with fluid. He laid the prints out one by one out on the table.

'Most, as you can see, are just shots of people partying like there's no tomorrow. Which, of course, is always possible these days.'

He put down a shot of a man and a much younger woman holding wine glasses and laughing. It was an informal shot, catching them unawares.

'I rather like this one,' Blithe said, raising his eyebrows.

'He's my father,' Sarah told him. 'And if we seem to be having fun, we didn't know the man who took these photographs would be dead within the hour.'

Blithe's smile faded. 'I didn't realise that, I'm sorry.'

The next photograph was more posed – two couples, facing the camera, smiles fixed and practised.

'Anyway,' Blithe went on, 'as I said, most are just the sort of pictures you'd expect.'

He laid down the three photographs he'd kept until last next to each other in front of them.

'And then, there are these.'

Sarah and Miss Manners stared in silence at the photographs.

'Oh my God,' Sarah said quietly.

CHAPTER 23

'Well, he certainly didn't look like that when we saw him,' Sergeant Green said.

The photos from the journalist's camera were spread out across the table in the conference room back at the Station Z offices. The three photographs that Blithe had held back till last were arranged together off to one side of the others.

Leo Davenport picked up one of the pictures, examining it closely. 'And these were developed in the normal way?'

Miss Manners nodded. 'Mr Blithe assures us that's exactly how they were taken.'

'The film was still in the camera and no one's tampered with it,' Sarah said.

'Curious,' Leo said.

'That's one word for it,' Green agreed.

Leo put the photo back down with the others. Each of them showed a general view of the reception J.D. Sumner had held. At the edge of one of the photos, Sarah herself appeared – half in and half out of the shot.

The common factor was that each of the three pictures showed the Ubermensch. In one, he was half hidden behind several other people at the back of the room. In the second he was visible between a waiter and one of the guests. In the third shot, the Ubermensch was off to one side, but very much in the foreground.

And in all three pictures, it was clear that the man wasn't human.

The clothes the creature was wearing looked normal enough. But in place of hands and head, there was a web-like network of interconnected lines, as if these areas had been scribbled over by a small child.

'Some sort of nervous system, do you think?' Miss Manners said.

'Or the fungus stuff that seems to replace the internal structure of the body,' Davenport said.

'But I don't understand why he looks like that here in the photos when we saw him as a normal human being,' Green said.

'Maybe it's to do with the way film works,' Sarah suggested. 'I don't really know much about it, but isn't it to do with light levels?'

'It is,' Miss Manners said. 'Perhaps the infected skin reflects light into the camera lens in a different way from other solid objects.'

'Oh, that this too, too solid flesh would melt, thaw, and resolve itself into a dew,' Leo said quietly. '*Hamlet*,' he added for anyone who was interested. 'There is another explanation. Well, probably several, but one that springs to mind.'

'Oh?' Sarah prompted.

'I assume your photographer used a flash gun?'

'You think this is due to exposure to the flash?' Miss Manners asked.

'Anyone close by would be blinded for a split second. The split second in which the Ubermensch was visible in this form. Well, as I say, it's just a possibility.'

'The important thing is we have a way of recognising them,' Green pointed out. 'We should tell the colonel.'

'He's rather out of touch at the moment,' Miss Manners pointed out. 'But it's certainly worth telling Elizabeth Archer. She may have some ideas.'

'Hang about,' Green said. 'She's got the body of one of these things in her collection.'

'It's badly damaged, almost charcoal the way it was burned,' Leo said.

'Even so, it might be worth taking its picture,' Green said. 'See how it turns out. With and without a flashgun.'

'Dr Wiles might have some ideas too,' Sarah said.

'I'll phone Bletchley,' Miss Manners said.

'Good idea,' Leo agreed. 'Now if you'll excuse me, I have to arrange to send a telegram. A friend of mine got married a few days ago, and I need him to know that my invitation never turned up.'

'Perhaps you weren't sent one,' Sarah said.

'Oh I'm sure I wasn't. And I couldn't have gone anyway as it was in America.'

Green laughed. 'You mean Cary Grant?' The actor's marriage to Barbara Hutton had made most of the papers.

'I do indeed,' Leo said. 'Seems only right and proper to send my congratulations to the happy couple.'

'Hasn't Cary Grant become an American citizen now too?' Sarah asked.

'He has. But with all due respect, my dear, I don't feel that is quite such a cause for congratulation.'

Dr Wiles was intrigued by Miss Manners' description of the pictures when she phoned him. She promised to send up a set of prints for Wiles to see.

'Not really that clued up on photography,' Wiles confessed. 'But Douglas dabbles a bit, I gather. He may have some thoughts. Send them up marked for my attention and Debbie can make sure they get to us.'

'Her name is Eleanor,' Miss Manners pointed out.

'Whose name?'

'Your assistant.'

'What, Eleanor? Well, of course it is. What are you talking about?'

'I sometimes wonder,' Miss Manners muttered.

'Actually, I had a note to contact you today anyway,' Wiles went on. There was a pause, and Miss Manners could hear the sound of papers being shuffled. 'Yes, here it is. "Call them," it says.'

'Does it say what about?' she asked with enforced patience.

'Oh, doesn't need to, I know. It's about Crete.'

Miss Manners leaned forward at her desk, telephone receiver pressed tight to her ear. 'What about Crete?'

'I know the colonel's interested in Crete, he asked me if we had any data about the island.'

'And did you?'

'Not that I haven't already passed on, which is mainly to do with UDT tracking. But that's because it isn't somewhere we were really watching. Well, I'm sure someone is, but *we* weren't, if you see what I mean. Anyway, I made arrangements for us to receive any unusual communications data from the area. The first batch came in yesterday. We're still analysing it, but recently there's been a lot of radio traffic that the Y Stations put down to interference or bad reception.'

'UDT transmissions?' Miss Manners guessed.

'Almost certainly,' Wiles confirmed. 'Quite a lot of activity. We're going back through whatever we can find in the historical data to see when it started. Don't know yet, I'm afraid. It might have been going on for years, of course.'

'Thank you. Let us know if you discover anything more.'

'There was some Ultra traffic that was passed to me this morning. Not sure if that's any use, but it seems that Colonel Brinkman isn't the only one interested in Crete.'

'There's a large German occupying force there, we know that. Over thirty thousand men, I believe. Not surprising given the strategic importance of the island.'

'This was a movement order, or news of one,' Wiles said. 'Probably nothing, but apparently there's a team from the Ahnenerbe heading for Crete. Whoever they are.'

Miss Manners frowned. She knew exactly who they were. 'The Ahnenerbe are part of the SS now. It's a group Himmler set up to look into ancient history and establish the Aryan origins of the German race.'

'Ancient history,' Wiles echoed. 'That can't be a coincidence.'

'No,' agreed Miss Manners. 'We have to warn Colonel Brinkman he may have company in Crete.'

'And how will you do that?' Wiles wondered.

'I have no idea,' she confessed. 'But I need to come up with something fast.'

A possible answer arrived that afternoon in the form of David Alban. He perched himself half sitting on the edge of Miss Manners' desk, smiling at her glare of disapproval.

'I'm not stopping,' he promised. 'Just wanted to let you know that my colleagues at SOE tell me Brinkman and Pentecross arrived safely in Crete. Well,' he qualified, 'perhaps "safely" is an exaggeration.'

Sarah had looked up from her desk at the mention of Guy's name. 'What do you mean?' she demanded. 'Are they all right?'

'They are now,' Alban assured her. 'But there was a storm. They lost their kit in the sea. Lost their guide too, apparently, poor blighter. But they've met up with their contact, and signalled on his scheduled radio transmission.'

'So we can get in touch with them?' Miss Manners said. 'There's a few things we have to pass on.'

'Oh?'

'I'll tell you in a minute. There are some photographs you need to see.'

'Sounds like fun,' Alban said. 'But getting the information to Brinkman won't be as easy as that, I'm afraid. Radio contact is infrequent and unreliable. Tell you what, though, the colonel asked for some replacement equipment. SOE agreed to send a plane in to make a drop in a couple of days. There's just about time to get a letter across to Cairo and have them include that with the gear.'

'A letter may not be the best way to communicate this,' Miss Manners said. She peered over the top of her glasses at Sarah, on the other side of the room. 'But I think, with your help, we can arrange something a little more appropriate and a lot more useful.'

Alban smiled. 'Are you suggesting what I think you're suggesting?'

'I'm suggesting,' Miss Manners said, 'that I find where Leo Davenport has got to, while Miss Diamond works out a flight plan.'

Alban nodded. 'I'll talk to SOE. They won't like it, of course. But that always makes for a more satisfying conversation. I'll be in touch directly.' He paused at Sarah's desk on the way out. 'Bring me back an olive, would you? I'm rather partial to olives. Especially in a good Martini.'

CHAPTER 24

The somewhat inauspicious home of the vast collection of art and culture that would one day be housed in the planned Fuhrermuseum at Linz was the basement and cellars beneath the Dresden Picture Gallery. An elderly curator armed with a clipboard, a pencil and dusty spectacles assured Hoffman that he would find the artefact requested.

'Everything is logged and catalogued,' he explained. 'We have a card index system set up by Dr Posse himself.'

Hoffman made a point of looking impressed, though he had no idea who Posse was and even less interest in finding out.

'Of course,' the curator went on, 'it will all be very different when we move to Linz. Let me show you. Come with me.'

He led Hoffman through a dimly lit passageway, past alcoves stacked with numbered crates and doorways that gave into more storerooms, all crammed with items on shelves and labelled boxes.

'We keep it down here to be safe from the bombing. Ah, here we are.'

They had arrived at a sort of hub, an open area where several passageways met. It was better lit, and in the middle of the area, directly under a hanging light, was a large trestle table. On the table was a model, buildings and streets manufactured from plain white card.

211

'Speer's design,' the curator announced proudly. 'This is what it will look like when it is finally built.'

It was certainly an impressive complex. Hoffman thought he detected similarities to the Haus der Deutsche Kunst in Munich.

'The railway station is on the site at the moment, so that will have to be moved, of course,' the curator was saying. 'Then here we have the monumental theatre, the opera house…'

'And this?' Hoffman asked, pointing to a third large building.

'The Adolf Hitler Hotel.'

'Of course.'

'All surrounded by wide boulevards. Oh, and a parade ground.'

'Will it take you long to locate the artefact?' Hoffman asked. The old man seemed happy to spend the whole afternoon pointing out items of monumental folly. 'It is rather urgent.'

'Oh, of course, Sturmbannfuhrer. I apologise. I shall leave you to enjoy the model while I locate the item you are interested in. I shan't be long. Ten minutes.' He made a show of consulting his clipboard before hurrying off along one of the passageways.

Hoffman was left waiting for nearer fifteen minutes, but even so he was impressed. However the card index system worked, it was certainly efficient. There must be thousands of artefacts and paintings stored down here. Finding just one small stone axe-head amongst them in a quarter of an hour was remarkable.

'I believe this is what you are looking for,' the old man said.

He handed Hoffman a plain cardboard box. Hoffman lifted the lid. Inside, nestling on a bed of cotton wool, was the axe-head, exactly as it had appeared in the photographs he had seen at Wewelsburg. It was about four inches long, and half as wide. He brushed his fingers across the surface, feeling the rough texture of the stone and the precise indentations where the runic symbols were carved.

'Will you want to examine it for long?' the curator asked.

'Examine it?'

'I'm sorry, I assumed that was why you are here. To examine the artefact.'

'No,' Hoffman told him. 'I am here to collect it. I shall be taking it away with me.'

The curator's mouth was an 'O' of astonishment. 'Oh no, no, no. I'm afraid that is not permitted. Nothing leaves here. We have pictures, of course,' he went on quickly. 'It was photographed for one of the Fuhrer's albums. Every Christmas and on his birthday we present the Fuhrer with a volume containing photographs of some of the artefacts in the collection.'

Hoffman closed the box and set it down on the edge of the model of the Fuhrermuseum. He took a piece of folded paper from his inside pocket and handed it to the man. 'Read this.'

The curator took the paper warily, as if afraid it might burn his fingers. He unfolded it, and his frown deepened as he read the letter.

'You will see that I have absolute authority to take whatever I please,' Hoffman said. 'Be thankful I merely want an old piece of stone which no one will miss for a moment.'

'But...' the curator protested weakly. 'But this is unprecedented.'

'Perhaps you would like to take the matter up with the Reichsfuhrer-SS,' Hoffman suggested, taking back the paper. 'It is, as you see, his signature on this letter.' That was a lie, of course. He had typed out the letter and signed Himmler's name to it himself.

'I'm sorry. Of course, the Reichsfuhrer must have the artefact if he so desires.'

'It's not a whim,' Hoffman told him sternly. 'This artefact could be vital to our future. By providing it so efficiently you have done the Reich great service.'

The curator blinked, his frown becoming a surprised smile. 'Well, of course, we here at the gallery are always more than happy—'

'As I shall make sure the Reichsfuhrer knows,' Hoffman

interrupted. 'Now, as I say, my time is pressing.' He picked up the cardboard box containing the stone axe-head. 'Perhaps you can show me the way out of this rabbit warren?'

Now that he had the axe-head, Hoffman needed to decide what to do with it. When he stopped concentrating, when it lacked focus, his mind all too easily became a conflicting mass of ideas and possibilities. He needed to take some time to clear his head and think things through. He had discovered that alcohol, paradoxically, helped him to concentrate. It deadened the voices and images that pressed in upon his thoughts, freed him to think for himself – provided he didn't overindulge.

There was a bar near the main station that senior officers frequented. It wasn't really to Hoffman's taste, but he could get a drink and remain undisturbed. The place was full of smoke hanging in the air like the dust in an ancient tomb. He pushed through a group of junior officers and made his way to an empty table against the wall. From here he had a good view of the bar, and of the stage. An elderly pianist was doing his best to disguise the tuneless voice of a young female singer. Since the woman seemed to be wearing only stockings and a short, tight jacket over a white shirt and bow-tie, the pianist needn't have bothered. No one was listening.

A waitress came to take Hoffman's drink. She wore almost as little as the singer but had compensated by slapping on a vast quantity of make-up which she presumably hoped would disguise her age. In fact she was probably only thirty, but glancing round the other women in the bar, that counted as elderly. Hoffman ordered schnapps, smiling and flirting with the woman briefly to make her feel better.

'If there's anything else you want,' she said as she returned with his drink, 'you know – anything at all. You let me know.'

'Just the drink will be fine.' He tipped her more than he needed to. 'You don't have to do this, you know,' he said, seeing her surprise as he handed her the money.

Her painted expression didn't change. 'With two kids and a dead husband? Oh yes I do.' She leaned closer. 'You'd be all right, though. I wouldn't mind with you.'

'Maybe later. What's your name?'

'Helena.'

'Thanks for the drink, Helena.'

He sipped at the schnapps, feeling it burn down the back of his throat. Her name probably wasn't Helena, and he wouldn't see her later. But he had no doubt she would find someone to subsidise her wages.

Helena sounded close enough to 'Alina' to make him think of home, of what he had left behind when he came to Germany and joined the madness. He pushed the thoughts to the back of his mind, and concentrated instead on what to do with the axe-head. It was a reassuring weight in his jacket pocket. But he couldn't just walk round with it hidden there, could he?

Whatever happened, he knew he didn't want the Vril to get it. What they needed it for was still only a vague impression in a corner of his mind. But if they wanted it, he wanted to keep it from them. Should he destroy it, he wondered? *Could* he destroy it? It had survived so long and in such pristine condition that somehow he doubted it.

So, his options were to keep it himself, to hide it, or to pass it on. If he kept it, he risked it being discovered on him and that could provoke difficult questions. If he hid it... Well, anything hidden might be found as he had proved himself today. But who could he pass it on to?

As he lifted it, he saw that his glass had left a wet ring on the table. He was seeing patterns everywhere now, he thought. He put the glass down, further across the table. Then he drew his finger through the ring, from the middle outwards. He did it several times, smearing the spilled liquid like a crude child's drawing of a sun with rays of light coming from it.

What did it remind him of? He'd seen it somewhere before, that pattern. Not just in his head, but somewhere else. Somewhere *real*. Lines radiating out from a central point. A photograph of... something. Something physical, not like rays of the sun. More like...

He glanced round for inspiration. At the next table,

someone struck a match and lit a cigarette. Yes, more like matchsticks laid out.

Hoffman drained his glass and waved to one of the waitresses. It wasn't Helena, but a younger girl. She was nervous, pulling at the hem of her short jacket, her lip trembling slightly as she came to ask him what he wanted. Her relief was obvious when he told her it was just another drink.

What about Pentecross and Davenport? They knew about the Vril. Hoffman didn't know much about the Allied organisation they worked for. But he had more confidence that they would not try to exploit the axe-head for their own purposes than he did that Himmler and Nachten wouldn't.

The girl was returning with his drink. On the way over, a man in a colonel's uniform grabbed her, pulling her over. His hand snaked its way inside her blouse as he whispered in her ear. She managed to extricate herself and hurry over to Hoffman. Her hand was shaking as she set down his drink.

'You should get another job,' he told her.

'There are no other jobs.'

'Find one anyway. What did the Herr Oberst say to you?'

'He said...' She swallowed. 'He said he'd see me later.'

'Go home. As soon as you can, go home.' He paid for the drink, and more. 'I'll make sure the Herr Oberst doesn't see you later.'

'Why?'

Hoffman wasn't really sure. 'Because you're young and he isn't. Because you have your whole life ahead of you, and he doesn't. Because although so many terrible things have happened, if I can make sure just one more doesn't then I'll feel a lot better.'

She pursed her lips and frowned. 'Do *you* want to see me later? Is that it?'

'I would love to. But sadly I have other things to do.'

She turned to go, then changed her mind and turned back. 'Thank you. I'm not used to kindness.'

He raised his glass. 'None of us is. Stay safe.'

The colonel looked up in surprise as Hoffman pulled up a

chair beside him. He looked annoyed, but struggled to hide it as he saw Hoffman's SS uniform. The colonel might outrank Hoffman, but he knew who had the real power.

'Herr Oberst, a word, if I may?'

The colonel nodded. 'Sturmbannfuhrer, what can I do for you?'

'The girl. The young one.'

'You noticed her too?' the man licked his lips.

'I think everyone has noticed her. Unfortunately for you – and, I have to say for me too – one of her admirers is my commanding officer. Gruppenfuhrer Streicher, perhaps you know him? He has quite a reputation amongst his SS comrades.'

The colonel shook his head. 'My apologies to the Gruppenfuhrer,' he stammered. 'I never intended, that is – I didn't mean...'

Hoffman waved his hand. 'Don't worry. You were not to know. Can I buy you another drink to compensate you for the loss of your evening's entertainment?'

'You're very kind.'

'Not at all.' Hoffman called over the nearest waitress.

'I am not usually...' the colonel said as he accepted another drink. 'That is, tonight is my last night here in Dresden. After that...' His voice tailed off.

'After that?' Hoffman prompted.

'My unit leaves tomorrow. We have been deployed to the Eastern Front.'

'I see.' Hoffman nodded sympathetically. 'I hear things are quite difficult there.'

'You have been to Russia?'

'Oh yes,' Hoffman admitted. 'One way or another I have spent quite some time there.'

'Our armies are making great progress, huge advances. But you hear stories – about the winter cold, the summer rain and mud, the barbaric fighting of the Russian scum. And it's such a long way from home, of course.'

'Yes,' Hoffman echoed. 'Such a long way from home.' He

drained his glass and signalled for another. 'So what unit are you with, and when are they leaving?'

He listened carefully as the colonel told him the details. He could have the man court-martialled for revealing such information. But that wasn't Hoffman's intention.

He had decided what he had to do. He'd been playing this deadly game for too long now. It was partly that he'd been away from Alina for too long – he didn't even know if she was still alive. But partly, he remembered where he had seen the pattern before, the radiating lines. It was indeed on a photograph. A set of photographs, spread across Stalin's desk when he sent Hoffman into Germany. If Stalin knew, then perhaps Hoffman's reports had not been ignored. Had he helped? Was someone in Russia aware of the Vril and, like the British, working to stop them? He had to know.

The axe-head could wait. He would work out what to do with it on the way. But first, Werner Hoffman – although that wasn't his real name – was going home.

CHAPTER 25

The sound of the small Lysander seemed a deafening roar in the quiet of the night, so far from civilisation. That, of course was why they had chosen this area. The fields were surrounded by woodland, so there was little chance of anyone seeing the plane. The only problem was the strong crosswinds, which had been picking up all day.

'They won't try to land in this,' Mihali shouted above the noise as the plane approached. 'They'll drop the supplies and keep going.'

'It's very low,' Brinkman pointed out.

The bright moon meant that the pilot would be able to see the field – and the people waiting – quite clearly. The disadvantage was obviously that the plane too would be more visible on its journey into enemy-held territory. It continued to descend, buffeted by the wind, until the wheels connected with the turf and the plane bounced and juddered across the field. Finally it came to a sudden stop, slewing drunkenly to one side.

'There's a pilot who knows how to fly,' Mihali said as they set off towards the plane. 'I don't know many who'd have attempted that.'

'I've an idea who it might be,' Guy said. He could tell from Brinkman's severe expression that he was thinking the same thing.

Sarah was pulling off her flying goggles as they reached the plane. She jumped down to the ground, and listened silently to Brinkman's angry rebuke before replying. Her insistence that she had brought vital information that he needed to hear in person went some way to appeasing him, as did the crates of supplies in the plane's hold. There were guns, grenades, explosive, and a replacement radio set.

'I also don't see,' Brinkman said as they unloaded the equipment, 'why it took two of you to relay whatever this information might be.'

Leo Davenport had jumped down from the plane after Sarah. He stared innocently back at Brinkman. 'Well, I had nothing much else on this week, and I thought you could do with some help.'

Brinkman made it clear that, if he could, he'd have sent them both back home immediately. But one of the wheel struts on the plane had buckled.

'I think I hit a rock or something,' Sarah confessed. 'I felt it go.'

'Easily done,' Mihali said. 'There's so many rocky outcrops round here, you're almost certain to hit something. Can you move the plane at all?'

'If I take it slow and careful. Certainly couldn't take off again, though, not till it's fixed.'

Once they had finished unloading, Sarah taxied the plane awkwardly to the edge of the wood, so it wouldn't be seen from the air. They covered it with branches and leaves. Mihali told them he would arrange for some of the partisans to assess the damage and do what they could.

'We have a blacksmith, he should be able to weld the strut back in place. But it'll take a day or two to organise.'

Sarah, Guy and Mihali went on ahead, carrying as much as they could load into their backpacks. Brinkman and Davenport followed with the rest of the equipment, carrying a crate between them by its rope handles. Out of Mihali's earshot, Leo brought the colonel up to date on the photographs from Sumner's reception, and Wiles's news that Himmler might also have people looking for the axe-head on Crete.

'Why do I feel like I'm playing gooseberry here?' Mihali asked, looking from Sarah to Guy.

'Probably because you are,' Sarah told him.

'Well, try to keep your feelings under control,' he told them both. 'Lose concentration or get distracted for a moment, and it could get you killed.'

'We'll stay focused,' Guy assured him.

They sheltered for the night in an old, deserted cattle barn, not far from the German fuel depot. Guy took first watch. Brinkman, Davenport and Mihali seemed able to slip immediately into a deep sleep. Sarah fidgeted, uncomfortable on a makeshift bed of straw. Finally she came over to join Guy as he sat close to the door, looking out through a gap between the planking of the wall.

She sat down beside him, pulling the thin blanket round them both and nestling into his shoulder. He put his arm round her, grateful for the warmth and affection of her body close to his. Their relationship so far was limited largely to moments like this – stolen hours together, hugging, kissing. He knew more would follow, but neither of them was in a hurry. It was strange, he thought. The danger and uncertainty of the war should surely hasten their relationship. But somehow it drew it out, made the slow, steady, growing feelings they had for each other all the more precious. All the more to be treasured.

'You shouldn't have come,' he said quietly. 'But I'm glad you did.'

Sarah didn't answer, and Guy realised she was already asleep.

After two hours, he gently roused Sarah, and led her half asleep to the back of the barn. He settled her down again before waking Davenport for his turn at keeping watch, Then he lay down beside Sarah, one arm protectively over her as he too drifted into oblivion.

Mihali's comrades in the local resistance movement met them at first light. Brinkman and Mihali had agreed their plan the previous night, and now Mihali briefed his men. He also arranged for the blacksmith and another man to check on the Lysander and mend the broken wheel strut.

The uniform was from a German lieutenant – an oberleutnant. It wasn't a particularly good fit, but Davenport assured Guy it would do.

'There should be a hat, surely,' Guy said.

The man who had provided the uniform laughed, seeing Guy looking for the cap. He was a broad-shouldered man with a mass of thick dark hair and a moustache that might have been borrowed from a villain of the silent movie era. 'There was a cap,' he told Guy in Greek. 'But it has a hole through it. Right here.' He pointed to the middle of Guy's forehead. 'How do you think we got the uniform?'

They had debated whether they should go at night. But Brinkman reckoned it was better so see what was going on. They hoped to find a way down into the ground, and hunting for that with torches in the dark would soon attract attention. Instead, the plan was to distract the Germans so that Brinkman and Davenport could search the area. Not really knowing what they were looking for, they also needed daylight to find it.

They cut the fence at the furthest point. There was a good view along the length of it, and there were no guards within sight. Mihali folded back the wire, letting Guy through, then pulled it back into place. Unless someone inspected it closely, they wouldn't know the fence had been breached.

Guy hoped he looked calmer than he felt as he walked back beside the fence towards the fuel depot. He glanced at the indented area beyond the pipeline as he skirted round it, but there was nothing to see except the rock and patches of sparse grass springing up through it.

He was almost at the first huts on the edge of the depot before he saw anyone. A German soldier walked past, heading out along the fence line on patrol. If he thought it odd that

Guy wasn't wearing his uniform cap, he showed no sign of it.

The trick was to find somewhere far enough into the complex – and far enough away from the indented ground – to draw attention away, but not too close to the fuel tanks. The first hut that Guy entered was occupied. Four soldiers sat round a wooden table playing cards. They leapt guiltily to their feet as Guy came in. He ignored their stammered excuses and apologies and left without comment.

He passed any huts that were obviously in use. From one he could hear raised voices – a heated argument about shift rotas. Through the window of another he could see a captain pointing out positions on a map of the complex to a group of soldiers.

Finally he found a small wooden building that was little more than a shed. It had been erected between two of the larger huts, which was ideal. Inside, there were shelves of paint, cleaning materials, pads of paper and other stationery materials. Guy closed the door behind him.

The only light filtered in through a grimy window on one side, but it was enough for him to lift down a pot of paint and stab his pocket knife through the lid. A quick sniff of the oil-based liquid told him it was likely to be inflammable.

For safety, he cut holes in several pots, then jammed folded paper torn from one of the notepads into the holes. He placed a pot against each wall, and another in the middle of the shelf of paint. Then, using a rather nice silver Dunhill lighter that Leo Davenport had lent him, Guy lit the paper.

A quick look round reassured him that no one was within sight. Guy walked briskly back the way he had come. As soon as the fire took hold, he would divert anyone heading out towards where Brinkman and Davenport were searching, sending them back to help fight the fire. Just so long as no one spotted the smoke and flames before it had a chance to take hold.

He need not have worried. From behind came the gratifying roar of an explosion as the paint in the sealed cans exploded. The shed was blown apart in a blast of splinters and fragmented paint cans. Burning liquid sprayed across the wooden huts either side and soon they too were burning.

Guy kept walking, shouting to anyone he saw to get across and help with the emergency. Black smoke drifted across the whole area, concealing how bad – or not – the fire really was.

Predictably, Sarah insisted on going with Brinkman and Davenport. 'I'll be safer with you,' she pointed out. 'If Mihali and his guys have to create another diversion, I'll be right in the thick of it. The whole point is to draw any attention away from what you two are up to. And I've been trained now.'

There wasn't time to argue, and from the amused way Davenport's moustache twitched, Brinkman knew he'd get no support from that direction if he objected. Besides, she was right. What was the use of sending her on the SOE training if he wasn't going to let her make use of what she'd learned?

'All right, But keep close to us and do as you're told.'

'Don't I always, sir?'

He didn't answer that. The three of them slipped through the gap in the fence, and hurried down the slight incline to the rocky area they had identified on the aerial photographs.

Smoke from the fire was drifting across, which was both a help and a hindrance.

'Means they can't see what we're up to,' Brinkman said.

'It also means *we* can't see what we're up to,' Leo pointed out.

'According to the photos, it looked like there was some sort of opening right in the middle of the area, at the back,' Sarah said. 'Where the two blades of the axe-head shape meet.'

They headed for what they hoped was about the right area. The smoke thinned slightly, blown away by the sea breeze. Even so, they had to stay close to each other so as not to get separated and lost.

'I think this could be it,' Leo called.

As he spoke, a gust of wind scattered the smoke and they could see clearly across the landscape. Leo was standing at the edge of a narrow hole disappearing down into the rocky ground.

'I'm not sure, but I think I can see steps further down. If we can squeeze through here—' He broke off as another figure approached – a figure wearing a German military uniform.

'So, what have you found?' the figure asked.

Sarah heaved a sigh of relief as she recognised the voice. "I thought you were staying to watch the fire,' she said as Guy joined them.

'It's managing very well on its own. I thought I'd see how you're getting on.'

Brinkman showed him the hole in the rock. 'Davenport and I will go down there, see what we can find.'

'We're coming too,' Sarah told him.

'Did you bring a torch?' Leo asked, brandishing his own.

'I brought a lighter,' Guy told him.

'And you take care of that,' Leo said. 'I don't want you using up all the fuel.'

'We need someone to stay up top,' Brinkman said. 'You can warn us if there's a problem, and signal Mihali if we need another distraction when we come out again.'

'We won't be long,' Leo assured them. 'Well, no longer than we need to be.'

Accepting the logic and necessity of the situation, Guy and Sarah helped Leo and Brinkman down into the hole. It was tight, but they managed to edge their way through.

'It's wider down here,' Leo called back.

'There are tunnels leading off,' Brinkman added. 'Might take us a while to explore them all, actually.'

'Don't wait up,' Leo told them.

The smoke was back, thicker than ever. It was almost a fog. Sarah took hold of Guy's hand.

'Looks like your fire is really doing the job.'

'I hope it doesn't do it too well,' he said. 'I don't fancy being anywhere near here if it reaches those fuel tanks.'

'I guess we just have to wait and see.'

'There's a dip in the rock just there. We should be able to keep out of sight even if the smoke clears.'

'Mihali will keep watch through binoculars,' Sarah said.

'We just have to let him know if we need his resistance guys to create another diversion so we can all get out again. What do you think they'll find down there?'

'Isn't it supposed to be the gateway to Hell?'

'But that's a metaphor, surely,' Sarah said.

'Let's hope so,' Guy told her. 'But a metaphor for what?'

The first tunnel came to a dead end.

'It's obviously deliberate,' Leo said. 'Not a rock fall or anything. The floor and walls are lined with stone. The roof too. This whole tunnel system was built, so there's some purpose to it all.'

'But what purpose?' Brinkman wondered as they retraced their steps. 'I'd suggest splitting up, which would make it quicker. But I have to admit I don't fancy wandering around down here on my own.'

'Me neither.'

They turned back along a side tunnel, which sloped gently downwards. This too reached a dead end.

'I thought this was the way back to where we started,' Brinkman said.

'So did I.'

Leo shone his torch along the side wall, revealing another opening, and another beyond that.

'You think we missed a doorway somewhere?' Brinkman asked.

'Seems likely,' Leo admitted. 'So, what now?'

'Now? Now, I think we're lost. Though we can't have come that far. We should be able to see the light shining in through where we came in. Let's try down that one.'

Ten minutes later they had still not found their way back.

'We should have brought a ball of string with us,' Brinkman said. 'Like the chap in the story.'

'Theseus. Yes, it is a bit of—' Leo broke off.

'What is it?'

'Don't you see? I was going to say it's a maze. And that's exactly what it is.' Leo shone his torch round, revealing the dark shapes of several doorways. 'But this isn't just any old maze of tunnels. We've found the actual ancient Labyrinth. And now, we're trapped inside it.'

CHAPTER 26

He wasn't a man who was easily scared, but the confined darkness of the tunnels was getting to Brinkman. The air seemed to be getting stale and though it was probably his imagination, the torch beams seemed less bright than they had just a few minutes ago. He leaned against the tunnel wall, feeling the damp, cold stone through his coat and shirt.

Leo Davenport crouched down. He took a fountain pen from inside the pocket of the rough leather jacket Mihali had provided him. The floor of the tunnel was layered with dust and fine sand, and Davenport scratched away at it with the back end of the pen.

'You trying to dig your way out?' Brinkman asked.

Davenport glanced up. 'Can you shine your torch down here?'

With more light, Brinkman could see that Davenport had drawn a circular pattern, with intersecting lines spiralling in towards the centre.

'I didn't realise it at first,' Davenport said, 'but I've been here before.'

'What?'

'Well, in a manner of speaking. Not actually *here* here. But I've seen a map of this place. Or of a section of it anyway.' He straightened up, putting the pen away and dusting his hands together. 'I've been keeping track of where we go, where the entrances and exits are and how the passageways interconnect, so far as I can tell.'

'And you can find the way out again?' Brinkman asked hopefully.

'Steady on, I didn't say that. But there's a definite structure to it, so we can start to make sensible deductions about a route through rather than just guessing.'

That sounded hopeful. Brinkman felt his head clear and the tension in his neck and shoulders ease a little. 'So where did you see this map?'

'In the Vril base in North Africa. Guy and I thought it was a puzzle, a maze we had to solve. Well, maybe it was. But this place seems to follow the same principles.'

'And you remember it?'

'I remember everything. Well, nearly everything. There are a few notices and reviews I do my best to forget. Now then, you ready to test my theory?'

'What had you in mind?'

'I suspect,' Davenport said, 'that if there is anything useful for us to find here, it will be at the centre of the Labyrinth.'

'Makes sense,' Brinkman agreed. 'So we head for the centre, following the map you remember so well.'

'That's the idea. Also, have you noticed how the ground slopes slightly? I think the centre of the Labyrinth will be the lowest point. And if we can find the centre of the maze, I'm pretty sure I can find the way back out again. Though, actually, that's not the bit that worries me.'

'Oh? What is it that worries you then?'

Davenport pointed to a doorway, and led the way through it and into the passageway beyond. 'What worries me,' he said, 'is what we'll find at the heart of the Labyrinth.'

The SS standartenfuhrer stood watching the fire, his gloved hands clasped behind his back.

'They have no idea how it started,' Hauptsturmfuhrer Grebben reported. 'But obviously, with the fuel so close it's a worry.'

Standartenfuhrer Nachten shook his head. 'It is a distraction.' A thought occurred to him as he spoke. 'A distraction in more ways than one, perhaps.'

'Sir?'

'We know the Allies are interested in the same myths and legends that brought us here, Grebben. Perhaps they are here already.'

'Then we should not delay.'

'No, indeed.'

Grebben pulled an envelope from his jacket pocket and slid out the aerial photograph inside. Together they examined the image, locating the fuel tanks, their current position, and the recessed area that looked so uncannily like an axe-head.

'That way,' Nachten decided, pointing away from the main installation and the noise and confusion of the fire. 'Bring the men.'

Nachten did not wait, but set off with his hands still clasped behind his back, his head slightly lowered and turning slowly from side to side as he scanned the surroundings like a hungry bird of prey.

The figures appeared out of the smoke, solidifying from vague shapes. Guy pulled Sarah back down into cover, beyond the lip of the recessed area. There were scattered clumps of ragged bushes here which afforded some cover. They crouched behind one, watching as the soldiers approached.

'Six of them,' Sarah whispered, though they were not close enough to hear unless she called out.

'SS,' Guy said grimly. 'Led by a standartenfuhrer – that's the equivalent of a colonel, so pretty high-powered stuff.'

'Do they know we're here?' Sarah wondered. Her voice was trembling slightly.

'I don't see how they could. Unless they guessed the fire was a deliberate distraction. But even then they wouldn't know exactly where to look for the culprit.'

'Could they be after the same thing as us, then?' Sarah asked. 'It's a hell of a coincidence if the SS just turn up at this exact spot out of the blue.'

'I suppose it's possible,' Guy said. 'You said Wiles was worried we might have company. Though how they know about it...' He shrugged.

The six men had spread out and were walking slowly across the area examining the ground. It did seem more and more likely they were indeed searching for something. For a moment, it looked as if they would walk right past the narrow opening. But just as Guy was about to heave a sigh of relief, one of the soldiers spotted the dark patch in the stone and went over to look at it. Moments later, the standartenfuhrer and the others were there too.

Guy and Sarah watched in horror as one of the soldiers – a hauptsturmfuhrer – clambered down into the narrow crevice. The standartenfuhrer followed, and then one by one the others also descended into the ground.

'We have to warn Leo and the colonel,' Sarah said. She hurried over to the opening, Guy close behind.

'I don't see how we can,' he told her. 'We just have to hope they don't run into each other.'

As they neared the crevice, they could hear the Germans speaking to each other. Guy gestured for Sarah to keep quiet. He lay on the ground, as close to the hole as he could without blocking any of the light and risking being seen.

'It's a maze down here,' one of the men was saying. 'Tunnels in every direction. We should prepare properly, sir. Come back with equipment.'

'The men have torches,' came the reply – from the standartenfuhrer, Guy assumed, speaking to his captain probably. 'And I have all the equipment we need here.'

Guy strained to hear. Was that the rustling of paper?

'I found this in Hoffman's notebook,' the standartenfuhrer said.

'A drawing? But, forgive me, how is that of help?'

'I don't know how he came by it, how he knew about this place, but I think it is a map.'

The voices faded.

'What did they say?' Sarah asked. 'Are they staying down there?'

'They are. And you're right, we have to warn Colonel Brinkman and Leo. Those Germans seem to have a map, or think they do. It's from Hoffman, so it's possible.'

'But, didn't he help you?'

'He did. From what they were saying, I don't think Hoffman knows they have it. Probably doesn't even know they're here.'

'So what do we do?'

'Only one thing we can do,' Guy decided. 'We go down there after them, and hope we find Leo and Brinkman before the Germans do.'

'I think this is it.'

Leo Davenport's torch picked out snatches of detail in the large chamber. A vaulted ceiling rose high above the circular space. At one end was what looked like a stone altar, or possibly a tomb. Its surface was adorned with runic symbols carved into the surface. There were two similar but smaller structures on other walls.

Brinkman paused as they made their way across the chamber, shining his torch down at the ground.

'You're the archaeology expert, Leo. What do you make of this?'

In the centre of the room was a large circular design, about six feet across, apparently engraved into the stone. A central circle, with jagged lines reaching out to the circumference. Leo stooped down, shining his torch round the edge.

'I think it's separate.' He ran his hand over the pattern. 'Ah – look!'

Brinkman watched as Davenport shone his torch into a cavity at the edge of the design. It was a shape he recognised at once.

'The same shape as the ground outside. The axe-head.'

'And about the same size as the artefact Miss Diamond saw at Sumner's house in Los Angeles. There are raised symbols in the indented area. How much would you bet that they fit into the engraved symbols in the axe-head?'

'There's another one over here,' Brinkman pointed out.

'And a third here,' Davenport said, shining his torch on it. 'Three axe-heads, and three sockets, or whatever they are.'

'But what's it for?' Brinkman demanded.

'Without the axe-heads, I have no idea. So, what else can we find in here?'

The sounds of the Germans' voices were getting fainter.

'We must have taken a different turning somewhere,' Sarah said.

They had been following, but now they seemed to be going in a different direction. Their only light came from the tiny flickering flame of the Dunhill lighter. They were standing at the intersection of several of the tunnels.

'Maybe no bad thing,' Guy said. 'Just because the Germans think they know where they're going, that doesn't mean that Leo and Brinkman have a clue. Given the size of this place we'll be lucky if any of us find the others.'

'You think we should head back to the way in?'

'That might be the best option. If we can find it. This place is a lot bigger than I thought it would be.'

'How long will that last?' Sarah said, meaning the lighter.

'Not long. Another reason to be getting out of here. Come on, this way.'

Sarah frowned. 'I thought we came in that way.'

'Are you sure?'

'No,' she admitted. 'Are you?'

Guy shook his head. 'If we're not careful, we might be stuck down here waiting for Brinkman to find *us*.' He sighed. 'Come on, let's try the way you said. It's as good as any.'

'Just so long as it's not my fault if we get really lost.'

Guy smiled. 'Promise.'

There were three raised plinths at the back of the altar stone. Resting on the central plinth, picked out in the light of Brinkman's torch, was a stone axe-head.

'Bingo,' Davenport said. 'Perhaps the trip was worth it after all.'

'Do you think we should try fitting it into one of the holes in the floor?' Brinkman said.

'I suspect it's all three or nothing. And I'm not sure I want to be here to see what happens anyway.'

'Well, at least we can take this one into custody,' Brinkman said.

He reached out across the altar and lifted the artefact from its position. It was not as cold as he had expected, but it was heavy. The carvings on its surface were clean and sharp, as if they were newly made.

'May I see?'

Davenport held out his hand. But before Brinkman could hand over the axe-head, there was a rough grinding sound of stone on stone. They both shone their torches back at the altar, in time to see the central plinth sliding down into the surface.

'That may not be a good sign,' Davenport said.

'They know we've taken this.'

'Someone knows,' Davenport agreed.

As he spoke, there was a muffled roar like a wild animal. A sudden thump, followed by an ominous cracking sound.

'And they're not happy about it,' Brinkman said.

They backed away, torches trained on the altar, as this was where the sound seemed to be coming from. There was another thump. More cracking. A split appeared in the front of the altar, starting at the top and travelling right down to the base. The whole stone edifice shifted.

'Time we were leaving.' Davenport had to shout above the sound of cracking stone.

They turned. Torchlight smeared across the walls, seeking out the way they'd come in – revealing dark figures approaching along the same tunnel.

Then, behind them, came a colossal crash as the front of the altar cracked again. Davenport whirled round, his torch beam finding the altar. Dust hung in the air like mist. The front of the altar was a crazy-paving of stone fragments that suddenly exploded outwards. A dark shape hauled itself into the torch beam, straightening up and bellowing in undiluted rage.

A massive creature stood in front of them, its shape masked by dark hair. But there was no mistaking the fact that the legs and torso were almost human. The arms, also covered with hair, ended in enormous fists. The fingers splayed out suddenly as it roared again – the sound thundering out from the snarling mouth set in the head of a savage bull.

'The Minotaur,' Davenport breathed. 'My God – it's real.'

CHAPTER 27

'Get down!' Guy's voice echoed round the chamber, and Leo Davenport and Colonel Brinkman threw themselves to the floor as Guy drew the Luger from his holster. Behind him, Sarah watched in horror, hand to her mouth, unable to believe what she was seeing. The sound of the shot in the enclosed space was deafening, echoing round the circular chamber.

The creature staggered back as the bullet impacted on its chest, ripping through hair and skin. At once, Leo and Brinkman dashed across to join Guy and Sarah in the doorway. Guy fired again, driving the beast further back towards the shattered remains of the stone altar.

'Is that really the Minotaur?' Sarah gasped.

'Could be what the myth is based on,' Leo told her.

'Let's debate the myth later,' Brinkman said.

Across the room, the creature had recovered from the shots. Orange tendrils caught the dancing torchlight, binding together over the bullet holes.

'Ubermensch,' Guy said. 'We won't stop it like this.'

'Uber-something,' Leo agreed. 'Follow me, I know the way out.'

'And we've got what we came for,' Brinkman added, showing Guy and Sarah the axe-head before stuffing it inside his sheepskin coat.

There was a thundering roar from behind them. Its massive head lowered, the beast was charging across the chamber. Sarah thought she could smell the hot, rancid breath from the flared nostrils. The deep-set dark eyes stared malevolently out of the bull's head. Guy grabbed her hand, dragging her with him down the tunnel.

'Be careful,' Guy called to Leo. 'There are Germans. We came to warn you. They must be heading this way. I don't know how we got ahead of them. Must have taken a short cut.'

Sarah risked a look back as she ran. Brinkman was behind her, and behind him the creature's huge body almost filled the tunnel – a black shape in the near darkness. She turned back – and almost cannoned into Guy as he skidded to a halt. In front of him, Leo had also stopped.

'Someone coming,' he gasped.

Torch beams scythed through the darkness ahead, rapidly approaching.

'This way!' Brinkman plunged through a dark opening in the tunnel wall, switching off his torch. Sarah followed, the others close on her heels. Behind her she heard the snorting of the creature, shouting, then gunfire.

The candles were lit, their guttering flames providing the only light now that the door to the corridor was shut. She sat alone at the circular table, the seventy-eight cards stacked face down in front of her. For the moment, Miss Manners ignored the letters and symbols round the edge of the table.

She sat absolutely still, eyes closed. It was a long time since she had done this. A long time since she had given in to the images that danced in her mind, the words and symbols that her imagination plucked out of the air. At first she had been excited by the gift, the power. When she first met Crowley and joined him, she had been entranced by the possibilities.

But gradually she had come to realise what a curse it was. A curse that still blighted Jane Roylston. Poor Jane – Miss Manners had not seen her for weeks. No, she thought – focus.

She pushed all concern for Jane to the edge of her mind. She needed to concentrate, to be sure she could still do this.

In her mind's eye she pictured Guy Pentecross and Sarah Diamond, making the image as clear and as detailed as she could.

When she was sure she had them, she opened her eyes. She reached out and spread the Tarot cards in a fan across the polished surface of the table. Picked a card at random from somewhere near the middle, and turned it over.

It was a card from the Major Arcana – The Lovers.

She replaced it, and shuffled the deck before spreading it out again. Now when she closed her eyes she thought of Leo Davenport.

It was another major card this time. But not the one she expected. She had thought it would be The Fool, but in fact it was The Magician. Perhaps she had underestimated him.

Time to move on, she decided. 'What are they doing now?' she said out loud. 'Colonel Brinkman – Oliver. And Leo, Guy and Sarah. Show me.'

She turned a card. Stared at it for several moments, her fingers still gripping the edge. A skeleton, sickle in hand.

Death.

She sighed, closed her eyes, leaned back. Then immediately she jolted upright again, eyes wide open in fear of the image that had appeared in her mind. A savage bull charging towards her, flame curling from its nostrils.

The creature caught in the torch beams was a horrifying mixture of man and bull. It charged along the tunnel towards Nachten, Grebben and the others.

'Is it possible?' Nachten murmured.

'Sir – do we fire, sir?' Grebben asked. The creature was almost on them.

In answer, Nachten raised his own pistol and loosed off three shots in rapid succession. The beast was knocked back by the impact, roaring in pain and anger. But it didn't stop. Head down, it charged back at them.

The whole tunnel echoed with the hammering of machine gun fire from the SS men. The creature was lost in smoke and dust, its snarls drowned out by the noise. Stone chips flew up from stray bullets as they hit the tunnel walls and floor. The noise cut out abruptly as Nachten raised his hand.

'Enough. We must retrieve the body.'

'If it's truly dead, sir,' one of the men said nervously. He was as battle-hardened as Grebben himself, but Grebben knew how the man felt. For a moment, as the creature charged at them, he had been as scared as he had ever been.

'Of course it's dead,' Nachten snapped.

But even as he said it, a dark shape coalesced out of the dusty air in front of them. Its chest was ripped apart. The face was pock-marked with bullet holes. Hair was scorched away from the ragged remains of flesh and skin. But the creature was alive, lurching forwards. A massive fist lashed out, at the nearest man.

It caught Nachten surprised and off balance as he backed away, hammering him sideways into the wall. Before Grebben could react, the creature had dragged the standartenfuhrer to his feet, lifting him off the ground. Then it hurled him back at the other men. There was a crack of breaking bone as Nachten hit the wall, then slid down to the ground. Unconscious, or dead.

'Back!' Grebben shouted. 'Everyone back! You.' He pointed at the nearest two men. 'Bring the standartenfuhrer. The rest of you – covering fire.'

The two men pulled Nachten down the tunnel, his feet dragging on the ground as they ran. Nachten's head moved slightly – he was alive then. But obviously badly injured. The other two SS men fired their machine pistols again, raking them back and forth as they fired into darkness and smoke. A discarded torch rolled along the tunnel floor. Its light gleamed for an instant, then went out as a foot stamped down on it.

One of the guns emptied. The soldier ripped out the magazine and slotted in another.

Grebben fired his Luger, knowing it would have no effect.

But what would? What could possibly stop the brute beast?

'Keep going – back to the way out,' he yelled, hoping they remembered the way. God knew what had happened to Nachten's map – even if he could understand it.

He grabbed the nearer of the two soldiers still firing. 'Grenade,' he demanded. He took the stick-grenade the man pulled from his belt and gestured for him to follow the others. 'Now – run.'

Grebben turned and peered into the darkness. The only light was from the torch he had somehow managed to keep hold of. It danced across the walls and floor as he used the same hand to grab the pin and pull it awkwardly from the grenade. Then he hurled the explosive at the creature that burst out of the smoke and dust and charged towards him, turned and ran.

He was counting, out of habit and under his breath. So he knew exactly when to throw himself to the floor and cover the back of his head and his ears with his hands. He was so close that the blast wave lifted him off the floor. He could feel it reverberating inside his chest. A rush of hot air. The roar of the explosion like a savage beast rolling down the tunnel. The crash of falling stone.

When he dared to stagger to his feet and shine his torch back down the tunnel, it illuminated a ragged wall of fallen stone. The roof above was a gaping maw. There was no sign of the creature that had been chasing them. Grebben watched for a full minute, hardly daring to breathe, expecting at any moment that the creature would burst through the rubble and debris and charge towards him.

Finally, Hauptsturmfuhrer Grebben turned and walked slowly back down the tunnel.

CHAPTER 28

He kept her chained in the cellar for a week. By then it seemed clear that Jane Roylston was not a threat. Crowley spoke the words of power, binding her to his will, every morning and evening. The holy man in Nepal who taught him the words, the incantations, had been vague about how – or even if – they worked. It was over thirty years since Crowley had learned them, and he couldn't even be sure he had them exactly right. It was hard to tell if the words had any effect, but it made him feel more confident. Less afraid.

After a while, he allowed her back to her room. She ate and drank little. She saw no one except Crowley. She rarely left the room – either sitting staring at the wall or lying on the bed, eyes closed. Perhaps she was asleep. He asked her questions, but the answers were now either noncommittal or non-existent.

Eventually, Crowley was sure the woman was no threat to anyone except Ralph, who was already dead. And probably he deserved it. Even by Crowley's standards the man had been a sadistic brute, though he had his uses. He considered admitting to Brinkman that Jane had returned. At least it would stop the man delving into her past.

One of the newer girls, Mary, took Jane's place at the ceremonies and séances. She had some innate ability, but nothing like Jane's talents. It wasn't long before Crowley realised that he needed Jane back. If nothing else, Mary might benefit from watching her, from seeing how the more experienced medium channelled the voices and messages from Beyond.

Crowley's Library doubled as a séance room. More than half of the bookshelves round the walls were empty. Candles and symbols of power replaced the books – animal skulls, phials of coloured liquid, statuettes and ancient sacrificial bowls. A curved dagger from Mesopotamia. The centre of the room was dominated by a large, round table. There was nothing so crude as an upturned glass or lettered cards. Whatever message came through would be delivered by the medium.

For the moment, Mary sat in the prime position, Crowley on one side of her. Jane sat opposite, eyes half closed, unspeaking. Where Jane was slight, Mary had a fuller figure. In contrast to Jane's short, dark hair Mary had blonde hair that reached almost to her waist.

Once the candles were lit, Crowley signalled for the lights to be extinguished. He allowed Mary to run the session, calling for Enlightenment, the fingers of her hand warm against his. The heavy bracelet scraped against the table top as she moved her hand slightly. It hung loosely on the woman's wrist.

After almost half an hour of going through the motions, it was obvious that Mary was making no connection today.

'Would you like to try?' Crowley asked Jane.

She was staring down at the table, but lifted her head at his words.

'Mary won't mind, will you, Mary?' he went on.

'No, of course not,' Mary said. From her tone, she minded a lot.

'You see.'

'I do not see,' Jane replied. 'Not clearly. Not now.'

'Then change places with Mary. Do you want to see?'

Jane frowned. 'I… I don't know.'

Mary stood up. The bracelet slid down her wrist. Jane's eyes followed it. 'Bracelet,' she murmured.

'It's mine now,' Mary told her.

'Bracelet,' Jane said again, louder, firmer. 'Bracelet.'

'Give it to her,' Crowley said quietly.

Mary hesitated for a moment, then pressed her thumb into the palm of her hand so that she could slide the bracelet off. 'I want it back.' She dropped it on the table in front of her, then stood up and walked round to where Jane was sitting.

Jane too stood up. 'No,' she said. 'You really don't.'

She took Mary's place in the chair next to Crowley. Hesitantly, she reached out for the bracelet. As her fingers touched it, the silver tracery round the outside flared a brilliant white. Crowley reached out to stop her – perhaps this was not a good idea.

But he was too late. Jane had already picked up the bracelet. The bright light from it faded to a glow as she opened it, and closed it round her thin upper arm, above the elbow. Her expression did not change. But the bracelet seemed to tighten in place. Blood oozed out from beneath it, dripping to the table. Mary gasped. The others at the table were pale as they watched.

Jane's eyes opened wide. They seemed to darken as she stared unfocused into the distance.

'*Now* I can see!'

'What do you see?' Crowley asked. 'Tell me. I must know.'

'I see who I am,' Jane said. 'What I must do. What will happen. And how it will all end when the Vril awaken and come among us.'

He gave up counting the bodies. German and Russian soldiers, peasants and civilians, horses… The road through the desolate, blighted landscape was like a pathway through hell.

The driver was a veteran. Hoffman had joined the detachment commanded by the officer he had met in Dresden to travel to the Eastern Front. But they had been diverted to the Caucasus, so he had been forced to find another unit moving up to join the troops advancing towards Moscow.

'It's nothing like what they tell you,' the driver said. He

was too weary and battle-scarred to worry about speaking his mind to an SS officer. Or perhaps he simply hadn't noticed the dark uniform beneath Hoffman's greatcoat. 'The plan is that the land we capture will supply the food we need. But it doesn't work like that.'

'Not when the retreating Russians burn the crops,' Hoffman agreed. 'Not when we kill the peasants who should be farming it.'

'That makes little difference,' the driver said, bumping the truck over another dead body. 'To farm land like this you need tractors. The Reds drove them all away. They evacuated the tractors, not the people. What's that tell you about them, eh?'

Hoffman didn't answer. It told him that someone realised that resupply was going to be a problem for both sides. It told him that his fellow Russians were prepared to sacrifice anything to protect their homeland. It told him that at some point – probably with the onset of another winter – the German advance would grind to a halt and might never get started again.

His hand strayed to his chest, resting over where the photograph of Alina nestled safely inside his jacket pocket. Was she still in Stalingrad? Was she waiting for him as she'd promised? Would he ever see her again?

The driver was still talking, but Hoffman wasn't listening. It didn't matter what he said. Nothing mattered. Alina first. Then he would think about getting to Moscow, and finding out what they already knew about the Vril.

Guy envied Leo his place in the repaired Lysander. Not just because he was sharing the small plane with Sarah, but also because the plane was a hell of a lot quicker than waiting for their rendezvous with the submarine and the subsequent journey.

They had managed to escape from the Labyrinth while the SS soldiers were confronting the Minotaur. Quite what had happened down in the tunnels, Guy didn't know. But from a safe distance outside the fence line, they had watched through the thinning smoke as the soldiers brought out their wounded officer who was quickly stretchered away.

Brinkman kept the stone axe-head with him. There was some value in getting it back to London as quickly as possible, but that had to be weighed against other considerations.

'I don't doubt Miss Diamond's abilities,' Brinkman confided in Guy as they waited on the shore for a signal from the submarine. 'But we can't count on anything. If the plane gets shot down, then the axe-head could fall into enemy hands. If our submarine gets hit, then we're all going to the bottom of the sea and the axe with us.'

'That's a sobering thought,' Guy told him.

Mihali rowed them out into the secluded bay where the submarine was due to meet them. It was a clear, summer's sky and the moon was bright despite being a mere sliver of a crescent, a contrast with the crashing, stormy sea and thunderous sky when they had arrived. The submarine was due to surface at 1am local time.

'It's hard to know exactly where it will appear,' Mihali told them.

'Hopefully, not right underneath us,' Guy said.

'I imagine they'll check their periscope first to make sure everything's safe,' Brinkman said.

'Well,' Guy said to Mihali, 'thanks for looking after us. But I can't pretend it's been fun.'

'The fun may not be over yet,' Mihali told them.

He was the one facing the shore, Guy and Brinkman sitting opposite him in the little boat as he worked the oars. They twisted round to see what Mihali was looking at.

Lights. A cluster of small lights, torches perhaps, on the shoreline.

'Not your people come to see us off?' Brinkman asked.

'Sadly not.'

As if to prove the point, there was a flash followed by a crack of sound. At the same moment as the noise reached them, something splashed into the water close to the boat.

'I think they've seen us,' Guy said.

Memories of Dunkirk rose unbidden in his mind as there was more gunfire. Bullets splashed into the water all around them like a sudden rain shower.

'Keep rowing,' Brinkman ordered Mihali. 'See if you can get us out of range.'

As he spoke, several shots hammered into the wooden side of the boat. A splinter whipped past Guy's face. He swore and ducked down low.

The sound of gunfire was drowned out as the sea around them began to boil. Caught in the wash, the boat dipped and rolled alarmingly. Water sloshed in over the side. More gunshots cracked past. A huge, dark shape reared up out of the bay, water gushing white and foaming off the sides of the submarine's conning tower as it thrust up into the clear night sky. A bullet pinged off the metal.

'Go!' Mihali shouted. 'Get yourselves on the deck.'

A hatch swung open at the top of the tower. A moment later, gunfire rang out from the submarine. The lights on the shore went out as the German soldiers turned off their torches.

'What about you?' Guy yelled at Mihali.

'Don't worry about me. I'll swim round to the next bay. Let them shoot up the boat, and assume we've all escaped on the sub.'

Mihali dropped the oars, and pulled Guy into a quick embrace as he pushed past towards the front of the boat. Brinkman got the same treatment. A bullet grazed past Guy's arm, ripping his sleeve close to the shoulder. Then he was leaping for the deck of the submarine, just clear of the surface of the bay. Water washed across it, making it slippery.

Brinkman grabbed Guy's arm – though whether to support Guy or for his own benefit it wasn't clear. The steel hull rang with a scatter of impacts. Guy looked back in time to see Mihali diving out of the small rowing boat and striking out strongly through the water, away from the submarine. He'd have to put some distance between them, to avoid being dragged down in the submarine's wake when it dived.

The ladder up the conning tower was on the far side,

shielded from the gunfire. Even so, it was a difficult climb up the slippery, wet rungs. At the top, sailors in lifejackets caught hold of Guy and Brinkman and bundled them quickly through the hatch.

Guy all but fell to the deck inside, half climbing half sliding down the ladder. He collapsed to his knees as he landed, before hauling himself upright in time to help Brinkman down. They turned to find a uniformed submariner watching them with amusement.

'I'm hoping you're the two chaps I'm expecting and not some unfortunate Greek fishermen who just happened to be passing.'

'I think we're your passengers,' Brinkman assured him.

'Then welcome aboard, gentlemen. I'm Captain Whitaker, and I expect you're about ready for a mug of tea.'

Above them, the hatch clanged shut as the last of the sailors descended to join them.

Mercifully, the rest of the trip back passed without incident. Brinkman and Guy delivered the precious axe-head to Elizabeth Archer at the British Museum as soon as they could, even before calling in at the Station Z offices.

'It's nothing much to look at,' she told them, as if they were somehow to blame for this. 'But I shall make a full analysis. It is remarkably well preserved.'

She shuffled through a pile of papers on her desk and handed several sheets to Brinkman. Looking over his shoulder, Guy saw that they were sketches of the room at the centre of the Labyrinth.

'I drew these from Leo's description of the chamber where you found this,' Elizabeth told them. 'I'd be grateful if you could take a look and tell me if there's anything we've missed or got wrong. Oh, and this one too.'

She pulled out another sheet – this one with a drawing of the Minotaur. Even though it was only a rough sketch, it made Guy shudder at the memory of the real thing. Here, back in London, it had all seemed so distant, almost like he had dreamed it. But the sketch brought home the reality of what they were dealing with like a hammer blow.

In a room lit only by black candles, four people sat at a round table, their hands on the polished wooden surface, fingers touching.

'Anything?' Leo Davenport asked.

'Shhh,' Miss Manners told him. 'I need to concentrate.'

'Waste of time, if you ask me,' Sergeant Green muttered.

'I don't think that's helping,' Sarah whispered back.

'Yes!' Miss Manners gasped. 'Yes…'

'Here we go,' Leo said quietly.

'Darkness,' Miss Manners breathed. 'We live in the dark places. Sleep in the depths beneath the earth. A few of us keep guard. A few of us watch and wait, learn and plan…'

'The usual story,' Green murmured. 'I told you – we never learn anything new.'

Sarah shushed him again and the sergeant lapsed into silence.

'Is she finished?' Leo wondered. 'I want to scratch my nose.'

'No,' Miss Manners told him sharply, glaring through the flickering light. The effect was just as forceful even without her spectacles. 'Keep the circle intact. There is more, I can feel it.' She closed her eyes again and took a deep breath.

'Speak to me,' she muttered. 'Speak to me again…' Then, abruptly, her whole body stiffened. 'We sleep,' she hissed. 'But our long sleep is almost over. We already have one key. We know where to find the second. The third will be brought to us…'

She lapsed into silence for several seconds. Then Miss Manners opened her eyes again. 'That's it,' she said calmly. 'A little more than usual, but whether it's of any use…' She raised her hands from the table. 'Now where are my glasses?'

'You mentioned keys,' Sarah said as they stood up. 'Three of them. Those must be the axe-heads.'

Green turned on the lights and set about extinguishing the candles. Dark smoky trails drifted upwards from the blackened wicks.

'It seems likely,' Miss Manners said, 'given what you've told us about what you found in Crete. But don't read too much into the word "key". What I say is my brain's best interpretation of what comes into my mind. It's like you're getting an imperfect translation of something I only dimly glimpsed.'

'But it all helps,' Leo said. 'Even if we don't yet understand how.'

'We'll see what the colonel thinks,' Green told them. 'He phoned just before we started to say he and Major Pentecross are delivering the axe-thing to Mrs Archer at the British Museum.'

Sarah's excitement at the news was evident. 'They're back? Safely?'

'So it seems.'

'Why didn't you tell us before?'

Green stifled a smile. 'Miss Manners is always saying we have to be calm and unemotional in here. So we didn't want you distracted. It might have interfered with the séance.'

CHAPTER 29

On 23 August 1942, the German 6th Army, together with support from elements of the 4th Panzer Army, crossed the river Don and laid siege to Stalingrad. Aerial bombardment by the Luftwaffe the same day reduced much of the city to rubble. Hoffman watched with a mixture of horror and fascination as six hundred planes passed overhead in a seemingly unending wave that turned the sky almost black. How many civilians were left in the city he wondered? How many would die today? And was Alina among them?

When the first German units entered the city, Hoffman was with them. But he didn't stay with them for long. At the first opportunity he struck out alone, down streets he barely recognised beneath the rubble that had been buildings and homes. He was answerable to no one here, but even if he had been there was so much death that he would not be missed any more than the men whose bodies already lay scattered across the rubble.

He spent the first night huddled inside his greatcoat jammed between the remains of a wall and the debris from its collapse. The next day he found a dead civilian who was about his size, and changed clothes with the man. Rigor mortis had set in, so he had to break the man's bones to get the clothes off him. When he was done, he stared at a reflection of himself in a muddy puddle, the water curdled with blood. He looked nondescript, ordinary, unremarkable.

The battle was already evolving into a new form of urban warfare the like of which had never been seen before. The German army was used to rapid advances – sometimes as much as fifty miles in a day. Here, they were forced to fight for every street, sometimes every building. The Russians retreated slowly, fortifying any structure that was still intact. Every house was potentially a fortress.

In the streets, the fighting was often hand-to-hand – Russian civilians attacking the advancing Germans with anything they could find. Shovels and spades with their edges sharpened were especially brutal and effective.

Snipers were a constant threat to both sides, but particularly the Germans as they pressed further into the city and entered new areas. Even without his uniform, Hoffman found himself a target for both sides. Anyone caught out in the open was likely to be shot.

The difference was, Hoffman didn't care. The first time a sniper's bullet ripped into his chest, he assumed he was dead. It was almost a relief. The impact knocked him backwards, into a bomb crater. He lay there in the mud staring at the clouds for a long time before he even realised he was still alive. Looking down at his chest, he saw the familiar orange filaments knitting the skin and flesh back together. Was the bullet still inside him? He neither knew nor cared.

There were other people, real people if you could call them that, as well as the soldiers and the armed civilians. People trying to survive in this devastated city. He caught glimpses of them scurrying through the wreckage, desperately searching for food or clean water. Rats were everywhere, but especially round the bodies of the dead. In less than a week the city had become an open grave, a charnel house. Even though there was almost nothing left, the bombing and shelling continued. As much as anything it seemed a matter of pride for the Russians to defend, and the Germans to destroy, the city that bore Stalin's name.

Only when he unearthed a street sign from beneath a

tombstone of bricks was Hoffman sure he'd found the right street – what was left of it. Outside Alina's ruined house he sank to his knees and wept. He didn't know he could still cry until that moment. A moment when he realised emotionally what he had known intellectually since he arrived. Alina was not here. Not any more. Please God she had left before the siege began...

With no chance yet of getting to Moscow, the rubble of Stalingrad became his home. If the Germans eventually won through and continued their advance, he would go with them. Or if he had the chance to join the Russians pulling back across the river, he would take that. But for the moment, no Russians were getting out of Stalingrad. The battle was fluid, moving back and forth through the city, and so he moved with it – to keep out of its way. He didn't seek out Germans, but if he came across them, he killed without thought or conscience. They had ripped the heart out of his country and whatever kinship he might have felt from his time masquerading as one of them had been ripped away with it.

Whatever he had become, Hoffman – he still thought of himself as Hoffman, one habit he could not so easily break – was cursed to be a perpetual survivor in a blood-red city of death. Even the rats seemed to sense he was different, dangerous, and avoided him.

He couldn't stay here for ever. If he did, then he would never find where Alina had gone. If he did, he would go mad with the scent and sound and sight of death all around him. The stone axe-head was a constant weight pulling at his pocket, and he had to decide what to do with it.

But he kept searching, despite knowing it was futile. And if he did find Alina, what then? If she was still in the city then she was either dead already or she was one of the emaciated, pale survivors – probably armed with a sniper rifle, knowing Alina. He smiled thinly at the thought. If she was here she was fighting, not scavenging.

So every day he searched another area, and every day he

found only the dead, the dying, or the killers. One morning he stood for an eternity staring down at a body. The sun was rising over the ruins, casting a jigsaw of light and shadow across the ragged landscape. The body was a young woman, of about Alina's age. Roughly her build and height. Dressed as she might well have been dressed. Her hair was the same colour. She was lying face down, the back of her coat a bloodied mess where the bullets had hit and she had bled out. He didn't dare turn her over.

He finally summoned the courage, finally convinced himself that it couldn't be Alina anyway, and turned her on to her back. One look was more than enough. He turned away and retched, heaving on an empty stomach. The rats had eaten away her face, down to the bone. It wasn't Alina. It couldn't be, not like that.

But from then on, he saw her everywhere. He caught glimpses of Alina in the shadows, watching him. He saw her duck behind piles of rubble and into the skeletal remains of broken buildings. He saw her shadow walking beside him as the afternoon sun gave the city an awful majesty. He heard her laughter in constant gunfire and the interminable explosions.

And one night, he saw her walking towards him down the street. She picked her way cautiously through the rubble, constantly looking round, alert for any trouble. Even so, she walked right into it.

There were three of them, two from one side, and another from behind. The field grey of their uniforms merged with the night shadows until they were almost on her. Hoffman didn't see them as he was too intent on the girl – tall and slim, though her body was smothered in shapeless clothes. Dark hair cut short, features slightly pinched but startlingly attractive.

Then suddenly, the German soldiers were on her. Two of them knocked her to the ground, holding her down while the third tore at her clothes. Her cries echoed round the ruins, lost in the constant sounds of battle and suffering – just more screams. She struggled, kicked, scratched, spat – more animal than human now. Desperate to survive, but knowing that she wouldn't, that this was it – this was the night she would be violated, discarded, killed.

Until Hoffman arrived.

The first soldier was standing over her, grinning as he shrugged out of his jacket. Hoffman grabbed him from behind, hands either side of the man's head then twisting suddenly. He heard the neck bones snap and the man went limp, dropping without so much as a whimper, falling across the girl's body and pinning her down.

The other soldiers reacted at once, their nerves strung out so tight and alert from the constant danger of snipers. One of them already had a rifle to the girl's head. He swung it up and fired, point blank, into Hoffman's body. He didn't even feel it. He grabbed the hot barrel of the gun and ripped it from the soldier's startled hands, swinging it hard at the other soldier. The blow crashed into the side of the man's head. He wore no helmet and the impact crushed his skull instantly.

The surviving soldier turned and ran. Hoffman watched him clamber over a pile of rubble, throw himself down the other side, reach the other side of the street and perhaps consider himself safe at last. Then Hoffman brought the soldier's own rifle to his shoulder, sighted, and shot him with it. The man's head exploded in a satisfying mist that was distinctly red even in the gloom of the night.

Hoffman dragged the dead weight of the first soldier's body away from the girl and offered her his hand. She took it warily, watching him all the time as he helped her up.

'Are you going to…' She couldn't bring herself to say it.

He shook his head. He didn't know if he was relieved or disappointed to see it wasn't Alina after all. She didn't look anything like Alina now he was close enough to see her clearly.

'He shot you – I saw him,' she said, taking a step away from Hoffman.

'He must have missed.'

She seemed to accept that, struggling to pull her clothes back into place, tucking in the ripped edges. She turned away, embarrassed at what he might have seen. That made Hoffman smile. How could human dignity survive in this place?

When she turned back, she was smiling too – with relief rather than joy. 'Are you hungry?'

He wasn't. Not really. 'Isn't everyone?'

'I was meeting my friends, in a cellar below the next street. We have some food – it's not much but... Thank you.'

Hoffman removed the pistol from the holster of the soldier he had killed first – an officer. He didn't bother to check the man's rank. There was no seniority among the dead. He handed the pistol to the girl. She took it without comment and pushed it into the waistband of her skirt. He hefted the rifle over his own shoulder and gestured for her to lead the way.

There were three of them, all women. The girl Hoffman had rescued was the youngest but the others weren't much older. They had a rifle between them, and Hoffman added the one he had brought. Some of the bricks round the top of the cellar had been removed so they could see out – and shoot at any German soldiers they spotted.

'We keep on the move,' the girl told him. They hadn't bothered with names, so nor had Hoffman. 'We'll need to leave here soon and find somewhere else.'

'We killed two of the bastards yesterday,' one of the other women said proudly.

'So that's five with the three you got.'

Hoffman acknowledged the praise with a nod. He ate a little of the food – they didn't tell him what it was they had boiled up on a fire made out of floorboards and paper. Probably rat. If they were lucky they might have caught a cat or even a dog, but there were hardly any left now. They had collected rainwater in a rusty can and took it in turns to scoop some out in a chipped tea cup.

'You can stay with us, if you want,' the girl told him when they'd eaten. 'I owe you my life.'

Hoffman wasn't sure exactly what she was offering, but he shook his head anyway. 'You seem to be doing all right without me. Smaller groups are safer.'

They all nodded their agreement. If they were disappointed they didn't show it.

'But there is something you can do for me.'

'Oh?'

'Not what you think,' he reassured her. He picked up the chipped cup. It would have to do. He could write letters on what was left of the paper with the charred end of a piece of wood from the fire.

The three women watched him with interest.

'What are you doing?' the one he'd rescued asked. 'Is it a game?'

'Everything is a game,' he told her. 'But no. Actually, if you're willing, I want to hold a séance.'

The three of them exchanged puzzled looks.

'A séance? Now? Here?'

He nodded. 'Now. Here.'

'I guess we all know lots of dead people,' one of the others said. 'Is there someone special you want to contact?'

'Yes,' he said. 'But not in the way you think.' Hoffman thought of Alina. But séances wouldn't help him speak to her – even if she was dead, and he hoped she was not.

'Well,' the woman he'd rescued said, 'I have nothing else planned for tonight. So I guess this is as good an entertainment as any.'

'Except killing Germans,' one of her friends said.

All he could do was try. He would keep trying, on his own if necessary, every night. Hoffman had no way of knowing if the message he was trying to send would ever get through. If it had any effect, he knew it would be thousands of miles away.

But as he sat with the three women, huddled over an upturned china cup in a ruined city of brittle buildings and rotting bodies, something stirred much closer to them.

The Volga was dark as a river of blood in the pale moonlight. But an even darker shape was forcing its way up from the silty riverbed. A skeletal tentacle broke the surface, testing the cold air. Another followed. A bulbous body like a misshapen football rose up above the water, its glistening eye seeking out the distant shore. Then the creature disappeared again into the murky depths.

Until, a few minutes later, it hauled itself out onto the bank. Moments later, another joined it. Then more. They stood poised, pulsating, glistening wet with water and mud for a moment beside the river. Then, like grotesque giant spiders, they scuttled off into the ruins of the city.

CHAPTER 30

After the excitement of the Crete expedition, Brinkman was aware that time seemed to be stretching out again. Elizabeth Archer was running tests on the axe-head, but with little to show for it. The UDT activity was about the same as usual, although standing orders now were for the RAF to keep clear of them. In several incidents planes had simply disappeared after making contact. So long as the UDTs were not actually attacking, it was safest to avoid direct contact. Dr Wiles continued to collate the tracking and interception data.

Leo Davenport and Sarah spent time searching through the British Library and the British Museum archives for any clues about the third axe-head, and Guy was helping Miss Manners and Sergeant Green organise the new photographic department.

'Department' was an exaggeration. With the help of Alban in MI5, Brinkman had managed to arrange for two secretaries at the Ministry of Information to look through photographs. With the discovery that an Ubermensch could potentially be identified in photographs, it needed someone to look through any photographs that might reveal one lurking.

Miss Manners had grand plans to station photographers on busy streets taking flash-lit photographs of crowds in the hope of finding any Ubermensch.

The arguments against were mainly logistic. But also, as

Wiles pointed out, unless you knew the identity of everyone in the photograph, seeing an Ubermensch in a crowd was hardly helpful except in confirming its existence. But in fact there was no evidence of any Ubermensch currently in Britain anyway.

The compromise was that the Ministry of Information, which had access to photographs taken every day all round Britain in other Allied countries, should check them for anything unusual. The two women given the job were told only vaguely what they were looking for, and that it was thought to be an experimental enemy camouflage technique used by spies to avoid showing up properly in photographs.

When she had time, which was rarely, Miss Manners retired to the Séance Room. Here she closed her eyes and tried to relax into a state where she might hear the voices, see the images. With the Vril becoming more active, the air must be alive with their strange communications. If she could tap into even a tiny fraction of that information it could prove invaluable.

Success was limited. The strongest signals were from UDTs over Britain. She caught images of the countryside seen from above, flying past at incredible speed. Little else made any sense. She could get stronger impressions, over greater distance if they actually held a séance of sorts. Perhaps the combined effort of several minds enhanced the signals. But still all she saw was the gloomy underground vaults and chambers so reminiscent of the North African base and labyrinthine tunnels that Leo and Guy had described...

She kept up her work photographing wives and children for the Snapshots from Home project, sending the pictures to the soldiers who were missing their loved ones.

Guy wasn't really sure what to make of the séances, until his name came up. It had become something of an end-of-day ritual to gather in the Séance Room and spend a few minutes helping Miss Manners settle into the relaxed, semi-trance state where she might glean further information about the Vril. It seemed bizarre, but Guy had to admit he had experienced far stranger things in the last year.

The frustration was that they seemed to have wrung as much information from the process as they could, and none of it was especially helpful. If they were lucky, Miss Manners might pick up some background detail or the shadowy realm where the Vril were located. She kept meticulous notes of every session. But without knowing the locations of the places she 'saw', or the details of the vague things she 'heard' it was all of limited value.

'If nothing else,' Guy joked to Sarah as they entered the room for the latest attempt, 'I get to hold your hand in the dark.'

'I'm putting you between Leo and Miss Manners,' she told him.

'Spoilsport.'

As usual, the four of them sat in the flickering candlelight, fingers touching, silent and still. Miss Manners breathed deeply several times as she settled herself. She murmured words and phrases that Guy couldn't hear, but which she had told them were to help her relax and put herself into a receptive frame of mind. Techniques she had learned from Crowley, he guessed.

'Glass!' she exclaimed suddenly. 'Someone – Leo – get the glass.'

'Of course.' Davenport got up and went to a side table where a tumbler stood next to a stack of squares of card.

'Are you all right?' Sarah asked.

Miss Manners was surprised more than anxious. 'I can see letters,' she told them.

'Are you sure it's the Vril?' Guy asked. 'They don't usually communicate in words.'

Leo positioned the upturned glass in the centre of the round table, then placed the pieces of card round the edge. Each was marked with a letter or number. 'Let's find out, shall we? Forefinger of the left hand on the top of the glass everyone, if you please.'

'Will it be in English?' Sarah asked.

'Possibly, or it could just be gibberish,' Miss Manners admitted. 'Now concentrate, everyone. Empty your minds of everything except the glass itself.'

He shouldn't really have been surprised, but Guy felt a jolt of astonishment as the glass moved. It slid smoothly and easily across the polished surface of the table, touching the card lettered 'N' before moving on to 'G'.

Leo had his pen in his free hand and a spare piece of card beside him. He noted down the letters as the glass travelled between them. Guy tried to keep track of the letters in his head, but they seemed to make no sense:

N G R A D P A V S H I K H B O R T S O V V W I

But gradually something seemed to resolve out of it. 'W I L L W A I T' he realised as the glass moved on. There was a pause, and he thought it was finished, but then the glass moved again.

P E N T E C R O S S

Startled, Guy pulled his hand back from the glass.

'Sorry,' he murmured, reaching out again. He gave up trying to follow the letters, his mind was numb. His name – how could it have spelled out his name?

'It's a loop,' Leo said eventually. 'We can stop now. It's the same thing coming round again.'

'But what's it say?' Guy demanded. 'It spelled out my name – who's doing that?'

'I think I know,' Leo said. He was smiling as he turned the lights on. 'I think you will too once I work out where the breaks in the words are in all this jumble. Tell me, does Pavshikh Bortsov mean anything to you?'

'It's Russian,' Guy said, looking at where Leo had written the words out on the paper.

'Which would make sense. See.' He showed them the full message.

PENTECROSS HAVE AXE MEET ME IN STALINGRAD PAVSHIKH BORTSOV WILL WAIT

'Our friend Hoffman, the Russian German?' Pentecross said. 'But how can he be sending us this?'

'He knows what we're doing, he must be hoping we'll intercept this.'

'But, how is he transmitting it?' Sarah said.

'I would guess,' Miss Manners told them, 'that he is holding a séance.'

'But what does it mean?' Sarah asked.

'We'll need a map of Stalingrad,' Leo said, 'but I suspect he is telling Guy where to meet him, and that he will wait until we get there.'

'We?' Guy echoed.

'Well I'm not letting you go on your own. And if Hoffman has the third axe as he claims then we can't just ignore this.'

'Pavshikh Bortsov could be a location,' Guy said. 'It means "Fallen Heroes" so it might be a monument or something.'

'I'll find out how you can get to Stalingrad,' Miss Manners said. 'Though I have to say I don't envy you the trip.'

'Don't be like that,' Leo told her. 'It isn't every day one gets an invitation from the spirits to visit one of the most dangerous places on Earth.'

If she had spoken English, she might have understood the significance of what she saw. The letters flashed through her ancient mind, imprinting themselves one by one. It was a repeating sequence, and she saw it most nights.

In her chamber – her sanctum – deep below the North Tower of Wewelsburg Castle that housed the Hall of Generals, the Seer sat alone in darkness. From here she saw so much. She could feel so much. The suffering and death from across the world; the aspirations and ambitions of the SS officers within the castle itself; the voices of the spirits that screamed desperately at the mortals who could not hear them; the cold, hard thoughts of Himmler himself.

And the dark, creeping malignancy of the Vril as they clawed their way through the deepest corners and recesses of their underground realm and of her mind.

Her thoughts were broken by the light from the door as it swung open. She struggled to her feet, ignoring the pain, and turned to see who it was although she had known he was coming. Her gnarled, crooked hand reached for a walking stick to support her weight.

The lights came on, gleaming on the high forehead and small round glasses of Heinrich Himmler.

'Have you anything to tell me?' he asked.

Her answer was scratchy and frail. 'Nothing that you want to hear.'

CHAPTER 31

It was a city full of predators where rats fed on the dead. Most of the predators were human, but not all.

One was little more than a ghost. The Germans called him 'The Dark One' – a living shadow that crept through the ruins and killed them one by one. There were stories that he had been shot and had survived. That he possessed inhuman strength. That he was on a mission to protect the Russian civilians who eked out a meagre existence in the rubble and had made it his goal to kill every last German in the city.

If you were the last man at the back of a patrol, he might get you. If you were separated from your unit, he could be lurking in the rubble, waiting. If you were a sniper, then as well as focusing your crosshairs on a potential target you might feel the real hairs on the back of your neck alert you to the arrival of death as it crept up on you.

Hoffman neither knew nor cared what the Germans thought of him. To his mind, *they* were the predators, intruders feeding on the last gasps of the ruined city. But they were a secondary consideration. He killed them when the opportunity arose, but he didn't go looking.

Every day he went to Pavshikh Bortsov – the Square of Fallen Heroes. What was left of it. Of all the city it was one of the most open spaces, which he hoped meant he would see Pentecross if the Englishman got his message and came.

The openness made it dangerous too, but Hoffman kept to the sides, hiding in the empty shells of the buildings that surrounded the square.

When the watching was done, he sat down in the near-darkness somewhere secluded and hidden. He set out the ragged paper and the chipped tea cup, and he concentrated his thoughts as he moved the cup back and forth, always spelling out the same message. Never knowing if it went any further than the edges of his own imagination. Life became routine. Like everyone else in the city he looked no further than the present moment, harboured no ambition beyond his own survival.

Hoffman's constant movement was how he survived. The Germans sought to avoid him, most doubting he really existed and assuming that 'The Dark One' was an amalgamation of Red Army soldiers and snipers, a bogeyman conjured out of the terrors of the debris.

But something was hunting Hoffman. Slowly, meticulously, tracking the stone axe that he kept either in his pocket or consigned to the safest of hiding places in the ruins. Its movement confused the Vril creatures, slowed them down. The death and destruction in the city didn't worry them. The Vril were at home clambering through narrow spaces and dark crevices, hiding beneath the ground and emerging only when night fell. But they were cautious. The humans were killing each other in the city, and the creatures were as vulnerable to bullets as any German or Russian. They moved slowly, warily, stealthily through the rubble.

One night one of the creatures almost died, caught in the open. It scuttled across what was left of a street, darting between the shadows. Two humans were picking their way along the same street, also hugging the shadows, holding hands, helping each other through the debris. One tall, the other shorter.

One of them slipped, foot almost colliding with the Vril as it tensed. It reached out with a brittle limb, ready to stab in self-defence. But the humans moved on. They had taken only another few steps when there was a crack of gunfire. The larger of the humans was hurled back as a bullet took her in the chest. The other dived for cover, close to the Vril.

The creature pressed itself into the darkness, aware of the danger. Soldiers were coming, hurrying down the street as the Germans pressed on through the city. There was a confidence in their movement, a renewed sense of victory. German forces had closed round the city, reaching the river Volga to the north. Surely it was only a matter of time now before they owned these death-trap ruins.

A rattle of gunfire hammered into the fallen human. The body, already dead, danced and juddered under the onslaught. The second human whimpered, pressed closer into the rubble. The Vril scratched at the ground, gouging out enough space to squeeze itself beneath a fallen wall. It stared out from its cover, eye glinting in the pale light of the impassive moon.

The soldier moved on, oblivious to the creature, not noticing the surviving human. The Vril could see the human's face pressed into the dusty ground nearby, wet with tears, pale with fright. The creature wasn't used to seeing its enemy so close. Usually they were so afraid their senses were heightened. They fled at the first sign of movement, the first unnatural sound, the merest hint that they were not alone.

But frightened or not, humans were an unpleasant distraction. Out of instinct as much as choice, the grotesque creature reached out a limb, turned it so the razor-sharp spines on the underside were exposed. Lashed out.

The soldiers were too far away now to hear the scream.

Crowley had finally admitted that Jane Roylston was back at Jermyn Street. But having had no contact with her friend, Miss Manners was sure that there was something wrong. Jane was often out of touch for a while, but never for this long. She knew that Brinkman wouldn't want to make waves with Crowley. He would tell her to bide her time, not to cause trouble.

But Miss Manners wasn't convinced Crowley was helping as much as he claimed. If she had managed to pick up the message from Hoffman, surely Crowley would have tuned into it at one of his séances or ceremonies. But he had never mentioned it... What else was he keeping to himself?

The more she thought about it, the more she convinced herself that a visit to Jane – to Crowley – was in the best interests not just of her own conscience but of Station Z as well.

It was impossible to tell if Crowley was pleased to see her. She knew from experience that his expression was likely to be as false as his words. But he made a show of welcoming her into the house like the friend she had once thought she was.

'What an opportune visit,' he said, smiling like a predatory animal. 'We were just about to hold a ceremony in the cellar. There was a time when you'd have been welcome to join us.'

It was clear she was not invited now.

'I wanted to see Jane. Just for a few moments.' She almost added 'if that's all right', but she wasn't going to ask his permission.

Crowley's face fell. 'Oh, but that is such a shame. Jane is preparing for the ceremony. I really don't think she can be disturbed just now.'

'Then perhaps I can wait. And see her afterwards.'

His expression darkened, just for an unguarded instant. Then he was all smiles again. 'But of course. We might be quite a while, and I have no idea how tired she may be afterwards. You know how exhausting these sessions can be. But please, wait in the drawing room. Help yourself to a drink, if you like.'

She left the door open enough to be able to see Crowley and his people heading towards the cellar. He had made it clear that Miss Manners was not welcome. She wondered why that was – she'd seen it all before. And worse. She waited until she could hear the faint intonation of the chanting coming from below, then made her way to the door down to the cellar.

There was no way of knowing if everyone was down there,

so she went carefully and quietly, easing the heavy door open. The sound of the chanting immediately increased in volume. She knew that because of the way the stairway turned as it descended she could not be seen from below until she was halfway down the steps. She went as far as she dared and listened for a few moments. Crowley was holding forth – reciting words of power in a guttural, indecipherable tone.

The scene below when she peered cautiously round the corner of the stairway was everything she had expected. The candles arranged round the edge of the chamber. The robed acolytes gathered in a semicircle before the altar stone. Crowley standing on the dais before the altar. And Jane, wearing a white robe so thin and so tight that it hid nothing of her body's form, stretched out on the altar, staring up at the ceiling.

Except… there was something different. It took her a few moments to notice, but something about the way Jane moved her head, the way her shoulders flexed drew Miss Manners' eye – and she saw that her friend was manacled to the altar, thick chains holding her down.

Perhaps it was nothing. Perhaps it was just another of Crowley's sadistic games. But it unsettled her. Miss Manners crept back up the steps and returned to the drawing room, where she waited. Soon she would know. If Crowley let her see Jane, then she could ask if everything was all right. If he didn't let her see the woman…

He still wore his robes when he returned, all apologies. 'I am so sorry. Jane really is very tired. I'm sure you understand.'

She forced a smile as false as Crowley's. 'Absolutely. I'll come back another day. But do please tell her I called.'

He almost managed to hide his relief. 'I will, yes, of course. Let me see you out.'

'There's no need. I know the way.'

He watched her to the front door. She glanced back as she went out, and saw that Crowley had turned and was heading back into the house. Hearing the door shut, he would know she was gone.

She waited in the hall, forcing herself to stand still, counting slowly to ten, before she slipped back along the hallway and down to the cellar.

The candles were still burning, casting an uncertain light across everything. Jane was still there, lying on the altar just as before, wrists and ankles enclosed in bands of dull metal.

'My God, Jane – are you all right?'

Jane struggled to raise her head slightly. 'Penelope? What are you doing here?' Her voice was flat, uninflected.

'I came to see you. Why's he keeping you like this?' She tested the chains, but they were too firmly secured for her to see a way of breaking or removing them.

'I tried to leave. I had... something to do.'

'And he's keeping you here? Like this?'

'For the moment.'

Miss Manners leaned over her, stroked her forehead and was surprised how cool Jane felt. 'I'll get help. I'll come back for you, I promise.'

'Thank you. Penelope?'

'Yes?'

'I haven't told him. But, your friend Pentecross... I heard a message. I keep hearing a message.'

Miss Manners nodded. 'It's all right. We know. We heard it too.'

'It mentioned an axe. Like the one I saw before.'

'We think there are three of them. Look, I'd better go before Crowley or someone finds me down here. But I'll come back. Soon. I promise.'

'Three axes? Is that what *they* want?'

'Yes, we think so. They have one. Another is in Stalingrad, if the message can be believed.'

'And the third?'

'It's all right. Don't worry.' She put her hand to her friend's cheek. 'We have the third one safe. They won't get it.'

Jane's eyes slowly closed. 'That's good. Keep it safe. And come back for me, Penelope. Please come back for me.'

'Of course I will.'

She stayed for another few moments, but Jane seemed to be asleep. Her lips moved slightly, as if she was speaking to someone in a dream.

CHAPTER 32

The last hints of sunlight were fading from the sky when the warden called. He was polite, deferential, but insistent. The woman who answered the door could see several more air raid wardens in the street outside. One was knocking at the next house. She went to find Crowley.

'We're hopeful it won't take long,' the warden said. 'Just got to make sure the thing's safe.'

'We've not had a raid here for months,' Crowley pointed out. The Blitz was over, and air raids on London were sporadic and infrequent now.

'God knows when it was dropped. But it's a big one.' The warden shrugged. 'Could take out most of the street, so the UXB lads reckon anyway.'

There was a steady stream of people coming out of the other houses on Jermyn Street now. The warden glanced back over his shoulder at them. 'We've told people if they wait in the pub in the next street, we'll let you know when it's safe to come back.'

'And do you have any idea when that might be?'

'A few hours at least. But before morning, I'm sure. Good excuse for a couple of pints, if you ask me.'

'And if we don't feel like a couple of pints?'

'Then it's your funeral. Maybe literally.'

Crowley's head turned from side to side as he considered.

Finally, he nodded. 'You'll let us know as soon as it's safe.'

'Don't worry, I don't want to be out here any longer than I have to be. Might even join you for a pint if I get a minute.'

'There's something to look forward to,' Crowley murmured as he went back inside. It was inconvenient, but it couldn't be helped. And the man was right – an unexploded bomb wasn't something to be taken lightly.

'What about Jane?' one of the girls asked as she headed after the others. 'I haven't seen her today.'

'I'll check,' he assured her. They didn't know that Jane was spending all her time down in the cellars now – the price of her attempted desertion. And a safeguard against what she had become. Well, she would probably be safer down in the cellar than anywhere else. The chances of the bomb going off, or causing any damage to the house if it did must be slight. Even so, he collected several of his most treasured books and put them in a leather briefcase to take with him.

'Was she with them?'

Miss Manners shook her head. 'No, Jane must still be inside.'

She and Alban were watching from across the road, hidden in the alleyway between two houses. The people leaving the houses were barely more than silhouettes in the fading light.

'No way of knowing if everyone's out,' Alban said. 'But at least we know Crowley isn't there any more.'

'I didn't see Rutherford,' Miss Manners said. 'He's a thoroughly unpleasant character.'

'Yes,' Alban agreed. 'But don't worry about him. He's...' He hesitated, choosing his words. 'He's no longer involved.'

'No longer involved in what?' Miss Manners asked, catching the tone in Alban's voice.

'In anything. If you take my meaning.' He stepped out of the alleyway and checked the street. 'Looks like it's all clear.'

It was the work of only a few moments for Alban to pick the lock on the front door. He stepped back to let Miss Manners precede him into the house. Alban produced a torch from his pocket, so they didn't need to put the lights on. She led the way to the door down to the cellar. The place was in darkness, but Alban's torch illuminated the stone steps leading down.

At the foot of the stairs, he shone the torch round the chamber and whistled. 'You could store a lot of wine down here, you know.'

'This way.'

Miss Manners set off towards the altar. Alban followed, shining the torch ahead of her. Only when he stepped up on to the raised dais did he see that there was a woman stretched out on the stone.

'Penelope?' the woman said, raising her head slightly as they approached. 'Is that you?' She blinked, dazzled by the torchlight after so long in the dark.

'It's all right. I told you I'd come back. We've come to get you away from here.'

'But – Crowley?'

'Out of the way for now,' Alban said. He examined the chains and manacles holding the woman down. 'Hold the torch for me, and I'll see if I can pick the locks.'

He had expected she would need help standing, let alone getting up the steep steps. But as soon as she was free Jane Roylston seemed to recover her strength.

'I'll take you to your room,' Miss Manners said. 'If we have time?' she checked with Alban.

He nodded. 'Good idea. She can't go out dressed like that. She'll need shoes at least, and a coat probably.'

He waited in the hallway. It wasn't long before the two women were back again, Jane now wearing a Macintosh, buttoned up with the belt pulled tight at her waist.

'I'll lock up,' Alban said, as they left the house. 'We'll give it an hour or so, then tell the warden that the bomb's been defused and everyone can come back again.' He grinned, suddenly looking like a mischievous schoolboy. 'Crowley will be livid.'

Sarah was waiting in the car a couple of streets away. Miss Manners opened the door for Jane to get in the back, then climbed in beside her.

'Do you know Sarah Diamond?'

Jane nodded. 'I think we've met. Or if not, I've certainly seen you.'

Sarah smiled a welcome, and put the car into gear.

'My place is so small,' Miss Manners said, 'and if Crowley comes looking for you it'll be one of the first places he tries. But Sarah has a spare room in her flat.'

Sarah glanced back. 'You're welcome to stay as long as you want,' she said.

'Thank you. You're very kind.'

'It's no problem,' Sarah assured her. 'And don't worry – you'll be quite safe.'

They were getting closer to their prey. They could sense it. They knew that the final key was being dealt with. That just left the key they were seeking, and they crept closer. Every day, their anticipation grew. Soon they would have what they needed.

A dark, bulbous shape clawed its way across a field of rubble. It clambered through a shattered window and into what had been a factory. From inside it stared back out across the devastated landscape, watching the humans picking their way through the debris. There were two soldiers, rifles clutched in their hands, alert for any sound, knowing that death could strike from anywhere at any time. They were probably looking for food.

Behind them, a small shape rose up from the cratered ground, watching the men as they moved cautiously forwards.

The girl was an orphan, her mother killed a few days earlier by men like these. She was too young to tell the difference between Germans and Russians. Too young to care. Men with guns were the enemy. Men with guns had left her alone in this world of death and destruction.

She kept a knife in her boot. Slid it carefully out as she hurried after the men, careful to make no sound. She was only small, but she was strong and every kill made her stronger yet.

The first man turned as she approached. His expression switched from fear to relief to the faintest smile as he saw it was just a child. A girl, no more than maybe nine years old, face grimy with dust and dirt, fair hair lank and darkened by sweat and blood.

Then surprise, and finally fear again as the knife blade gleamed in the pale September sunlight. It was the one thing she kept clean. His grunt of sudden pain as the blade entered his stomach was loud enough for the other man to swing round, his rifle raised.

The girl twisted the knife savagely, her face frowning with the effort. Then she ripped it out again, her hand and arm spattered red.

He had time for one shot. It went wide, hammering into the remains of a wall a hundred yards behind the girl. She hurled herself forwards, catching the soldier off balance, knocking him to the ground. He landed on his back, his head cracked into the rubble blurring his vision.

But he could feel her weight on top of him as he struggled to bring up the rifle again. Could see her unfocused silhouette, arm raised. Could feel the thump of the impact as the blade sliced into his chest, again and again and again.

In the shadows opposite, a dark creature squatted malevolently watching through a single darkened eye. The setting sun caught the mist rising from the soldier's chest, and stained the ruined landscape red.

CHAPTER 33

One way to get to Russia was on an Arctic convoy, delivering military supplies from the UK to Archangel or Murmansk. But after the disastrous losses suffered by convoy PQ17 in July 1942, Guy wasn't convinced this was the safest or the most comfortable route.

'Besides,' Brinkman told him, 'I gather they're suspending convoys now until probably December. And I agree with you – time is of the essence.'

The simpler option, if it could be arranged, was to fly to Moscow.

'The Prime Minister managed, on an American bomber,' Davenport pointed out.

'You are not the Prime Minister,' Brinkman told him.

'Hmmm, but are you sure?' Davenport asked in a passable Churchillian voice.

Brinkman stifled a smile. The last thing Davenport needed was any encouragement. It was with reluctance that Brinkman had agreed that Guy should go to Stalingrad. He was even less persuaded that Davenport should accompany him. But it was hard to argue with Leo, who contended that if anything happened to Guy he was the only one that Hoffman knew and would trust.

'But you don't speak Russian,' Brinkman had told him, exasperated.

'I didn't speak German but you sent me to Wewelsburg. And anyway, Hoffman speaks pretty good English.'

So it was decided. Brinkman would do his utmost to arrange air transport for Guy and Leo to Moscow, and from there they would make their way to Stalingrad.

'And hope the Germans haven't completely overrun the place by the time you get there,' Brinkman said. 'Ismay won't agree to send a plane just for you, so let's hope there's a delegation going anyway and you can hitch a ride.'

'I'll get on to Chivers at the Foreign Office,' Guy said.

'He the chap you used to work for?' Leo asked.

'That's right. He may have some diplomatic contacts out in Moscow who can help us travel on from there.'

'I should think he'll have something to say about being asked for directions from Moscow to Stalingrad,' Leo said with a smile.

Guy laughed. 'I expect he will. But it'll be what he always says: "Rather you than me".'

It turned out there was a flight in a few days that they could get on. After the meticulous and frustratingly slow research of previous weeks everything was now happening very fast, Guy thought. He would have liked to spend more time with Sarah before he left, but she was preoccupied with Jane Roylston.

'It's like she's sort of gone into her shell,' Sarah told him over a quick drink after they left the Station Z offices the evening before his flight to Moscow. 'I don't like to leave her on her own for too long. God knows what those monsters did to her. She hardly speaks. Never smiles.' Sarah reached across the table to put her hand against Guy's cheek. 'I'd like to spend more time with you, really I would.'

He put his hand over hers. 'It's all right. I understand. I hope I shan't be gone long.'

'Come back safe.'

He smiled. 'With Leo looking after me, what can possibly go wrong?'

They kissed long and hard outside the pub, ignoring the looks of passers-by. Then they walked hand in hand to the nearest tube, and went their separate ways, not knowing when or if they'd meet again.

In fact, they met again the next morning, much to Guy's surprise. He had agreed to meet Leo not at the offices but at the British Museum. Elizabeth Archer was already at her desk. And sitting beside her was Sarah.

'Come to see us off?' Guy asked.

'Not exactly.' She glanced at Elizabeth, who stifled a smile. 'I'm coming with you.'

Guy couldn't disguise his surprise. 'To Stalingrad?'

'Just as far as Moscow.'

'But – why? Not that I'm unhappy about it,' he added quickly.

'Blame Elizabeth.'

'I had a word with Colonel Brinkman,' Elizabeth confessed. 'Did you know that the Kremlin has a hidden Archive, rather like this one though on a much smaller scale. Well,' she added, 'I suppose you wouldn't, as very few people do. But I was lucky enough to visit it once, long ago...' Her voice tailed off and she stared into the distance through watery eyes.

'Elizabeth thinks they might have some information about the Vril that could be useful,' Sarah said.

'The problem is, I don't know if Vasilov is still the curator. It was a long time ago.'

'You're still here,' Guy pointed out.

'True enough.'

'So my job is to try to find Vasilov and persuade him to show me anything they have on the Vril.' Sarah picked up an envelope from the desk. 'Elizabeth's written me a letter of introduction.'

'Even so, you'll have to be careful,' Elizabeth warned. 'Trust no one except Vasilov. Since Stalin's rise to power, most of the old guard have been removed. Executed. Knowledge about the Archive was severely restricted even before Stalin arrived. Now...'

'I get the idea,' Sarah said.

'I'm afraid you may have a wasted journey.'

'We won't know unless we try, though,' Guy pointed out. 'What sort of thing is Sarah looking for?'

'Oh, Elizabeth's given me all sorts of clues and pointers,' Sarah said. 'But I'd better get home and pack. I didn't know I was going anywhere until Brinkman called me in this morning and sent me over here.'

'I assume you can write in Russian as well as speak it?' Elizabeth said to Guy.

'I'm not sure I do it quite as well, but passably.'

'Good, then you can make yourself useful and address Sarah's envelope.'

She handed Guy a pen, and Sarah gave him the blank envelope.

'What do you want me to put?'

'Address it to the Senior Archivist of the Kremlin Library.'

Guy did as he was told. 'But the letter inside, I assume, is in English.'

'Vasilov can speak and read English,' Elizabeth told them. 'And if the letter doesn't go to Vasilov, then it probably doesn't matter if it can't be read.'

Guy blew on the ink to make sure it was dry, then handed the envelope back to Sarah.

'Make sure she's safe,' Elizabeth said to Guy when Sarah had gone. 'It may not be as straightforward as she seems to think.'

'I'll look after her,' Guy promised.

'And yourself too.'

Their eyes met for a moment, and just for a second Guy could imagine her as a young woman – perhaps the same age as Sarah. Then she returned her attention to the ancient manuscript laid out on her desk. It seemed to be written in a language consisting entirely of interconnected lines and a few dots. It looked like a cross between Chinese and a child's scribbles. At the side of the desk rested the stone axe-head. She seemed to be using it as a paperweight to hold down a pile of meticulous sketches of the artefact and the symbols carved into it.

'Ancient Morse code?' Guy suggested.

'Linear A,' she said without looking up. 'It's an ancient language only found on Crete.'

'Ancient?'

'Prior to 1500 BC.'

'So when were you in Russia?' he asked.

'Oh, a long time ago. Before all that nasty revolutionary business.'

'And you think this Vasilov might still be there?

'I hope so.' She leaned back. 'He was a good man. Extremely learned and well read. Clever, good at his job. It would be sensible to keep him in charge as long as possible. But,' she went on, 'there's precious little sense in what has happened in Russia. So who knows? We can but hope.'

Leo Davenport joined them a few minutes later. 'You got my souvenir ready?' he asked.

'I thought a souvenir was something you brought back from a trip,' Guy said.

'Pedant,' Leo accused.

'I've got it here,' Elizabeth said, opening a drawer in her desk. She brought out a heavy metal bracelet and handed it to Davenport.

'You're never going to put that on?' Guy said. He knew these bracelets could fix themselves to a wrist, burrowing into the flesh.

'It's all right,' Elizabeth said. 'That's the one you recovered from the Vril base in North Africa. It's useless, inert. Just for show.'

'Which is why I want it, of course,' Davenport said, snapping it closed on his wrist. He held his hand up. 'Rather fetching, don't you think?'

'Very,' Guy said. 'But why bother?'

'It just struck me that we don't know what we'll find in Russia. But run into an Ubermensch, and this might just convince it I'm on its side. At least for a while. Call it insurance.'

Guy nodded. That made sense. 'Just so long as I'm covered as well.'

285

'I'd offer to help,' Leo said, looking over the papers spread out across Elizabeth's desk, 'but sadly we have to be going.'

'That's all right. Penelope Manners said she'd spend the afternoon here with me. She's a bit more tidy and a lot more responsible than you are, Leo.'

'And rather more clued up about all things pertaining to the occult,' Leo agreed.

'Why not ask her if her friend Jane can help too?' Guy said. 'Sarah says the woman's at a loose end, a bit withdrawn. Doing something useful might help.'

Elizabeth nodded. 'I'll suggest it. Now be on your way, you two. I don't want you missing your plane and blaming me.'

'You're sure you'll be OK?' Sarah asked, pulling on her coat. She had to hurry to make it to the plane.

'I'll be fine. I'm feeling a lot better,' Jane told her. 'Really I am. Tell Penelope I'm looking forward to seeing her this evening.'

With Sarah away, Miss Manners had asked Jane to join her for supper.

'Make yourself at home while I'm away. You're welcome to whatever food you can find, but I'm afraid there's precious little. And I've no idea when I'll be back.'

'I'll manage,' Jane promised. 'And thank you.'

Jane watched the door close behind Sarah. Her left hand went unconsciously to her right upper arm, just above the elbow. She could feel the heavy bracelet through the material of her jacket, hidden beneath the sleeve. She waited for several minutes, then she started in Sarah's bedroom.

She emptied each drawer carefully, replacing the contents exactly as they had been once she had looked through them. Once she had searched the drawer thoroughly for any clue as to how much Sarah and her colleagues knew about the Vril, or where the axe-head might be.

Hoffman had long since lost track of time. But it was the evening of 6 September when it found him.

He was working his way through a maze of buildings. They were little more than burned-out shells. The upper floors had collapsed into the basements, leaving the remains of joists and beams like broken ribs above him. There was machine-gun fire from somewhere nearby, the solid crump of explosions from further off.

The axe-head was heavy in his coat pocket as he moved through the buildings – a constant reminder of who he was. He had found no trace of Alina, but she was still uppermost in his thoughts as he searched through the city. Soon he would head for the square and see if the Englishman had arrived yet. It would take him time to get here – if he ever came. But perhaps, just *perhaps* it might be today.

He didn't tire easily, but he stopped to get his bearings, staring out through a shattered hole that used to be a doorway, working out the best route to the Square of Fallen Heroes. He heard they'd renamed it Red Square. He hoped that wasn't true. The fallen heroes of Russia deserved better than that.

A moment longer and he would have been too late. But he turned just as the darkness leaped at him. A black shape coalesced out of the shadows, leaping towards him. Gnarled limbs extended, claws snapping at their ends. A single eye staring hungrily at him. If Hoffman could die, then this was what could kill him. It knew what he was, and what he had.

He lashed out with his arm, out of pure instinct. The sharp spikes down the creature's leg ripped through the sleeve of his heavy coat, but his fist connected with its bloated body and knocked it aside. It landed amongst the dust and rubble, squatting, pulsing, staring back at him, tensing on its limbs ready to leap at him again.

Hoffman grabbed a length of broken, charred wood, maybe a broken floorboard, dragging it out of the rubble. The creature was on him before he could swing it, clamped to his shoulder, its eye staring into his own. A cold, twisted leg clawed and tore at the small rucksack on his back. He dropped the length of wood and dug his fingers into the creature's body, feeling it squelch and squirm as he struggled to tear it away.

It shrieked and squealed as he somehow managed to break its grip. He heard his coat tearing, felt the burning of it lacerating his flesh as he finally dragged the creature off his shoulder and hurled it away.

The creature smacked wetly to the ground, rolling and skidding, legs flexing and skittering as it righted itself. But before it could come at him again, Hoffman had grabbed the wooden strut and slammed it down, sharp end first, like a stake into a vampire's heart.

Its whole body seemed to compress. Then the wood pierced the bulbous, gelatinous flesh, rupturing the creature's body. Dark, viscous liquid squirted out. It shrieked louder, legs drumming desperately on the ground. The eye stared up angrily at Hoffman. As he watched, it clouded over, becoming as dark as the deflated body. The legs stuttered to a halt.

He pulled out the makeshift stake. The creature spasmed once, then seemed to contract, the legs drawn in, curling up like the husk of a dead spider.

Hoffman kicked it out of sight, into a gap in the rubble, tossing the wooden strut after it. He stood for a moment, catching his breath. Then he crouched down and shrugged off the rucksack. He took out the teacup and the pieces of paper, looking for a flat area to spread them out. It was close enough to the right time and this was as good a place as any.

The girl watched from the other side of the building. He saw her as he laid out the paper, weighing each piece down with a stone to stop it blowing away. She realised he had seen her, but she didn't run.

'You can help me if you like,' he called.

Warily, she edged out from the shadows and he saw she was only about nine years old. Maybe less. Her hair had been blonde but was now lank and greasy, and her eyes were incredibly dark.

'You want some company?' he asked. 'I like company. It's no fun being alone, especially here.'

She edged closer, to see what he was doing as he set down the upturned teacup in the middle of the circle of letters. He leaned forward and put his finger on top of the cup, ready to move it. She still said nothing. Maybe she was too traumatised to speak – that wouldn't be surprising.

'I won't hurt you,' he said quietly. 'I only hurt men with guns.'

Her face cracked into a half smile. She sat down next to Hoffman, and reached out to put her own finger on the top of the cup next to his.

CHAPTER 34

The previous year, the Germans had got to within sixty miles of Moscow. But Russian reinforcements brought in to defend the city drove the enemy back. There was still danger, but the Germans were over 150 miles away, and increasingly preoccupied with the battle for Stalingrad.

'Not the place I'd choose for my holidays,' Paul Tustrum told Guy and Leo.

Tustrum was the man Chivers had told Guy to contact. He was a veteran of the diplomatic service, in his mid fifties but fit and healthy with a full head of greying hair and an impressive moustache.

Sarah was with them, sitting in Tustrum's office at the British Embassy. He had arranged for her letter to be delivered to the Kremlin – though he made it clear he had no control over what happened to it once there. He had also provided Sarah with a small room on the residential floor in the Embassy building. As Tustrum apologetically pointed out, it was hardly the Ritz, but there was a bed, a small wardrobe, and access to a shared bathroom. Guy and Leo got to share a room on the same floor for their single night's stay.

Warned of their arrival, Tustrum had already investigated how best to get to Stalingrad. 'You'll have to loop round behind the city,' he explained. 'Stalingrad's south-east of us here, and the only way in is from the east, across the river

Volga. The Germans control everything on this side.'

'I hope we don't need to swim across,' Guy said.

'I hope so too,' Tustrum said. He smiled. 'No, they resupply the city across the river. So long as the Red Army controls the landing stages in the city side, they can keep ferrying in men and munitions. Food too, though they seem less worried about that.'

'Are there still civilians there?' Sarah asked.

'Oh yes. Fewer every day, of course. Stalin could have evacuated them, but he reckons the soldiers will fight harder if they're defending real people. Plus he had them digging defences and setting up barricades right up until Jerry arrived. Then the Luftwaffe bombed the hell out of the place and created far more effective barricades of their own. We'll fly you down tomorrow morning on a freight plane and you can catch a ride across the river on an ammunition box or something.' His smile widened. 'Nothing safer.'

'Sounds delightful,' Leo told him. 'So, do we get to have dinner with Uncle Joe before we leave?'

'I wouldn't recommend it,' Tustrum said. 'Between you and me, you're safer on that ammunition box.'

'Not a pleasant character?' Guy asked. That was certainly received opinion about Stalin.

'This is a man who entertains himself by listening to records of dogs barking,' Tustrum said. 'And right now he's pretty hacked off with us. The Arctic convoys have been suspended, though he sort of understands why. He's happy that the Yanks have agreed the "Germany First" policy rather than concentrating their attention on the Far East and Japan. But he's impatient. He thinks we should be invading mainland Europe in the next few months and certainly by the summer of next year, rather than pissing about in Northern Africa and making noises about Italy.'

'I guess he wants the pressure taken off,' Sarah said.

'He certainly does. They're suffering huge losses – the enemy too, I'm happy to say. But if casualties in Europe are in the thousands, here they're in hundreds of thousands. Millions even. And the very worst of it, I'm sure you'll be pleased to hear, is in Stalingrad.'

'I hope we won't be staying long,' Leo said. 'So, any good news for us?'

'I've got you a street map, as requested,' Tustrum said. 'But I doubt it'll bear much relation to what you actually find when you get there.'

Sarah went with Tustrum to see Guy and Leo off on their plane. It was early in the morning and she had hardly slept. Her bed was unfamiliar and uncomfortable. She almost dozed off in the car back to the Embassy. She had already decided to return to her room on the pretext of working and try to catch up on her sleep.

Tustrum dropped Sarah at the front of the building and then went on to park the car. As she entered the foyer, the woman on the front desk called Sarah over.

'Miss Diamond?'

'That's right. Is there a message?' Could Vasilov have got back to her already? Elizabeth's letter of introduction had only been delivered the previous afternoon.

'Not exactly, miss. Someone to see you.' The woman nodded to a young woman sitting in the waiting area nearby.

She was in her early twenties with dark hair and narrow features. She looked pale and undernourished, but there was a hint of fire in her eyes as she came over.

'Sarah?' she asked in a heavily accented voice. She sounded nervous, glancing round as she spoke.

Sarah nodded. 'That's me. Who are you?'

'Sarah,' the woman repeated, heading back to the empty waiting area, obviously intending Sarah to follow her.

'What is it you want?' Sarah asked.

The woman sat down and gestured for Sarah to sit opposite. She said something in Russian – a question.

'If you're asking if I understand you, then no, I don't.' She shook her head emphatically to make the point.

The woman frowned. Then she pointed at herself. 'Larisa.'

'I'm guessing that's your name,' Sarah said. 'And that this could be a long conversation.'

But the conversation, such as it was, had finished. Larisa handed Sarah a folded piece of paper. She watched as Sarah opened it and read the brief note inside.

```
    I  have  received  the  letter  of
Elizabeth  Archer.  Forgive  me  for
not  coming  to  you  in  person  but  my
absence  would  be  noted.  Our  meeting
should  not  be  noticed  if  I  am  to
help  you  as  Elizabeth  asks.
    Please  meet  Larisa  tonight  at  9.
She  will  wait  for  you  in  the  narrow
street  opposite  the  Embassy.  She
will  bring  you  to  me.
    I  hope  you  will  have  news  of
Elizabeth  and  that  she  is  in  good
health.  Also  George,  to  whom  I  owe
my  life  and  more.
```

It was signed 'Feyodor Vasilov'.

Sarah refolded the piece of paper. She had no idea who George was, but she would worry about that when she saw Vasilov later.

Larisa was watching Sarah as she read the letter, waiting for her response. She raised her eyebrows. 'Sarah?'

Sarah nodded. 'I'll be there,' she said.

In response, Larisa stood up. When Sarah stood up too, the young woman offered her hand. There was the first hint of a smile on her face as they shook hands.

She ate as little as Hoffman did, and she never spoke. But she evidently understood what he said to her. They evolved their own way of dealing with the Germans. Meeting the little girl had impressed upon him more than anything the horror and the injustice of what the Germans were doing to the city. To Alina's city – *his* city.

Every day he checked the square. Every evening he and the girl found a secluded place to hold their séance and send the message again. And every day they sought out enemy soldiers to kill.

They weren't the only ones of course. The conflict had moved to a new phase and General Chuikov was sending many more snipers out into the city. They waited on rooftops and in shattered buildings, picking off the enemy. The constant fear and demoralising uncertainty their presence instilled was far more effective than their firepower.

Hoffman and the girl were more opportunistic. Whereas a sniper set up his – or her – position and waited for a target to present itself, Hoffman simply killed any of the enemy he came across. The girl – small and agile – provided a distraction. Hoffman approached and killed. Occasionally he was wounded, but the girl seemed to take it for granted that he was indestructible.

'I'm waiting for a friend,' he explained in answer to her curious glance as they watched the square over the top of a broken wall. 'I'm not sure he will come, but I think he will. I hope he will.'

She leaned her chin on her hands and watched with him as the sun dipped down.

'It's the same friend as we send the messages to. I have something for him.'

She looked up at this, head tilted, questioning.

'Oh, don't worry. It's well hidden. Only I know where it is.'

She nodded thoughtfully, and returned her attention to the square. Hoffman put his hand on her shoulder – she was so small, so fragile-looking and yet so resilient. He wondered what had happened to her that was so awful she couldn't bear to speak of it. Or anything else.

'I did carry it with me,' he explained. She seemed to like to hear his voice, maybe because she had been robbed of her own. 'But there are others who want it. I don't want them to get it. One of them found me. I had to kill... him. But if I hadn't, they would have got it, the thing I have hidden. I want my friend to have it. But better that it stays buried for ever here in the rubble than *they* get it.'

She heard them before he did. He had been too busy talking, and hadn't checked over his shoulder. The girl turned abruptly, eyes widening.

Hoffman turned just in time to dodge the rifle butt that slammed into the wall beside his head. He grabbed the gun and wrenched it away from the German soldier. Ammunition was valuable. If the Germans could kill without wasting a bullet, that was preferable. And there was the danger of someone hearing the shot.

The second soldier grabbed the girl, dragging her back, laughing. Hoffman couldn't let them take her, couldn't lose her. He had no qualms about wasting another man's bullet, didn't care who heard. He turned the rifle and fired in one movement. The soldier beside him was slammed backwards, feet skidding from under him on the uneven ground.

Hoffman stepped over the body, ignored the foaming blood, the rasping curses, the hand that clawed at his ankle as he passed. Focused entirely on the second soldier as the man produced a pistol and pressed it to the girl's temple. Hoffman shouldered the rifle, but he didn't dare shoot for fear of hitting the girl. The soldier swung the pistol, aiming it at Hoffman, grinning as he pulled the trigger. Hoffman didn't move. He smiled back.

The moment the shot rang out, Hoffman ran towards it. The bullet ripped into his shoulder, knocking him off his stride. He stumbled slightly, but kept running. The soldier was about to fire again, but the girl ducked out from under his arm, grabbing his wrist and wrenching it sideways so the shot went wide. Somehow she tripped the man, knocking him to the ground. As he fell, she twisted the gun from his hand.

He landed on his back, staring up at them, his face now a mask of disbelief and fear. He had underestimated what a child could do in order to survive. The girl looked up at Hoffman. She held out her hands, offering him the pistol. He shook his head.

'It's all right. You can do it.'

The shot echoed off the shattered walls. The girl took his hand and together the two survivors walked away through the rubble.

CHAPTER 35

She took the Underground to Holborn and walked the few hundred yards from there to the British Museum. Miss Manners had told her to come to the main entrance. Miss Manners did not tell Jane the details of where they were going as she led her friend down into the vault beneath the building. There was no need for her to know anything more than she was helping with some research into an ancient artefact held by the Museum.

If Jane was surprised to be taken into such an enormous subterranean storage area, filled with crates, boxes, display cabinets and bookshelves all packed with artefacts and manuscripts, she gave no sign of it. Miss Manners was happy for her to believe this was a typical storage area for the Museum, although in fact it was nothing of the sort.

Elizabeth Archer was expecting them, waiting at her desk in the middle of the maze of shelves and storage. She had already prepared a collection of volumes and manuscripts that were worth checking for any reference to the axes and the associated legends, or for the symbols carved into the artefact. It helped that Jane knew something about the axe already.

'So far, we haven't made an awful lot of progress,' Elizabeth confessed. 'I can't even tell you what sort of stone the thing is made from. In fact, I'm beginning to think it might not be cut from stone at all, but manufactured.'

'Really?' Miss Manners said. 'You think it might have been cast rather than carved?'

'It's possible. The material seems more like a durable ceramic in some ways. And it is so remarkably well preserved.'

'May I see it?' Jane asked.

'Of course,' Elizabeth told her. 'I'll get it later, I have to put some of these notes and drawings away in the same section when I've finished with them.'

They worked steadily and quietly through the morning. Jane took meticulous notes on any reference she felt might be relevant and added them to the notes that Miss Manners and Elizabeth Archer were compiling. It was almost noon when they were joined by Sergeant Green.

'I've just come from the meeting,' he told Miss Manners. 'Alban's on his way too. He took notes which the colonel wants typed up – a copy for us and one for Alban and MI5. I'm afraid I volunteered your services as everyone else is rather under the gun.'

'That's all right,' she told him. 'I could do with a break. I have a few things to finish here, but I'll come up with you and see Alban. You can tell me anything important on the way.'

She excused herself from Elizabeth and assured Jane she would be back soon. 'Perhaps we can find lunch somewhere before I go back to the office.'

'I'd like that,' Jane agreed.

As soon as Miss Manners and the sergeant were gone, Jane went over to Elizabeth.

'How are you getting on?' the older woman asked. 'What I've looked at so far is very precise, very useful.'

'It would be a help if I could see the axe-head now,' Jane said. 'It might focus my thinking, so I can decide what's actually relevant.'

Elizabeth put down the manuscript she had been examining. 'Of course. I'm sorry, I meant to fetch it ages ago. Time rather runs away with you down here, especially when you're busy. I get lost in my own little world, I'm afraid.'

'That's quite all right,' Jane said, following Elizabeth

down a narrow passageway between two sets of bookcases. 'I understand.'

The axe was in a wooden box on a shelf, anonymous amongst other boxes. Elizabeth lifted it down, setting it on the top of a nearby packing case. She opened the lid, to reveal the stone – or possibly ceramic – axe-head nesting inside on a bed of straw.

She turned to say something to Jane, but froze. The change in the woman was startling as she stared fixedly at the box. Her eyes were wide and dark and all colour and expression seemed to have gone from her face.

'Are you all right?' Elizabeth asked. 'Do you want to get some air? It can get quite stuffy down here.'

Jane did not reply. Instead she shoved Elizabeth roughly aside and reached into the box for the axe-head.

'Careful!' Elizabeth caught hold of a bookcase to keep her balance. 'What are you doing? I think you'd better put that back.'

'Keep out of my way,' Jane said, voice level and devoid of intonation. She lifted the axe-head, examining it carefully. 'I don't want to kill you. But I will if you try to stop me.'

'Put it back,' Elizabeth said firmly. 'Now!'

In response, Jane grabbed the front of Elizabeth's blouse, dragging the old woman onto the tips of her toes. Elizabeth clutched at the young woman's arm, trying desperately to break free. Her hand closed on something hard around Jane's upper arm. Even through the material of blouse and jacket, Elizabeth knew at once what it was. Then the younger woman hurled her aside. She crashed into the bookcase, and slumped dazed to the floor.

The next thing she knew, Miss Manners was helping her to her feet, face etched with concern.

'What happened? Did you fall?'

'Jane...' Elizabeth gasped. Her mouth was dry and her head throbbing.

'I passed her just now. She said you told her to get some air.'

Elizabeth shook her head, her vision blurring with the effort. 'No – she took the axe.'

'What? Jane?'

'I think she's possessed. Or worse.' Elizabeth pushed Miss Manners' supporting hand gently away, standing on her own. 'She's wearing a bracelet.'

'Oh no,' Miss Manners breathed. 'What have they done to her? What did she do to you?'

'I'll be fine – just get after her. Get that axe-head back. Go on!'

By the time she reached the top of the stairs again, Miss Manners was out of breath. She forced herself to keep going. There was no sign of Jane as she hurried down the main corridor to the museum entrance, then out and down the steps into the courtyard outside.

At last she caught sight of her friend, just turning out onto the quiet street. And parked close by was Alban's car. She thought he'd have gone, but Sergeant Green was talking to him through the open window.

'Green!' she shouted. 'Green – stop her!'

The sergeant straightened up, looking round to see who was calling him.

'Stop Jane – she's got the axe.' She pointed at the figure a few yards away from the car.

At once Green was on the move, running after the woman. For his burly figure, he was fast. Miss Manners reached the car just as Green reached Jane.

'What's going on?' Alban asked.

'I wish I knew.' She bent over, hands on her knees as she struggled to get her breath back. 'Jane took the axe-head. She must be controlled by the Vril.'

'Good God.'

In the street ahead of them, Green had grabbed Jane by the shoulder and turned her round to face him. She lashed out, her hand holding the heavy axe-head. It crashed into the side of Green's head, knocking him sideways. But he kept hold of her shoulder, grabbing her wrist with his other hand to stop her striking him again.

It was an unequal struggle. She shrugged off his grip, wrenching her arm free. With her other hand she grabbed the front of Green's uniform jacket, hoisting him off the ground like he weighed no more than a child's doll. Then she hurled him away from her. Green hit the ground hard, cartwheeling across the pavement.

Jane turned and walked quickly away. She did not look back.

Alban swore. 'More than just controlled,' he said. 'Converted. Mind out.'

Miss Manners stepped away from the car as Alban slammed it into gear. The engine roared as he accelerated down the road. Jane was just stepping onto the pavement when she seemed to hear the car, and turned to look back.

A split second later the bonnet hammered into her, knocking her through the air. She hit the front of a building on the other side of the pavement, and slid down the wall to land in a crumpled heap on the ground. Her head lolled sideways across her shoulder. The axe-head slid from her hand.

Alban tore open the car door, running to where she had fallen. The few other people on the pavement stared in shock and horror. But before Alban reached her, Jane's body jerked back into life. Her head straightened. She reached for the axe-head, grasping it tightly, then got to her feet as if nothing had happened.

Before Alban could get to her, she turned and ducked into a narrow alleyway between two buildings.

'Come on!' Miss Manners urged, catching up with Alban. 'We'll have to follow her on foot.'

Alban glanced back at his car – half on and half off the pavement. Behind it, Sergeant Green was staggering uncertainly to his feet.

'Green – look after my car!' Alban yelled. He didn't wait for a reply, but raced after Miss Manners down the alley.

'I am so glad I wore sensible shoes today,' she told him as they ran.

The alleyway came out on New Oxford Street. It was busier here, and it took them a few moments to spot Jane amongst the other pedestrians. She was cutting across the road, heading towards Shaftesbury Avenue.

'Have you any idea what we'll do when we catch up with her?' Alban asked.

'None. But I'm open to suggestions.'

Jane had quickened her pace. Either she knew they were following, or there was some urgency to her journey.

'Where the hell can she be going?' Alban wondered. They had to run now just to keep her in sight.

'Trafalgar Square?'

'Or Charing Cross. Maybe she's catching a train.'

'Not very likely.'

Alban forced a short laugh. 'None of this is very likely.'

They almost lost her at Charing Cross. Miss Manners wondered if she really had gone into the station, but then they spotted her heading down a narrow street to the side. St Martin's Lane.

'The river?' Alban suggested.

'We'll soon know.'

They found themselves at Embankment tube station, caught in a tide of passengers spilling out onto the street. They managed to force their way through, and emerged on the Victoria Embankment beside the river.

There was no sign of Jane Roylston.

'Damn!' Alban thumped his fist down on the stone wall running along the side of the river. 'Where did she go?'

The Embankment was busy, but they should be able to see her among the other people.

'What do you think?' Alban said 'You go one way and I'll go the other? Maybe one of us will spot her. Or I can head back up to the station and find a telephone. We could get a search team here in half an hour maybe.'

'I don't think there's any need for that,' Miss Manners told him. Her voice was quiet, but strained. 'She's down there, look.'

Alban turned to see where she was pointing. Further along there was a landing stage. There was no boat, but steps led up to the stage, and then down the other side, into the water.

Jane Roylston was walking slowly, calmly, deliberately down the steps on the other side of the wall. As they watched, she reached the river. Her feet disappeared below the surface. And she kept walking, kept descending.

'Jane!' Miss Manners yelled.

Jane glanced up. Maybe she smiled – it was too far away to tell. But she didn't hesitate. The water was up to her waist. Then her chest.

Finally, the murky waters of the Thames closed over Jane Roylston's head, as if she had never been there.

CHAPTER 36

The day passed slowly. Sarah tried to catch up on her sleep, and dozed for most of the afternoon. But her mind kept coming back to the meeting with Larisa planned for this evening.

Could it be a trap? She had no way of knowing if the letter was actually from Vasilov. But surely, she reasoned, if the Russians for some reason wanted to trap her, then they would have sent someone who spoke English, who could persuade her. She didn't want to have to explain to Tustrum what she was doing, except in the vaguest terms. But it seemed prudent to let him know she was meeting Larisa.

Predictably, Tustrum advised caution. 'It could be genuine,' he agreed as they sat in the Embassy dining room making the best of a thin soup and rather dry bread. 'In fact, it most likely is. This all seems too ad hoc and amateur for an official set-up.'

'That's what I thought,' Sarah said.

'And the Russians want to keep us sweet,' Tustrum went on. 'If they don't want to help you, then the easiest thing for them would be to ignore your letter to this Vasilov. Do nothing. But even so, I'd take care.' He considered for a moment. 'Are you armed?'

Sarah shook her head. That wasn't an option that had occurred to her.

'I'll get you a gun,' Tustrum said. 'Something small you can keep hidden. I assume…?' He let the question hang.

'Oh, I can shoot,' Sarah assured him. 'I've done the SOE training too, so I can look after myself.'

'Let's hope so. And good luck. Let me know when you're back safe and sound, won't you?'

She could feel the reassuring weight of the small pistol Tustrum had provided in the small of her back where she had it tucked into the waistband of her trousers. Her grey coat covered it. The evening was cold, so Sarah wore a sweater as well. She hoped it would cover the bulge of the gun if she took the coat off.

The street outside the Embassy was deserted as she crossed the road. There was a hint of rain in the air. Like London, the city was in near-darkness. There was only one street off the main road that Vasilov could have meant. It was little more than an alleyway between two high brick-built structures. Sarah peered into the narrow opening, but it was impossible to see anything in the darkness. She should have asked Tustrum for a flashlight.

The ground was uneven, and she couldn't see more than a yard or two ahead. Should she wait, or continue down the alley? Was it safe to call out?

She decided to risk it. 'Larisa?'

Silence.

Sarah turned back towards the main road, wondering how long she should wait before she gave up and went back to the Embassy. A dark shape moved across the entrance to the alley, barely more than a shadow. Something brushed against Sarah's arm, and she stifled a cry.

'Sarah,' a voice breathed, close to her ear. Then a gloved hand took hers.

She recognised the woman's voice and, relieved, allowed herself to be led down the alley. In fact, it wasn't far before they emerged into another street. There was enough light now to see Larisa's reassuring smile.

'Where are we going?' Sarah asked. But she got no reply.

They passed few other people, and Sarah wondered if there was a curfew. Tustrum hadn't mentioned it. Their destination became apparent long before they arrived. Its towers and turrets stark against the night sky, the Kremlin was far larger than Sarah had imagined. How many people, she wondered, had admired the sight of it as they approached and then never left? Would she be one of them?

Larisa led the way to a side entrance. They passed through a small entrance hall where a guard sat behind a desk. He glanced up at them, and nodded – obviously recognising Larisa. They exchanged some brief words in Russian, and the guard nodded for them to go on. Sarah wondered what the woman had told him, who the guard thought she was.

The part of the Kremlin they were in was like a cross between a castle and a country house. The corridors were bare, the rooms they passed sparsely furnished. But the floor was polished marble and the ceilings were adorned with ornate plasterwork.

Finally, Larisa opened a heavy wooden door and gestured for Sarah to go inside. She found herself in a large room lined with books. A huge chandelier hung from the ceiling, casting a glow across the centre of the room. A cluster of several small armchairs was grouped round a table beneath the chandelier. The only other light came from a lamp on a small desk in the corner of the room – the man sitting behind it almost lost in the huge space. He rose to his feet as Sarah entered, Larisa closing the door behind them.

'So, you are Sarah,' he said, his voice thick with the Russian accent.

'That's right.'

A few wisps of white hair clung to the man's head. He was shorter than Sarah, and seemed shorter still because he stooped, his shoulders hunched. As he approached, Sarah could see that he was ancient, his face lined with experience and his movements dulled with age. But his eyes were bright and alert.

He reached out to shake Sarah's hand. 'I am Feyodor Vasilov.'

Larisa said something in Russian, and Vasilov nodded and replied.

'Larisa is my granddaughter,' he explained to Sarah. 'I am afraid she has never learned to speak English. But please, take a seat. We have much to discuss, I am sure. Take a seat,' he repeated, gesturing to one of the armchairs. 'And then I have things to show you.'

As soon as they were all seated, the old man asked, 'How much has Elizabeth told you about me?'

'Not very much,' Sarah admitted. 'She didn't know if you would still be here.'

Vasilov shrugged. 'Life goes on.' He leaned forward, glancing at Larisa before asking: 'And how is George?'

Sarah had wondered how best to reply to this. She had decided that it was probably best to be truthful. 'I'm afraid I have no idea who George is.'

The old man nodded slowly, his expression unreadable. 'But you know Elizabeth, yes?'

'Of course. She said that you have a similar role to hers. I assume you are some sort of curator?' Elizabeth had told her as much, but she wanted to keep the conversation going.

'Our own archive here in the Kremlin is rather smaller than Elizabeth's, or so I believe from how she described it to me.'

'When did you meet her?'

'Oh, many years ago now. Many many years. So much has changed. And yet, some things remain the same.' He stood up, apparently invigorated by their brief conversation. 'But Elizabeth asks, in her letter, that I give you any information I can about what she calls the Vril.'

'They live underground,' Sarah explained, not knowing how much the letter had told him. 'Creatures of darkness—'

He waved her to silence. 'Then underground and into darkness is where we must go.'

He turned to speak rapidly to Larisa, who nodded. She went over to the desk where her grandfather had been working, and opened a drawer. She returned with three torches, handing one to Vasilov and another to Sarah.

'If anyone speaks to you, let one of us reply,' Vasilov warned as they left the room. He closed and locked the door behind them.

'Where are we going?' Sarah asked.

'First, to the Arsenal Tower, and then you will see.'

There were as few people inside the Kremlin as out on the streets. Or at least, there were in the secluded, barely lit passageways that Vasilov led them along. They descended a stone staircase, and continued along a narrow passageway with whitewashed walls. It wasn't long before Sarah was hopelessly lost, with no idea how she might ever find her way out again on her own if she had to.

'The Kremlin is like a city,' Vasilov told her. 'Built for the whole population of Moscow to retreat into and take shelter if necessary.'

Finally they reached another stairway, this one made of iron, spiralling down into the cellarage. At the bottom was a large iron gate, secured with a heavy padlock. As Larisa opened it, Vasilov explained they were below the Arsenal Tower.

'There are many tunnels beneath the Kremlin, and several converge below this tower. There are underground rivers too, all manner of secret ways. Most of them have been blocked off now, for security reasons.'

The other side of the gate was a wide, low passage. There was no light here, so they turned on the torches. Larisa and Vasilov concentrated their beams on a large flagstone a short way along the passage. Under the old man's instructions, Sarah helped Larisa slide the flagstone to one side, revealing a dark cavity below.

'Down there?' she said.

'There is more room than there seems.' He smiled. 'Don't worry, I shall go first.'

In fact, there were steps down, leading into another tunnel.

But the opening was narrow, and Sarah felt the gun tucked into her waistband catch on the edge as she climbed down. She paused for a moment at the bottom to reposition it. The walls, floor, and arched roof were lined with white stone that almost glowed under the glare of the torch beams.

'There are other ways in,' Vasilov said as he led the way down the tunnel. 'But this way is unguarded. Even Stalin does not know it exists.'

'We're avoiding the guards?'

'The less they know the better,' Vasilov said.

Larisa caught her grandfather's arm, speaking rapidly and urgently to him. The old man frowned and glanced back at Sarah before answering.

'What is it?'

'Larisa is worried that there may be guards at the Archive. But I have assured her this is unlikely. They guard the entranceways, the other access tunnels, but not the Archive itself.'

'The Archive? Like Elizabeth's department at the British Museum?'

'It was a library originally,' Vasilov explained as he led the way along the tunnel.

The air was damp and close. Somewhere Sarah could hear water dripping.

'Don't the books get damp?'

'The Archive itself is dry enough. But you are right, it is a worry, especially as the books are so old. They come from Constantinople.' He glanced back at Sarah, who shrugged.

'Sorry, ancient history isn't really my thing.'

'The city fell in 1453,' Vasilov explained. 'The library was said to be unsurpassed. But the only books that survived were taken by the Emperor's niece Sofia, and brought here to Moscow.'

'Why Moscow?' Sarah wondered.

'She married a Russian prince. Her grandson was cruel and sadistic, but also learned and well read. He added to the library, and kept it hidden and secret. He created these tunnels by diverting underground rivers. Anyone who knew of the library's location was put to death.'

'That seems a bit extreme,' Sarah said.

'They did not call him Ivan the Terrible for nothing.'

They walked on in silence for a while.

'For many years the library was lost,' Vasilov said. 'Most people think it still is, if it ever really existed. But we maintain it, and we have added to it, as you shall soon see.'

The tunnel ended in two enormous metal doors. Vasilov produced a large key, which he handed to Larisa, who unlocked one of the doors. It swung open easily. Vasilov went inside first. Sarah saw him reaching for a switch on the side wall, and a light came on overhead.

The chamber it illuminated had been made by blocking off a section of the tunnel. It extended into the distance, fading into darkness and shadow. Wooden shelves lined the walls, stacked with metal strong boxes. The floor was a maze of wooden crates and packing cases. Sarah could see an immediate and obvious similarity with the vault beneath the British Museum, although this was on a smaller scale. And unlike the Museum vault, everything here seemed to be packed away, nothing left out on display. She guessed this was to protect the artefacts, books and papers from the damp, as Vasilov had said.

Larisa pushed past Sarah, heading for one of the nearest crates. She murmured something to Vasilov as she passed, and he nodded grimly.

'This is impressive,' Sarah said.

'And now that you are here,' Vasilov said, his voice suddenly harsh and angry, 'now that we have brought you where you wanted to come, I think you should tell us who you really are and what you want here.'

'You know who I am,' Sarah said, surprised at his sudden change of tone.

'We know nothing about you, except what was in the letter that is supposed to come from Elizabeth Archer.'

'It does,' Sarah protested. 'She gave it to me herself. She's a friend, or at least a colleague.'

Vasilov was shaking his head. Larisa reached into a crate and pulled out a revolver. She trained it on Sarah, gesturing for her to put her hands up.

'You claim Elizabeth sent you,' Vasilov went on. 'Yet you do not know George. And you have a gun. Don't deny it, Larisa saw you reach for it earlier.'

'I wasn't reaching for it,' Sarah protested. 'Look, let's just talk about this, can we?'

Larisa was right in front of her now. The gun held steady, aiming at Sarah's chest.

'Take off your coat,' Vasilov ordered. 'Carefully. Slowly.'

Sarah did as he said, dropping her coat over the nearest crate. The old man reached behind her and removed the small handgun Tustrum had given her. He put the gun down on top of a nearby crate.

'Now,' he said. 'Tell us the truth, or Larisa will shoot you.'

But Sarah barely heard. She was staring past the young woman, into the darkness beyond, watching as a patch of shadow coalesced into a shape. Long, crooked limbs reached out over the top of a crate. A bloated, glistening mass hauled itself up, crouching behind Larisa's shoulder.

'Tell us,' Vasilov demanded. 'Now!'

Larisa braced herself, legs apart, holding the gun in both hands ready to fire.

Close behind her, the hideous creature shivered and tensed as it prepared to launch itself at the woman.

CHAPTER 37

They crossed under cover of darkness. There was a near-constant stream of boats ferrying men and equipment across the Volga to the wooden landing stages on the other side of the river. As they approached, Guy's senses were assaulted by the city: the constant noise of gunfire and explosions; the flashes of light and guttering flames; the smell of cordite, smoke, decay, and death.

'I have to confess I've never been in a real battle before,' Davenport said.

'This isn't like any battle I've been in,' Guy told him.

They were wearing Russian army uniforms, armed with pistols rather than rifles. Neither of them intended to kill anyone at long range, and up close if they needed to defend themselves a pistol was likely to prove more useful and effective.

An officer they knew only as Malinov was responsible for getting them across the river and into the city. He shook hands with them in the shadow of the embankment. Several trucks were lined up under cover of the high bank, huge sets of rocket launchers arranged on a framework on the back of each, ready to fire.

'Katyusha,' Malinov explained. 'We reverse them back, fire the rockets over the bank at the German positions, then drive forward under cover again before the rockets have even hit.'

'That's a lot of firepower,' Guy said. 'But why the name?' Katyusha was a form of Katya, equivalent to Katherine in English.

'Katyusha is a girl in a traditional story, who waits for her lover to return from the war.' He shrugged. 'I believe the Germans call them "Stalin's Organ" because of the arrangement of the pipes and the God-awful noise it makes when it fires.'

Davenport laughed when Guy translated. 'Well,' Davenport said, 'I guess it rather emphasises the differences between the two peoples, doesn't it? The Germans with their prosaic bombast and the Russians with their romantic notions of pining lovers.'

Guy told Malinov what Leo had said, and the Russian grinned. 'They don't like the music we play on them, that's for sure. Now, I have work to do. Maybe I'll see you on your way back. If you come back,' he added. 'I have to tell you that most people don't.'

He pointed them in the rough direction of the Square of Fallen Heroes, then returned to supervise the unloading.

Negotiating the ruined streets took longer than Guy would have imagined. As far as possible they kept to the darkest areas, cutting through the empty shells of half-demolished buildings. It was hard to imagine that anyone still lived in here, but occasionally they caught sight of other shadows flitting through the darkness – Russian soldiers, or civilians struggling to survive?

'Abandon hope,' Davenport muttered at one point. 'Dante had it easy compared to the people here.'

The Vril moved fast. It launched itself from the crate at Larisa. But Sarah was faster. She dived towards the young woman. Larisa fired. The shot grazed past Sarah and ricocheted off the metal door behind her.

Sarah's shoulder collided with Larisa, knocking her backwards – out of the way of the Vril. The creature landed on the floor nearby. Vasilov cried out in surprise and terror, backing away. He stumbled, falling to his knees, staring in incredulous horror.

Larisa hadn't seen the hideous shape that almost hit her. Her eyes were full of rage as she struggled to hold on to the gun. But Sarah's training had kicked in, and she twisted the handgun easily out of Larisa's grasp. She rolled away from the woman, landing on her back and bringing the gun up.

The Vril was moving again – scuttling rapidly across the floor towards them. Larisa did see it now, and screamed. Her hands came up in front of her face as the grotesque shape leaped straight at her.

The bullet stopped it in mid-air, knocking the creature sideways. Its ghastly, inhuman scream echoed round the chamber. A trail of dark, viscous liquid hung from its body as it landed awkwardly on the ground, smearing across the pale stone floor.

Sarah fired again. Two shots in rapid succession hammered into the Vril's bloated body. The first punctured it, sending out a spray of the dark liquid. The second ripped into the damaged body and out the other side, bursting it like a balloon full of brackish water. Larisa screamed again as the dark sludge spattered across her hands and body. Vasilov crawled across to her, speaking quickly but nervously.

'It's all right,' Sarah said. But she turned slowly, checking every shadow for more of the creatures. She clicked her torch back on, holding it aligned with the gun, checking the furthest, darkest corners for any sign of movement.

Nothing.

'You asked me about the Vril,' she said, putting the torch down and kneeling beside Vasilov and Larisa. 'Well, now you know.' She held the gun out to Larisa. 'Yours, I think.'

But Larisa shook her head, wiping her shaking hands on her coat. Sobbing quietly in her grandfather's arms.

'I know you don't trust me,' Sarah said. 'And I guess I understand that. But everything I told you is true. That letter I sent you really is from Elizabeth Archer.'

Vasilov was smoothing Larisa's hair, still speaking gently

and quietly to her.

'I don't know who George is,' Sarah went on. 'If he used to work with Elizabeth, then I'm sorry but I've never met him. There is someone who helps her. Keeps himself to himself. He's quite old, but she calls him "Young Eddie" not George.'

Vasilov looked up at that. 'Young Eddie,' he repeated. 'He would not be so young now. But how can you not know George Archer? He is the Curator of the Department of Unclassified Artefacts.'

And suddenly it made sense. 'Elizabeth's husband?'

'Of course.'

'I'm sorry.' There was no easy way to tell the old man. 'Elizabeth has never told me her husband's name, or if she has mentioned it, I didn't remember. But – Elizabeth is a widow now.'

Vasilov looked up at her, a frown creasing his already wrinkled face. He wiped his hand across his eyes and murmured something in Russian.

'I'm sorry,' Sarah said.

'So am I,' Vasilov said. 'And grateful,' he added. 'For the life of my granddaughter.'

They helped Larisa to her feet and she sat on one of the metal strong boxes, still breathing heavily. She seemed to notice the mess down the front of her coat for the first time, and quickly pulled it off, throwing it away from her.

'That beast,' Vasilov said. 'The Vril. What did it want here?'

Sarah shook her head. 'I have no idea. I wasn't expecting it.'

'You said they live underground.'

'But you're right, it came here for a purpose. There must be something here that it was after.'

Vasilov nodded slowly. 'There are many things here that it might have wanted. One section in particular, stored away from the other artefacts. A section that holds especial interest for Comrade Stalin...' He paused, letting out a long breath. 'Yes, that would make sense of many things. I store the items, but I am forbidden from investigating them.'

'What are these things?'

'They were recovered from the same area, the same *incident*. Thirty-five years ago, it must be now.'

'Can you show me?'

Vasilov nodded. 'Of course.'

He turned to speak to Larisa. She looked pale, but her breathing was back to normal. She stood up, slightly shakily, and walked with them through the chamber.

They needed their torches again as the back of the area receded into shadows. Sarah was listening keenly for any hint of sound, of movement. There was another set of metal doors. There was a grille above the doors, the bars too close together for anyone to get through. But wide enough for the Vril to have entered from, Sarah assumed, the tunnel beyond. But when Larisa unlocked these and swung them open, she revealed another chamber beyond.

Lights flickered on, and Sarah saw that this chamber was smaller than the first. Again, it was filled with crates and metal boxes. The centre of the floor was covered with the shattered debris of a broken crate. Straw spilled out of the remains.

'I think we can see what they came for,' Sarah said.

'And how they got in,' Vasilov added.

He nodded towards the side of the chamber. The distinctive white stone had been torn away, leaving a ragged dark hole.

'They took something away with them,' Sarah said. 'Something that was inside that crate. But what? And why?'

It was surprising how quickly they got used to the constant background noise, the smell, the need to stay alert at every moment. When the first light of dawn filtered through the haze of dust and smoke, they found themselves in a surreal landscape. Brick chimney stacks stood as industrial sentinels as far as the eye could see, like petrified trees in a desolate winter forest. The ground was uneven, but layered with dust and ash rather than rubble.

'Incendiaries,' Davenport said. 'I've seen similar in parts of London, but nothing on this scale. The air raids burn out the wooden buildings but leave anything brick or stone almost intact.'

Beyond the forest of chimneys, they moved back into the shattered remnants of more robust structures. Several buildings they passed were obviously occupied by Russian troops. Guy saw them watching from windows, gun barrels poking out from upper storeys and field guns on the ground floor. With the arrival of a misty daylight, they became even more careful, hugging the shadows and avoiding open ground. They should be safe from the Russian snipers, but as they moved into areas that were not completely controlled by either side, there would be German snipers too. The bodies crawling with rats were a continual reminder that death was never far away.

They hid on the upper floor of a building, watching through a hole punched in the wall, as a group of Germans advanced across one area. Two of them carried flamethrowers, spraying liquid fire across walls and rubble. Guy knew that the fire would find the tiniest way through. If there was a sniper hiding the other side, the flames would find him. Or her.

But the sniper was further away and higher up, judging by where the shot seemed to come from. One of the soldiers collapsed clutching his chest. The others scattered.

'Didn't kill him, though,' Leo pointed out as the other soldiers dragged their comrade into cover.

'Probably didn't aim to,' Guy said. 'A badly wounded man can't fight, but he ties up resources. Just getting him out of here will slow the others down and make them easier targets.'

It was late afternoon before they found what they hoped was the Square of Fallen Heroes. It was still recognisable as a square, but the buildings on one side were all but gone and on the other three they were little more than burned-out husks. A tattered red flag fluttered in the breeze, hanging from a pole angled off a shattered balcony. It was the only colour in the whole grey landscape – the colour of blood.

'No street signs, and no policeman to ask,' Davenport complained. 'But assuming this is the place, what do we do now?'

'I don't know,' Guy confessed. 'To be honest, I didn't really think we'd get this far. I guess we have to hope that Hoffman will be looking out for us.'

'Just so long as he hasn't given up and gone home.'

They gathered up enough wood to make a fire in the doorway of one of the buildings. Guy took a charred piece of wood from the fire and scraped a large letter 'H' on the wall behind the fire. With luck it would attract Hoffman's attention. Of course, the fire was likely to attract the attention of anyone else in the area too. So they watched from another building fifty yards away.

The fire was dying with the sunlight as evening drew in. There was no let-up in the sounds of the battle. If anything it had intensified in the last hour. The figure was so slight they almost missed her – a little girl picking her way round the edge of the square. She paused by the fire, perhaps looking at the 'H' on the wall, or perhaps just warming herself. She turned, looking round. Another figure, a man, joined her. He too turned and looked round. It was too dark to make out his features.

'Could be him,' Davenport said. 'He's about the right height and build. So far as you can tell from here.'

'He's not a German anyway,' Guy said. 'Could be a civilian. Let's go and talk to him.'

'Is that a good idea?'

'Keep your hand on your pistol just in case.'

Even in the fading light, they recognised Hoffman as they approached. He had also evidently realised who they were, walking briskly towards them, the girl following behind.

'There are German patrols nearby,' he said in English, greeting them each with a slap on the back and a handshake. 'We should get under cover, then we can talk. Come with me.'

They followed him into a burned-out building, then through it and out the other side. The girl came with them.

'I guess you don't speak English,' Davenport said to her as she walked beside him.

'She doesn't speak at all,' Hoffman said over his shoulder. 'I don't even know her name, she's sort of adopted me. God knows what happened to her, poor child.'

Davenport reached out to take her hand. The girl hesitated before accepting. She was staring at Davenport's wrist and it took him a moment to work out why. The bracelet he wore was glinting in the reflected light. It seemed to fascinate her. Hoffman saw it too, and stopped.

'Is there something you need to tell me?' he asked.

'This?' Davenport held up his hand. 'No. It isn't real. Just a precaution.'

Hoffman nodded. 'I'm pleased to hear it.' He looked round. They had stopped outside the doorway of what might have been an office building. 'This will do for now.' He shoved the remains of the wooden door open and led them inside.

'We got your message,' Guy said. 'A clever way to get in touch.'

'A desperate way, more like,' Hoffman said. 'I had no way of knowing if it would actually work.'

Light filtered in from a nearby fire, picking out their faces in flickering orange and red. Hoffman had taken a knife from inside his coat.

'But these are desperate times,' he said.

As he spoke he drew the sharp blade of the knife across the palm of his left hand. The skin parted, and Guy expected blood to well up from the wound. But instead orange tendrils licked out, pulling the skin closed again and sealing it up. In moments it was as if the cut had never been made.

'Don't worry,' Hoffman said in response to their startled and worried expressions. 'My mind is still my own. Most of it. I can hear them inside my thoughts. Trying to take control. But I managed to resist taking a bracelet and without it I can keep them at bay.'

'How did it happen?' Davenport asked.

'In the Vault, at Wewelsburg?' Guy guessed.

Hoffman nodded, slipping the knife away again. 'The Vril from the tank. A deep scratch is enough for it to infect you. It takes a while, but if the initial attack doesn't leave you dead, then it leaves you like this.'

There was a rattle of gunfire from close outside the building.

'We should move on,' Hoffman said. 'I have something for you, something they must not get.'

'The axe-head?' Guy said.

'One of three. The Vril already have one of them, I know.'

'We have the other,' Davenport told him.

The girl still held Davenport's hand as they skirted another square and headed off down a road lined with rubble and debris.

'You think we can trust him?' Guy asked quietly as they followed Hoffman.

'We don't have a lot of choice. But why bring us here at all if he's working for the Vril?'

'To find out how much we know, maybe?'

'He could just have asked us. He didn't have to show us he's an Ubermensch.'

'True,' Guy conceded.

At the corner of the next street, Hoffman told them they were almost at their destination. 'I've hidden the axe. Somewhere safe. Once I've recovered it, you have to get it away from here and make sure the Vril can never find it. I'll tell you all I know before you go.'

They came at them without warning out of the darkness. The leading soldier fired his rifle from the hip as he ran. The bullets slammed into their target, knocking him backwards – Hoffman.

Guy had his pistol out and had shot back before Hoffman recovered. Davenport pushed the girl behind him, bringing up his own gun and firing in one fluid, practised movement.

Two of the four Germans went down at once, including the one who had shot Hoffman. A third charged towards Guy, yelling and brandishing a bayonet. Hoffman rose up from the ground beside him, grabbed the man as he ran past, twisted his head viciously sideways and let his body drop lifeless to the ground.

The last German had a Luger. His first shot cracked into the brickwork close to Guy's head. Davenport shouldered the man sideways and he stumbled on the uneven ground. Guy's shot caught him as he was off balance, spinning him round to fall face down across a pile of rubble.

Davenport had fallen heavily after knocking the soldier aside. He struggled to his feet, but one leg was painful when he put weight on it.

'Probably just bruised,' he assured Guy. 'It's not broken anyway. I'll be all right in a minute.' He sat on the rubble and tried to massage some feeling back into his leg.

'You wait here with the girl,' Hoffman said. 'Pentecross, come with me and we'll get the axe. Then we'll find somewhere safe so we can talk.'

The girl came and sat beside Davenport. She watched him rubbing his leg, and frowned. She reached out and tapped the heavy bracelet on his wrist.

'It intrigues you, doesn't it,' Davenport said. His leg was feeling better. 'We'll maybe find you something pretty to wear.' He stood up and tested his leg. It seemed to take his weight now, though it was still painful. As he turned, he caught sight of movement in the near darkness. The German he had knocked down was moving, groggily shaking his head. Guy's shot hadn't killed him.

The girl saw it too. She ran towards the soldier.

'No!' Davenport shouted.

But he was too late. The soldier was sitting up. In his hand he still held the Luger he had fired at Guy. As the girl rushed towards him he fired again. The force of the shot twisted her round, knocking her backwards. Anger taking hold of him, Davenport grabbed his own gun. But the girl was on her feet again almost at once, up and running at the soldier, blocking Davenport's own line of fire.

She was on the German before he could get off another shot, knocking the gun from him. Her hands raked down his face, nails biting into the man's neck, twisting and squeezing, pushing him back down on to the rubble. He was still groggy from the initial fall, hardly able to defend himself as she grabbed his head and slammed it down on to broken bricks and stone. He cried out in pain. The cries became a whimper as she slammed his head down again. Even in the uncertain light, Davenport could see the dark stain spreading over the rubble as he limped over to help the girl.

Dark shapes approached out of the night. Davenport brought up his gun, then sighed with relief as he saw it was Hoffman and Guy coming back. He knelt down beside the girl.

'Are you all right? He shot you – let's see how bad the wound is.'

With any luck, the shot had gone right through, leaving only a flesh wound. Once the adrenalin wore off, she'd feel the pain. He didn't envy her that.

Gently, Davenport turned her so that what light there was illuminated the shoulder where she'd been hit. He could see the ragged hole torn in her clothes, the skin exposed beneath. And the orange tendrils flickering out of the wound as they repaired the damage.

'Good God,' he murmured. He turned to call out to Guy and Hoffman.

Just as the girl grabbed his legs, pulling them away from beneath him. Her hands curled into claws, stabbing towards Davenport's face.

CHAPTER 38

The Thames was boiling. Several minutes after Jane Roylston had disappeared beneath the surface, the whole middle area of the river erupted. Bubbles burst to the surface. A sudden, impossible wave curled upwards close to Westminster Bridge, between Miss Manners and the Houses of Parliament.

'What the hell?' Alban said. 'Did your friend do this?'

Miss Manners shook her head in disbelief. She had no answer.

People paused on the Embankment, staring out incredulously as the waters churned, turning from muddy brown to foaming white. A dark shape forced its way to the surface. Water cascaded from the huge, bulbous craft as it broke the surface. It rose slowly, ponderously, water sluicing off it as it came clear of the river. Boats were tossed about like wooden toys, their crews struggling to keep control and avoid being washed overboard.

The shouts and cries of the people watching were lost in the roar of the massive engines glowing beneath the craft. It climbed higher into the air, pausing for a moment before turning slowly on its axis. It was slightly elliptical, short, stubby fins jutting up from the back end, as big as a double-decker bus. Then suddenly a light so bright it hurt the eyes flashed out from the back of the craft. In moments it was screaming away across the river, climbing over the Palace of Westminster.

'They've got the axe,' Miss Manners said, staring after it.

'Jane gave them the axe.'

'Is it important?' Alban could see the answer in her expression. 'I'll get on to the RAF. Maybe they can intercept it.' He was already running back towards Charing Cross to find a phone.

'It might be quicker to run to the Air Ministry,' Miss Manners murmured. But Alban was probably right. He'd have more success phoning MI5 to put in an urgent, formal request than trying to get past the front entrance to the Air Ministry without the requisite clearance.

For the moment, there was nothing Miss Manners could do except wait for Alban, assuming he came back. She stared out across the Thames. The surface was still choppy from the Vril craft's emergence. If nothing else, she now knew what a UDT looked like. It matched the descriptions she'd taken from pilots who'd seen one – including Sarah Diamond. There were quite a few more people who'd seen one now, though of course they'd have no idea what they had really seen.

She was about to turn away and follow Alban when she saw something in the water. At first she thought it was just a piece of driftwood or rubbish. But as she watched, it was drawn closer by the flow of the river – a shape emerged. A body. Lying face down in the water, just the head and shoulders breaking the surface. She could make out the short dark hair, plastered to the back of the neck. Jane.

The current was taking Jane's body towards Westminster Bridge. She ran along the Embankment, trying to keep the body in sight. Could she have survived – was it possible?

She was almost at the bridge when the body seemed to come to life. Jane's head lifted. Water gushed from her open mouth as she looked round. Then she struck out for the bank, swimming strongly with even, almost mechanical strokes.

Miss Manners increased her speed. But she wasn't going to get there in time. Already Jane was hauling herself up a slipway, then on to the Embankment. Apparently oblivious to her appearance, she headed off towards Westminster Bridge. People glanced at her curiously, taking in the sight of a young woman drenched from head to toe hurrying barefoot along the pavement. But most had seen more improbable sights.

Turning onto the bridge to follow, Miss Manners lost sight of Jane for a second. Was she crossing the bridge, or had she turned the other way? Miss Manners looked round, trying desperately to spot her. Instead she saw another familiar and distinctive figure – Alban's red hair meant he stood out easily in the crowd.

'Did you see her?' Miss Manners gasped as she reached Alban.

'See who?'

'Jane.'

He just stared at her.

'She swam to the bank. Climbed out. I lost her.'

'She got out of the river? And came this way?'

Miss Manners nodded, breathless.

'Then let's follow her.' Alban pointed at the pavement at their feet. The area closest to the river was wet from the water cascading off the Vril craft. Trails of wet footprints led off in all directions.

'How does that help?'

'It might not,' Alban conceded. 'But if she's been in the river, she'll stay wet longer than most people's shoes. Show me where she was heading and we'll see if she left a trail.'

'She's barefoot,' Miss Manners said. 'That will help. And the RAF?' she asked.

'If they can get a trace, they'll try to intercept. Well, they might get lucky.'

The UDT had reached the English Channel before the Spitfires found it. Three planes from RAF Manston intercepted over the Kent coast. None of the pilots had seen anything like it before, but their orders were clear – the craft was hostile and to be brought down.

'Some sort of dirigible, maybe,' Bert Tanner, piloting the lead aircraft, thought as he closed in, approaching from ahead of the craft as it raced at him.

The other two Spitfires were close behind and on either side. Tanner opened up with his Browning .303 machine guns. If the bullets impacted on the craft in front of him, they had no effect. He kept firing, but the craft was moving rapidly towards him and he had to bank rapidly to starboard.

As soon as Tanner was out of the way, the other two planes opened up. Their fire had as little effect, and they too had to turn rapidly to avoid collision.

'Bring it down at all costs' had been the order. Tanner barely gave a thought to what he was doing as he swung the plane round and dived back towards the strange craft. He pushed the throttle to its full extent, the acceleration driving him back into the seat. The Merlin engine's note deepened to a throaty roar as it propelled the plane towards the enemy craft at almost 500 miles per hour.

He closed his eyes at the moment of impact, taking his hands off the controls and breathing out. Only at that moment did he think about what he was doing. About Gracie and the children.

A brilliant white light burned through his eyelids. That was it, he realised, and suddenly he felt calm and relaxed.

Then a deafening thunderclap of sound shocked him back to reality. He opened his eyes and grabbed for the joystick. His plane was still diving, powering through the low clouds. The distinctive elliptical wings of two Spitfires cut through the sky above him as Tanner pulled the plane out of the dive and levelled off.

A streak of white disappearing into the distance was the only sign of the craft he had been attacking.

CHAPTER 39

Sarah slept better the second night, not waking until almost eleven. She lay in bed for several minutes thinking back over the events of the previous night.

As he had promised, Tustrum had been waiting in the Embassy dining room when she returned from the Kremlin. He was dozing in a chair, his feet stretched out under the table, an empty whisky glass in front of him.

He jolted awake as Sarah pulled out the chair next to him and sat down. She felt every bit as exhausted as the man looked.

He wiped his eyes. 'Sorry, what time is it?'

'Almost two in the morning.'

'Christ – where have you been?'

'I probably shouldn't tell you,' Sarah said.

He nodded. 'Fair enough. So long as you're all right.'

'The evening had its moments, but yes, I'm fine. I'll see you tomorrow.'

Sarah and Vasilov had cautiously checked there were no Vril lurking in the shadows or waiting behind the hole they had torn in the wall of the Archive. But it seemed the one that attacked them was alone. Perhaps it had been left on guard, or been sent back to obtain some other item.

'Or it somehow got separated from the others,' Sarah suggested.

'I need to tell the Kremlin commandant what has happened,' Vasilov said. 'We need to block off this opening. Make sure they cannot return.'

'Do you know what they took?' Sarah asked.

Vasilov nodded. He looked pale. 'I believe so. I shall have to check to be certain. But first I must alert the commandant. You should go.'

'I need to know why the Vril were here,' Sarah insisted. 'What they took.'

Vasilov shook his head. 'You cannot stay here. I will check what is missing, and get a message to you. Or, no,' he decided, 'I shall write to Elizabeth. You will see she gets the letter?'

'Of course.'

'Then Larisa will bring it to the Embassy. Tomorrow.' He called her over, giving her rapid instructions. 'But now, she will take you back while I find the commandant.' He glanced at the gaping hole in the wall. 'The fact that one of them was still here – it could mean that others will return.'

'It could,' Sarah agreed. 'We should all get out of here. Let the soldiers sort it out.'

They returned through the white-stone tunnels to the opening into the Arsenal Tower above. Then through the metal gate and up the spiral staircase. At the top, Vasilov left them. He shook Sarah's hand, then leaned forward and kissed her gently on each cheek.

There was a different guard on duty at the exit, but he spared Larisa and Sarah little more than a glance as they left. Outside, it was raining. Larisa shivered, but declined Sarah's coat when she offered it. They walked briskly back to the Embassy, parting company in the same narrow alley where they had met several hours previously.

As Sarah turned to go, Larisa pulled at her sleeve, turning her back. For a moment, the woman stared impassively into Sarah's face. Then she pulled Sarah into a fierce hug. When they separated, Sarah took off her coat, and this time Larisa accepted it.

Vasilov was as good as his word. When Sarah finally

emerged from her room the next day and checked with the front desk, there was an envelope waiting for her, addressed to 'Mrs Elizabeth Archer, care of Miss Sarah Diamond'. She recognised Vasilov's handwriting from his earlier letter. She considered opening it, reading what Vasilov had discovered.

But no, she decided. There was likely to be more than just a note of what the Vril had taken. Whatever friendship Vasilov, Elizabeth, and Elizabeth's husband George had enjoyed was not hers to share. She pushed the envelope into her pocket, and went in search of Tustrum. He might have news of Guy and Leo. But whether he did or not, it was time for her to head home...

The Vril had scratched her as it hid from the soldiers – the same soldiers as moments earlier had shot the girl's mother. She screamed from the pain, the last pain she ever felt. Being so small, the infection spread rapidly through the little girl's body. So young and inexperienced, so innocent and naïve, her mind was easy to control even without a bracelet to focus the Vril influence.

Her instructions were simple: find the rogue Ubermensch, and get the axe from him. Now it was almost within her grasp. The man with the bracelet was a problem. She had thought he was with her, was an Ubermensch. But then he had been injured, so either he was not yet fully absorbed into the Vril, or he was not an Ubermensch at all. Either way, he knew what *she* was, he had seen.

Somehow Davenport managed to grab her wrists, pushing her away from him. But the girl was incredibly strong.

'Help me!' he yelled. 'Get her off!'

Guy and Hoffman were running, scrambling over the rubble to get to him. He felt her nails rake down his cheek, the warmth of blood. Then Hoffman was there, one arm round the girl's waist as he dragged her away. Her legs were kicking, arms flailing. He couldn't hold her and she broke free, hammering at Hoffman's chest.

The axe-head he had been holding fell from his grip and

landed amongst the other fallen stone. The girl dived for it, grabbing it with both hands, scrambling off across the broken landscape.

Guy threw himself at her, dragging her down. She swung her hand, the heavy axe connecting with his shoulder. His grip weakened, she tore herself free and was off running.

But Davenport was back on his feet and in her way. She didn't try to avoid him, but lowered her shoulder like a diminutive rugby player, crashing into him and sending the bigger man sprawling. He managed to grab hold of her sleeve, pulling her off balance. It slowed her down enough from Hoffman to launch himself at the girl. The axe-head went flying again and the girl wriggled out from Hoffman's grasp and scrambled after it.

It skidded through a doorway, falling over the threshold. The wooden floor had burned away, leaving the blackened spikes of charred timbers jutting from the remaining walls. The girl fell to the ground that was several feet below. The fall should have winded her, perhaps even fractured her leg. But she was unaffected, immediately searching round to see where the axe had fallen. Within the walls, the light from the distant fires was dimmed and the whole place was in near-darkness.

Hoffman jumped after her, Guy and Davenport clambering down more cautiously, Davenport trying not to put weight on his injured leg. The girl eyed them cautiously. Then she caught sight of the axe, the white stone picked out in the grey ash and soot covering the ground. She ran across and picked it up. Holding it in one hand, raised like a weapon, she edged round the walls, inside the broken timbers.

There were only two ways out of the shell of the building – back the way she had come, past Hoffman, or through a side door where Davenport was now standing. She feinted towards Hoffman, then ran at Davenport, axe raised ready to strike.

Guy's first shot caught her in the shoulder. It barely slowed her. The second shot hammered into her chest, knocking her sideways. But she kept coming at Davenport. He stepped aside at the last moment, so that the axe swept down onto nothing. The vicious force of the blow unbalanced her, and she stumbled into the low side wall. One of the sharp wooden joists ripped through her clothes, scraping past her side. She ignored it, and started to scramble up towards the doorway.

Davenport grabbed for the axe as she climbed, but she swung it at him, holding on to the side wall with one arm. The blow knocked him backwards.

Then Hoffman was there. He grabbed her round the waist with both arms, dragging her back, staggering to keep his balance as she thrashed and squirmed and hammered at him with the axe.

'Now what?' Davenport yelled.

The sky above burst into brilliant light as a series of explosions rang out nearby. The flashes strobed across Hoffman and the girl, giving their movements the staccato quality of an old movie. As if in slow motion, Hoffman lifted the struggling girl to shoulder height. Then he shoved her violently away from him, towards the jagged, broken joists jutting out of the wall.

Two of the wooden struts pierced her body, one erupting from her chest, the other through a shoulder. A gelatinous mass of orange tendrils squirmed out, pulsing and throbbing round the wounds. The girl screamed – the first sound any of them had heard her make. She shuddered, tensed, rocked back and forth as she tried to free herself, but she was stuck fast on the wooden stakes.

Hoffman grabbed her hand, holding it tight in his as he prised open her fingers and removed the axe-head.

'I'm sorry,' he said quietly in Russian. He turned to Guy and Davenport, who were both watching in horror and disgust as the girl writhed and snarled. 'Let's get away from here.'

'A scratch from that creature in the Vault at Wewelsburg was all it took,' Hoffman said.

The three of them sat round a small fire in the cellar of what was left of a house. Davenport and Guy had food with them, but Hoffman assured them he wasn't hungry.

'It was a few hours before the infection took hold. Then I was numb. Like I didn't know what to do. After a while, there was a voice, if I can call it that. Someone else's thoughts inside my head – more pictures than words, feelings and cravings. I had to get one of the bracelets from the Vault.'

'But you didn't?' Davenport said.

'No. I've spent so long pretending to be what I'm not, locking my thoughts away and ignoring them as I play at being someone else, that I could resist the urge. When I first became German, there were times when the stress was so intense I just wanted to tell someone: "This is all a lie. I'm not Werner Hoffman at all, I'm a Russian who had the misfortune to be born to a German mother and speak her language." It was a bit like that, resisting an overwhelming desire to do something I knew was stupid. Suicidal.'

'The bracelets are how they control an Ubermensch,' Guy said. 'We know that.'

'They don't always need the bracelet though,' Hoffman told them. 'I imagine it enhances the control, amplifies it. That girl, she didn't have a bracelet but the Vril evidently controlled her utterly. A young mind, easily influenced...' He stared into the dancing firelight. 'She was dead already,' he murmured.

'Tell us what happened,' Guy said. 'After you were infected, if that's the right word.'

'The Vril still tried to control me. I saw images of the axe-head, amongst other things. Nachten – one of Himmler's archaeologists – he was searching for it too. But you probably know as much as I can tell you about the axes.'

'We know there are three of them,' Guy said. 'And we know they slot into some sort of mechanism buried on the island of Crete.'

'The Vril are everywhere,' Hoffman said. 'Thousands of years ago they came to our world.'

'But what do they want?' Davenport asked.

'I don't know exactly. But they are colonists, imperialists, conquerors. To be honest, I can only see what they show me, and that's less and less each day as they realise I'm of no use to them. Some things still sort of seep through. But I couldn't tell you if the Vril are any more active now than they have ever been. Perhaps it's only now, as we develop flight and the ability to detect their craft and transmissions, that we've noticed them. Or perhaps they've decided we're ready to be… harvested.'

'Harvested?' Guy said. 'What do you mean?'

Hoffman shrugged. 'When the Vril first arrived, the human race was undeveloped. They're nothing if not patient, and incredibly long-lived by our standards. So the Vril waited until humanity reached a point in its development where we'd be useful to them. But useful for what, I'm not sure.'

'Not a very pleasant thought,' Davenport said. 'But what do these things do?' He pointed to the axe lying beside the fire.

'The Vril left colonies here. A few of the creatures are active, but most sleep in huge hibernation caves deep below the ground.'

'And there's one of these below Crete?' Guy guessed.

'The axes are actually the keys that will unlock that chamber, and awaken a vast army of Vril. We have to stop them. Make sure they sleep on.'

'Well, they only have one of the three keys,' Davenport said. 'So that must be a good start. We have that one, and another back in London.'

Hoffman closed his eyes for a moment. 'No,' he said when he opened them again. 'We only have this one.' He picked up the axe-head and weighed it in his hand. 'The one you had in London has been recovered by the Vril.'

Guy was shocked. 'Are you sure?'

Hoffman nodded. 'Certain.'

'Then what's happening back in London?' Davenport said.

CHAPTER 40

She was standing at the end of the bridge, absolutely still, gazing out across the water. It had taken Alban and Miss Manners twenty minutes to find her, following different trails of wet footprints. It looked like she had been standing here all that time. Silent and still.

'Let me,' Alban said, gesturing for Miss Manners to wait. 'You saw what she did to Green.'

'She's my friend,' Miss Manners told him.

But she hung back while Alban approached the woman. Passers-by were looking curiously at Jane Roylston as they passed, taking in the sodden clothes, the wet hair plastered to her scalp. Her blouse clung to her, the shape of the metal bracelet on her upper arm clearly visible through the thin material.

'Miss Roylston?' He touched her arm. She didn't react. 'Miss Roylston, are you all right?'

There was no reply. Alban glanced at Miss Manners and shrugged. She joined him, and when Jane still did not respond took her friend's arm and gently turned her away from the river.

'Penelope?' Jane said, puzzled. 'I'm sorry. I was… waiting.'

'What are you waiting for?' Miss Manners asked.

'To be told what to do. I must know what to do.' She frowned, and clutched at Miss Manners' hand. 'Do you know what I should do?'

'I think you should come with us. Come on.'

With Alban following close behind, Miss Manners guided Jane, leading her back towards the Station Z offices.

'Is this a good idea?' Alban wondered.

'It's the only idea I have. What about you?'

'She seems calm enough now, I suppose.'

Jane walked as if in a trance, not seeming to notice what was happening around her. Not hearing Alban and Miss Manners as they spoke.

Green was already back at Station Z. He had been bruised in his encounter with Jane outside the British Museum, but was otherwise unhurt. He looked up in surprise as Jane came in, Miss Manners and Alban close behind.

'It's all right,' Alban assured him. 'She seems quite calm now.'

He and Miss Manners told Green what had happened. Jane sat quietly at Sarah's desk, her hands clasped on her lap. Her clothes were still wet, water dripping to the floor.

'I checked on Mrs Archer,' Green said, 'after you two ran off and I lost you. She's a bit shaken, but she'll be all right.'

'Thank goodness for that,' Miss Manners said. She was ashamed to realise she had completely forgotten about Mrs Archer.

'She's a tough old bird, and no mistake,' Green went on. He nodded at Jane. 'Not the only one, it seems. I'll make her some tea.'

'Your universal remedy?' Miss Manners joked.

'The poor woman's soaked through. I'm sure a hot drink will do her good.'

'If she's an Ubermensch – or Uberfrau, I suppose,' Alban said, 'why's she just sitting there? The others have all tried to kill us. So did she, less than an hour ago.'

'She's delivered the axe,' Miss Manners said. 'That was her mission. Now she's waiting for orders, I think.'

'Then how do we make sure she doesn't get any?' Green asked. 'Because you can bet they won't be healthy for us.' He headed off to put the kettle on.

'If I've understood this,' Alban said, 'they transmit instructions into her mind, like a radio message – yes?'

'As far as we can tell,' Miss Manners agreed. 'The people Guy and Leo saw at Wewelsburg, drawing, they intercepted the messages going back to the Vril.' She gently touched the bulge on Jane's arm where the shape of the bracelet was still visible. 'These bracelets must be how the instructions are relayed and received, don't you think?'

'They must be something to do with it,' Alban agreed. 'So maybe we can block the transmissions somehow. Stop her new orders from ever coming through.'

'We can try,' Miss Manners said. 'And I'm sure it would help if we could get that bracelet off her arm, which might also be easier if we can block the signals, at least for a while.'

'And how do we do that?'

'Well, given that we can tap into the Vril's communications by holding a séance, maybe there is an occult way to exorcise them from her mind completely.'

'Exorcise?' Alban echoed.

'There are ancient ceremonies, rituals, handed down through time. Some of them at least seem to the derived from the science and knowledge of the Vril,' Miss Manners said. 'What if an exorcism isn't just some form of religious words and symbols, but the remnants of something more tangible, more applicable?'

'Vril science?' Alban shook his head. 'You think an exorcism could actually be some sort of scientific process?'

Green returned with a mug of tea in time to hear this. He set it on the desk in font of Jane, and gently lifted her hands and clasped them round the mug. After a moment, Jane lifted the mug and sipped at the steaming brew.

'Did I hear that right – you're going to hold an exorcism?' Green asked.

'Well, it can't do any harm I suppose,' Alban said.

Miss Manners was at her desk, opening one of the drawers and pulling out her camera. 'But I think we should wait until she's got her strength back. It's likely to be a rather traumatic experience, so she may need a day or two to recover. And before that, I want to take Jane's photograph.'

'We have to move,' Hoffman decided. 'The Vril will know what has happened. They know we have one of the axe-heads.'

'Can you walk?' Guy asked Leo.

Leo stood up, tentatively putting weight on his bad leg. 'Just about,' he decided. 'So long as I don't have to run, it should be all right.'

'They will be heading this way,' Hoffman said. 'I can feel them, probing my thoughts, trying to assert their control.'

'So do we try to keep out of their way, or take the fight to them?' Guy asked.

'Do they know where we are?' Leo wondered.

Hoffman shook his head. 'I don't think so. They are in contact with the girl. They know I am in the city, and was close by. But without a complete, direct link they don't have any more information than that.'

'Many of them?' Guy asked.

'I don't think so,' Hoffman said.

'I vote we take the fight to them,' Leo said.

'Risky,' Guy pointed out.

'This place is bad enough as it is,' Leo told him. 'Imagine if they start turning more people into their Ubermensch creatures. God knows what it'll be like then.'

'The Vril themselves are easier to deal with than the Ubermensch,' Hoffman agreed.

'We still have to find them,' Guy said.

'Or let them find us,' Hoffman suggested. 'I can feel them inside my mind. If I let my guard slip, they will see what I see. They will know where I am.'

'Draw them to us?' Leo said.

'Exactly. And choose where we face them.'

Despite Leo's insistence that he was on the mend, he was still limping and so they made slow progress through the shattered city. As dawn's first light began to break over the ruins, they found themselves in the broken remains of another square. There was movement on the far side, figures picking their way through the fallen debris.

Guy, Leo and Hoffman ducked into cover behind what was left of a wall. Across the rubble-strewn area they could see the German soldiers making their cautious way towards them. There were six in total. The soldiers moved between areas of cover, slowed by the uneven ground. But there was a space to one side of the square where they were exposed. The buildings along that side had been completely demolished, leaving little by way of shelter.

They crossed the open area one at a time. The first soldier stumbled as he ran across the rubble. His comrades watched anxiously as he recovered, kept moving, and finally made it to the cover on the other side. Relieved and emboldened, three of the others made the journey together. They were midway when the shots rang out.

The noise echoed round the area. One of the soldiers was flung backwards by the force of the bullet that caught him in the chest. A second fell sideways, clutching at his leg just above the knee. Another shot ripped into him as he stumbled. The third soldier hesitated, then ran on, leaving his colleagues behind. His legs seemed to keep running even when the front of his chest disappeared in a red haze.

Answering fire from the two soldiers still on the far side of the square hammered into the building where the snipers were hidden.

'They must have seen the muzzle flashes,' Guy said.

Closer to them, the soldier who had made the first journey across the square rose up from his cover and hurled a stick grenade. It turned end over end in the air, disappearing into the ruins of the building where the shots had come from. A moment later, smoke and flame billowed out of the ruins, followed by the percussion of the blast.

A volley of shots from one of the other Germans gave his colleague the chance to hurry across the square and join the one who had thrown the grenade. The man moved awkwardly, hampered by the heavy cylinders attached to his back.

'Flamethrower,' Hoffman said grimly.

Even as he spoke, a jet of liquid fire shot out from where the two soldiers were sheltering. It bathed the outside of the broken building with orange, leaving the brickwork charred and black where it had been. The third soldier dashed across to join them as the fire ate into the ruins.

'This way,' Hoffman said in a low voice.

To Guy's surprise, he led them not away from the Germans, but towards them. Skirting round the shattered buildings, they approached the soldiers from behind and slightly above. Edging closer, Hoffman drew his handgun. Guy didn't realise what he was intending until he rose up above a broken section of wall and fired.

The first soldier was hit in the chest, knocked backwards. The second got off a single shot, which ricocheted off the brickwork close to Leo. Then Hoffman's bullet dropped him like a stone. The third soldier was firing the flame thrower and didn't seem to notice the fate of his comrades. His face snapped from grim determination to abrupt surprise. He fell backwards, a stream of flame arching up over the building as he toppled back, before it cut out.

Hoffman jumped down into the rubble, picking his way past the fallen soldiers towards the building.

He called out in Russian: 'Are you in there? It's safe – they're dead.'

Guy and Leo followed him as he clambered up into the wrecked house. Guy expected at any moment a bullet from the sniper would hammer into his chest. But they got inside with no problem.

What remained of the internal walls was as blackened as the outside of the building. Several small fires still burned on the floor, and one in the remains of the ceiling. At the back of the devastated room, a dark shape lay stretched out – as if it had been trying to claw its way through the back wall. It was impossible to tell if it had been a man or a woman. All that remained was a smoking, blackened mess in the vague shape of a human being. The charred remains of a rifle lay twisted and melted close by.

Movement in the far doorway. A rifled aimed at them. Guy swung round, bringing his gun up.

'No!' Hoffman shouted in Russian.

The woman – barely out of her teens – stared across the room at them, eyes filled with a mixture of hatred and fear.

'It's all right,' Hoffman said gently. 'The Germans are dead. I shot them. We're on your side.'

The woman's rifle wavered slightly, but she didn't lower it. Instead she kept them covered as she edged across to the window and peered out at the bodies below. She stared down for a moment, then spat. The gun lowered, and the woman collapsed slowly to the ground, sobbing suddenly.

Guy instinctively moved to comfort her. But Leo caught his arm. He pointed out of the window across the shattered square.

'We've got more company.'

Another group of German soldiers had appeared. They made their way cautiously through the rubble.

'They must have heard the shots,' Guy said. 'Maybe even seen what happened.'

Hoffman helped the woman to her feet as Guy and Leo watched the smudges of field-grey uniform almost invisible in the colourless landscape. Without comment, the woman levelled her rifle, steadying it on the broken edge of the window. She glanced back at the blackened mess on the other side of the room, then set her eye to the rifle sight.

'Is this a good idea?' Leo asked. 'I can't help feeling we're both outnumbered and outgunned.'

But before Guy or Hoffman could reply, the rifle kicked back in recoil. The sound of the shot was deafening inside the ruined room. Out in the square, a soldier cried out and collapsed behind the wall he had been clambering over.

The woman worked the bolt on the rifle, muttering to herself as she did.

The next shot kicked up a thin shower of dust from the

rubble, missing its target by inches. The woman cursed, and reloaded.

'Leo's right,' Guy said. 'We should go. Can we persuade her to leave, do you think?' he asked Hoffman.

'I doubt it. But we may not have to.'

His words were punctuated by a scream from outside. Guy turned quickly back to the remains of the window.

In the distance a German soldier was silhouetted against the ruins. Upright, back arched, mouth open. A dark spear was thrust through his body from behind, emerging in a bloody mess from the front. As Guy watched, a dark shape reared up over the dying man. Its sharp, serrated tentacle withdrew abruptly from the soldier. For a moment the man didn't move. Then he collapsed, falling straight down like a string-severed puppet.

Hoffman spoke quickly to the woman. Her face was pale and her eyes wide, but she nodded, aimed, and squeezed the trigger of the rifle.

The bullet hammered into the bloated dark body of the Vril. It exploded in a mass of tissue and viscous, steaming liquid.

The other German soldiers were running, all thought of cover gone as more Vril emerged from the ground beneath them.

'They must have burrowed under the rubble,' Leo said. 'Persistent buggers, aren't they?'

A soldier screamed as his legs were ripped from beneath him by a mass of dark tentacles. Another turned to fire at the Vril, but was dragged down before he could get off a shot.

'How many can you see?' Guy demanded.

'Half a dozen,' Leo said.

'I count seven,' Hoffman told them.

Another soldier dropped, this time from a bullet fired by the sniper beside them. Her next shot severed a Vril's tentacle, and the air was filled with inhuman screeches of pain, until she fired again and the creature was splattered across the ruins.

The last of the soldiers was almost at the edge of the square when two Vril erupted from the broken ground beside him, hammering into his body and knocking him down. He was carrying a rifle, bayonet fixed to the end. It scythed through the glutinous body of one of the creatures, ripping it open. But the other Vril's tentacles tore the gun away and the man's screams faded and died.

'Five left to deal with,' Hoffman said grimly.

'They'll just hide in the rubble,' Leo told him. 'We'll never pick them off from up here.'

'And if we go down there...' Guy said. 'Well, we've seen what will happen. Unless...' He leaned forward, peering out of the remains of the window to the bodies of the first group of soldiers, lying sprawled below.

'What are you thinking?' Hoffman said.

'The flamethrower,' Guy told him. 'As long as there's still fuel in those tanks.'

'You know how to operate it?' Leo asked.

Guy shook his head. 'Haven't a clue.'

'I do,' Hoffman told them. 'Come on.' He turned to the woman. 'Keep us covered, as best you can. But if things get too dangerous, just go. Leave us.'

She started to protest, but Hoffman shook his head. 'Just stay safe,' he told her. 'Keep doing what you do best. You're a good shot.'

Hoffman went first, clambering over the window edge and dropping easily to the ground on the other side. Guy followed, reaching up to help Leo down. Even so, Leo winced as he put weight on his injured leg.

'We should hurry,' Hoffman said.

Across the ruined landscape they could see dark shapes oozing up from between piles of rubble, scuttling towards them.

'They know we're here,' Leo said.

'They can sense me, now they're close,' Hoffman said. 'The axe too.'

Together they struggled to unbuckle the heavy fuel cylinders from the dead soldier. Above them the woman's rifle cracked out several shots. One caught the edge of a Vril, sending it scuttling away, a dark trail leaking behind it.

As Hoffman and Leo finally managed to get the flamethrower free, Guy drew his gun. He scanned the nearby rubble and debris for any sign of movement, any shadow that was just a little too dark. Something moved in the crevice between a fallen wall and the ruins of a doorway. Guy's shot ricocheted off the stone.

'Ready,' Hoffman announced.

He strode forward across the rubble, flanked by Leo and Guy. The rifle barrel in the window above them tracked their movement. As they neared the area where the Vril had attacked, they could see that the ground was a mass of squirming shadows. Sensing their approach, the creatures rose up suddenly in front of them.

A rifle bullet took one immediately, splattering the gelatinous creature across its fellows. Undeterred, they surged forwards. Just as Hoffman ignited the end of the flamethrower. Fire jetted out, raking across the ground and scorching its way into the Vril. Black smoke billowed out. The shrieks of the creatures filled the air, and the sudden stench was impossible to ignore.

Slowly and methodically, Hoffman worked his way across the square, squirting flames into the smallest opening in the rubble. Off to one side, a Vril suddenly hurled itself out of the ground, scuttling rapidly towards them. Guy's shot knocked it sideways. A bullet from the sniper burst into its body. A sweep of the flamethrower reduced it to a charred mess imprinted on the rubble.

It was not just the Vril that were the enemy. Guy was acutely aware that there might be more Germans in the area – drawn by the noise or following their comrades. Both he and Leo paid as much attention to the edges of the square as they did to the ground closer to them.

Most of the Vril seemed to have been caught by surprise in Hoffman's first assault. Another was trapped and burned in a narrow crack in the debris. Others might well have been incinerated as Hoffman made his way through the ruins. It was impossible to tell.

Eventually they reached the end of the square. Hoffman sprayed flames across an area of unmarked ground, leaving a black trail. But the flames were less fierce than they had been as the fuel started to run out.

'Is that all of them, do you think?' Leo asked.

'I don't sense any more,' Hoffman said.

'But some of them could have got away?' Guy said.

Hoffman nodded. 'It's possible,' he conceded. 'There are always more.'

'So what now?' Leo asked.

'Thank our friend,' Guy suggested, glancing back towards the building where the woman was concealed. 'Then I think it's time we got out of this godless place.'

CHAPTER 41

She needed a bath after the flight. Sarah wondered if Jane Roylston would be there. But there was no sign of the woman. Either she was far more tidy than Sarah, or her bed had not been slept in. In fact there was little evidence that she had been there at all.

Not that Sarah was too worried. Miss Manners would know where she was – she'd be sure to be keeping an eye on her friend. And if the woman had recovered from the ordeals inflected on her by Crowley then that had to be a good thing.

Soap was a luxury that Sarah had not enjoyed for several days. She lay soaking in the bath, the water right up to the 'plimsoll line' painted on the inside to show how much she was permitted. But finally, she had to get out and face the real world again.

Sarah went straight to the British Museum from her flat. But the door down to the vault below the Great Court was locked and there was no sign of Elizabeth. Hunting through the building, she finally found the elderly man that Elizabeth called Young Eddie sitting drinking tea in a storeroom.

'Just taking a quick break,' he apologised. 'Elizabeth has left me a list of things she wants moved or sorted or catalogued.'

'Where is she?' Sarah asked.

'Just having a day off. Or as close as she gets. She'll be reading up on something or writing about something else.

351

Then she'll go and see a play, if there's anything good on. She always wanted to be an actress, you know.'

Sarah wasn't sure what she would find at Station Z or where she might be sent by tomorrow, so she entrusted Vasilov's letter to Eddie to pass on.

'I'll see she gets it,' he assured her. 'Vasilov is one of the good guys.'

'You know him?'

'We met. A long time ago. You ever heard the term *Vrolak*?'
Sarah shook her head.

'Well, pray you never do,' he said, pushing the envelope into his jacket pocket. 'Right then, best get back to work. No peace for the wicked – and if they don't rest, neither should we.'

Hoffman had his own uniform stashed away together with his identify papers not far from the Square of Fallen Heroes. Heading back that way, Guy and Leo stripped the uniforms from two of the German soldiers they had killed earlier in the day. It was an unpleasant process, made more horrendous by the fact the rats had already found the bodies.

'You sure about this?' Guy asked, not for the first time as Hoffman buttoned his jacket.

'This place is just a sample of how the world will be if the Vril take over,' Hoffman said. 'I came here to find someone, hoping she was here waiting for me. Alive and well. Now I hope to God that if she's still here then she's dead already. But whatever happened to her, she's lost to me, I know that.'

'But the risk,' Davenport said. 'Not just to us. You're suggesting we gamble *everything*.'

'It's already in play. The Vril have two of the keys. I don't know if they have another they can use. But I do know that we can't destroy this one.' He picked up the axe, and slammed it hard against the remains of a shattered wall. 'You see,' he said, showing them, 'not even scratched. And if we keep it or hide it, the Vril will seek it out. They can *feel* it. It calls out to them. You thought you had one of the keys safe, and now they have it. Eventually they will get this one too. Oh, it might take

months or even years, but they'll get it, and when they do...'
He turned a full circle, his arms out to show them. 'Well, you
can see for yourselves.'

'The axes stayed hidden for thousands of years up till now,'
Guy pointed out.

'It's only now they want them back,' Hoffman told him.
'Perhaps it's only now that they found they were missing.'

'What puzzles me,' Davenport said, 'is how they went
missing in the first place. They were all down in the Labyrinth
originally, we saw where they were kept. Who took them and
why?'

'I don't know,' Hoffman said. 'But I think I can guess. The
legends have some truth in them. And we are not the first
people to fight back against the Vril.'

'Theseus and the Minotaur?' Guy said. 'Well, we saw the
Minotaur in the Labyrinth, so that much is true.'

'Did he rescue the girl or retrieve the axe?' Davenport said.
'Two of them perhaps. And so a legend is born.'

'And the Minotaur?' Guy asked.

'The Vril have been here a very long time,' Hoffman said.
'Most of them are sleeping, deep underground, but not all.
They experiment constantly. And that includes perfecting their
Ubermensch technology – developing how they administer the
infection, how they control people like me afterwards. Who's
to say they haven't experimented with other creatures – bulls,
hybrid humans?'

'And people knew about them before,' Guy said. 'Was that
writer, Bulwer-Lytton, picking up on the legends and myths,
do you think?'

'More likely his mind had some affinity with the Vril,'
Hoffman said. 'They control the Ubermenschen by putting
thoughts into their minds and enhancing those thoughts and
instructions with the bracelets. But not everyone needs a
bracelet to hear them. Bulwer-Lytton probably thought the
ideas came to him in a dream, or that he just imagined them.'

'Whereas in fact there was a mental link of some sort, he
picked up on the actual Vril transmissions and thoughts,'

Davenport said. 'H.G. Wells too, perhaps, to a lesser extent. Well, it would also explain why the book caught on. The notion of Vril energy became a very popular one.'

'I'd never heard of it before,' Guy said.

'Oh yes you had,' Leo told him. 'You ever had Bovril?'

'Of course.'

'That's where the name came from. The "bo" from bovine, as it's derived from beef. And the "Vril" was to imply it gives you mysterious energy. If Hoffman here is right, these creatures have been influencing our lives, our evolution, to a greater extent than we ever imagined.'

'So let's get out of this hell, and do what we can to stop them,' Hoffman said. 'At least, to prevent the Vril hibernating beneath Crete from ever waking up.'

The greatest danger now they were in German uniform was from Russian snipers. They moved cautiously, keeping inside buildings as far as possible. Hoffman had a good idea of where the Russian strongholds were located. Being shot was barely more than an inconvenience to him, so Hoffman tested the open ground they had to cross by going first.

It took them all night to reach the German lines, the sounds and smells of the battle enveloping them and the darkness constantly dispelled by fires and the flashes of explosions. But once they were behind the front line, Hoffman's uniform got them out of the ruined city. They walked through fields of wounded men lying on the ground, the lucky ones getting some rudimentary attention.

'They evacuate the ones that have a chance of surviving,' Hoffman said. 'If I can get us on an evacuation flight back to Germany then we can arrange transport to Crete.'

'As simple as that?' Guy asked.

'I work directly for Heinrich Himmler,' Hoffman said. 'I may have been rather out of touch, but I'm hoping that will still count for something.'

'How much does Himmler actually know?' Leo asked. Speaking in English, he kept his voice low. 'About the Vril, I mean?'

'Enough. But he's more interested in how he can exploit their knowledge and technology than in the threat they pose. He doesn't see that at all. Most of what he knows comes from a Vril craft that crashed near Freiburg in 1936.'

'The remains we saw in the Vault at Wewelsburg. And the creature,' Guy said.

'The creature is dead, but he has others hidden away in another Vault. I didn't know that then. How much more he has...' Hoffman shrugged.

'And the first Ubermensch came from Tibet, I believe,' Leo said.

Hoffman was surprised. 'How do you know that?'

'Standartenfuhrer Streicher mentioned it. He was rather drunk at the time. And to be fair, he wasn't very specific but it was enough for me to draw my own conclusions.'

'I never thought I'd say this,' Guy told them, 'but whatever the Nazis are up to and whatever threat it poses, it will have to wait for the moment.'

Several hours later, as their plane took off, Guy looked down through a side window. The city below was a wasteland, smoke from the fires and explosions drifting across the rubble. It was hard to believe that he had actually been down there in that hellish place. But if Hoffman was right, unless their plan succeeded the whole world would soon be reduced to the same state.

The Séance Room was the obvious place to hold an exorcism. Jane was docile and compliant, but she seemed more aware of what was going on now, more herself than she had been a few days ago. Miss Manners spent several minutes explaining to her quietly and carefully what they were planning.

'And then you should be free of the Vril presence in your mind. You do want to be free of it?' she asked.

'I... I don't know.' Jane considered. Then: 'Yes,' she decided abruptly. 'I want to be free of it. I want to be able to think again. My mind is just so *numb*.'

Whatever Sarah had thought she might find when she

returned to the Station Z offices, this wasn't it. Brinkman welcomed her back, listening to her brief account of her time in Moscow, before leading the way through to the Séance Room.

Jane was lying on her back on the circular table. Her bare legs emerged from the loose dress she wore. Her arms were outstretched on either side, the bracelet still clamped tightly in place above her elbow.

'Don't you need to be a priest to do this?' Sarah said as she helped light the candles.

'Only for a Christian exorcism,' Miss Manners replied. 'And there's nothing very Christian about this. In fact, the words I shall use are taken from one of the texts in Crowley's library. It's been handed down since time immemorial.'

'Will it work?' Brinkman asked. 'Do the Vril respond to, what would you call this, magic?'

With the candles lit, Miss Manners ushered Sarah, Brinkman and Green to the side of the room. 'They do seem to have some affinity with the occult,' she said. She lowered her voice. 'And Jane will understand what's happening. This is as much for her benefit as it is for theirs.'

'How do you mean?' Green asked.

'She's sharing her mind with them at the moment. I'm hoping that the text is derived from actual rituals and ceremonies established either by the Vril, or by their enemies in ancient times. But whatever the origin, if Jane *believes* that this process has weakened or expelled their influence, then perhaps her own mind will be better able to reassert itself.'

Sarah nodded. 'Restoring her self-confidence, I see. And removing the bracelet will also weaken their control, I guess.'

'If we *can* remove it,' Brinkman said. 'I assume she wore it above the elbow so no one would see it. But the thing's pretty much welded into her skin. There's sure to be some... damage.'

'Can't be helped,' Miss Manners said. 'But you know, I'm not sure she'll care – or even notice.'

With the lights turned out, the room was lit only by the

candles. Sarah and the others were too far away to hear clearly what Miss Manners murmured as she moved round the table. There was a bowl of water on a side table. She dipped her fingers in it, then shook the water over Jane's supine body, sprinkled it on her face, traced it down the palms of her hands.

Jane's body tensed, her back arching up off the table and her face contorted in apparent pain, eyes wide open. Her breath came in sharp gasps as Miss Manners continued with the words, standing at her head and staring down into her friend's eyes.

Finally, Jane gave a cry – a sound that combined pain and sadness and loss. Her teeth clenched together and she began to writhe uncontrollably on the table.

'Hold her!' Miss Manners ordered. 'Hold her arms down.'

The woman's legs were kicking and thrashing. Brinkman and Green hurried across, each grabbing one of Jane's arms. Green leaned his weight down on her shoulder, holding her forearm with both hands.

Miss Manners grabbed Jane's hand, which was clenching and unclenching. She worked at the bracelet on the upper arm, unclasping it and folding it open. As it moved, the orange tendrils connecting the inside of the bracelet to the flesh rippled and pulled, desperately dragging the bracelet shut again.

'Sarah – help me with this.'

Sarah grabbed one half of the bracelet, working her fingers beneath it. She could feel the thin tentacles squirming round them, imagined them burrowing under her own skin, and felt sick. She swallowed, concentrating on the task of tearing open the bracelet.

Miss Manners had hold of the bracelet on the other side of the central hinge. Like Sarah, she was working it back, prising it slowly open. One of the tendrils snapped. Then another. They curled back in on themselves, retreating into the bracelet at one end, the flesh of the arm at the other.

With all her strength, Sarah ripped the bracelet open. Jane gave an almighty scream, her whole body rising up from the table before sinking back down again as her cry faded away. Skin tore from Jane's arm where the tendrils struggled to keep hold. An orange wound opened up, like a second visceral bracelet. But already the skin was beginning to reform as the tendrils closed it up again.

Jane's gasping breaths slowly subsided. Her eyes were closed now, her head lolled to one side. A thin strand of saliva hung from the side of her mouth like a spider's thread. Slowly, warily, Green and Brinkman let go of her shoulders and arms and stepped back.

'Is that it?' Green asked, his voice tight with nervous energy.

'I don't know,' Miss Manners admitted.

'She seems to be asleep,' Sarah said.

'I'll stay with her,' Miss Manners told them. 'We'll see how she is when she wakes.'

The dreams were vivid and terrible. A confused jumble of nightmare images, part memory, part vision. It was like when she saw through the eyes of the cat – gazing out through eyes that were not her own. Some of the things she saw had already happened; some were visions of things that were yet to come. Plans and aspirations, intentions and strategy.

She had only the vaguest memory of how she had become like this. Her skin crawled and tightened as she recalled something moving up her naked body. A stab of pain. The bracelet heavy on her arm. But the details were an unfocused blur.

More clearly, she could see a field of rough grass sloping down towards the sea. Rocky outcrops piercing the vegetation, the grass becoming thinner and disappearing as an area of stone thrust up through it. A shelf of rock scattered with patches of shadow. Beyond and to the side of this there were buildings, a utilitarian industrial landscape juxtaposed with the natural one. Huge storage tanks dwarfed wooden huts, metal pipes snaking away out of sight.

Then the rock seemed to come to life. The dark shadows were moving. Creatures hauled themselves up out of the holes in the rock. Long gnarled limbs reached up, searching for purchase before levering bulbous dark bodies out of the blackness. The huge bloated creatures scuttled across the rock, into the field, more and more of them – almost liquid in their density, a viscous wave of grotesque spiders spilling out of the ground and staining the fields black.

'I dreamed terrible things,' she asked weakly. 'What do they mean?'

'I don't know,' Miss Manners sighed. 'Some of it is probably your memory of what Crowley did to you. The rest…' She handed Jane a glass of water. 'How do you feel? Are you… yourself?'

'My head is clearer. But there's still something, at the back of my mind. Like when you can't quite remember something that you ought to know well. A shadow across my memories and thoughts.'

'Hopefully it will clear.'

'Am I free of them?'

'Perhaps. But your body has obviously undergone quite a change. Mrs Archer might have some ideas, but I can't tell you anything much you don't know yourself. Your dreams suggest you're still linked to the Vril. If you can resist their influence, that might help us.'

'You think I can see what they are doing, or intending?'

'You have a gift,' Miss Manners said. 'If we can focus that, see what the Vril are doing just as you saw what the cat saw in Los Angeles, then perhaps.'

'It may be too late,' Jane said. 'I can't explain exactly what I saw. But I do know it was the end of the world.'

Miss Manner sat down beside her. 'Then you'd better tell me what you saw. Every detail.'

'It does sound like the place we found in Crete,' Brinkman agreed.

'And either the hatchway you saw has been opened, or the Vril intend to open it.'

'Releasing thousands of the buggers,' Green added. 'Millions.'

'That would tie in with the stories about opening the gates of hell and awakening vengeful gods, or whatever it was,' Sarah said. 'But how do we stop it – assuming this is a prophecy and it hasn't happened already?'

Brinkman's phone rang, and he gestured for Miss Manners to answer it. 'Unless it's urgent, I'm not here.'

She lifted the receiver. 'Colonel Brinkman's phone, Miss Manners speaking.' She listened for a moment, then covered the receiver his her hand. 'Wiles,' she said quietly. 'I think you'd better speak to him.'

'So I'm a message service now am I?' Wiles said as soon as Brinkman took the phone. 'Not like I've anything else to do, now, is it?'

'I'm sorry,' Brinkman told him, 'but I have no idea what you're talking about.'

'I'm talking about a message picked up by several of the Y Stations, that's what.'

'What of it?' Brinkman asked, nonplussed.

'Well, I can't think why it was passed straight to me, but let me read it to you. This was received at nine-seventeen GMT today. And it reads: "FAO", that means "For Attention Of", by the way.'

'Yes, thank you, I did know that.'

'Well, that's a start. Anyway, it says: "FAO Dr Wiles." That's me, by the way. "Tell Ollie", and I assume that is you, "Tell Ollie we are off to meet his shepherd friend most urgently. All help appreciated. Guy and Leo." And for the record I have no idea who this shepherd is.'

'It's all right,' Brinkman told him. 'I know who he is.'

'Oh? A codename is it?'

'No, he's a shepherd.'

'Well that's clear as mud then,' Wiles said. 'I've sent a copy down to you by motorcycle, as Eleanor assures me that's the quickest way. There's a bit more, but it's just dates and times which may make more sense to you than to me. But the whole thing is so cryptic I assumed it must be urgent.'

'It is,' Brinkman agreed. 'Thank you. You may not appreciate it, but if you get any more messages like this, please do pass them on as soon as you can.'

'Oh, it's all right,' Wiles said. 'I'm just a bit miffed that it sounds like some people are having more fun than I am.'

'So what was that about, sir?' Green asked as Brinkman hung up.

'I think we were right: what Jane saw is related to our excursion to Crete. That, by a rather roundabout route, was a message from Mr Davenport and Major Pentecross.'

'Really?' Sarah's excitement was obvious. 'Did they get to Stalingrad? Where are they now?'

'I'm afraid I have no idea,' Brinkman told her. 'But I know where they're going.'

CHAPTER 42

Hoffman had returned to Wewelsburg from Russia, Guy and Leo Davenport travelling with him. Rather than risk getting into the castle again, they waited in the shed where Hoffman had a radio set hidden – and from there sent a cryptic signal they hoped would get to Brinkman without making much sense to anyone else who intercepted it. Now in SS uniforms, they had travelled with Hoffman back to Crete.

'The whole area is off limits now,' Hoffman told them. 'Nachten was flown back to Berlin for treatment. He broke some ribs and an arm, nothing too major. But he's still at Wewelsburg, recovering. I persuaded him I should come back to Crete to check on how his man Grebben is doing. Lucky for us, Nachten left instructions that no one is to go back down into the Labyrinth until his return.'

They spent as much time as they could going over the plan time and time again. It wasn't perfect – no plan could be. But there didn't seem to be any realistic alternative.

'Will you have time to get away?' Davenport asked Hoffman.

'Does it matter if I live or die?' he asked. 'It doesn't to me.'

'We'd hate to lose you,' Guy told him.

Hoffman did not reply.

So far as Mihali was aware, it was the fuel depot they were interested in. Hoffman insisted on a full inspection of the facility as soon as they arrived in Crete, taking Guy and Leo with him. Having seen everything they needed to, Guy and Leo slipped away from the quarters they had been given on the edge of the fuel depot, and headed for where they hoped to contact Mihali.

The dates and times they had put in the message to Brinkman had been of necessity vague, and they had no way of knowing if the message had even got through. But Mihali was waiting for them at the edge of the wooded area where he and Guy had hidden to observe the depot almost three months earlier. He raised his eyebrows as he saw the uniforms they were wearing.

'I suggest you delay your plan for twenty-four hours,' Mihali said when Guy and Leo gave him an edited version of what they intended.

'Why's that?' Guy asked.

'Our mutual friend Ollie Brinkman is due to arrive tomorrow evening. Organising my people at short notice won't be easy, and what you're asking requires some skill. My chaps are better at blowing things up, and to be honest I'm not sure why you're not just setting explosives.'

'There's something under that area of rock that we need to make sure is destroyed,' Leo told him. 'Just blowing up the fuel depot won't do it.'

Mihali nodded. 'I see. We haven't noticed any construction in that area, but maybe they tunnelled through from the fuel depot or under the cliffs.'

'Maybe,' Guy said. Neither he nor Leo were ready to tell Mihali that it wasn't a German installation they were targeting.

Explaining why they were staying on for another day at the facility was a potential problem. But Hoffman simply asked to see the paperwork relating to fuel transfers for the past six months. It didn't take him long to come up with a list of difficult questions and demands for further information. The depot supervisor was relieved when Hoffman offered to stay an extra day while the administrative staff sorted out what he wanted.

'The last thing either of us want is for me to report back, and to be told I missed something and have to return,' Hoffman said. 'Better to be thorough now, and then we can leave you in peace.'

'And some time in the next twenty-four hours,' Guy added, 'we shall want to test your emergency evacuation procedures. There will be no prior warning, except that I shall require you to sound the alarm at a time I specify, of course.'

'Will the evacuation include Hauptsturmfuhrer Grebben's men?' the supervisor asked nervously.

'It will,' Hoffman told him. 'But if you prefer, I shall inform the Hauptsturmfuhrer myself of the exercise.'

It was clear the supervisor certainly would prefer this.

Guy was not surprised at the reaction when they met Grebben. The Hauptsturmfuhrer had requisitioned a hut on the edge of the facility, close to the shelf of rock where the entrance to the Labyrinth was hidden.

'My orders from Standartenfuhrer Nachten are to stay here, sir,' he told Hoffman.

Guy and Leo kept to the background and made no comment. Leo, of course had little idea what was being said, though Guy followed the discussion easily.

'Well, now I am giving you fresh orders,' Hoffman replied.

Grebben shifted uncomfortably, aware that his own men were watching too. 'Can I ask the purpose of this evacuation exercise?'

'It is to make certain that this facility can be evacuated effectively in a timely manner, that is all.'

'And why is an assistant to the Reichsfuhrer-SS so interested?'

Hoffman waited a few moments before he answered, allowing Grebben to wonder if he had perhaps gone too far.

'You have been down into the Labyrinth,' Hoffman said at last. 'You have seen what is down there. Do you really need to ask why we might have to clear this entire area as rapidly as possible?'

Grebben did not reply. A nerve ticked rapidly at the corner of his left eye.

'When the alarm sounds,' Hoffman went on, 'you and your men will take part in the drill, and evacuate this area along with the other personnel. Is that clear, Hauptsturmfuhrer?'

They waited in the middle of nowhere. The fields were bordered by woods on one side, the ground rising to rocky mountains on the other. It was the perfect landing zone, well away from any habitation. The plane was flying high, so as not to be heard, and with a light wind there was a danger of drifting. But right on schedule, Guy spotted the three pale parachutes floating down towards them.

'Has Brinkman done this before?' Guy wondered.

'Who knows,' Davenport told him. 'The colonel keeps himself to himself rather. I think Green's seen a lot of service though. Wouldn't surprise me if he hasn't made a few drops in his time.'

The two men came down at the edge of the area, close to the woods. The third parachute landed nearby – a wooden crate of equipment attached to it. With the help of Guy, Davenport and Mihali, Brinkman and Green detached themselves from their 'chutes, and bundled them up and out of sight.

Mihali helped Green open the equipment crate and they split the contents between them.

'We need to get moving, sir,' Guy told Brinkman. 'We start at first light.'

Brinkman nodded. 'You'd better tell me all about it on the way.'

The easiest and quickest way back into the facility was through the fence. The first light of dawn was breaking across the sea in front of them as they reached the edge of the woods. The hole they had cut back in July was still unrepaired, the fence folded back into place so that it didn't show.

'They obviously don't inspect the fence very often or very well,' Brinkman said as they reached it.

'I'll tell Hoffman,' Leo told him. 'He can make an official complaint. I expect there's a form he can fill in.'

A complication was that the area below them, around the rock shelf, was now patrolled by Grebben's SS men.

'They'll be gone soon when we set off the alarms,' Guy said. 'Hoffman's ordered them to evacuate with everyone else.'

'Just so long as they do,' Green said. 'If not, then it could get interesting.'

The metal pipeline running round the edge of the rock shelf and then off to the jetty was obvious.

'Leo and I took a look yesterday,' Guy told the others, 'as best we could, without it being obvious what we were doing. Anyway, there seems to be a valve about halfway along that section there. Probably for venting air or drawing off excess fuel if they need to clear the pipe.'

'Or if that doesn't work, you may have to just make a hole in it,' Leo added. 'Without sparks flying, of course.'

'I still think we should just blow the thing up,' Mihali told them.

'Not an option, I'm afraid,' Brinkman said. 'You can never guarantee success, of course,' he went on, 'but this seems to be as good a plan as we could put together under the circumstances. Good luck to everyone, and hopefully we'll meet back at the drop zone in a few hours.'

Mihali and Green folded back the wire and Guy and Leo squeezed through the gap in the fence. Brinkman passed Guy a small backpack, which he slung over his shoulder.

The SS patrol had passed a few minutes ago and was out of sight, so they should be safe for a while. Even so, they hurried down the slope, putting as much distance between themselves and where they had come through the perimeter as possible. It was fully light now, but if Grebben's men saw them, they would assume Guy and Davenport had come from the fuel facility.

Hoffman was waiting behind one of the huts, close to the largest of the two main fuel tanks. Together they made their way along to where a network of pipes joined together in a complicated junction of valves and flow controls before entering the tank.

'Your people ready?' Hoffman asked.

'They're ready,' Leo told him. 'As soon as Grebben's men are out of the way they'll get to work on the pipe.'

'I need to get down there before they open the valve,' Hoffman said.

'Are you all set?' Guy asked.

Hoffman pulled back the cuff of his jacket to show the inert bracelet Davenport had given him clamped to his left wrist. From his pocket he produced the axe-head. 'There's just one other thing I need.'

Guy slipped the small backpack off his shoulder and handed it to Hoffman, who opened it to check the contents. He placed the axe-head inside, and closed it up again.

'Thank you,' Hoffman said grimly. 'Now I'm all set.'

CHAPTER 43

The alarm was like the wail of an air-raid siren. It cut through the early morning air, easily audible at the edge of the wood where Brinkman was waiting with Green and Mihali.

'Right on time,' Green said, checking his watch.

Some of Mihali's men were in position further along the perimeter, out of sight but ready to give covering fire if it was needed.

'So far, so good,' Mihali said, watching the fuel depot through binoculars. 'There are people leaving, in rather a hurry. I guess they think it's a real emergency.'

'The SS men are heading back to the depot too,' Brinkman said. 'We'll give it a couple of minutes, just to be sure there are no malingerers.'

All the activity was concentrated on the far side of the facility. People hurried to designated safe areas, and trucks ferried staff further away from the huge fuel tanks. Mihali led Green and Brinkman back down to the fence, pulling it open to let them through.

'I'll stay here so I have a clear view of the whole area. If I see any activity, I'll fire a warning shot. If nothing else, that should draw the enemy away from you.'

'Remember Hoffman, the SS major, will be coming this way in a few minutes,' Brinkman said. 'Don't shoot him by accident, he's with us.'

'I'd still like to know how you pulled that off,' Mihali said. 'Good luck to you both.'

'And to you, mate,' Green said. He took the canvas bag that Mihali gave him, then helped him fold the fence wire back into place.

They walked briskly down the slope towards the pipeline. If they ran, they knew they were more likely to attract attention. Rapid movement could draw the eye, and it would look more suspicious. The valve was where Davenport had told them it was. They knelt down beside it, Green opening the bag of tools they had brought.

The pipe was larger than Green had expected – almost a foot in diameter.

'There'll be a lot of fuel flowing through this,' he said.

'Just so long as Pentecross and Davenport open the valves at the other end, and keep them open.'

Brinkman handed Green an adjustable spanner and the sergeant set to work on the valve mechanism. It was set above a threaded socket where another pipe could be attached then secured. The socket itself was covered with a metal cap, which Brinkman unscrewed. The valve hadn't been used for a while, if ever, and the locking nut was stiff.

'It might even have been painted over,' Green complained as he strained at the spanner.

'Here, let me,' a voice said from behind them.

Both men turned in surprise. Brinkman already had his hand on his pistol. But the uniformed figure watching them seemed unconcerned.

'You must be Hoffman,' Brinkman realised.

'Some of the time.' Hoffman stepped past them and took over from Green. He gripped the spanner tightly in both hands. For a moment, nothing happened. Then the spanner turned suddenly. Dark, viscous liquid dripped out from the socket below the valve.

'There you go.' Hoffman straightened up.

'You're stronger than you look,' Green said.

'Sadly, that is true. Give me a few minutes, then open it

fully. Your colleagues are opening the valves at the tank.'

'Thank you,' Brinkman said. 'We'll see you later,' he added, speaking in German.

Hoffman smiled. 'We both know that is extremely unlikely. But anything is possible.' He continued down the slope towards the rocky shelf.

The evacuation drill was scheduled to last for an hour. Guy hoped that would be long enough. But the chances were that no one would think to check the valves at the fuel tanks for a while after they were allowed back inside the facility.

'That should be long enough for Brinkman to get the upstream valve open,' Leo said. 'You want to do the honours?'

Guy turned the wheel that controlled the flow through the pipe. 'I hope this is the right one.'

'Trust me, it's the right one.' Leo had traced the pipe back through the various connections and junctions. 'But there's a gauge here on the side. If we've got the wrong pipe, it won't be open at the other end and the fuel just won't flow. It's a safety measure; both valves have to be open at the same time, in case one fails.'

The wheel reached the end of its run and stopped.

'We could break the wheel off, so no one can close it,' Guy suggested.

'No, I think that will just draw attention. As it is you have to check the gauge before you can see the valve is open.' Leo peered at the small glass panel, checking the position of the needle behind it. 'Yes, that's flowing.'

'In that case…' Guy bent down and scraped a handful of dirt and mud from the sole of his boot. He smeared it across the glass, obscuring the gauge.

'Good idea,' Leo said. 'So, now what?'

'Now we get the hell out of here before the fireworks start.'

In theory, the two of them should be the only people left within the installation now it had been evacuated. But as they reached the edge of the main buildings, Guy could see a group of soldiers a short distance ahead of them making their way towards the fields behind the facility. They wore the distinctive darker uniforms of the SS.

'Where the hell are they off to?' Leo said.

'I don't know,' Guy replied. 'But if they keep going they'll run right into Brinkman and Green.'

'Then we've got to stop them.' Leo broke into a run, Guy close behind.

'Halt!' Guy yelled in German.

The soldiers stopped, waiting for Guy and Leo to reach them.

'Where do you think you're going?' Guy demanded, breathless, as soon as they were close.

'We are just following orders,' one of the soldiers – a corporal – replied.

'Whose orders?' Guy asked. But he could guess. 'You're with Hauptsturmfuhrer Grebben, aren't you? Did he order you to ignore the evacuation drill?'

The corporal shifted uncomfortably and glanced at his colleagues. 'We have our orders,' he repeated.

'And I have mine,' Guy told him. 'What instructions did the Hauptsturmfuhrer give you? You can either answer to me, or to a court martial. It's your decision.'

The corporal stiffened to attention. 'Our orders were to wait for the drill to start, and then join him in the tunnels, under the field. There is—'

'I know about the tunnels,' Guy interrupted. 'You said you were to join Grebben. Is he already in the tunnels?'

'He is, sir.'

'Then we will find him,' Guy said. 'If he has a legitimate reason for disobeying Sturmbannfuhrer Hoffman's direct orders then he can explain it to me. You and your men will join the evacuation drill. At once.'

As soon as the soldiers were out of earshot, Guy told Leo what the corporal had said.

'If Grebben's down in the Labyrinth, he could ruin everything,' Leo said.

'We have to find Hoffman and warn him,' Guy decided.

'He's probably in the Labyrinth already,' Leo pointed out as they started to run.

'Then we go in after him and make sure nothing goes wrong.'

It was like he had been here before, in a dream, or so long ago he only half-remembered. The fields sloping down to the rocky ledge that itself then sloped down towards the sea. Hoffman knew exactly where the opening would be, and what it looked like.

He climbed down through the narrow gap, easing himself into the subterranean Labyrinth. They were expecting him, which was good.

Dark liquid poured out of the socket in the side of the main pipe, splashing to the already sodden ground below. A vast pool of fuel oil was spreading down the slope, becoming a river flowing towards the rocky ledge.

Brinkman and Green watched from the other side of the pipe. The smell was nauseating and getting worse.

'We should probably get well clear, sir,' Green said. 'I've seen what that stuff can do to a man if it ignites.'

'Back to Mihali,' Brinkman agreed. 'We can watch the progress from there, and make sure it gets to the where we need it.'

'And if it doesn't, sir?'

'Then we pray.'

CHAPTER 44

By the time Guy and Leo reached the pipeline, fuel oil was pouring across the landscape. It collected in a slight dip in the field, forming a large pool. But soon it would lip over the edge and run across the rocky outcrop, then down into the tunnels. There was no sign of Hoffman.

'You sure about this?' Leo asked.

'I don't think we have much choice.'

'Then let's be quick.'

'Agreed,' Guy told him. 'I'd like to be in and out of there before we get flooded.'

They set off round the edge of the growing pool of oil, and clambered quickly across the rock shelf. In moments they were lowering themselves down through the narrow opening and into the Labyrinth.

'Once more unto the breach,' Leo muttered. 'I keep hoping someone's going to shout "Cut!" and give us notes.'

'At least I have a torch this time,' Guy said, pulling from his pocket and shining it down the tunnel.

'I bet you were a boy scout, always prepared.'

'I do my best. So, can you remember the way to the main chamber?'

'What the hell are they playing at?' Brinkman said.

He and Green were on their way to join Mihali, but

Brinkman had looked back in time to see Leo and Guy hurrying across the rocky shelf and down into the Labyrinth.

'No idea,' sir,' Green replied. 'But I don't think there's much we can do to help them.'

Brinkman had to agree. 'Whatever it is, let's hope they're quick about it.'

Hoffman was expecting company. He walked slowly through the tunnel, light still filtering in from behind and above. They knew he was coming, and it was only a matter of time before something came to meet him.

But the figure that stepped from a dark opening further along the tunnel was not one that Hoffman expected. 'What are you doing here?' he demanded.

'I might ask you the same thing,' Grebben replied. 'Sir,' he added, though there was no respect in his tone. He was holding a Luger, pointing it at Hoffman through the semi-darkness.

'That is none of your business.'

'Oh, but it is.' Grebben stepped closer. 'Standartenfuhrer Nachten ordered me to allow no one down here without his express permission. No one at all. He was very precise in his instructions, and the lengths I must go to in order to preserve this site.'

'You think that applies to me? Or that I don't have his permission?'

'I have my orders. Just tell me what you are doing down here, sir.'

Hoffman started down the tunnel towards Grebben. This was wasting time – time he didn't have. 'I don't have to tell you anything. Get out of my way.'

'I checked with Wewelsburg,' Grebben said, stepping in front of Hoffman and blocking his way. 'No one knows you are here.'

'No one you spoke to, I'm sure. Did that include Reichsfuhrer Himmler?'

There was a flicker of uncertainty in the shadows of

Grebben's face. He stepped back, the gun still raised. 'You're alone. Whatever happens between us down here, no one will ever know.'

Hoffman gave a short laugh. 'That's certainly true. Now, I am in a hurry, so either get out of my way or shoot me.'

'And if I shoot you?'

'Then you are a dead man.'

'No,' Grebben said quietly. 'No, that's not how it works.'

The flash was sudden and bright in the near-darkness. The sound of the gunshot echoed off the tunnel walls. Hoffman was knocked back several paces by the force of the bullet that hammered into his chest. He looked down at the smoking hole in his jacket, brushed at it with the back of his hand as he felt the flesh below begin to knit back together.

Grebben stared in disbelief. 'But – that's not possible,' he gasped.

'Oh, I can assure you it is,' Hoffman told him. 'And I did warn you.'

Hoffman's bullet caught Grebben in the throat. He staggered backwards, dropping his own gun, clutching his neck. Dark liquid poured out over his hands, splashing to the floor. His whole body heaved, choked, convulsed. Then he was spewing blood, collapsing against the tunnel wall, sliding slowly down until he was a crumpled heap on the ground, the blood pooling darkly around him.

Hoffman paused for long enough to take a torch out of his backpack. He shone it across Grebben's body, waiting until the final spasms had subsided.

He turned at the sound of running footsteps behind him. Torchlight flickered across the tunnel walls. Hoffman raised his gun, ready to put paid to any further delays.

'No, wait – it's us!'

He lowered the gun as Guy Pentecross and Leo Davenport were revealed by the light of his own torch.

'I see you found Grebben,' Davenport said.

'We ran into his men heading this way,' Guy explained. 'It's all right, he added quickly, 'we sent them off.'

'Then you should get out of here too,' Hoffman said. 'The Vril are waiting. I can feel them scratching at my mind.'

'We'll come with you,' Guy said. 'Some of the way at least. Just in case Grebben wasn't alone.'

'I think he was,' Hoffman said, glancing down at the body at his feet. 'You should go back. It isn't safe down here. You may already have left it too late.'

'You mean the fuel?' Guy said.

'Not just that. The Vril can sense my approach. They know I have the key – the axe. They will close off the Labyrinth behind me to be sure I get to the main chamber.'

'You mean we could be trapped down here?' Leo said.

Hoffman nodded. 'Go,' he repeated. 'And good luck.'

'You too,' Guy told him.

They shook hands. It seemed a strangely formal farewell. Then Hoffman continued down the tunnel. Guy and Leo watched him turn the corner, and disappear into darkness and shadow.

The liquid ran more quickly across the stone, pooling in hollows. The pools gradually joined as more liquid flowed in, finding its way down hill towards the cliffs. The way the ground dipped into the indented shape of the axe-head drew the liquid in. It poured down, like water over a weir. At the centre of the indentation, it sought out the opening into the labyrinth.

A torrent of the dark, viscous fluid crashed down into the tunnels. The oil washed across the body of Hauptsturmfuhrer Grebben, and on down the gently sloping tunnel, gathering speed and momentum. A wave of fuel crashed through the tunnels, towards the lowest point.

Retracing their steps was not as easy as Guy had expected and hoped. They had hurried towards the sound first of voices, then a shot. But neither he nor Leo could find the way back again. It was as if the walls had moved, the tunnels rearranged themselves as they passed through. Remembering Hoffman's warning, Guy began to wonder if perhaps they had.

'Turn the torch off,' Leo suggested.

'How will that help?'

'We might be able to see light coming in.'

Guy turned off the torch. There was some light, just enough to make out Leo's shape close to him. But not enough to be sure of a direction.

'I thought your memory was infallible,' Guy said, turning the torch back on again.

'Yes, well, I was hoping you'd forgotten that.' Leo smiled, despite the situation. 'Though I should point out that there's quite a difference between memorising lines and remembering a route taken in haste underground and in the dark.'

'So you've no idea?'

'Well, I think it's that way.' He gestured to an opening a short distance ahead of them. 'And I think we should hurry.'

'Obviously.'

Leo caught Guy's arm. 'No, I *really* think we should hurry.'

He moved Guy's arm so the torch was pointing down at the floor of the tunnel. Thick, dark liquid was running along the ground. It filled the narrow gaps between the paving slabs, then welled up again and spread across the width of the passageway. It lapped against their boots, licking over the toes and on down the tunnel.

The tunnels sloped down to the central chamber. He could feel them getting stronger inside his mind, probing, searching. He concentrated on what he wanted them to know – that he had the final key.

At some point, he wasn't sure exactly when, another figure joined him, walking just behind. It was a good job that Pentecross and Davenport had not come with him. There was no chance of retreat now, even if he decided to go no further. He could hear the massive creature snorting like the bull it partly was.

He could see two of them, vague shapes in someone else's memory, standing on a deserted shore as they waited for the

Vril craft to surface. Striding out into the sea, to return with the two keys that had been recovered – one from Los Angeles, the other from London. Bringing them back here through the maze of tunnels that ran down to the cliffs below.

It was an effort not to think about what he was doing. What he was *really* doing. He concentrated on the axe-head in the rucksack, mentally emptying it of everything else he was carrying and leaving just the axe – the final key – nestling inside. If he felt his thoughts drifting to anything else, he turned them to Alina, to her smile, the sound of her voice. The single cracked photograph of her that he possessed…

Entering the central chamber, he saw the shattered stone where the Minotaurs had emerged from their long sleep, ready to awaken their masters. Think of the axe. And Alina. Nothing else.

A dark scuttling at the edge of the torch beam. A Vril edged into view – little more than an extension of the shadows at the edge of the chamber. But he could feel it inside his head, as if the grotesque creature's spindly tentacles were groping round inside his mind.

'Where is it?'

The thoughts appeared as a mixture of images and feelings that he translated into words. It was easiest to speak the reply, and let them hear the thoughts behind the words.

'I have it here.'

'We thought you were lost to us.'

He made sure the torch beam fell across the bracelet on his wrist as he shrugged out of the rucksack. He didn't dare look inside, but felt for the axe-head, withdrawing it through the smallest possible opening.

'Why do you think of fire?'

He froze, desperately emptying his mind of everything except the axe. 'This world will burn,' he said.

'Empires are forged in fire and war. What survives is the strongest, the most useful to us.'

He held up the axe in one hand, shining the torch at it with the other. The Vril crept forwards, into the light, as if drawn towards the object. Brittle gnarled legs reached upwards.

Hoffman glanced back towards the entrance, shining the torch at the dry, dusty ground. Nothing. He strained to hear, but the only sounds were the stentorian breathing of the Minotaur and the scraping of the Vril's limbs across the floor.

The other two keys were already in place, slotted into the sockets at the side of the circular hatchway. The Vril was squatting beside the empty third socket, pulsing with suppressed excitement.

'Open it!'

Their feet splashed in the heavy liquid as Guy and Leo hurried along the tunnel. It was getting deeper by the moment, washing past them. They turned into a side tunnel, where the ground was dry. The fuel ran like a river down the main passageway.

'We should think about this,' Leo said.

'We should keep going,' Guy told him. 'If we keep to the side tunnels we can move quicker.'

Leo was shaking his head. 'No, the fuel's pouring in through the entranceway. Which is where we need to get back to.'

'Obviously.'

'So if we follow the fuel back, against the flow...'

'We reach the entrance, where it's coming in.'

'But you're right, we need to hurry,' Leo said. 'The deeper and faster it gets, the harder it'll be to move against the flow. And if we're still down here when...' He didn't need to finish the thought.

'Come on, then,' Guy said.

He stepped back into the main tunnel, hurrying forwards. The pressure of the liquid running past them was already making it difficult. In the torchlight, the whole floor was a heaving, black mass. A wave of darkness crashed towards them, slamming into Guy's legs. They were wading through it now, covered in oil. The smell was stifling, thick fumes making it difficult to breath.

'It can't be far,' Leo gasped.

'Let's hope not.'

As Guy pushed onwards, the torchlight danced across the surface of the liquid, up the walls, over the roof of the tunnel. At first he thought it was a reflection – the undulating liquid somehow mirrored above them. But then in a sudden stomach-dropping shock he realised what he could see. He stopped abruptly, Leo almost knocking into him as he waded alongside.

'What?'

Guy said nothing, just shone the torch directly upwards – at the creatures clinging to the roof of the tunnel. Dark, bulbous shapes hanging above them, swaying and rippling as they moved. Thin, brittle limbs scraped across the stone, seeking out crevices and openings where they could cling on.

'Are they watching us?' Leo said quietly.

'Who knows.' Guy waded onwards. 'It's like they're just waiting. They must know we're here.'

'Maybe they don't like the fuel. It stinks to high Heaven.'

'Not sure they have noses,' Guy said. 'But you're right, they may just be keeping out of it.'

He shone the torch upwards again. It looked as if the roof further on was clear of the creatures. But as they waded forwards, there was a sudden splash in front of them. Drops of oil spattered across Guy's face. The light played across the walls as he wiped it away. Then back onto the surface of the flowing liquid – onto the dark creature rising up in front of them.

Leo had his pistol out, taking aim as the Vril moved rapidly towards them.

'No!' Guy warned. 'A shot might ignite the fuel.'

'You got a better idea?' Leo demanded.

A serrated tentacle whipped past Guy's face as the creature reared up. He ducked out of the way just in time. There was a blur of movement beside him as Leo lunged forwards. A flurry of tentacles, oil splashing over Guy's face again. He blinked it away in time to see Leo's hand slash down at the bloated black shape. The tunnel echoed with the Vril's screeches. A spray of dark liquid coated the walls – not oil this time.

The oil bubbled as the creature thrashed and fought. But it was weakening, Leo waded away from it – a deflated dark mass floated past Guy, a limp tentacle brushing against him. He turned to watch it float away down the tunnel.

'Pocket knife,' Leo explained breathlessly. 'Not that I'd want to go through that again, so let's get moving.'

But Guy's attention was fixed on a point behind them, down the tunnel. Where a dark shape was emerging from a side tunnel – not the bulbous, scuttling form of a Vril, but something larger. A figure, silhouetted against the torchlight reflecting off the shiny surface of the oil. Huge, muscular, its torso covered in matted hair, and with the head of a massive bull. Steam erupted from its nostrils as it turned towards them. A bellow of rage echoed round the tunnel as the body of the Vril that Leo had killed floated past the Minotaur.

Then it turned towards Guy and Leo, forcing its way through the liquid towards them.

'I'm guessing he's quicker than us,' Leo said.

'And I'm guessing your pocket knife won't stop him,' Guy said. 'Come on.'

They waded forwards as fast as they could. But the liquid was getting deeper – above their knees. Behind them, Guy could hear the splashing of the Minotaur as it waded towards them, closer with every massive step.

Hoffman could smell it now. He thought he could hear it, a low rumble in the distance. He concentrated on the axe – on how it felt in his hand, how it fitted into the socket.

As soon as he released the key, it dropped fully into place. With a scraping, rasping sound, the circular hatchway dropped down, and then slid aside. Hoffman's torch illuminated a dark chasm beneath. The light gave out before it reached the bottom.

There was another sound now. More scraping and sliding of stone on stone echoing up from deep below. The clattering of hundreds – perhaps thousands – of tentacle-like limbs. The depths of the darkness seemed to deepen and swell. Glimmers of reflected light as malevolent eyes stared upwards. Then the first of the Vril appeared in the torchlight, scrabbling up the shaft, hauling itself towards the surface.

The Vril at the top of the shaft scuttled forwards, to the edge.

'They are coming!'

'Yes,' Hoffman agreed. The axe or Alina. Nothing else existed. He reached down for the rucksack and lifted it up.

'What are you thinking?'

'Only of victory.' That much was true. He pulled open the top of the rucksack and reached inside.

'No.' The Vril was moving round the opening, towards Hoffman. 'You are thinking about another human.'

Dark, crooked tentacles reached out over the lip of the opening. Contorted limbs scrabbled to get a grip. The first of the Vril hauled themselves up and out, stalking towards Hoffman with the other Vril.

'You are thinking about a woman.'

The rumble behind Hoffman became a roar as a wave of fuel crashed in. The Minotaur staggered back, unbalanced by the weight of liquid that swept into its legs. The Vril in the chamber reared up on their back legs, front limbs raking the air.

'Her name is Alina,' Hoffman had to shout about the roar, though they would have heard his thoughts anyway.

The wave swept across the chamber. He braced himself against it to keep his balance. Fluid poured over the lip of the open hatchway, a sudden violent waterfall crashing down. Most of the Vril in the shaft were swept away, screeching and howling. Some managed to cling on, desperately reaching upwards, clawing their way through the constant flow of falling fuel.

Hoffman waded through the sticky liquid, finding where it was shallow but close to the shaft, pulling the packages from the rucksack.

A Vril splashed towards him through the liquid, and he kicked at it viciously, sending it rolling away in a mass of whirling tentacles. It toppled over the lip and down the shaft.

They were tearing at Alina. In his mind, the Vril clawed and ripped at her, shredding her dress. But she was only a picture, an image, a photograph. It tore away, and for the first time he allowed himself to think about what he was doing. For the first time the Vril saw the image revealed behind the mental picture as it disintegrated into a ball of fire.

Torpex was short for 'torpedo explosive'. A combination of TNT and the more powerful RDX laced with powdered aluminium that would prolong the explosive pulse, it was designed to burn even underwater. Hoffman tore across the tops of the friction strips. He watched the fuses burst into intense flame, burning down towards the explosives.

He had dropped his torch, but through the stuttering light of the fuses, he saw the Minotaur hurl itself across the chamber, head down as it charged towards him. He didn't move. Made no attempt to get out of the way. Waited until the last possible moment – so that the fuses were almost spent and as much fuel as possible had poured down into the Vril's hibernation chambers deep below. Then he threw the explosives towards the open shaft.

The bull's horns hammered into Hoffman, lifting him off the ground and tossing him across the chamber. He rolled as he landed, splashing through fuel, somehow getting to his feet – running.

He had always known he was going to die here, but now that there was nothing he could do about it, now that there was no turning back, he was running for his life – out of the chamber and up the tunnel, against the tide of flowing fuel.

Behind him, the Torpex exploded as it neared the bottom of the shaft. The fuel vapour ignited first, blasting up through the shaft. Then the fuel itself burst into flame, scorching through the lower levels and sterilising them of Vril. Dark shapes burst into brilliant light. Shrieks and screams were lost in the roar of the explosion.

The percussive force hit Hoffman harder than the Minotaur had done. It propelled him up the tunnel. A ball of fire erupted from the shaft and blasted through the chamber. The Minotaur disappeared in a blaze of orange flame.

The fire swept up the tunnel, running along the river of fuel, hurtling after Hoffman as he ran for the opening so far ahead. His torch was gone, but the whole tunnel system was bathed in the light of the fire. He stumbled and lurched against the tunnel wall. His hand disappeared through an opening and he fell through into the tunnel on the other side.

That was it. He couldn't outrun the fire now. He staggered back to his feet, ready to step back into the main tunnel and the charging flames. Except – the tunnel here was dry. The fuel didn't run through it as it sought out the shortest way downhill to the main chamber. If Hoffman could get far enough along this tunnel, away from the fuel and the flames then perhaps he had a chance.

Then he felt the heat on his face. The flames roared past and the world exploded into red.

The Minotaur was so close that Guy could hear the creature's roar behind him, feel its hot breath on the back of his neck. The roar became a low rumble from deep in the Labyrinth. The breath was a wave of heat moving through the tunnel.

A massive hand closed on Guy's shoulder, wrenching him back. The torch went flying, disappearing into the shadowy liquid that was gushing past them, up to their waists.

But as the Minotaur dragged Guy back, he realised that he could still see. There was light above them – shining down through a hole in the rock, illuminating the dark torrent of oil that crashed down in front of them like a waterfall.

The creature's painful grip loosened slightly as Leo hammered his shoulder into the Minotaur's side. With an almighty effort, Guy tore himself free of the monster's grasp. He turned, pulling his gun from its holster. The Minotaur reared up, dark oil dripping from its glistening body. One powerful arm lashed out, sending Leo spinning away.

Then Guy lunged forwards – straight at the creature, gun raised. The smallest spark would be disastrous. But the time for caution was gone. Deep in the Labyrinth, the rumble was becoming a roar. Flickering orange and red lit the roof of the tunnel behind them.

The Minotaur reached out for Guy again. Leo struggled towards it, thumping at its back, but with no effect. It opened its jaws, saliva mixing with fuel oil, teeth glinting orange and red. Without thinking, Guy rammed the barrel of his Luger into the creature's mouth and pulled the trigger.

For a moment it was still. The sound of the shot was lost in the growing bellow of the explosion and fire. Then the Minotaur staggered backwards, stumbling and falling into the flowing oil. It struggled back to its feet, but in those few moments it had been swept back down the tunnel several yards. Far enough for Guy and Leo to have time to reach the side of the crevice.

Oil poured past them as they clambered up the other side. The rock was slick with fuel, slippery and treacherous. Guy felt himself sliding back down, but Leo's hand grabbed him, and helped him regain his grip.

Suddenly, they were in daylight, and the stench of the fuel was mitigated by the sea breeze. Slipping and stumbling, they scrambled across the rock shelf and towards the field. They had moments – seconds at most – before the area became a raging inferno.

Up the slope, away from the pipeline and the torrent of fuel washing down towards the rocks and into the Labyrinth. Finally, they collapsed, gasping and exhausted.

The roar of the explosion erupted like a wave of sound from the rocky depths behind them, Looking back, Guy saw a single figure emerge from the entrance in the rock, climbing up through the lake of fuel.

It stood knee-deep in the liquid, bellowing in rage. The head of a bull and the body of a man, standing defiant as flames erupted from the ground behind it. The figure was immediately enveloped, burning as it staggered forwards, through a sea of fire.

The flames spread across the surface of the fuel, rushing

towards the pipeline higher up the hill where liquid still poured out.

Further up the hill, Brinkman watched Guy and Leo scramble away from the fire. He could feel the heat of the flames that reached the pipe and clawed their way inside. He could imagine the fuel in the pipe igniting, a shockwave roaring inside. At one end was a closed valve where the ships would attach for refuelling. At the other…

The entire massive fuel tank exploded in a moment. A second later, the blast wave thumped into Brinkman's chest like a physical blow. The air was full of flame and debris. Then the second tank exploded, blasting the remaining buildings in the facility to matchwood.

There were further, smaller detonations as more pipelines and backup fuel tanks exploded. Liquid fire rained down across the whole area.

'Probably time we were leaving,' Mihali said as the sound of the explosions died away. 'I've a feeling that might have attracted some attention.'

'I'm hoping it did more than that,' Brinkman said.

CHAPTER 45

Dr Wiles passed round a sheet of paper. It was a table of numbers divided into columns that were themselves numbered. It meant nothing at all to Guy, who passed it on to Leo. When Sarah, Sergeant Green and Colonel Brinkman had also looked at it, Miss Manners passed it back to Wiles. It was clear from their faces that no one understood it at all.

'You'll see that the figures speak for themselves,' Wiles said unhelpfully.

'Perhaps you could summarise for us?' Colonel Brinkman suggested.

'If you think that's necessary.'

'It's necessary,' Miss Manners told him.

'Well, in that case...' He held the paper up, pointing at parts of the table as he explained. 'The columns are by date, recording the number of UDT transmissions and other Vril communications by month. This table records only those UDTs detected in the area of Crete bounded by these grid references noted here, and the other communications which either emanate from or appear to be directed towards that area of the Mediterranean.'

'And what do the numbers tell us?' Brinkman asked.

'They tell us that Crete was something of a centre for Vril communications and activity in the last six months, which is partly why we focused our own attentions there, of course.

But in the last week, since you and your colleagues returned from your last expedition to the island…' He held up the paper again, and gestured emphatically to it with his other hand, like a Shakespearean actor. 'Nothing.'

'Nothing?' Guy echoed.

'Not a jot. Nothing. Which, it seems to me, rather suggests that your expedition was a complete success.' Wiles put the paper down on the table in front of him and stared at it. 'So, well done.'

'That doesn't mean our job is finished, though,' Brinkman said.

'Far from it,' Wiles agreed. 'If anything, the Vril activity in other geographical areas has increased. Probably messages toing and froing about what we've been up to and what they can do about it.'

'Do we have any way of knowing exactly what that is?' Green asked.

'Jane's visions of the Vril have faded,' Miss Manners said. 'But she still has the dreams, and she can still connect to them at times. Her visions are still stronger than I can achieve. If we can interpret what she sees, that might help.'

She opened a folder and took out a large glossy black and white photograph. 'This might interest you. It's a photograph I took of Jane Roylston when we first brought her back here, once we knew she was working for the Vril.'

The picture showed a corner of the Station Z offices. But the figure sitting on a chair by a desk looked nothing like Jane Roylston. The areas emerging from her clothes were a mesh of interconnected and tangled lines, as if someone had tried to clothe a human figure constructed out of different types of string and wool.

'I took several, but this was using a flash. Without the flash, she looked quite normal.'

'Interesting,' Wiles said. 'I wonder if it's to do with capturing the image, the reflection of light from the flash effect, or if it's an artefact of the developing process when a bright negative is produced.'

'Could it be related to the way vampires cast no reflection in a mirror?' Davenport asked.

'There's no such thing as vampires, Leo,' Sarah told him.

'Really? You should tell Elizabeth Archer that. I think she might take issue quite strongly.'

'A conversation for another time, I think,' Brinkman said, cutting across Sarah's reply. 'Anything else?' he asked Miss Manners.

'Yes, this.' She produced another photograph from the folder. It was a different angle on the offices, and the subject of the picture was standing against a wall. Although the features were again overlaid with tangled lines, the effect was less blatant, and the standing figure was obviously Jane Roylston.

'It's like someone just scribbled over her face,' Sarah said.

'And this was taken, when?' Guy asked.

'After our little exorcism ritual.'

'You think it cured her?' Green said.

'It's certainly a step in the right direction,' Miss Manners replied. 'But whether this is the first stage in an ongoing change, or a temporary improvement, or simply the effect of Jane no longer being directly controlled, who can say?'

'We still have a lot to learn about all this,' Guy said. 'Where's Jane now?'

'She's at the British Museum,' Brinkman told them. 'Mrs Archer is doing some experiments to see if she can tell us more about the Vril under mild hypnosis. In fact, she's asked to see me this afternoon. I gather Miss Diamond here left her some rather interesting correspondence.'

The body was held open by long metal pins which pierced the skin. The pins were fixed into the wooden board. Inside, a spongy orange mass was revealed in place of flesh and organs. More pins held the legs spread-eagled.

Two men stood at the workbench, looking down at it. The older man took a pencil from his pocket, prodding at the animal's insides experimentally. He tapped the metal collar round the creature's neck. The man beside him watched impassively through pale blue, watery eyes. He wore a dark suit and a dark blue tie.

'The President doesn't need to know about this, Agent Cooper,' the older man said. He wiped the end of the pencil on the edge of the workbench before returning it to his pocket. 'The President has enough to worry about already. Though I think we could do with some help on this.'

'Who do you suggest, sir?' Cooper couldn't take his eyes off the body of the cat. It was unsettling, macabre... Frightening.

'The British must know something. They were there. And Sumner, of course. Be worth a few calls.'

'I'll arrange it, sir.'

'And get that thing out of sight,' ordered John Edgar Hoover, Director of the Federal Bureau of Investigation.

On the workbench, the cat, spread-eagled on the board, its skin folded open and pinned back, raised its battered head and gave an angry hiss.

'The whole place was destroyed, by fire and rock falls.'

Nachten listened in disbelief. 'But, how could this happen?'

'And just as you were almost recovered,' Himmler said. He leaned back in his chair and regarded the two men standing in front of him carefully. 'A pity.'

'An attack by Greek partisans?' Nachten still could not believe it.

'Hoffman?' Himmler prompted.

'It would seem so,' Hoffman agreed. 'It was lucky I was there. I ordered the evacuation of the fuel facility at the first sign of trouble. Sadly, Hauptsturmfuhrer Grebben was one of the casualties. I gather he tried to protect the site from escaping fuel.'

'A tragic loss,' Himmler said. 'But perhaps now we should focus our attentions closer to home. It is not all bad news. Did you know that with the help of expertise and material provided by us from the Freiburg crash, von Braun and his team last week achieved a successful launch of the A4 rocket?'

'I gather we are now calling it the V2,' Hoffman said. 'A great triumph, Reichsfuhrer.'

'We are all to be congratulated. And it should serve as an encouragement to redouble our efforts, to determine what other technology and weapons we can derive from the Vril Project.' He waved his hand to dismiss Nachten, but gestured for Hoffman to stay.

'It is lucky that you were on Crete when this attack took place,' Himmler said.

'If I had got there sooner, I might have managed to avert the attack, or protect the site.'

'No matter. It is good to have you back, Werner.'

'It is good to be back,' Hoffman replied levelly.

'You will keep me informed if you decide to go on any other ad hoc adventures, yes?'

'Of course, Reichsfuhrer. I was merely following a lead, a hunch. I had no idea if it would pay off. And sadly, of course, it did not.' He opened his hands apologetically.

Himmler removed his spectacles, polishing them slowly on his handkerchief. 'Luck was not on our side this time, it seems. No matter. It was the right decision. But as I say, in future keep me informed.'

'Of course.'

Himmler replaced his glasses and stared up at Hoffman. 'Just so long as you were not injured in the explosions and fires on Crete.'

'Not at all, Herr Reichsfuhrer,' Hoffman said. 'Although I confess, I did feel the heat of it.'

Jane Roylston was drawing. She sat at Elizabeth Archer's desk in the vault below the British Museum, a pencil in her hand. She stared straight ahead, but her eyes were unfocused, her expression blank.

'That's good, Jane. Very good,' Elizabeth said quietly.

Jane's hand lifted from the paper. She took a deep breath, her eyes focusing again.

'What did you see?'

'Terrible things,' Jane said. 'I always see terrible things.'

'Can you be more specific?'

'Fire climbing into the sky, then falling back to the ground. Death and destruction. Vengeance.' Her gaze fell on the picture she had just drawn. 'This is what I saw.'

The drawing showed a ruined street, bodies strewn across the pavement and over the rubble. Elizabeth lifted the sheet away. She put it on top of the first picture Jane had drawn – a sleek elliptical shape climbing into the sky, fire spewing from the engines beneath it.

They kept her in a cage for their own safety. When he came to see her, she stared back at him through the bars, her dark eyes defiant, her hands curled into claws.

'Show me,' he ordered.

In response, one of the guards took out a pistol. He stuck it through the bars and shot the girl. Twice.

The bullets drove her back against the bars of the cage. But almost at once she flung herself forwards again, at the man with the gun. He withdrew his hand just in time, stepping back quickly.

'She killed two men when they found her,' the guard captain explained. 'Another as they put her in the cage.'

'And she does not wound?'

'No, comrade. We have tried shooting her, stabbing her...' He shrugged. 'I've never seen anything like it.'

'Then you are one of the lucky ones. You say she was found in Stalingrad?'

'Impaled on wooden joists in a ruined basement. God knows how she got there. The injuries healed as soon as my men removed her.'

'And then she killed them.'

'Yes... What should we do with her, sir?'

'Take her to the Kremlin Archives,' Stalin ordered. 'Tell Archivist Vasilov that I want her stored with the items recovered from Tunguska.'

*

'Tunguska?' Brinkman shook his head. 'I've never heard of it.'

'It's a place in Siberia,' Elizabeth Archer explained.

The two of them were sitting either side of her desk in the vault beneath the British Museum. Elizabeth had Vasilov's letter in front of her.

'And why is this place relevant?' Brinkman asked.

'There was an explosion there.'

'There *is* a war on,' Brinkman pointed out.

'This explosion was in 1908,' Elizabeth told him. 'On 30 June, to be exact. Vasilov says that the archive the Vril broke into was where the Russians stored what they recovered after the blast.'

Brinkman nodded. 'He thinks the Vril were somehow involved?'

'He does,' Elizabeth confirmed. 'Because this wasn't just a bomb going off. Luckily it was in an uninhabited area, but even so it devastated the forests.'

'Is this what Jane Roylston saw in her vision?' Brinkman asked.

Elizabeth shook her head. 'What she saw was on a much smaller scale. The Russians estimate that the Tunguska explosion destroyed eighty million trees.'

Brinkman stared at her. 'Eighty *million?*'

'Over an area of about 800 square miles.'

Brinkman leaned back in his chair. 'That's a hefty blast. I'm surprised there was anything left to recover.'

'Not much,' Elizabeth admitted. 'But, according to Vasilov, they found something buried under the ground right at the epicentre of the blast. He doesn't know much about it. He says they spent years examining the device, but without learning much.'

'It wasn't damaged by the explosion?'

'Probably, but Vasilov's working assumption was that it was somehow involved in *causing* the explosion.'

Brinkman let out a long breath. 'I can see why Stalin and his comrades would be interested in finding out how it works. And this device was created by the Vril?'

'If not, then they certainly know about it,' Elizabeth said. She picked up Vasilov's letter, quickly reading back over it. 'And now, they have it.'

'What?'

'That device is what was taken from the Kremlin Archives. Vasilov couldn't learn its secrets, but we have to assume the Vril already know them.'

'It's a weapon,' Brinkman said grimly.

'Obviously. But what, or whom, are they planning to use it against?'

'And when?' Brinkman added. 'And how do we stop them?'